Nor Shapes Of Men

The Shattered World Saga Volume 3

Brian Koscienski & Chris Pisano

HELLBENDER BOOKS

an imprint of Sunbury Press, Inc.
Mechanicsburg, PA USA

**HELLBENDER
BOOKS**

an imprint of Sunbury Press, Inc.
Mechanicsburg, PA USA

For information about special discounts for bulk purchases, please contact Sunbury Press Orders Dept. at (855) 338-8359 or orders@sunburypress.com.

To request one of our authors for speaking engagements or book signings, please contact Sunbury Press Publicity Dept. at publicity@sunburypress.com.

FIRST HELLBENDER BOOKS EDITION: June 2022

Set in Adobe Garamond Pro | Interior design by Crystal Devine | Cover by Victoria Mitchell and Lawrence Knorr | Edited by Sarah Peachey.

Publisher's Cataloging-in-Publication Data
Names: Koscienski, Brian, author | Pisano, Chris, author.
Title: Nor shapes of men : the shattered world saga volume 3 / Brian Koscienski & Chris Pisano.
Description: First trade paperback edition. | Mechanicsburg, PA : Hellbender Books, 2022.
Summary: Those who lived through the events of *Fearful Symmetry* must now survive a power-hungry senator appointed by the federal government to hunt them.
Identifiers: ISBN 978-1-62006-799-4 (softcover).
Subjects: FICTION / Superheroes | FICTION / Science Fiction / General | FICTION / Fantasy / Urban.

Product of the United States of America
0 1 1 2 3 5 8 13 21 34 55

Continue the Enlightenment!

CHAPTER
1

Harrisburg, Pennsylvania

Vincent "Stone" Carvello wiped his right hand against the guard's arm. It didn't get rid of all the blood, but enough. The blood splatter on the wall took on an unnatural hue of brown, the streetlights not strong enough to make it this far down the alley. He didn't mean to make such a mess, but it wasn't his fault, really. He couldn't judge how hard the hits were.

"Sorry about that, buddy," Stone mumbled to the corpse as he pocketed the guard's access badge and unclipped his keys. "But sometimes there's a price for working for the wrong people."

Stone didn't mean to kill the guard—Randy, according to the name pinned to the front of his shirt—but he needed to get into the building. Rather unassuming at five stories tall, the basement and subbasement held secrets. Secrets Stone needed to access.

The plan was simple. Knock out the camera to get the guard's attention, then knock him out. At this time of night, there would be a single guard in the monitor room watching the cameras; when one went out, he'd have no choice but to investigate. The unmarked door in the alley was the best one, watched by a lone camera. It was hidden, tucked in the corner of the overhang just big enough to keep the rain off anyone standing there, but Stone knew where it was. He used to live here, after all.

Six months ago, the building owner died, and his wife shut down all operations within it. Rumor had it that she needed time to examine the companies her dead husband left behind, especially those with questionable intent. The happenings inside this building were *very* questionable. The widow hired a security firm to guard the assets inside and keep it from looking abandoned. Stone spent the last five months casing it and asking around about the place.

He needed to get inside, and he couldn't wait any longer. His condition was getting worse.

Keys to get in and a badge to fool the sensors into thinking he belonged here, he left Randy where he lay. He once belonged; these hallways were a part of his home. And home to others like him.

Dim emergency lights were strong enough for Stone to see where he was going. He wasn't smart enough to grasp the deeper aspects of his unconscious, so when his path took him by his old room, he viewed it as a coincidence.

The quarters were small but nice. One bedroom, a living room with kitchenette. He had his own bathroom. It wasn't anything as nice as when he lived in his brother's house after killing him and taking over his business, but Stone's time there was brief. Compared to some of the places he stayed these past six months, this simple apartment was a paradise. A few nights in the forests of West Virginia were bad, but he had no other place to stay as he trekked back to Harrisburg. The piece-of-shit truck he stole broke down an hour after he took it. The worst was the one night he spent in a homeless shelter along the way. The smells. The fucking crazy people. Never again. He hitched. He walked. He stayed in cheap motels using the money he stole from the people he hitched rides from. It took a month to get back, and his world was not as he had left it.

By the time he got back to Harrisburg, the widow of his deceased boss had taken over and clamped down. Over the following five months, he studied the building and watched the amount of security dwindle to one guard, down to Randy. Stone lost his home, but what he needed from within the building was more important. What he needed wasn't in his old room but in a lab further down the hall. One last look as he weighed the pros and cons of spending a night in his old bed. It'd be comfortable, but there might be some form of check-in between the guard he just killed and the security agency. He wasn't here to look for sleep; he was here to look for help.

The building was old, retrofitted for today's technologies but still retained some of its quaintness. The room he wanted had a thick wooden door. The guard's badge unlocked one set of locks, a faded silver key on Randy's keyring to turn the deadbolt.

The room was dark. The door closed and locked behind him. In the basement, there were no windows. At first, he cursed himself for not bringing a flashlight and forgetting to search the guard for one. Then he remembered—if there were emergency lights, the building was still getting power. A quick feel along the wall, and he found the switches.

The flashes of white lights bursting to life were intense. His eyes should be watering. They should be stinging, and he should be blinking and using his hand to shield them from the brightness. But he couldn't even feel that anymore. He didn't believe in God and had been called a devil over the years, but he prayed anyway, prayed that he could find what he needed in this room.

Not sure where to begin, he started down the main aisle. As wide as a two-lane road, it split the room in half. Desks, worktables, and counters populated the left side, equipment and computers taking up every available space. Normally Stone would have been thinking of ways to haul them out of here and come up with names of who could give him the best prices for them.

"The office," he mumbled to himself. Places like this always had at least one office in the back of the room. Maybe he could find what he was looking for there.

"Hello?"

The question came from the right side of the room, followed by the sound of bare feet shuffling along the concrete floor.

"Who's there?" the voice called out again, closer.

Shelves of computer components and machine parts turned the right side of the room into a labyrinth, not protected by a minotaur but by a spider.

"I assure you, I'm friendly," the tone befitting the words.

Stone knew who it was and what he said was true. But six months was a long time to be trapped in a room. Nothing in this room could harm him, but he clenched his fists when a tower of metal boxes shook as the guardian of the room passed by. Old habits die hard, some not at all.

The owner of the voice was getting closer, hurrying down a row of shelving and causing the rainbows of dangling wires to dance as he passed by. The shelf rattled as the guardian of the room stepped out.

Bob.

"Hey, my name is Bob. Sorry for my appearance, but . . . Stone? Stone, is that you?"

Stone had seen some weird shit over the past couple of years, but Bob was still hard to look at. Like a middle finger to nature, Bob had two torsos, one stacked on the other, and four legs. The last time Stone had been in this room, Bob had four arms. Now pieces of metal capped the sockets of all four of his shoulders.

"Yeah," Stone grunted. "Where'd Kevin go?"

Bob walked closer, lumbering awkwardly. Each of his four feet pointed in a different direction, and titanium joints connected his thighs to an aluminum alloy sphere, the skin from Bob's lower torso hanging over it like a fleshy apron. Black tubes ran from the base of his spine and along the floor, disappearing into the darkness of the room's far corners. Bob had blathered all the details of his existence once to Stone about a year ago. Stone never cared to know that the tubes were the conduits to the freak's life, circuitry and oily white fluids containing synthetic nutrients. He never cared to know anything about Kevin's bizarre experiments. "Kevin? Oh, yeah, I can tell you about Kevin. But you'll need to do me a favor."

"A favor? You're charging me for information?"

"No, no, no. Nothing quite so dramatic. I'll need you to do something you've done plenty of times before. Real simple."

"Yeah? What?"

"Kill me."

Bob smiled through a thick, unkempt beard, but Stone knew the outward expression wasn't real, just a part of some computer program. It was his eyes that told Stone. A curtain of straight brown hair almost covered Bob's eyes, but it couldn't hide the desperation and pain of a tormented soul.

Stone shrugged. "Yeah, sure. What do ya got on Kevin?"

"He left."

"No shit, asshole. I figured as much before I got here. I was hoping to find some clue where he'd gone."

"Well, our hometown is Pittsburgh."

"Fuck you." Stone turned and walked back to the door.

Bob hurried past Stone and then blocked his path. "Kill me! I gave you the information you were looking for, so now you gotta kill me."

Stone pushed the abomination aside. "I wanted answers. Pittsburgh's not an answer."

"That's the only answer I have."

"Then good luck with life, asshole."

"Yeah? Well, good luck to you, too, since you're gonna spend it with me!" Bob yelled as he scurried to a nearby shelf. It was a smaller unit, small enough to tip as Bob pressed his body against it. Should that shelving unit fall, it would hit a larger set of shelves with enough force to topple it into another set, this one even larger. If that structure fell, it would hit what Stone thought to be a leg of a giant robot. No matter what it was, the piece of machinery was ten feet tall and weighed well over half a ton. If it fell, it would block the door and Stone would be fucked.

Killing the freak was now the only option.

Stone ran down the aisle of shelves, looking for a weapon. A long piece of metal with a jagged edge. A leg torn from a metal shelf maybe. It would have to do.

When Stone approached, Bob turned to face him and yelled, "Show me what you got, big guy!"

A response was pointless, so Stone shoved the pseudo-spear into the gut of Bob's lower torso. It pierced with ease, going all the way through, but it didn't have the desired result.

Bob looked down at the milky white fluids trickling from the puncture site and then back up at Stone. With eyes wide and mouth stretched into a maniacal smile, Bob yelled again, "Come on, you fucking loser! You have to do better than that!"

Why's everything gotta be harder than it should be? Stone thought as he pulled the jagged metal from Bob's belly. The white fluids flowed out faster. Bob yelled and gnashed his teeth as he advanced.

Surprised, Stone jumped back and used his weapon more like a knife, slicing upward. The jagged metal split Bob's flesh along both torsos. Sprays of white fluid splashed Stone's face.

Temporarily blinded, Stone backed away and wiped the oily liquid from his eyes. As soon as he opened them, Bob was on him. "You have to do better than that, pussy! You have to do better than that!"

Bob threw himself at Stone and knocked him off balance. Stone reached for a nearby shelf, but his hands were too slick, and he fell to the floor, Bob flopping on top of him. Squirming and gnashing his teeth, Bob continued to yell, "You have to do better!"

"Get off!" Stone pushed, but his hand went inside Bob's chest, releasing a wave of fluid. Struggling to keep his eyes open, Stone grabbed and pulled some sort of organ out of Bob's upper chest, a spaghetti ball of wires attached to it. It wasn't enough to stop the writhing or screaming, so he reached in with both hands and pulled out another gloppy mass. And again.

Stone didn't know if he yanked on tubing or intestines, lungs or compressors, organs or components. The consistency of the fluid thickened with every pull, splashes turning to chunks. Stone grabbed and pulled faster, screaming along with Bob, until there was only one person screaming.

Finally, able to push Bob's corpse off him, Stone rolled over, careful with his balance as he stood up. He didn't get the answers he was looking for, but he had a place to start. And he hoped like hell that Kevin didn't have any more freaks like this.

CHAPTER
2

Camp Hill, Pennsylvania

"Michael's right."

Sitting in her living room, on her couch with Michael, Claire Roseman cringed at those words. She loved her husband and often agreed with him, but in this particular situation, those words were inflammatory.

Michael smiled and gestured to Colton McGrath, the man who agreed with him, like a trophy he had won. Both Bree Storm and Sister Angela Vazquez frowned.

Bree's real name was Aubrey Austin but felt "Bree Storm" was a better name for an artist. Her facial piercings—her right eyebrow, left nostril, and bottom-right lip had hoops, while a sparkling faux diamond stud had been implanted in her left cheek—made her sneer even more aggressive. Her shoulder-length blue hair fell over her left eye, the right side of her hair trimmed close to her head. "How is it any different than what I do?"

"You cure addiction," Colton answered, frowning. "People prone to addiction can't help themselves. What the nun does is fuck with people's heads. She can make them forget things. She can change people's personalities. We're talking about stripping away someone's free will."

Sister Angela slouched, crushed by Colton's heavy words. She ran her fingers over a lock of her long hair, so straight and black that, at first glance, one could mistake it for the veil of a traditional nun's habit. Sister Angela opted for a long black skirt and thin gray sweater over a white blouse buttoned all the way to her neck. "I just want to help people."

Colton ignored her statement and continued arguing with Bree. "And you shouldn't even be using your powers anyway. That's the whole point of these meetings."

"That is *not* the point of these meetings. We're meeting because we're a unique community of individuals with unique needs. We're meeting to prepare ourselves for when the rest of the world finds out about us and how to best represent ourselves. And don't tell me you don't use your powers."

Claire liked Bree and admired the passion that burned within her. The girl was more than a decade younger but had been through so much, falling victim to drug addiction as well as those who preyed upon young women with such addictions. She liked Sister Angela as well. She, too, had endured more than her fair share of hardships. She was almost twice Bree's age, and Claire was comfortably between them at "late thirties."

"I'm a real estate agent, and I can 'push' things with my brain," Colton snapped. "What the hell am I gonna do with that? Push potential buyers from room to room in houses I'm showing them?"

The same ability as her husband. "Monodirectional telekinesis," as she once heard it referred to. However, Michael had used his ability well beyond Colton's limited scope of imagination. He saved people. He killed people. He killed people to save her life. It had been six months since the incident in Mills Hook, and his nightmares had been subsiding, none within the past month. Because of what Michael had seen, done, lived through, it was no surprise when he agreed with Colton. "If we don't use our powers, we have no fear of the rest of the world finding out about us."

Claire used her telekinesis to hand a drink to everyone in her living room, including her husband.

"Thank you," Michael said, plucking the drink from the air. He opened his mouth to continue expressing his opinion but closed it when he realized what Claire had done, prompting a flat-browed look of accusation. Bree laughed and Claire shrugged a shoulder.

"Thank you, Claire," he said again with a slight growl to his voice. "But this is exactly what I'm talking about. If we don't use our powers, we have nothing to fear. The more we use them, the more we invite trouble."

"I respectfully disagree," Claire said. Michael's expression softened, giving his full attention to her. Despite his many faults, he always listened to her when she talked. "Preparing for an unwanted scenario is very different than inviting it. Making a will isn't inviting death. Buying insurance isn't a plea for calamity. In fact, being unprepared creates many other problems."

"Those are just bridges to cross when it comes time. The more we collectively use our powers, the faster we sprint to those bridges."

As a lawyer, Claire was used to dealing with people who refused to listen while twisting whatever words they heard into nonsense. Her first thought was to call him a small-minded ass, but she had enough willpower to keep that to herself. Luckily, Bree added credence to Claire's argument. The young woman tapped away at her phone and then said to Colton, "I just sent you a link. Just posted today. How about you click on it and show the class?"

Colton mumbled something to himself about manners, and Claire smiled at the irony. A few taps later and his screen came alive with a video. Senator Alistair Varney from Alabama stood behind a podium with a beaming smile for the small crowd of people clapping and cheering. Thirty seconds of adulation later, the senator leaned forward just enough to speak clearly into the microphone. "Thank you. Thank you all for coming. Six months ago, an issue came to light that threatens your safety. *Our* safety. There was some debate about this issue. Accusations of chicanery ran amuck, but you, the American people, spoke and I listened. Five months ago, I stood before my fellow senators and demanded in *your* name, in *your* voice, to start this task force, one dedicated to finding the truth. One month ago, our task force became fully operational with a state-of-the-art facility in Arlington, Virginia. A miracle that this government could move that quickly, right?"

Senator Varney, fit for his age and handsome enough to make his gray hair an asset, paused to allow the crowd to share a chuckle within itself. A "silver fox," as Claire had heard some women refer to him. While he waited for the right time to speak again, a phone number and website appeared at the bottom of the screen, below the senator. He continued, "But they did, because of this new threat, because of these potential *impurities* within our system, we needed to discover if they exist or not."

The camera pulled back to capture most of the screen behind the senator, parading a slideshow of images. A grainy image of a man with wings. A picture of a man-sized lizard walking on hind legs. A video clip of a carload of people driving away from a small town that had been leveled into smoldering ruins. That one produced a sting within Claire's chest. She was in that car.

The senator didn't wait for the crowd's murmurs to die down; he just moved closer to the microphone. "During this last month, our task force gave you, the American people, a way to contact them any time you suspected that someone was an impurity. Well, I'm pleased to tell you that thanks to the tireless efforts of the task force, we have captured one."

The crowd gasped. Before anyone could collect their thoughts, the senator hurried to say, "We caught one, thanks to the tips you provided us, but unfortunately, I am not at liberty to give any more details than that. I needed to share the good news with you, and I encourage you to keep the tips coming in."

The crowd cheered and the video stopped. Colton put his phone away as the room fell silent.

"He calls us impurities," Sister Angela whispered.

"He does," Bree said. "And he has the rest of the country calling us impurities."

"Vainglory. Noun. Excessive elation over one's own perceived achievements, usually hollow pomp and show," Michael said. "That's all we saw."

"He said he caught one of us," Sister Angela said. "Maybe he has reason to boast about his achievements?"

"I doubt he's caught anything more than an STD from a hooker he used taxpayer money to buy," Colton argued. "If he does provide 'proof,' it'll be like a carnival sideshow where he gives you a fetal pig in a jar and calls it a human soul."

"It doesn't matter what he can prove. It only matters what people believe. As history has shown us time and time again, people are stupid fucking lemmings more than happy to jump from a cliff because their messiah told them to," Bree said.

Colton flicked his fingers as if shooing away a fly. "A tiny little crowd of undereducated idiots kissing the ass of a pretty politician. That rally was held at the local fire hall. Who could take that guy seriously? Have you read the comments? The people think he's a joke. They said some pretty scathing things. No one truly believes that he found anything, just like no one believes that the photos he used as 'proof' are real."

"But *everything* in the photos *is* real."

Michael leaned forward and smiled at Bree. "Like *you* said—it doesn't matter what's real, only what people believe."

It frustrated Claire when her husband got like this. He, too, was in the video the senator played; he was driving the car. Michael was too caught up in the argument, too enamored by another person agreeing with him that he deprioritized other viewpoints, like how he was being demonized. It was time for Claire to change the topic. "We could debate how politicians twist the truth to manipulate the masses all night, but that's not the purpose of these meetings. Yes, we need to discuss what we should do as a community, but we can't forget that we aren't the only ones in this community."

It was Claire's turn to tap away at her phone. Within seconds, Colton's phone buzzed. "Why is my phone the one for community viewing all of a sudden?" he mumbled but clicked the link in his inbox.

Another crowd, larger than the one in the senator's video and more uproarious, clapped and cheered after every statement made by the speaker, a man wearing an ill-fitting suit that accentuated how spindly he was, a bolo tie that looked like used shoestrings, and a white Stetson hat too small for his head. With a microphone in one hand and a Bible in the other, his erubescent face glowed, shimmering with sweat after every statement.

He promised the word of the Lord.

He promised salvation for those who believed and paid.

He promised all ailments would be healed.

But it wasn't he who had the power of God's touch—it was a boy in his early teens sitting on a chair next to him on stage.

A line of people quickly formed, the crowd doing its best to make way for those who wished to be touched. The boy seemed quiet, only smiling and nodding, offering a soft, "You're welcome" if the person he healed thanked him. He might have been center stage, but the people he healed were the stars of the show, each gleefully screaming and crying, laughing or flailing, as if God had reached from the heavens and shook them Himself. Canes were dropped by those who didn't need them anymore, and wheelchairs were abandoned, their owners dancing free from their rolling prisons. Cancers were destroyed and the blind could see, all thanks to this boy.

"His name is Horatio Jackson," Claire said when the video ended. "He's fourteen and can channel the word of God to heal people."

Both Colton and Michael moaned and rolled their eyes. Michael started with, "Claire, there is no way that you believe God is talking to—"

Claire stopped her husband by placing her hand on his and giving him a gentle squeeze. "No, I don't believe it's God, but I do believe Horatio could be one of us. Before you and Colton start mansplaining how charlatans work, trust me, I already know. Even though his pastor clearly is a fraud, I don't think there's any trickery going on. I've been watching Horatio for months now, and the crowds keep growing. A lot bigger each video."

Colton leaned back in his chair and crossed his arms. "I'm not going to mansplain anything, because that's not what I do—" The women groaned, even Sister Angela. "—But you can't believe everything you see on the internet. The past videos might have some trickery to encourage such a big crowd to bring their wallets in this video."

"That would certainly make sense if this were a troupe traveling across America. All of the videos were filmed in locations close together. There's a good chance that a lot of these people are neighbors and friends who knew each other before the big healings. They're in Georgia, so I suggest that we go down there and meet Horatio."

"Georgia," Colton and Michael moaned in unison.

"How many more videos before it attracts Senator Varney's attention? Or before someone who believes that young man is the minion of the devil and not an angel from Heaven and calls the tip-line? We have a chance to outsmart the government. How often do you two get the opportunity to say that?"

"We can't just go to Georgia on a whim," Michael said. "We still don't know if this is real. How about a compromise? We'll keep an eye on him. If, and only if, he does something deemed exceptional, then we'll investigate in person."

"I'm not going to fucking Georgia," Colton spat. Everyone else agreed with Michael.

"We should talk about the new crop of—" Bree started but was distracted by her phone's ringtone. She declined the call and continued, "—people like us appearing six months ago. That's three different times that—" Her phone rang again. "Sorry, but it's Thelma. She's only this persistent if it's important."

Bree took the call but didn't speak, only listened. She concluded with, "Okay. We'll be right there."

Colton looked at Michael and huffed, "So, I guess the meeting is over?"

"Not quite," Bree said. "We just need to move it. Thelma said there was a break-in at one of her buildings. She's there now and we need to meet her."

"See, this is what I'm talking about," Colton snipped. "A woman of extreme wealth is trying to get us to solve a problem meant for the authorities."

Bree stood and turned her back to Colton. She looked at Claire and said, "This particular building had a few of her late husband's laboratories where he had his people conduct some of the more illicit research. Trust me—this is very much an 'us' problem."

CHAPTER
3

Hotel, Miami, Florida

Carol Carole's tits bounced. Lying on her back, she loved the sensation. But not as much as she loved the old man's hands around her throat. He was going to town, the headboard of the king-sized bed smashing against the wall, her ankles on his shoulders—there'd be bruises on her ass from his hips. That would be an issue tomorrow, if she'd even live to see it. Darkness infiltrated her peripheral vision, steadily conquering her world. When she could see nothing other than his eyes, his angry, angry eyes, he removed his hands from her neck and grabbed the sheets by her head as he came. The gulp of air intensified the orgasm wracking her entire body.

Grunts and thrusts ended his performance. Carol giggled as sweat dripped from his chest and splashed her cheek. She ran her hand through the white curls of his chest hair, creating a fine mist. She then licked her fingers.

Edward Edwards sneered at her. "You're disgusting."

"Considering where your dick is right this second, what does that make you? I mean, I'm not blackmailing you or paying you, and you're probably not under any form of mind control. I know the popular idiom is men let the little head think for the big head, but unless your dick somehow got online, stole your credit card number, and booked you a flight from Pennsyltucky to Florida, then that means you *willingly* put it in the disgusting."

Rolling his eyes, Edward left the bed and strode across the room to the couch, where a towel was draped over the arm. Drying off, he said, "Just killing time before our meeting. You're one step above masturbation. Although my hand doesn't talk to me afterward."

"So, it talks to you *during* masturbation?" Carol rolled over onto her belly and propped herself up by her elbows. She made a loose fist with her right hand, her thumb straight. Using her thumb as the bottom jaw, she moved it to simulate a mouth in time with a cartoonish voice. "Oh, Eddy, give me your big cock, big guy. Right here. Oh yeah." She made gagging sounds as she inserted her left index finger into her hand-made mouth.

Edward dropped the towel on the floor and walked over to his clothes, scattered about the armchair in the corner. If not for his white hair, short but just long enough to need a comb to style, there was no other evidence that he was in his sixties. The wrinkles on his face were few and shallow; Carol assumed that was because he never smiled. His tall frame was sturdy, built by thick muscles. She enjoyed looking at him, but he made his thoughts about her perfectly clear. "With you as head of one of our shops, it's no wonder the organization collapsed."

Carol jumped from the bed and pointed at her lover. "Easy with that talk, mister. My head might be filled with rabid weasels, but I assure you they know what the fuck they're doing when it comes to control and manipulation. My shop might have been responsible for the fucksplosion in Mills Hook, but it was Matthew Matthews's ineptitude that got the organization nervous to begin with."

Underwear. Pants. Shirt. "*You* were the reason Matthews started phases one and two without the organization's approval. You confessed this yourself."

"Excuse me, I was responsible for convincing him to start phase one without the organization's approval. Phase two was all his idea. It's not my fault Little Carol makes boys do stupid things." To emphasize the topic of her statement, she used both hands to gesture to her crotch while thrusting her hips forward. Edward paused putting his socks and shoes on to close his eyes and shake his head. "And don't forget," Carol continued, "before the organization tucked their tail, took their toys, tapped their tits, and ran, you were gung-ho about us partnering up to find other shops who wanted to start phase two."

Edward had no reply, tying his tie in silence, his moves fast and hard as he took his frustration out on the material. This made Carol smile. She tried to think of other ways to piss him off, but she was interrupted by a knock on the door.

"Can you at least pretend to be professional and put some clothes on?" Edward asked.

She debated participating in the meeting while naked with sex-mussed hair, but the man on the other side of the door was a letch, and Carol wanted this meeting over as soon as possible. On her way to the door, she grabbed the robe from the closet and ran her hands through her shoulder-length, ombre hair, black at the scalp and ending in bright purple. She tied her robe closed just before opening the door.

The shock of red hair on the man's head always surprised Carol. Styled differently every time she saw him, she kept forgetting that it was so orange it seemed to glow. Today was an upward swept muss. His teeth gleamed unnaturally white and stood out, even against his pale skin. His eyes were blue and piercing. They'd be nice if they didn't make it so obvious that he was calculating ways to fuck over anyone he looked at. His lips shined as he smiled; Carol expected to see a line of drool dangle from the corner of his mouth. After inhaling deeply through his nose, he said, "Mmm . . . Smells like daddy issues. Can anyone play, or are there age restrictions?"

Conner O'Conner. Carol didn't get to choose her name—the organization changed it once they put her in charge of a shop. She often wondered if somehow Conner conned his way into choosing a name so befitting the stereotype he portrayed. Or did he alter his image after the organization gave him his name? Either way wouldn't surprise her.

Carol held her hands ten inches apart and looked down at his crotch. "Sorry, leprechaun, you must be this tall to ride the ride."

Conner sauntered into the room, shouldering past Carol, and addressed Edward. "Well done to you and yours, sir. Well done, indeed."

Carol hated Conner, but she loved how he got under Edward's skin. She didn't trust anyone she couldn't control. Edward was difficult to manipulate but not impossible. The more time she spent with him, the more tricks and traps she learned. Crudeness was a distaste of his, as evidenced by him walking to the table in the middle of the room, pulling out a chair, and huffing, "If you two are done behaving like children, then maybe we can get on with this meeting."

On his way to the table, Conner cocked his head to address Carol. "He's still grumpy after his daddy-daughter dance? I'm no longer curious about your abilities since they clearly seem to be lacking."

Conner's suit was a navy blue that shimmered, a thin layer of opalescence playing in the light. His shirt was black, a void with his tie being the only thing it couldn't swallow, the same shining blue of his suit. It fit perfectly, the material neither stretched nor puckered as he sauntered about the hotel room, but it didn't move right. Like an extraterrestrial attempting to blend in with the populace by donning human skin. Or like a pet wearing clothes.

Carol took a seat as far from Conner as possible. "How would you know? The only viable point of comparison comes from your girlfriends being made of 'lifelike' vinyl and inflated by tire pumps."

"May we *please* begin?" Edward snarled.

Conner frowned and leaned toward Carol. "Boring company aside, why is he so grumpy?"

Keeping her gaze fixed on Edward, Carol leaned toward Conner and said in a mock whisper. "Because his girlfriend is mad at him for not bringing her along on this business trip of his."

"Clearly she doesn't trust him."

"I know, right? Trust is the cornerstone of every relationship."

"Enough!" Edward barked. "There's no need to talk about her."

Carol's tone went cold, and her precise words cut like a surgeon's scalpel. "Oh, Edward, there is *absolutely* a need to talk about her. Isn't this meeting about phase two of our shops and who the best specimens are? I think our bidders would be very interested in a sixty-five-year-old woman who is the perfect killing machine. She's a real-life video game character. Fast, accurate, lethal. Our bidders would pay millions."

"We are not bringing her in."

"Why not?" Conner asked. "She'd be easy to capture. All you'd have to do is lure her into a trap."

"She'd never do what any of the bidders would want her to do."

"I'm sure these people have ways of making others do what they want. Even if she didn't cooperate, all we need from her is a demonstration. We need to show the bidders what our product is capable of creating."

"No. I'm using her to keep tabs on other phase-two candidates."

"Oh, yes," Carol said. "The little club that Michael and Claire started? With the girl who can cure addictions, the nun who can fuck with memories and personalities, and the real estate agent with monodirectional telekinesis, the *exact* same ability as Michael."

"Monodirectional telekinesis? What the hell is that?" Conner asked.

"He pushes things away with his mind. Kind of like how you push women away with your words."

Conner laughed and shook his head. "Okay, then what about the nun? She sounds impressive?"

"No. Right now, it would be too difficult to separate her from the others," Edward said.

Perfect, Carol thought. She didn't want the nun or Emma or any of the ones in that little group. She just needed a few more names thrown around until she could get to the one she wanted.

"Fine," Conner waved his hand as if erasing the last conversation. "Then how about the Indian guy who does the fire thing?"

"Went missing six months ago," Carol answered.

"Okay, then the guy who can see what other people see?"

"Last seen with the Indian guy who does the fire thing."

"The guy who does the weird cybernetic machine computer thing?"

"Went missing six months ago."

"Are there any left? I mean, does my shop have to start phase one?"

"There are plenty of candidates left," Edward said. "Do not start phase one. That's what we want the potential buyers to bid on, remember?"

Now was the time. "Have you two seen the kid in Georgia who can heal people by touching them?"

Conner sat straighter, eyes wide with anticipation. "Can he only heal people, or can he do what that Marvin guy from Matthews' shop could do?"

"Marvin Carver," Carol said. "We're not sure yet."

"We don't even know if what he's doing is real," Edward said. "His family runs one of those revivalist churches known for their scams and trickery."

"But you've said before that he was definitely one of your phase-one candidates. He took a bad spill riding his bike one day and needed surgery to fix the broken nose and cheek."

"Yes, but we all know that the nanobots were completely ineffective in over half of the candidates."

"Oh, come on, Eddie. Yes, his family is using him to bilk cash from their inbred neighbors, but this is too much of a coincidence."

Edward stared at the center of the table as if communing with it, ferreting out the answers he needed from the wood pattern. A smile crept along his face, small but noticeable. "Our shops are jumpstarting the next step in human evolution. This is an exciting time to be alive and not only witness such a miracle but guide it. Since we have no better candidate at the moment, let's investigate this one further."

Conner clapped his hands together and whooped. "The amount of money we're gonna get for this kid is gonna be enough for me to swim in."

"All right, boys, it looks like we have a plan," Carol said. A plan for the candidate she wanted. The candidate she needed. She was more than happy to collect the metric shit-ton of cash they would receive for this candidate, but before that happened, she wanted him to take care of the lump in her breast.

CHAPTER
4

Montgomery, Alabama

Devlin Varney awoke with a hand on his dick. The young woman to whom the hand belonged was still asleep, her body positioning unintentional. After three rounds of sex last night, he was very well satisfied and had no interest in an early morning attempt. Plus, he had to take a leak.

When he finished and exited the bathroom, he regarded the sleeping girl. At first, he was irked that she was still in his house, but he saw her phone on the nightstand by her side of the bed. Her password was 1234; he had seen her tap that combination plenty of times last night. All the pictures and videos she had taken chronicled the events that led from the nightclub to his bedroom and were easy enough to find. It took only a few taps to delete the past twelve hours.

She was perfect. Well, her face and body, at least. He knew little about her, but how amazing of a human being could she be if she aggressively jumped into bed with the son of a famous, rich politician? Hell, he couldn't even remember her name. He thought about grabbing his phone and taking a few pictures for his memories, but why bother? He could find a dozen more like her tonight if he wanted. That was the whole point of being rich, right?

Poverty defined his childhood years. A shitty shack to grow up in and shittier parents to raise him. Back then, Devlin was weak and had no future. Fate knocked him around some more, pushing him headfirst into the depths of Hell. But within that torture, there was opportunity. There was Alistair, Devlin's adopted father.

Every wish had been fulfilled for Devlin. Money was the salve for any wound. His shitty old world had been torn down and replaced by an amazing new one with fame, respect, a promise for a better future. And hotties willing to fuck him all night long just to get a fleeting glimpse into his world. He hated the name "Devlin," though.

Without the slightest bit of tenderness, he sat on the bed by her feet. That was enough to cause her to stir. Tapping her foot with the back of his hand, he said, "Hey."

Full lips turned into a sleepy smile. She moaned and propped her head on her hand, her tits shaming the concept of gravity. "Hey, Devy."

Devlin couldn't stop the quick laugh aimed at her stupidity. "Yeah, we're not gonna do that."

Hair as gauzy as pulled cotton candy, she sat up. "No? Do you prefer Devzie? Devver? Devinator? Devilicious?"

Her toes curled around his finger and pulled at his hand. He was in no mood for that either. "I prefer that you head out now."

The playful toes stopped their kneading. The young woman tilted her head but still smiled, a practiced move. "Oh? You have a busy day? I can hang out if you'd like."

Now that he had her attention, Devlin slipped on a pair of two-hundred-dollar pajama bottoms and walked to a set of windowed doors that led to the balcony. "Nope and nope. I'd like you to get dressed and get out. Actually, I don't care if you get dressed or not—just get out. And please leave by the back door."

Smiling turned into frowning, and cute became fierce. "What? You can't be fucking serious."

"About what? Leaving?"

Getting dressed consisted of slipping back into her skintight party dress and heels. "Yes, about leaving, asshole."

"What? You were expecting this to be some rom-com? Where I'm suddenly in love with you because you threw your pussy at me?"

Hair into a ponytail, she stormed over to him as he opened the door. "No, but you could at least be a decent human being."

"Why? You're not."

She wielded her phone in front of her like a weapon, ready to record the moment. "Yeah? Well, the whole world will see what an asshole you are, asshole."

Before she could hit record, Devlin snatched the phone from her hand and tossed it over the balcony. "Nope."

Considering what she did to him last night, Devlin had a pretty good idea just how wide she could open her mouth, but watching her jaw drop to this extreme was surprising and cartoonish. He chuckled again. Had she shown any emotion to indicate she was hurt by this maneuver, he would have felt bad. Instead, she crossed her arms and stomped away while mumbling obscenities— the price he had to pay for being him.

When she reached the bottom of the stairs, he shut the door and went downstairs to the kitchen. His father had to pay a price as well, and it was sitting at the kitchen table. Devlin only knew the man by his last name—Samuels. He assumed it was his last name, even though there was no title in front of it. Samuels's buzzed hair, white and thinning, could no longer hide the random liver spots on his head. Far from fat, he had the paunch all men got after a certain age. Few wrinkles, though, as if his hard eyes were frightening enough to keep them at bay. This man used to have a title, but Devlin couldn't remember what it was or where it came from. General? Colonel? Army? Marines? All Devlin knew was that Samuels was retired from wherever his title originated, and he had never seen any man look angrier to be in a suit.

Samuels sat at the kitchen table with Alistair, folders overflowing with papers spread between them. Alistair greeted his son with, "So excited to tackle the day you forgot to put a shirt on, son?"

Devlin laughed and opened the refrigerator. He never had a body like this in high school, and now that he could afford the time to keep it perfectly sculpted with lean muscle, he never wanted to wear clothes again. "Be thankful I'm wearing pants, Dad. Good morning, Samuels."

Samuels returned the greeting with a simple head nod before drinking from his coffee mug.

Ex-army or navy or whatever aside, Devlin thought Samuels was cool. "So, what's with the folders? Intel on other potential targets?"

"Yes," Alistair answered, "and information about the one we captured."

Samuels had a permafrown, his emotions displayed by the depth of his forehead creases. After Alistair's comment, the frown deepened slightly as Samuels shifted in his chair.

"So, what you said at the conference yesterday was true? You captured one?"

"Me, personally? Oh, Heavens no. The task force? You bet your Bible-loving ass they did!"

Samuel's frown turned into a full scowl. He shifted in his seat again, this time accompanied by a harrumph.

Devlin loved his adopted father. Even as a millionaire politician, he loved to make people in power squirm. And Samuels had power. Few people knew the Pentagon was funding the task force. The money needed to keep it up and running was merely lint found in their deep pockets. The deal gave them the right of first refusal for any and all findings derived from researching the individuals in question if they had special abilities. If the target wasn't valuable and the money was wasted, then so what? Easy enough to hide a small set of numbers within a larger set of numbers. "So, what's the guy you caught do?"

Alistair opened his mouth, but Samuels hurried to cut him off. "We don't know yet. This is sensitive enough information as it is, so it would do more harm than good if we made any kind of speculation."

Devlin hid his smile by bringing a glass of orange juice to his lips. But he almost spat it out when his father said, "Don't worry, son, I'll tell you all about it later."

This resulted in Samuels sitting straight and organizing the folders. Devlin felt a lecture coming on, but it was halted before it could begin. Samuels's phone buzzed. As he read the text, his frown became shallower, yet somehow more ominous. With no warning, he stood and said, "Well, it looks like a few questions are about to be answered. The subject we captured is finally awake."

CHAPTER
5

Harrisburg, Pennsylvania

Michael stopped in his tracks. Not only had he been to this building before, but he'd been inside it. Someone he knew died in this building during a failed attempt at heroics. Someone he didn't know had been mutilated before his eyes, and he subsequently felt like a coward for doing nothing. He still had nightmares about those experiences, and late at night, when he had no other recourse than to stare at the ceiling, he'd debate if there was anything he could have done differently. Inevitably he'd come to the same conclusion each time. The man who committed both murders was to blame—Thelma Carver's late husband, Marvin.

Claire took Michael's hand, causing him to jerk. Voice soft and soothing, she said, "Hey. Let's keep moving to get you out of the middle of the street."

"This is the building," he replied but allowed her to lead him off the street and onto the sidewalk.

A breeze blew along the city streets, cooling his cheeks. The night was quiet, the surrounding buildings devoid of life, except for a few late workers and custodians moving around in the ambient lights.

"I know, sweetie."

"It's . . ." a symbol of why using their abilities was wrong. "It's . . ." a testament to the abuse of power. "It's . . ." everything wrong with the situation. He wanted to point at the building and say, *This! This is why no one should have these abilities!* Instead, he said, "It's just as terrifying as I remember."

Claire wrapped her arms around his left arm, a subtle hug. A display of love, comfort, and support.

Marvin Carver was a sociopath. Not only did he have the ability to alter a person's biology by touching them, but he could somehow absorb the abilities of other special people. Marvin was the personification of avarice. He hurt people, controlled people. Michael had a tenuous grasp on the reasons for organized religions and how they viewed the sliding scale of morality, but he knew Marvin was evil. That was why Thelma killed him and left his body to burn in the town of Mills Hook.

Michael loved Claire and appreciated the constant support she gave him. He needed that support now, needed to share the feelings that swirled around in him like a colony of discontented bats. However, that would have to wait as the other three caught up.

"Your girlfriend does pretty well for herself, huh?" Colton said to Bree while looking at the building.

"She doesn't even use this place," Bree replied.

"There's a reason for that," came from the alleyway next to the building. Thelma Carver.

Normally she wore suits with the right accessories in the perfect color combinations to exude power. As a woman who acted as the president of a multi-million-dollar company, she was already at a disadvantage when trying to garner respect from important people in the business community. Add to that the way she looked, and she faced an uphill battle any time she stepped foot into a boardroom.

Not needing to exert her influence, Thelma wore a baggy sweater and fashionable jeans. Her clothes were meant to hide her cartoonish figure but failed. Her tiny waist was so out of proportion with her massive breasts and rolling hips that she could only exist in a fantasy graphic novel drawn by a teenager with no other means of easing his libido. A twist, a turn, a bend, a stretch, exemplified her figure. Most men found her sexy—Colton's gaze lingered longer than it should have—but Michael found no interest in her. He found her curious.

She was one of the people Marvin had changed. Michael didn't know her exact age, but he calculated late forties. Not that long ago, she was bone thin and comely at best. Marvin had transformed her into this. Would the effects one day disappear, and she'd go back to looking like an emaciated woman in her fifties? Or would she age naturally from here on out, roughly the same point in her journey through life as Bree? He didn't know. Neither did anyone else. And *that* was what terrified him. He had so many questions and issues to bring up, but now wasn't the time. He just wanted to get away from this mausoleum of bad memories. "Why are we here, Thelma?"

Thelma hurried to Bree and hugged her. She then led them to the front doors and said, "Glad you asked. I think it'd be better if I showed you. Just be warned—it's pretty gruesome."

Michael had seen gruesome, had seen it in this very building. He didn't want to see any more, but he followed along anyway. Whatever they'd find, he would use it as a talking point in future argument with this group.

"Why were you in the alley?" Bree asked as they walked through the dark foyer and darker hallways. Emergency light cast a faint blue glow, creating broad and bizarre shadows, a strange sorcery that hinted at potential monsters dwelling within.

Thelma took a deep breath and exhaled slowly, stalling to find the right words. This unnerved Michael, as if she were preparing to start a campfire tale that he had no desire to hear.

"All of you know Marvin did some bad things—some very bad things. This was one of the buildings that housed some of his laboratories. As soon as we came back from Mills Hook, I assumed control of his companies, much to the chagrin of some board members. I wanted his experiments to stop, so I evicted everyone from this place and locked it up. I . . . I couldn't bring myself to deal with his sins right away, so I hired a private security company to keep an eye on it, make sure no one snooped. Minimal security, usually one guard to roam around. Well, the security guard is dead."

Claire and Bree gasped. Sister Angela whispered a prayer in Spanish. Colton blurted, "What the fuck? Have you called the cops? You *did* call the cops, right?"

"No. I can't. There would be too many questions about why I was here in the middle of the night."

"Jesus Christ, I didn't sign up for this."

"None of us did," Bree snapped. "This is exactly what I'm talking about."

"Exactly what? I have *no idea* what you're talking about. I have no idea why Thelma is here at this time of night or why she won't contact the *proper* authorities. I have no idea why *I'm* here."

They had taken many turns and walked through a series of doors labeled "Authorized Personnel Only" until Thelma finally stopped. "This is why we're all here. Apparently, Marvin kept his finger on the pulse of everything going on in this building, even to the point of receiving an email notification if there was an unauthorized entry into any of the labs. Well, guess what I received an hour ago. After I open these doors, you'll see why you're here. Again, I need to warn you—it's gruesome."

Thelma pulled out a badge and swiped it through a card reader next to a massive wooden door. It opened and the light inside was so bright everyone shielded their eyes. Claire was the first one to speak. "Oh my God. What is that?"

More gasps from Bree and Angela and another "What the fuck?" from Colton. On the floor was the body of a naked man intermingled with machine parts, wires, and tubes, all covered in white grease. No blood.

"I believe this was one of Marvin's experiments," Thelma said. "I don't know what it is, and I never knew what he was doing. I feel stupid even saying that."

Bree took Thelma's hand, a gesture of love and support.

Colton turned away from the mess on the floor. "Other than to turn our stomachs, why are we here? This is clearly a break-in at your late husband's secret robot lab. I'm sure there's some sensitive intellectual property here, but I don't see any reason why you think we should be handling this and not the police."

"When it comes to Marvin's secrets, they're never as simple as they seem. Whatever he was doing in this lab, I can guarantee it was regarding people with abilities," Thelma said.

"So, why was he making these robots? Why did he make them look like people?"

"They might be robots made out of people," Michael said. Another horror he had experienced, another nightmare he had lived through. There was a man who could control machines, use them in terrible ways. Marvin had been with Michael on that adventure and stopped that man by offering him a job. The body on the floor was another reminder of the past—a reminder of why these abilities were wrong.

"That's pretty messed up," Colton said to Michael.

"Marvin was a messed-up person." Yes, this reminded Michael of that experience those many months ago. The creepy house and creepier basement. Wires and machine parts moving as if living things. Wires and machine parts *comingling* with living things. He hadn't even realized that his hand was trembling until Claire grabbed it and squeezed, her eyebrows arched, eyes wide, face a portrait of concern. Calmer now, Michael returned her gesture and whispered, "I'm good."

"Has anything been vandalized?" Bree asked. "Or stolen?"

"I don't know. Nothing as noticeable as . . . whatever is on the floor. But Marvin was paranoid. Whoever broke into the building knew enough about it to come here but didn't know that Marvin had cameras in here not connected to the main server. I think we can access them from the back room, but I don't know how. Would any of you know?"

Colton shrugged. "I have experience with security systems from the more upscale places I've sold. Couldn't hurt to see what I can do, right?"

The back room was half storage, half office. Unopened boxes of computer components were stacked in the far corner, wedged between the wall and a metal shelf full of office supplies. Desks lined two walls, half of them holding banks of monitors. Colton made himself at home in front of a keyboard and mouse. "Okay, let's see what we see."

As Colton clicked and tapped away, Michael's attention waned and turned to Thelma. Her face. Her beautiful, perfect face. He didn't like it.

"Hey, perv, you're going to stare a hole right through her clothes," Claire teased.

"I'm not looking at her clothes."

"No?"

"No. I'm looking at her face." It wasn't her face he didn't like. Thelma had been a strong woman through this ordeal of everyone in her life getting special abilities, and she had been generous with her money. It was what her face represented. The uncertainty of power. "Do you see even the slightest wrinkle anywhere? I sure can't."

Claire crossed her arms and cocked her hip. "You know, there is a jealous monster that rages inside my tight and toned body, and the only thing that keeps it from bursting free and mauling the world around me is your sweet comments about my tight and toned body."

"Wait . . . what? You can't be serious." Michael stopped examining Thelma and looked at his wife. Claire raised an eyebrow. That was all it took for Michael to realize that she was indeed serious. "Okay, first of all, you know that giant boobs and asses aren't my thing. You. You are my thing. You are a goddess. You are number one in my book, and there is simply no second place."

Claire smiled and kissed his cheek. "I know. You make me feel like that every day. I just wanted to tease you for ogling."

"I wasn't ogling. I was just looking for any signs of aging. I mean, is she going to look like that forever?"

"Huh," Claire grunted, squinting as she studied Thelma. "That's a good question."

Michael smiled. Now was the perfect time to bring up his point about using their abilities, his fears, his questions. Just as he opened his mouth, Colton called out, "We got it working."

Everyone gathered around the monitors as they each blinked to life, gray visions of different parts of the laboratory, three showing the body on the floor. Colton clicked away with the mouse, the time displayed on the monitors moving backward. As quick as a blink, the thing on the floor popped up and seemed to talk to someone. Michael prayed he wasn't seeing what he thought he saw. When the man disappeared, Colton clicked a few more times, commanding the playback to move forward in real-time. Michael wondered if the power of prayer only worked if it was used more than once a decade. "I know him. In fact, I know them both."

"Oh, God, Michael. I'm sorry," Claire said. He had told her the stories but not all of the details—just enough to piece together his puzzle of anguish.

"The big guy's name is Stone. He has impenetrable skin and is a fucking psycho. He's the monster Emma and I had fought at the hospital in Harrisburg. The robot isn't a robot. His name is Bob, and I'm guessing the person who made him was running this lab. Also, a fucking psycho, just in a different way."

The black and white images on the screens showed what happened, eliciting gasps from everyone watching and a prayer from Sister Angela. As soon as Stone left the room, Colton rewound the footage.

"What in God's name are you doing?" Thelma asked.

"I don't want to see it again either, but the big guy was here for a reason. Unless you're going to call the cops in on this, we should at least make an effort to find out why he was here."

Michael couldn't watch. He turned his back to everyone else as Colton replayed the conversation between Stone and Bob. It became a game, each player making guesses about what each person on the screens was saying. He didn't care. He didn't want to know. All he wanted to do was go home.

"It looks like Stone is saying, 'Where is.' He's looking for someone," Bree said. "Maybe the guy in charge of the lab? Whoever made Bob?"

"Look at how Bob's lips move here," Colton said. "He's saying a word with two *p*'s or two *b*'s in a row."

"Fuck!" Michael yelled as he kicked a nearby wastebasket. It bounced against the supply shelf, boxes of pens falling to the floor. He couldn't control his emotions anymore. This was how his father would have reacted, and the icy claw of guilt gripped the base of his throat. But he just couldn't take this. All he wanted was to play silly games with his daughter, engage in meaningful conversations with his wife, and teach the disenfranchised youth in his English classes. Whether it was the kid in Georgia or the government task force in Virginia or where the large bald man in the security footage was going, it would be a long time before Michael could go back to doing what he enjoyed.

"Michael?" Claire whispered, her hand tentative on his shoulder as if she were afraid to touch him.

"Pittsburgh," Michael answered, his fists clenched so tightly that his fingers hurt. "The big psycho is looking for the other psycho, and he lives in Pittsburgh."

Michael wondered if he'd ever see home again.

CHAPTER
6

Baltimore, Maryland

Laney Pederson studied a page of six photos: The three on the left were in black and white; the three on the right were the same images in color. The person in these photos had answers, if she could just figure out who it was.

These were taken six months ago at the town of Mills Hook, West Virginia. The town was no longer there, and Laney had witnessed its demise. She and her partner, Charles "Click" Lickman, had arrived to watch every building set aflame, the citizens dead or dying. She and Click were too far away and too late to help, so they filmed the waning minutes of Mills Hook. After all, she was a journalist and he was her cameraman. It was their duty, no matter what future nightmares they'd be inviting. They were obligated to record a team of black-clad soldiers gunning down hundreds of men while the ordnance from their tanks and helicopters demolished buildings. Every citizen was a man, the exact same height as each other, the exact same face as if it were an entire town of identical twin brothers. Hundreds of them. Click captured that on video as well. He did his job—he created the questions. Her job was to manifest the answers, but she had failed to do so.

The person in these photos had to have some answers. Somehow, some-way, six regular-looking people—four women, two men—escaped the burning town, escaped the horde of lookalike men, escaped the armed soldiers in black combat gear, and drove away in the most popular make and model sedan sold in the country. Just five seconds of the video with no other details. But one of the women seemed familiar. Her shape, her hair, something special hidden in the blurry image of her face. This woman wasn't just a person, but someone famous enough to make Laney swear to God that she had seen her before. Laney had studied these pictures, comparing them to every model and actress that had any similarity. Nothing. Even now as she looked at these six pictures, she could feel this information torture her by playing keep-away with her mind.

"Pulitzer Prize to Laney!" Click yelled. "Did you hear anything we said?"

Marvelous heels propped on her desk, she refused to look away from the photos. Of course, she heard them talking. It was a bigger office than her last one, but it was still too damn small. "No politicians. You know that."

"But this one's different. He's been on the radar ever since he got the U.S. government to back this special task force of his to find the kind of people you and Click have been looking for. He just announced that they found someone," Dean said.

Dean signed her paychecks and was generally a nice guy, so she always tempered her responses to him. Sometimes it was difficult, like minutes ago when he asked her to waste time investigating Senator Varney. Deep breath. "He's on the radar because he preys on the uneducated and mentally feeble."

"We're gonna get scooped."

"Is that still a thing? Getting scooped? If it is, there's nothing to scoop. He's a politician. He's going to say and do anything to get as many eyes on him as possible. Trust me, when it comes time for the 'big reveal,' he'll come up with some excuse why it didn't happen and then dole out more empty promises. Classic bait and switch. Don't fall for it."

Dean leaned against the doorframe and removed his wire-framed glasses to pinch the bridge of his nose. He was only in his mid-thirties, but his ability to lecture made him seem much older. "Laney, you're by far the best journalist we have, probably the best in the field of online journalism, but—"

"But what have I done for you lately?"

"No!" Dean snapped. Standing straight, he pointed at Laney, glasses dangling from between his third and fourth fingers. "That is not what I said or meant. You've been all but frozen since Mills Hook. Unless you've been writing in your diary at night, you haven't produced a single word."

"That story tripled your subscriptions."

"And now they're falling."

"They're still way healthier than they were six months ago."

"Yes, but there was a cost to that, Laney. Or did you forget about the nonstop investigations?"

"A few cops with some stupid questions."

"And the army confiscating our hard drives."

"And they gave them right back."

"There were death threats."

"Yet, we're still alive."

Dean returned his glasses to where they belonged, then scrubbed his short blond hair with his hands. "For the love of God, Laney, we need something new."

"We'll get it. You just need to have patience. There's something bigger than Mills Hook and I'll find it. Yes, it's been six months, but look at the number of hits our video keeps getting. Look at the comments section. That video is still *relevant*. People are *still* talking about it."

Dean sighed and put his hands in his pockets. *Oh, no. Fatherly advice time.*

"I'm worried, Laney. I don't know what's going on with you, and you're not talking to me. I don't know if you're afraid that Mills Hook was the best you'll ever do. I don't know if you now set your expectations too high. I don't know if you're obsessed. All I know is you've rejected every lead Click and I have thrown at you for months now."

Laney wasn't obsessed. Being obsessed meant putting her life on hold to focus solely on one thing. She couldn't be obsessed because . . . because . . . her life consisted of eating takeout alone in her apartment, devoid of human contact other than the person she saw in the mirror. Waking up, hitting the gym, coming to work to pour over pictures and video she'd seen a billion times. She still denied that she was obsessed, but she admitted that she needed to look at something new, something different. Think about something other than what happened six months ago.

Dropping her feet to the floor, she rolled her neck and worked out the kinks of leaning back in an office chair for over an hour. "Okay. What do we got other than a politician?"

Click and Dean looked at each other, clearly surprised that Laney agreed to listen. Click tapped away at his keyboard while Dean hovered behind him to study the monitor. "There's a kid in Georgia who can cure people by—"

"Touching them?" Laney interrupted. "The one with the charlatan parents? Why is it when a group of rubes gets together, it becomes news? I'd sooner believe the politician than whatever it is the kid's pretending to do in those videos."

"Okay. Let's see what else we got," Click mumbled as he squinted at the screen.

"Have you two thought about going back to Virginia to look for that birdman you saw?" Dean asked.

"You mean the one you originally said no to and then we sold the story to a grocery store rag-mag? Haven't heard anything about him since then. Is there anything newer?"

"Hmmm," Click hummed. After a few seconds of agonizing silence other than the scroll wheel of his mouse, he muttered, "Some rich widow in Pennsylvania had one of her office buildings broken into."

"So?"

"So, it seems like the building had been empty for a while, and when asked about what's in the building, she became really cagey. Stressed the confidentiality of proprietary and intellectual property. Obviously, she's hiding something and . . . whoa!"

Both men reacted with wide-eyed surprise.

Laney sat straight up, ready to jump from her chair. "What? What's wrong?"

"Ummm . . ." Click stammered, his cheeks turning pink. "They included a picture of her and . . . uhhh . . . please don't take me to HR . . . but she's gorgeous."

"She *really* is," Dean whispered, clearly not realizing he had spoken.

Laney rolled her eyes. "Oh, good God. Does this gorgeous widow of mysterious secrets have a name?"

"Thelma Carver. Isn't her husband the one who went missing six months ago?"

Thelma Carver.

Laney's heart stopped and it wouldn't start again until she saw a picture of this woman. She jumped out of her chair with enough force to knock it over, crossed the room, and pushed Dean out of the way to look at Click's computer monitor. Yes, her husband went missing six months ago, but that was after she herself had gone missing. Holding the page of photos next to the monitor, Laney barked, "Search for images of her."

"Okay, okay. You're so bossy when you get like this," Click whined but still did as instructed.

The screen filled with dozens of images of Thelma Carver. Laney shook the page of photos with one hand and repeatedly smacked Click's shoulder with her other. "That's her! That's totally her!" Her voice came out too shrill, but she didn't care. There was a certain orgasmic quality about defeating her own memory.

"I know you don't want to hear this—" Dean started.

"Then don't say it," Laney cut him off.

"I have to! What in God's name makes you think the woman in those blurry photos is the woman on the computer screen?"

"Goddamnit, Dean! It's her. I don't know how I know, but I just do. It's a gut fucking feeling."

"It's grasping at straws!"

"It's intuition! It's instinct! It's whatever the hell it is that makes me a good journalist. That's Thelma Carver. I'd be willing to stake my career on it."

Dean's blue eyes looked unnatural in his reddening face, but he looked more hurt than angry. "I'm not willing to do the same, Laney. If it's her, I'll pay for everything. If it's not . . ."

The unsaid words were louder than those spoken as he left the office. Laney stewed in regret, wondering why her mouth worked faster than her brain. Her first thought was to apologize to Click for gambling with his career as well as her own, but he was trying hard to stifle a chuckle. "What in the world are you trying not to laugh at?"

"You said, 'gut fucking.' I have no idea what that means, but it sounds really gross and really funny, almost like a grandma from a foreign country trying to swear in English."

Laney sighed. The ninety-minute ride in his van to Harrisburg would feel like an eternity.

CHAPTER
7

Field outside of Augusta, Georgia

Horatio Jackson peeked out from behind the curtain. The biggest crowd yet. Mother thought it was because people had been hearing the word of God. Father thought it was because of the videos he had been posting online, as well as this location being closer to a city than those rinky-dink towns. Father was right and Mother was an idiot.

Backstage, she pranced around in her lime green pantsuit and high heels. She was too round of a woman for heels that thin and pants that tight, especially since it took Father and Mr. Seltzer to keep her from falling while they crossed the moist ground of the field. But, in her mind, a woman of business—of power—was the only type of woman who wore pantsuits. What kind of power could she possibly wield if she didn't understand the simple concept of marketing? Horatio was only fourteen and knew their social media channels increased attendance, not dictates from Jesus.

Mother was busy bossing Father around and treating him like a production assistant while she planned the logistics of their next event with their manager, Mr. Seltzer. As much as Horatio hated seeing his father being fussed at by his mother, it gave him a rare moment of being left alone—of peace. He hadn't had many of those moments since he laid hands on Grandfather Jackson six months ago. A man dancing a jig after being in a wheelchair for fifteen years was certainly a miracle. And a way to make money.

Mother and Father had always had their traveling congregation, accepting donations everywhere they preached. Barns. Fire halls. Parks. Social halls. Horatio always liked God and the stories from the Bible. However, this didn't feel right. The word of God in his mind was "Love everyone." The Bible stories were tales of perseverance. Yet his parents preached exclusion; gays and anyone non-white weren't invited to sit at the Lord's table. When Mr. Seltzer joined the operation, he informed Horatio's parents that gays and people of a different color had money as well and were willing to give it away just as quickly. They were still referenced as "Them" on his parents' lips, just not as vehemently as before. Horatio had a different definition of "Them." Everyone else was "Them." Horatio's world now consisted of him and "Them." A perfect example was the girl in the front row.

While everyone in charge of Horatio's life was still distracted, he continued looking at the world through the split in the curtain. The size of the donation determined the order in which he laid hands. The front row had given the most money to his parents' church. How the money could help a church that had no permanent structure, Horatio couldn't understand, but he noticed that both Mother and Father drove much nicer cars now.

The girl looked about his age and sat next to her parents, all three looking smart in their Sunday best. They were black—a "Them" to his parents. As the girl waited for the event to start, she played on her phone, tapping and swiping away—a "Them" to Horatio. Someone who could do what he couldn't. Play a game. Watch a video. Check social media. Instead, he had to learn scripts, memorize cues, smile and wave upon command. Be surrounded by people who leached off him and allowed strangers to grope him.

Slouched and tired-looking, the girl seemed nice. Her hair was pulled tight across her head into two puffs, and she wore a pink dress with a white bow and pristine white shoes. Horatio wanted to meet her, talk to her, find out what games, movies, music, websites she liked. Interact with her the way he used to interact with his friends before Mother pulled him from school. Father, even more powerless than before, allowed her.

Just as the girl looked up, Mother grabbed Horatio's shoulder and pulled him away from the curtain. "Horatio! Don't ruin the surprise."

"They all know what I look like," he said.

She huffed her words with a proud southern drawl as if she took pride in being out of breath. "I'm not talking about you, silly! I'm talking about the surprise of the Lord."

"They all know what he looks like, too, Mother."

"They do not, or else they wouldn't be here. Now, get ready. Your father is about to start. You have all your lines down?"

Horatio thought about the girl with her phone and how different her life must be from his, how she could make choices that he couldn't. "I'm not doing my lines this service."

"What? Horatio August Jackson, you will most certainly be doing your lines!"

"Look at how many people are out there for me to lay my hands on them. This is the most we have ever had and will be the longest service. I don't think we should make it any longer than it has to be."

"Thinking is not your part of service to our Lord."

"Belle, you leave our son alone," Rutherford Jackson scolded his wife. Ready to step out from behind the curtain onto the stage, he had a Bible in hand. It gave him the courage to stand up to Mother. Horatio wished his father carried a Bible more often. "He's right. This is our biggest turnout yet, and I think I'm going to shorten my sermon to accommodate."

Mother scowled and crossed her arms over her chest in the unholiest of ways. The tiniest of smiles touched Horatio's lips. She found the nearest mirror to primp her overdone hair and remained quiet as her husband took the stage. Arms raised to the heavens, he accepted the thunderous applause.

After basking in the adulation of strangers, he beckoned everyone to return to their seats and calm their spirits so their hearts could open up and accept the Word of the Lord. His words were as warm and creamy as melted butter poured on freshly baked biscuits. So emphatic, Horatio almost believed them.

Thirty minutes. Horatio watched the time tick away on his phone, an old flip thing his grandparents would use. No games or music or pictures. He desperately wanted to look through the curtains again at the girl but was too afraid of what his reaction might be. Too afraid he'd do something untoward in the eyes of God. His father did not shorten his sermon, too caught up in the desperate faces and hands clasped in prayer to God. Prayer to him.

Mr. Seltzer gestured for Horatio to join him and get ready to go onstage. Horatio did as instructed; anything else and Mother's bottled-up wrath would become uncorked. The buildup was intense, and the people's emotions had substance, as if hope and expectation were guests of each individual crowding the space under the tent beyond its limits. Father had everyone stand up and then had his ushers manage the line.

It was time. Horatio left one set of confines to enter another as he stepped through the curtain and greeted everyone with a forced smile and a wave. A mix of reactions. Relief. Glee. Excitement. People waved or thrust their hands to the sky. Many cried, some cheered. A few even dropped to their knees and spoke to the glory of God. Horatio didn't react to any of that; he had neither the time nor inclination. Instead, he gave a courteous bow and aimed for the cushioned chair in the middle of the stage. His mother appeared as if summoned from the pits below to escort him the rest of the way, bright smile exposing newly bleached teeth. At least the chair was comfortable.

The black girl in the front row was first. This was the only joy in the entirety of Horatio's day. With a simper on her face, her hands wringing together, she approached by herself, her parents staying back and holding each other. This also made Horatio happy. With the murmuring of the crowd and his parents crossing the stage to greet as many donors as possible, there was no one to hear his conversation with her. His smile at her was real. "Hi."

"Hello," she whispered, almost out of breath. Her eyes were yellow, and her skin held a tint of jaundice. As any proper young woman would before someone important, she curtsied. It was shallow and her face twitched with pain.

Horatio extended his hand for her to take but not too far from his body, forcing her to come closer. "What's your name?"

Putting her tremulous hand in his, she said. "Molly, sir."

Sir? Her parents had coached her. Horatio smiled and shook his head, wordlessly telling her that such formalities weren't necessary, even though his next question was rehearsed. "What seems to be the problem, Molly?"

"Sickle cell anemia. Chronic and severe. I'm always in the hospital. Well, it feels that way, at least."

Horatio was supposed to ask questions like, "Do you accept Jesus as your Lord and Savior?" and "Do you accept God, and only God, into your heart?" Instead, for Molly, he placed his other hand on top of hers. No theatrics. No practiced prayers. Her eyes lightened and her skin darkened. She took deeper and deeper breaths. The pain disappeared from her face. "How do you feel?"

Part of him expected her to withdraw her hand and run to her parents. So many people ran off after he healed them, forgetting that he was sitting right there. He lost count of how many times people older than him, people who would be first to criticize bad manners, left without any form of gratitude as soon as he gave them his gift. His heart sang when she squeezed his hand and said, "Thank you."

"No problem."

Tears rolled over her cheeks and flowed along the creases of her smile. She placed her other hand on top of his. "I . . . I don't know what to do. Is there anything I can do?"

"The game you were playing."

"Excuse me?"

"You were playing a game on your phone earlier. What was it?"

She giggled and shook her head, his question not one her parents had pre-pared her for. "The game? It was 'Crazy Fish Food Fight.' It's . . . it's really stupid."

"The title is awesome. Is there a two-player mode?"

Something in her eyes changed, something for the better. A realization that Horatio wasn't some kind of vending machine that dispensed miracles but rather a boy her age who wanted to meet her, get to know her. Be her friend. "I don't know. I can check. Are . . . are you on Instasnapbook? My username is—"

Mother cut her off by pulling her away from Horatio and pushing her toward her parents. "Come now, sweetie. I'm sure your parents are excited to witness firsthand the miracle of God."

"Molly!" Horatio called out, reaching for her. He was too late. Once she got close enough to her parents, they snatched her up with hugs and scrutiny, examining every inch of her through tear-filled eyes. As they left, Molly looked over her shoulder, a sadness in her eyes.

"You were the one whining about time," Mother hissed into Horatio's ear. "So don't waste all of your time with Them."

To fend off the sadness, Horatio turned the other worshipers into a game, although that led to a different kind of sadness.

Fifty-seven. Fifty-seven miracles he had performed. Fifty-seven human be-ings he healed. Only six thank-yous, and three of them were from children younger than he. Four God-bless-you-childs from men and women older than his grandparents. But that meant forty-seven people gave him zero recognition for his deed. One woman who had the shakes of Parkinson's yanked her hand from his as soon as she was cured and turned to the waning audience and yelled, "My faith has healed me! My prayers have worked!"

When the line finally shrank to ten people, Horatio became engaged. The stragglers looked destitute, and they were the ones who would make Horatio feel better about this situation. The homeless *always* thanked him. Not this time, though.

Four ushers congregated in front of the stage to halt the progress of the last ten people. Horatio stood from his chair, legs sore from two hours of sitting. His mother halted his pained steps. "You're done for the day, son."

"I can get those last people, Mother. They need my touch just like everyone else."

"But they did not donate; therefore, they cannot accept God into their hearts."

A woman with gray hair and seeping lesions on her cheeks pushed her way closer to the stage and reached for Horatio. "I ain't got nothin' to donate other than my eternal love for my Lord, Jesus Christ."

Horatio tried to make his way around his mother, but she was too strong, too determined to exact her rules. His struggle was useless, and it didn't stop her from saying to the homeless woman, "We have different views of the Bible, and mine are right while yours need some work. You may go back to wherever you came from and revisit the Good Book."

The ten individuals in front of the stage started to cause a commotion, resulting in two more ushers coming to help, as well as Mr. Seltzer. As Mother led Horatio away, the older woman yelled, "You will pay for this, you charlatan. You will pay!"

The words were directed to his mother, but Horatio knew well enough that he would be the one who had to pay the price.

CHAPTER
8

Camp Hill, Pennsylvania

"Mommy! Daddy!" Sarah Roseman squealed as she hugged her parents. Michael lived for these moments. His eight-year-old daughter between him and his wife, squeezing their necks. She had attacked them as soon as they crouched down to greet her.

Michael stood to greet his father in the doorway, no hugs or handshakes for him. "How was she for you and Mom?"

"I was great, as always," Sarah answered.

"It's true, she was." The only time Timothy "Buck" Roseman smiled was when he was talking about his granddaughter. At least, in Michael's mind, that's how it was. He wondered if love somehow skipped a generation; he got none of it so his daughter could get all of it. As a father, it was a fair trade for Michael. He would do anything for Sarah, give anything for her happiness, even if that meant being raised by a man who cared more about sportsball players than intellectuals. "She's as quiet as a church mouse."

"See, Dad!" Sarah yelled. "Grandpa says I'm quiet!"

Michael wasn't sure if she was too young to understand the irony or if she was precocious enough to master the finer points of sarcasm. Either way, she was her mother's daughter.

Claire laughed. As she stood, she gently pulled Sarah's long hair into a ponytail and then released it. A curtain of blonde fanned out across her back. "Yes, you most certainly are, sweetie. And guess what? Your father and I have to go out again today. I know you just got home, so we're going to make it up to you next weekend. But I'm going to call Cindy to see if she can come over and watch you."

Sarah bounced on the balls of her feet and clapped. "Awesome! I like Cindy!"

"I thought so. I'm going to call her now." Claire kissed the top of Sarah's head and left the foyer. At least Michael had Sarah to keep him company while he hurried to shoo away his father. Or so he thought.

Like a magician with rabbits and hats, Buck produced a juice pouch from behind his back and handed it to Sarah. Pumping her fist, she accepted it. "Thank you, Grandpa!"

"Dad. You know Claire and I don't want you and Mom giving her all that sugar when she stays with you guys."

"We don't. We wait for when we drop her back off to you to give her sugar." For his next trick, Buck produced a candy bar with his other hand. "Here you go, princess."

"Grandpa's the best!" Sarah announced as she bounded up the staircase, her stomping feet knocking dust from the ceiling as she ran to her room.

"Wow, Dad. Truly amazing. Ignore my requests about sugar and make me look like shit in front of my daughter."

"Trust me, sugar is nowhere as harmful to a child as absentee parents."

"That's not even close to what's happening here."

"And where you off to today?"

"Pittsburgh."

"Ahh. I assume it's for some writing symposium for part-time English teachers. I'm sure that's more important than spending time with your only daughter."

A ball of pain swelled within Michael's skull, and he considered it a minor miracle that his right eye hadn't popped out. There were so many things wrong with this conversation, from his father accusing him of being absentee when he, himself, took very little interest in Michael's life as a child, to making a dig about his chosen career, as he did every conversation. A father should be a son's aspiration. Instead, Buck was the mold for men that Michael wished to avoid. He was a near-perfect specimen of humanity, taller and more muscular than most people, with a full head of hair and a perfectly centered mustache even though he had crossed the threshold of sixty. He could fix entire car engines with nothing more than a paper clip and some duct tape, but he thought all men not matching his characteristics were inferior. Michael was none of those things and hated how his father made him feel inadequate for being happy with who he was. Michael wanted to yell at Buck about how terrible of a job he did as a father and to get the hell out of his house. Instead, he said, "No. A conference about new taxation laws that affect a few of Claire's firm's bigger clients."

Buck stroked his chin and nodded. Michael hated how he did that, too. "Okay. Well, that makes sense. Since she's the sole breadwinner of the house, she should definitely keep up with that kind of stuff."

Michael started to shut the door and said, "Okay, Dad, always a pleasure. Thanks for watching Sarah last night. Tell Mom I said hi and I love her."

Buck's typically hard face softened. Had it been anyone else, Michael would have guessed it was sadness, but his father had no room for that emotion in his heart. "Bye, son."

The door latched and Michael leaned against it, eyes closed, gasping for breath like a drowning man making it to shore. The rhythm of his heart thudded through his entire body as he forced his anger down. *Calm. Don't be like Dad. Don't react to every aggravation with anger.* He whispered, "Don't scare the devil."

"What did you say?" Claire asked, a lilt to her voice.

Michael opened his eyes. "It's something stupid from my dad. When he'd get mad—really mad—he'd say he was mad enough to scare the devil. Well, I was alone with my dad for two full minutes, so . . ."

"So now you're beyond flustered and need to calm yourself down."

"Yep."

Without another word, Claire pulled him in, hugging him tightly. "It's okay, sweetie."

This. This was what Michael was fighting for by fighting against everyone else. His wife. His daughter. This was why electricity went screaming through his body when the doorbell rang.

"Is that Cindy?" Sarah called down from her bedroom.

"No," Claire answered. "But she'll be here soon!"

"Yaaaaay!"

"We should really make her come down to talk to us instead of encouraging the use of screaming as an acceptable form of communication."

Claire stroked his cheek, a calming mechanism. "We will. Let's take care of this first."

Michael nodded and kissed her hand. "Okay. Let's do this."

Bree and Thelma were waiting hand in hand when Michael answered the door, and Bree pointed her thumb to a vague location behind her. "Was that your dad? I see a little resemblance, but he's so much bigger."

"Yeah, yeah, yeah," Michael moaned. "Very funny. Just come on in. You're the first to arrive.

"I wasn't joking," Bree mumbled. Michael ignored her as Claire gestured for them to go to the living room.

Before joining them, Claire handed Michael's phone to him. "You need to call her."

Michael sighed. "Can't you do it?"

"I could, but she might say no. She was along when you first went to Kevin's place, and you said you couldn't remember where he lives. We're going to need her help, and if you can humble yourself long enough to ask for it, she'll better understand the gravity of the situation."

"Fine." Michael took his phone and dialed the number. After two rings, she answered. "Emma? It's Michael Roseman. Please don't hang up. I need your help."

CHAPTER
9

Williamsport, Pennsylvania

"There. Pull over there," Laney said.

"Are you crazy?" Click whined but did as she had asked, guiding his van to a stop along the curb. "They're gonna see us."

"They're not going to see us. We've driven behind them for an hour and a half and they haven't noticed."

"You haven't noticed if they noticed or not. If they haven't, they're either stupid or my driving skills are amazing."

Click left the keys in the ignition and slipped into the back of the van as Laney slid over into the driver's seat. Camera with telescopic lens in one hand and parabolic microphone in the other, Click sat in the passenger seat. Laney remained quiet as Click attached headphones to the microphone, a device with a handle and small dish on the front. With the headphones on and pointing the device at the house across the street, Click looked like something from a 1950s science fiction movie. He brought the camera to his eye to complete his cyborg look. "Okay, all five are getting out of the car. Four of them look very nervous."

"Nervous? Like they have to deliver bad news?"

"Scared like they made the bad news. The professor-looking guy keeps saying something about someone not liking him."

"Who? Does he say who?"

"No, but I'm assuming it's the owner of the house." Click aimed the camera toward the house, and Laney looked over his shoulder. A small ranch with a screened-in porch. The living room curtains were open. When the five visitors rang the doorbell, two figures stirred in the living room. "Whoa. I may need to rethink my lifestyle choices."

"Do I even want to know why?"

"They're both white-haired senior citizens, but she's a GILF and he's a silver fox."

"Ew, you're so disgusting."

"Usually, but I might not be this time. She looks like she could win a triathlon if one suddenly broke out, and he looks like he could bench press a weightlifter while he's bench-pressing a car."

From her angle, Laney could see that Click was right. Their white hair wasn't befitting their general athletic shapes. She couldn't see their expressions, but they were courteous enough to invite the visitors inside. "What are they saying?"

"I don't know."

"I thought you have state-of-the-art equipment."

"I have state-of-the-whatever-I-can-buy-on-sale-off-the-internet equipment. This thing has about a three-hundred-foot range and isn't really good at piercing walls. I'm not James fucking Bond here. I can only do so— Whoa. The old couple certainly doesn't like the professor-looking guy."

Laney craned her neck and squinted—anything to get a better look. All she could see were the backs of bodies. "Why do you think that?"

"I can hear the old lady yelling at him, and the old dude is putting his arm around her to guide her away from him. I think the old lady can do something special."

Fear and excitement spiraled up and down Laney's spine. "Really? Is she doing something?"

"Not really, but when she points or gestures, everyone winces. They look like they're scared shitless of her."

"That doesn't mean she has special abilities. My whole family was scared of my grandmother when she was still alive."

The rapid fire of the camera shutter filled the van. Click then handed the camera to Laney and adjusted the headphones. "She ain't your grandmother, and these people ain't your family."

Click was right. Laney flipped through the pictures on the digital camera's screen. Everyone was turned defensively, almost cowering. Maybe the old woman did have some special ability? Maybe something dangerous? There had to be a reason why one of the richest women in the state and four other people were willing to drive ninety minutes to talk to an older couple.

"What are they saying now?" Laney asked.

"The old woman who lives here is telling the professor-looking dude that she can't believe how loud the woman is in the van parked conspicuously down the street."

"Don't forget this is *your* windowless van and you were the one who chose to get it painted predator-white. Was psychedelic-rock wizard shooting lightning bolts from his fingers already taken?"

"Ha, ha. There's a reason those people paint their vans white. No one notices a common color when their overly aggressive coworker forces them to park on a neighborhood street to spy on people."

"*Those* people? You mean suspicious characters who own white windowless vans?"

"You are being exceptionally mean right now."

"I just don't want to miss this."

"Miss what? We followed Thelma Carver from Harrisburg to Camp Hill to here. If she and her friends go somewhere else, we'll follow them there."

"It'd just be nice to know where they're going. It might be a place where we have contacts."

Click turned away from the window, his eyebrows pinched and mouth open. Slowly shaking his head, he said, "What contacts? In all the years we've worked together, I've never seen you associate with anyone other than me and Dean. When could you have possibly made any contacts?"

"I meant you. Don't you have a guild for cameramen?"

"A guild . . . ? Guilds are for craftsmen and wizards."

"How about your slut-whores. With the number of them you have, the laws of statistics dictate that at least one of them will be useful."

"Wow! You are Queen Mean abusing the court jester. What is going on with you?"

"I just . . . I just don't want to lose this story."

"We won't, Laney. We're the only people running in this race, so we're already winning."

A race. A competition. That was how she viewed her career. A contest. She couldn't help it. She had been competing in beauty pageants since she was two years old. Her mother had always told her she'd be insignificant if she lost too many times. Although that was true, winning didn't help. She'd get a crown, a bouquet of flowers, and streaked makeup from fake tears while accepting the audience's applause. Then the very next week, it was a different city where she started back at zero, back at anonymity in the general public's view. Her best stretch was three wins in a row, and she had the same level of fame recognition as she did after her worst stretch of seven losses in a row. None.

All her devotion to pageants from the time she was a toddler to her twenties landed a few modeling gigs and a couple acting auditions. Her mother had motivated her by instilling a fear of losing something she never had. Significance. Laney wanted to do something that mattered. Mattered to her, mattered to the rest of the world.

Her poise and pretty face helped her acclimate to the world of newscaster, but she lacked the big story to break her out of her current situation and rise to the next level. Showing the world what happened in Mills Hook could have been it, but the viewers of an online newspaper were too cynical, and she had suspected this. What motivated her to keep digging was her time with a person with special abilities.

Six months ago, she and Click stumbled upon a story they couldn't tell. A young woman named LaKeisha had the ability to project her feelings onto others through pheromones. Laney didn't know how this woman could do what she did, but she needed to find out, needed to find more people with special abilities. "I know, I know. I've just been thinking a lot about LaKeisha lately."

"Oh, I know. You've been obsessed with trying to find people like her ever since our time with her."

"Can you blame me? I feel so violated by the situation."

"You? I was the one who was raped."

"Charles Lickman! That's a very harsh term for what happened."

"Okay, sorry. Yes, you're right—it's not the right term. But what happened between me and her was non-consensual."

"Really? I've seen some of the women you've met in a bar and taken to this van. LaKeisha was not the worst. I'm sure you would have had sex with her had you met her in a bar."

"Yeah, but I'd have had a beer or three in me."

"So, what's the difference between numbing your mind with a few beers and numbing your mind with pheromones?"

"Did you just compare being drunk to being roofied? Come on, Laney, I'm serious. No matter how handsome a guy you're flirting with is, how would *you* feel if he affected *your* mental capacity by using pheromones? Or what if I were a woman and LaKeisha were a guy? Just because I'm a dude doesn't make what she did to me right."

Laney turned away, too ashamed that she caused the hurt within Click's eyes. LaKeisha activated desires within Laney that made her feel uncomfortable. Made her look at Click in ways she had never dreamed of. She understood how his teddy bear aspects—his dadbod-like fluff, mussy brown hair and soft beard, chubby cheeks, and a smile that promised warmth—made him appealing to a lot of women, but that wasn't what she looked for in a man. He was never her type, even now after having experienced thoughts that had made her look at him with a more lustful eye. Her attraction level for him returned to zero once she was away from LaKeisha's influence, so there were no lingering effects other than the nagging, low-level terror that someone messed with her mind like that. Made her experience feelings that weren't hers. How many other people had special abilities, and what could they do? Was there a connection between LaKeisha and what happened at Mills Hook? "You have some valid points. Sorry if I trivialized your feelings. It's . . . she affected me too. It's not what happened to you, but it still freaked me out. I guess I was projecting my frustrations onto you."

Click smirked as he took the camera from Laney and went back to watching the house. "I stand corrected about me and Dean being the only people you associate with. Clearly, you've been seeing a therapist behind my back, because that's some seriously enlightened shit."

"You're an asshole."

"Yeah, but I'm the only asshole willing to spy on people and follow them to Pittsburgh," Click said as he yanked off his headphones and handed his equipment to Laney. He hurried to the back of his van.

Securing everything on her lap, Laney asked, "Pittsburgh?"

"Where is it? I know it's here," Click mumbled to himself as he rummaged through boxes. "I'm fairly confident that's where they're going. I heard them say the word about a hundred times. Got it!"

"The old couple too? I thought they hated the professor guy? And what the hell are you doing?"

Click slid into the passenger seat and grabbed the door handle. Winded from the exercise, he took a few deep breaths to calm down and held a small disc between his fingers, an inch in diameter. "Maybe that's his special ability—convincing senior citizens to take unplanned road trips. And this is a transponder. Riding behind them on the Turnpike for four hours without being noticed would be impossible. We'll need to be inconspicuous, and that means there's the risk of losing them. I'm gonna plant this transponder on his car. Cover me."

"Cover you? What does that even—"

Click slipped out of the van and crouch-walked along the street to the Ford Expedition they had followed all day. Laney was surprised at how deftly he slipped the transponder under the rear wheel well.

Something was going on with these people. Click suggested that the older woman had a special ability. What if she could do what LaKeisha could do? What if they all could do what she did?

There was a fine line between fear and excitement, and Laney no longer knew which side of the border she was on.

CHAPTER
10

Pittsburgh, Pennsylvania

The last few rays of the setting sun washed over the slightly ramshackle house as Stone pulled up in the gray Dodge Charger.

"Well, this is fuckin' creepy," he muttered as he dragged himself out of the car. He shut the door a little harder than intended, spooking himself with the echoing sound, the neighborhood adding to his unease. Everything in this city seemed to be built on a hill, including these houses. The road sloped sharply, enough that Stone would have engaged the emergency brake if the car were his. Eight houses lined the hill before the road made a hard curve. All of them were two stories with porches and lattice-work accents. Brown. Old. Dirty with overgrown lawns. A dark forest lurked behind them as if the mountainside put the houses there to lure in unsuspecting victims.

"Get a grip, man," he muttered to himself. "This dude might be a fuckin' freak, but you're Stone. You got this."

As he walked alongside the car, his fingers traced its sexy lines, although he was oblivious to its smoothness. When he got to the front of the car, he looked back at the driver's front side fender. It was still a little stained. *Have to hit a carwash after I deal with this guy,* he thought, remembering how the true owner of the vehicle had exploded in a pulpy mass when Stone had pushed the car over him. He hadn't expected such a big mess. It had seemed simple, really. The guy had been washing the front end of the car, all hunkered down right in front of the tire, when Stone gave the vehicle a good shove. It had happened so fast that the guy hadn't even had a chance to yell. He was still alive when Stone checked on him, the wheel solidly resting atop his upper abdomen.

"Please," he had whimpered to Stone, blood escaping his lips on a foamy cloud of spittle. Stone had thought the man wanted him to end his misery, so he obliged by climbing up on the hood of the car and testing the shock absorbers, just like a surfer taking a wave. The man had died quickly after that, staring open-eyed at Stone but not in an accusatory manner. It was more in the nature of a silent thank you—an acknowledgment of the help that Stone had provided him against his pain. So, Stone took his car. After all, the dude no longer needed it, and Stone had needed to get somewhere fast. He had turned the hose against the affected area of the car and then fished the keys out of the dead man's pocket before heading west. Three hours and a couple of ignored tollbooths later, Vincent Carvello had found himself in Pittsburgh, outside a weathered two-story house, looking for a guy who made his skin crawl. Luckily the guy who once owned the car had a phone. Stone was no genius, but he could use the internet and GPS to find Kevin's house.

He did his best to stretch a little bit on his way up to the front door. The idea made him chuckle since he had no reason to stretch. He felt no cramping or tightness, just muscle memory repeating an action he had done so many times before in similar situations. He was dragging this out, plain and simple, procrastinating from the unease he felt at confronting this guy. Kevin could help him with his problem, but the freak might be the only person in the world who could hurt him. First, he needed to convince the house's locked door to open, whether it wanted to or not.

He hit the door with his shoulder, taking care to grasp the knob so it didn't crash against the wall, but it was still louder than he intended. Inside, the house was a dump. Motes of dust flashed darkly in the stark rays of the waning daylight, playing with his mind as his vision adjusted to the gloom inside the room. Stone pushed the door closed and walked farther into the house.

Stone considered sneaking through the house but nixed the idea. Kevin had to be aware of his presence. Nothing to lose. He wanted to give this meeting a chance to be civil, so he opted to hold back on threats for now. "Hey, Kevin! Kevin, it's your buddy, Stone. Remember me? We worked for Marvin. I need to talk to you." No reply came back to him. "You sick, fuck," he added quietly as he looked around.

The foyer was small and opened to a living room. The stairs leading to the second floor were in front of him, a small room to the left. Stone went into the room to the left.

A wisp of movement disturbed the darkness in the far corner. "Wha's that?" Stone jerked his head and clenched his fists, positive that something had moved, disrupting some boxes in the corner. "Probably a cat," he mumbled to himself.

This room was meant to be a dining room, but instead of a table and chairs, there was nothing but boxes and stacks of magazines. The lone window had its blinds down, so Stone's eyes needed to adjust. His skin was impenetrable, and he had killed more people than the average serial killer, but he was still spooked. Very few things unnerved Stone. Kevin was one of them.

Stone knew fear. Not as a consumer but rather as a producer. He knew how to manipulate them using fear. Except for Kevin. Every time Stone had tried to interact with him in the past, he was met with a blank stare and minimal words. It was as if Kevin didn't recognize another human being as one of his own kind.

Stone continued to the kitchen. It appeared to have seen no use in months. Empty sink, except for the stain of a leaking faucet. The counters were bare. A few of the cupboard doors hung limply half-open. Inside he saw pots, pans, plates, and . . . *what the fuck just moved?* Not a cat. A rat, maybe? Stone flung the cabinet door open and braced for the teeth and claws of a rodent, another muscle memory he no longer needed. Nothing. For the second time in as many days, he wished he had a flashlight. He tried the next cabinet and was greeted by a flash of bright white light.

Arm up to shield his face, he growled, lurched away from the cabinets, and slammed into the refrigerator. The already opened door suddenly shut on him. He shook his head to shoo away the random bursts of color. When his vision returned, he discovered he couldn't move.

The refrigerator was not a normal model; Kevin had modified this one in deadly ways. The door pressed against him, but that shouldn't have been enough to keep him pinned. Metal claws reached from the door to the fridge. It wasn't large, but Stone struggled. He was stronger than most people, having prison muscle and the lack of pain sensation to limit his efforts gave him quite the advantage, but his thrashing yielded nothing, the claws' grip too strong.

The overhead light popped on, and a person appeared in the kitchen doorway. Too small to be Kevin. Stone barked, "Who are you?"

The figure stepped awkwardly into the kitchen, and Stone would have reeled back if he could.

Debra.

Just like Bob, Debra was an amalgam of flesh and machine parts, but her naked body had a far more human look. Only her joints weren't real. Black metal protruded from her limbs to create ball and socket connections. And her right eye was no longer there, replaced by a telescoping camera lens.

She took a few more steps closer, dragging behind her the tubes and wires connecting her to something larger somewhere else. "Hello, Stone."

Trapped or not, Stone looked at her tits and said, "Hey, Debra. Lookin' gorgeous as always."

With jerky motions, she reached up and squeezed her breasts. "You always say the sweetest things."

"Where's your boyfriend? I need to talk to him."

Her hands dropped to her sides as if she had forgotten how to use them and her head cocked to the right. "Kevin is here. He wants to know why you're here."

"I need his help."

"He wants to know why he should help you."

"Because I can help him."

"He wants to know how you can help him."

Stone growled and fought to move again. "Come on, Kevin! Let me the fuck out of this thing and let's talk!"

Still standing like a stored marionette, Debra continued, "He wants you to know that you two are talking."

"Face to face!"

"He wants you to know that he finds no added value to that, especially in your agitated state."

"I'm agitated because we're not talking face to face. I find value in it. I promise I'll calm down."

Debra remained still, a faint pulse of red light glowing from somewhere within her body. Without as much as a twitch, her right index finger snapped and folded away as if on a hinge. A metal tube extended from the new opening, snaking its way through the air to Stone. A small scalpel point topped the end of the tube, Stone was ready to say something macho and insulting to boast about how useless that would be until it pierced his right shoulder.

It went in less than an inch, but that was deep enough to cause pain and draw blood. The pain was glorious, almost orgasmic. A sensation he hadn't felt in months. The blood was so rich in its redness that it shimmered almost black under the kitchen's light and oozed from his wound like paste. *Does that circulate through me now?* Stone thought. *Or is it glue holding me together?*

"He knows you respect violence. He wants you to know that he *can* hurt you."

"Tell him I understand," Stone replied.

The blade exited his skin, and the metal tentacle retracted into Debra, her finger snapping back into place. The claws of the refrigerator opened and released Stone.

Wiping his hand over his shoulder, Stone smeared his blood over his fingers. He couldn't feel it, but it didn't seem right. What was happening to his insides?

"He wants you to know that he's in the basement," Debra said. As a punctuation, the kitchen lights went out, and a small light came on from behind a door at the other end of the room.

Debra was gone in an instant, and the feet of a million ants scurried down Stone's spine. Was he willing to descend into the basement of a house where the one person who could hurt him lived? What he needed couldn't be found anywhere else. He opened the door, and down the stairs he went.

The little overhead light didn't reach the bottom of the steps. Stone swore he saw more movement and paused one last time to weigh his options. Still no other solution came to mind, so he continued down the stairs, each one creaking under his weight. Once he stepped on the floor, the entirety of the basement lit up.

A wall of heads greeted him. Fifteen faces in a three-by-five arrangement tried to talk to him. There were no words, just the tacky sound of lips opening and closing. Blood vessels, both organic and artificial, ran from the base of their necks to another section of the room, a wall of organs. Fifteen beating hearts, then thirty lungs, expanding and contracting. Livers, kidneys, spleens, stomachs. The massive tangle of intestines filled an entire wall, so it appeared as if they supported the ceiling. Tubes lined the tops of the walls, excreting thin sprays of a muculent liquid to keep the twitching organs moist and shimmering.

For the first time in a long while, Stone was thankful he had only two senses left. He was certain the sights mixed with the sweet, earthy smells would have made him puke. "What the fuck is wrong with you?"

"I don't know," Kevin answered from a different room. "I'm trying to understand people better."

Stone continued through the room of horror, and an archway of wriggling toes and curling fingers marked the border between this room and the next one, where Kevin was. Stone was thankful to leave the room of body parts but wasn't certain this one would be any better.

Black tubes as thick as arms ran along the walls and ceiling, each offering an occasional shudder as if a few large animals ran through a bizarre Habitrail. Dozens of clear tubes intertwined with the larger black ones. Liquids of various colors flowed through them as they trembled in rhythmic ways, the veins and arteries of a giant creature. Thousands of wires flowed like a chromatic river among the tubes. In the center, the heart of this macabre beast, was Kevin.

"Understand people better, huh?" Stone started as he stepped closer. He almost tripped over more tubes and wires along the floor. "I can help with that."

Naked, but with enough belly flab to cover his privates, Kevin sat upon a metal chair attached to an arm extending from the wall. The arm moved, swinging Kevin closer to Stone. "How?"

Stone hated talking to him. When most people conversed, they sprinted from one topic to the next. With Kevin, he tiptoed. "I can get you more people."

Kevin gestured to the room behind Stone. "I can get people."

"The lights are off in the surrounding houses. If the families of the people who live there haven't noticed yet, they soon will. I'd say you have a few days before the cops come knocking. I'm honestly surprised they haven't already."

A metallic arm protruded from a different part of the wall. As it moved toward Kevin, the end divided and shifted around, forming a sort of hand. The chair Kevin sat upon moved, passing him off, and the newly formed hand brought him closer to Stone. "I've been monitoring and manipulating the information the police are receiving."

"Not enough. You're still thinking of people as puzzles. You think if you put the right pieces in the right order, then you get a picture. That ain't how people work."

More metallic arms reached down from the ceiling, lined with black foam. They curled around Kevin's limbs, cradling him like a swollen baby, and moved him closer to Stone. He was glad he couldn't smell, imagining the disgusting stenches surrounding Kevin's unwashed body. He hated talking to Kevin.

"If people aren't puzzles to solve, then what are they? How can I learn more about them?" Kevin asked.

"Music," Stone answered. Back when he was in high school, before he dropped out, he had banged some hippie chick from the drama club. She started talking about this shit right after they had finished. Coincidentally, that was also when Stone learned he hated pillow talk. He was now proud of himself for remembering her stupid words for so many years. "People are like music. All of us are just different songs played by different instruments by different composers and orchestras."

"And you can teach me this music?"

Stone shrugged a shoulder. "I can help you learn a note or two."

Kevin stared at Stone, assessing this new information. Fluids pulsed through the tubes as wires slowly scraped along the floor and walls. Only God knew what machinery lurked behind the walls, ready to strike upon command. If Kevin didn't go for this, then Stone was fucked. "What do you want in return?"

Stone smiled. Now he was getting somewhere. But before he could voice his request, red lights started flashing. Three monitors extended from behind the tubes and wire along the walls and stopped in front of Kevin. There were people at the front door.

CHAPTER
11

Sandeep Masir hurt. The pain floated with him through the darkness, an unwanted companion he couldn't leave behind. He wondered if he was sleeping and this was just a dream. No, he was conscious. Wasn't he? Didn't everyone feel like they were conscious in nightmares?

What happened? What's the last thing I remember? It hurt his head to travel through memory's corridors, but he got to where he needed to go. Slots. He was at the slot machines. No? Yes. Yes, he was, but he got bored.

It had been time for a cash run. He and Jonathan weren't running low on funds, but it was time to add to them, especially if they wanted to enact their plan. The casino was the best place to do just that—win a ton of cash. Well, it was the place for Jonathan to do that. Sandeep no longer had a place.

Tapping at the slot machine's video screen, Sandeep shook his head to remove the thought. He had a place, just not at the moment. Six months ago, he and Jonathan escaped from the happenings in the town of Mills Hook. More importantly, Sandeep escaped from under the thumb of Marvin Carver.

News reports had stated that Marvin was dead, and his widow assumed ownership and operation of his multi-million-dollar empire. That wasn't enough to make either Jonathan or Sandeep comfortable using their real names in an attempt to return to a normal life. Sandeep had worked for Marvin, while Jonathan had been offered the same opportunity. What if the authorities uncovered the malfeasance that Marvin wallowed in and saw the names of Jonathan and Sandeep? What if the other freaks, like Stone or Kevin, came looking for Jonathan and Sandeep? What if the widow wanted to pick up where Marvin left off? No, neither Jonathan nor Sandeep felt comfortable using their real names. Thus, the need for fake names.

Again, Sandeep needed to depend on Jonathan for this part of the plan. Coming up with fake names to tell the women he met at bars was easy and required nothing more than an ethnic-sounding word. To insert himself back into the workforce? To open and maintain asset accounts? To purchase and sell real estate? A *verifiable* name was necessary for that. Meeting women at bars—that was an area where Sandeep excelled. His swarthy complexion, coupled with a mysterious and remarkable smile, made that easy. Meeting individuals capable of creating fake identities was not an area Sandeep was familiar with, having no experience with the dark and dirty world of the street-level criminal underbelly. That was Jonathan's area of expertise. That and winning tons of money at the poker tables, the perfect place to use his special ability. Sandeep didn't like the one he had and found no non-violent ways for it to benefit him.

While Jonathan won at the poker tables, Sandeep was relegated to wasting time at the slot machines and meeting women in bars. And the slot machines now bored him.

Leaving over a hundred dollars in credit on the machine that had dulled his mind for the past two hours, Sandeep strolled to the casino bar and took a seat. Everything was clean and unblemished, no scuffs or dings on the bar's top, no holes in the seats. A false sense of luxury. There were three women at the bar, one of them conversing with a man. Either of the other two women would satisfy Sandeep's appetite.

The bartender was a pretty blonde with a smile and smoldering eyes that could convince a man to tip more than normal. She wore a vest, tie, and collared shirt and guarded a wall of different colored boozes from around the world. So many to choose from, the drink combinations were endless. He wanted something high-end but not so rich that the women didn't know it. He kept it simple. "Blue Label, please," he answered after the bartender asked him what he'd like.

Both women noticed.

The one with shoulder-length black hair and barracuda eyes got up from her barstool. She wore a smart business suit. Not a hooker. Probably in town for a conference. With a faint smile and a surety she wore like a cloak, Sandeep assumed sales or marketing of some sort.

She arrived at the stool next to him just as his drink appeared in front of him.

"Good or bad?" she asked.

Sandeep smiled and took a sip from the glass. "Oh, very good. Some say Johnnie Walker Blue Label is the best."

"Not talking about your overpriced scotch. I'm talking about the reason you ordered it."

The question threw him for a loop. He ordered it to get her attention, but he wasn't about to tell her that. "Excuse me?"

She sighed, but her faint smile didn't disappear. Nodding toward the casino floor, she said, "Your experience in there. Good or bad? Whenever someone orders Blue Label, it's either because they had a good day and they're celebrating or it's because they had a bad day and they say, 'Fuck it, I had a bad day, so what does it matter if I spend more than I should on a drink.'"

Sandeep chuckled. A real laugh, not a practiced one he had used so many times to placate the ego of a woman whose comment or observation wasn't as clever as all her social media likes made her believe. "How do you believe I did?"

The woman sipped from her drink and made zero effort to conceal that she eyed him from head to toe. Sandeep exercised as much as possible, giving him a toned body and six-pack abs, yet he still felt the need to sit up straight and suck in his gut. Placing her glass back on the bar with precision, she said, "Well, you're not crying, so that's a sure sign you did well. And the fact that the old lady who took your seat at the slot machine started playing right away without putting any money in tells me you walked away with quite a few credits still in there. No way a loser does that. Only a big winner."

Sandeep was impressed. "That was quite observant."

"I need to be for my job."

"Which is?"

Her smile grew, her teeth perfectly white. She took another sip, this time ending with the slight lick of her lips. "Your turn to guess."

"Sales."

"Nope."

"Marketing?"

"Getting warmer."

"Acquisitions?"

She chuckled. "Something like that."

"Are you in town for an acquisitions conference?"

"No, but I am in town for business."

"What kind of business?"

"That question is for a later time."

That answer gave Sandeep pause. He believed she was being truthful. No need to withhold information if she was going to lie about it. If she was telling the truth, maybe she found him more interesting than just a warm body to have for a few hours of fun in her hotel room? "May I have a name?"

"Linda. And your name is?"

"Pakishashisharama."

She laughed. "That is most certainly not your name."

"No?"

"No, because that is nowhere close to an Indian name."

"It's Pakistani."

"It's not that either. It's a made-up name. It's such a made-up name that if I tried to say it, it would be considered a hate crime."

Sandeep laughed. This woman was interesting and smart enough to know he was lying. Of course, grifters were smart people, able to assess a mark in mere seconds. Sandeep decided to play it safe. "Okay. You got me. My name is Raj."

She squinted, clearly dubious. "I still don't believe you, but I appreciate the better effort."

"I'm glad to hear that. However, I'm now curious if Linda is your real name. It sounds too American."

"It's Canadian."

Sandeep laughed again. Yes, she was suitable for his appetite. Maybe she had a personality that would entice him to stay for pillow talk? Encouraged, he turned on his stool to face her. "It sounds like you're being coy."

Linda turned on her stool to face him as well. She slid her right hand up his thigh while her left hand slipped into her jacket pocket. Leaning in closer, her voice the purr of a hungry jungle cat, she said, "Oh, Sandeep, we are well past coy."

Sandeep? How did she know his real name?

A pinch in his upper thigh. A gun? Linda held a gun to his thigh. No, not a gun—they shoot, not pinch. A syringe of some sort? He looked up and his world wavered, then tilted. Two large men with clenched fists in black suits approached. Invisible dirt poured into Sandeep's mind, filling it and weighing it down, making it harder to use. The men looked like casino security. Good! This woman drugged him, and he wanted to report her. As he stood up, his legs melted, as did the world around him. He collapsed right into the arms of the two men . . .

. . . and now he was floating in darkness. No, not him. His mind. The woman he had met at the bar . . . Linda, wasn't it? Yes, Linda. She drugged him and now . . . ?

Sandeep opened his eyes.

His arms and legs were secured to a hospital bed, an IV tube leading from his arm to a hanging bag. Mouth pasty with a slightly metallic taste. Head still foggy but clearing up by the second, he struggled against the restraints. The thudding of his heart intensified every inch of his body, throbbing to the increasing rhythm. Muscles burned. Joints ached. Finally, he screamed and stopped fighting.

Panting, he dropped his head back into the pillow, rivulets of sweat flowing over his face.

"Are you done with your hissy fit?" A woman's voice. Familiar.

Sandeep turned his head. Standing next to his bed in a white lab coat was Linda, typing away on a tablet. He frowned, which sent a lightning bolt of electricity through his forehead. "Bitch."

"There's the charm I was expecting."

"Who are you?"

She paused from her typing to address Sandeep, looking him in the eye while displaying that faint smile. "Linda. I was hoping our time together had meant something to you."

"Fuck you."

Linda placed her fingertips to her heart and reeled back with mock indignation. "Oh my. Do you kiss your mother with that mouth? Actually, I know for a fact that you don't. You haven't seen her for over a year now, ever since you got your abilities. You haven't seen your father, either. They disowned you because they thought you tried to commit suicide."

Sandeep turned away. What she had said was accurate. There had been an accident because of his abilities, and he almost died. His parents assumed the worst about him and said he cast shame upon them and their family.

"Must be lonely," she continued, her tone less antagonistic. "No family, no career that you used to love. No real friends. Other than your brief stint working for Marvin Carver, you've really had no one in your life. Of course, we're not counting all the nameless, faceless trollops you hook up with at bars."

"Shut up," Sandeep whispered.

"Sorry, my employers won't let me."

"What do you want?"

"That all depends on what you want, Sandeep. If you want to remain thigh-deep in dirty hussies, you're in for a rude awakening. If you want to have purpose again, to be something more . . . well, I can offer that to you."

Sandeep didn't like where this conversation was going. He had heard this sales pitch before. Trying as best as he could to strip away all emotion from his face, he turned back to her. "Where am I?"

"What a coincidence," she said as she pressed a button on her tablet. The back half of Sandeep's bed lifted, moving him to a sitting position. "The people who have more answers have arrived."

The lone door to the room opened, and two men in suits entered. Both men were old enough to sport gray hair. One had a buzz cut and looked grumpily uncomfortable in his clothes, adjusting his tie twice, from the door to the side of the bed. Sandeep assumed ex-military officer who took a civilian job. The other man smiled and wore smarm like a cologne. He was the one who would do all the talking. With a bit of southern in his accent, he started, "Sandeep! Very happy to see that you're awake. I'm sure you have a lot of questions, but I feel introductions are in order first. You've already met our head of research, Linda. I'm sure you learned pretty darn fast that she is quick-witted and sharp-tongued, but trust me, her intelligence exceeds all of that. My associate here is . . . let's just call him Mr. Samuels. He likes that. And me? My name is Senator Alistair Varney, and you, my friend, are now the property of the United States of America."

CHAPTER
12

Pittsburgh, Pennsylvania

Emma Montgomery recently turned sixty-five years young. She married once, a firefighter who died in the line of duty, but never had any children. Instead, she devoted her life to her religion and her community, to anyone who truly needed help. Her life was comfortable for many years, content to follow her daily plans week in and week out. Sometimes life did funny things with comfort and plans, though.

Unusual abilities were bestowed upon her, and she assumed it was a test from God. It was, but in ways she never could have imagined. She never imagined she'd meet another man who could interest her as much as her late husband. She was wrong about that too.

Sixty-five years young and she had a boyfriend. That concept always made her chuckle whenever she was alone with her thoughts. A woman her age, rapt with such fanciful emotions, one reserved for starry-eyed girls, yet she longed for him whenever he went on his business trips, and she texted him or chatted with him face-to-face via her phone. The mere thought of him released silly butterflies that drunkenly flittered through her belly. He made her feel like a teenager in love. All she wanted right now was to be with him, but she was stuck with . . .

"Are you sure this is the right road?" Michael asked, leaning his whole body into the sharp turn up the hill. Emma assumed his movement was exaggerated to make a point.

"Yes, I'm sure." She was upset with herself for being so short with him—it wasn't very Christian of her. While she viewed her special abilities as a blessing, he viewed his as a curse. At his core, he loved his family wholeheartedly and didn't want one iota of that happiness to change. She respected him for that, but dear blessed God in Heaven, did he have to lash out like a child at anyone who held a different opinion than his?

Doing ten miles under the speed limit, he leaned forward and squinted. "Are you really sure—"

"Michael," Claire interrupted from behind him, her voice calm, soothing. "She was sure the last three turns she told you to make."

Emma thought about asking Sister Angela to bless Claire, but that would worsen Michael's mood. Instead, she offered a silent blessing in her mind. The whole reason Claire was in the car was to keep Michael under control. Of course, the whole reason Sister Angela was in the car was to keep Emma under control.

She would have loved to have Edward in the car with her. So charming. Fun. Interesting. They had been dating for less than a year, so she might still be swept up in the euphoria of something new. But she didn't care. It was so intoxicating to be with someone so charming, fun, interesting. Edward followed behind, driving Thelma and Bree in his Chevy Equinox. She appreciated how supportive he was, never once trying to convince her to use her abilities for any purpose other than what she deemed necessary, and insisting he join her on the misadventure Michael had brought to her door. Not that she had much use for her abilities in her day-to-day life. It's not often the local churches and charities need a killing machine.

A tingle raced through her, plucking her nerves like harp strings. It'd be so easy to subdue Michael, take the wheel, and call an end to this trip. But they had come too far, and if it was true that two evils might be working together, she had no choice but to help stop them. She decided to appeal to his sensitive side and said, "Michael, it was the most terrifying night of my life. I remember everything about that trip, down to the exact turns."

"Sorry," Michael replied. Neither Michael nor Emma knew Kevin's last name, so they couldn't look him up. Thelma searched employee files, but his name wasn't there either. Michael now leaned forward so far that his chest touched the steering wheel. "I didn't mean that I don't trust your judgment. I meant, how can you tell we're on the right road? There are no lights. No streetlights. Not one single light on inside or around any of the houses."

It hadn't registered with Emma that there were no lights until Michael mentioned it. Even with the high-beams on, the darkness put up an unyielding border. The lights from Edward's SUV behind them only added to the eeriness. Under-maintained two-story houses lined one side of the road; the other side was a too-steep drop down the mountain. Between each house was plenty of room for another house or two; instead, unkempt bushes and overgrown lawns filled the spaces, replete with children's toys, lawn furniture of all types, and grills. The landscape was a graveyard filled with discontent ghosts begging for escape.

The road curved slightly and took them to one house with a soft glow inside it, dimmed lights emanating from the basement windows. As Michael slowed to a stop by the house, Emma's gut tightened. She remembered this house. This house of horrors.

"Michael?" Claire whispered. "This is it, isn't it?"

Michael replied with a tremulous nod.

Emma stared at the two-story house, maintained just well enough to keep from collapsing. She didn't see the peeling paint curls on the porch or the waist-tall weeds in the front lawn dancing in the slight breeze. She saw the bodies. The blood. The blank look of soulless eyes. That was when Emma learned that evil wasn't always enticing or wrathful, but instead cold, absent of feeling. All she saw now was evil.

Sister Angela whispered from behind Emma. "What do we do now?"

Emma wondered that herself. The question hadn't left her mind since Michael and the others brought this problem to her doorstep. Stone had to be stopped. Kevin had to be stopped. But how?

Sister Angela jumped and Emma almost put her fist through the window when Bree knocked on the passenger side window. "Oh my God, I'm so sorry. I didn't mean to scare you!"

Emma didn't know what to think of Bree—she seemed like such a hellion. For some reason, Thelma was dating her, and Claire once described her as strong and independent. It must be a generational thing. But Emma liked her more than Colton. She had never met him, but Claire and Sister Angela shared stories. Rude. Pushy. Forcing his opinions without listening to others. According to them, he was worse than Michael, even though Emma found that difficult to believe. Michael disagreed with his wife and the nun, of course, but it was obvious to Emma there was great relief among everyone else that Colton had declined the invitation to come along.

"It's okay, dear," she said as she exited the SUV. Seven people congregated between the parked cars, Edward's lights still on.

"So, what's the plan?" Bree asked. Emma didn't like her tone of excitement. "We go in and stop them, right?"

"Are we sure we don't want to alert the authorities?" Edward asked.

"The authorities aren't equipped to handle what's going on in that house," Bree replied.

"Unfortunately, we don't know what's going on in that house."

"We know it's nothing good."

Bree was right. Emma had shared with Edward her encounters with Stone and Kevin as well as her dealings with other people like her, but she glossed over the details. He respected her enough not to push or ask too many questions. The downside to that was she muted the impact of the experiences. The fear. The tension. The grief of loss.

"Even though we all agree that both Kevin and Stone are evil, we don't actually know what they're doing or what they might be planning to do," Claire said. "We don't know if Stone is here. We don't know the terrain or the layout of the house."

"Do you think it's a trap?" Thelma asked.

"I don't know. What I do know is we can't just storm the house without gathering more information."

"More information?" Bree asked. "Claire, look around. There's not a single light on along this road. There's no people. It's a ghost town. It's obvious they're up to something."

"Are you sure we can handle them?" Sister Angela asked, her face the portrait of fear.

"Michael and Emma did."

Emma tensed and Edward put his arm around her shoulders. "Handled" wasn't quite the right word. Blessed to have made it out alive was a more accurate explanation.

Claire cleared her throat for everyone's attention. "Michael? I know you don't want to think about it, but it might be time to remind everyone about your experience with Kevin in this house."

Shoulders slumped, hands in his pockets, Michael kept a vigilant eye on the house but looked primed to jump back into his SUV. "We almost died. The . . . 'person' . . . who lives here can control machines and computers and electronics, down to making the wires move. The only reason —and I mean *only* reason—we're still alive is because Marvin offered him a job."

It was Edward's turn to talk. "Emma told me the story as well. As much as I don't want to put good men and women in harm's way, I think the authorities should be the ones who handle this first. Let's report the unusual blackout and direct them to this house. We can intervene if things get out of hand."

"You'll be sending them to their graves," Thelma countered. "I don't know all the details of this monster, but unless one of the first responders is a millionaire like my deceased husband, they're going to die. And that's not considering

Stone's motivations. Michael and Emma faced him too, and they said he threatened to harm children. He's dangerous and made even more so because we don't know his motives."

Edward shook his head. "I don't know. I hear what you're saying. I really do hear you, but it just doesn't feel right to take the law into our own hands. We're debating about being a bunch of vigilantes smashing down the door of a man's house who, by law, should be presumed innocent. Maybe we just take a step back and really think about how to proceed."

"Innocent" was another word not meant for the individual living here. But Emma didn't know what to do. Edward was a strong, hard man, but he had no special abilities, no way to effectively defend himself against this threat. Nor did Thelma. Nor did the first responders they debated calling. Emma abhorred violence, but the creatures they were talking about needed to face judgment. There was no non-violent way to do that. The internal debate became moot when Bree took matters into her own hands.

"We didn't just drive four hours to get here and do nothing," Bree snapped. "And we're not going to *smash* the door down."

She ran across the street and onto the porch.

Then knocked on the door.

CHAPTER
13

Sandeep paced like a zoo animal. He *was* caged, after all.

It was a twenty-by-thirty-foot room with more amenities than the traditional prison cell, and it felt more like a small studio apartment—nice bed, comfortable couch, desk, chair. Thanks to an elaborate transfer system along part of the back wall, he was supplied plenty of food for his mini-fridge and pantry to cook in the microwave or on a hot plate. Sandeep didn't need those appliances to heat his food, but he didn't like to use his abilities in such a confined space. When his abilities had manifested, he immediately discovered he wasn't immune to them.

The bookshelf in the corner was full, mostly with books covering the topics of business practices, theories, and histories, all topics he enjoyed. He was in no mood to read, stuck in this cage for three days now. Or was it four? Could it actually be five? When it was time to sleep, the lights dimmed, but there was no other way for him to tell how many days had passed. Agitated by this, he paced, looking through the clear wall. There was nothing to see other than a wall painted an institutional white on the other side of the hallway, but it was the perfect screen to view the happenings in his mind clearly.

Flames danced in bright reds and yellows and oranges, consuming this building and all the people in it. His fantasies specifically showed Alistair Varney and Linda aflame again and again. His frustration burned as hot as he imagined those flames were. He was so close to starting over, so close to Jonathan getting enough money for a new identity to begin a new life. So close to freedom. This was the exact opposite, the very fears he had been running from.

Jonathan. Sandeep wondered about his fate. Images of Jonathan danced along the white hallway. At a poker table. Maybe on a clean beach kissed by crystal clear water, a drink in one hand, a girl in the other. Or maybe he was captured by the task force as well? They were both in the same casino, after all. Sandeep doubted he'd ever see him again. Even if Jonathan avoided capture, they weren't friends, just acquaintances temporarily partnered together by fate. There was not enough of a connection between the two to motivate Jonathan to search for him. Sandeep was on his own.

Escape plans swirled through his mind. He eschewed them, not having enough information about his captors or where he was being held. Whenever he decided to break out, he'd have only one attempt. There were more luxuries here than compared to other prisons, and they would surely disappear if he ran and got caught. That was even if they wanted him alive after an escape attempt. No, he needed to plan, to study, to learn.

Footsteps echoed from down the hallway, getting closer. Sandeep stopped pacing and feigned confidence. He expected Linda or a uniformed soldier, the only people he had seen since waking up in this room three or four or five days ago. Much to his surprise, it was neither.

A young man in his mid-twenties, based on his smooth face and arrogant posture, stood in front of Sandeep's cell. From his expensive sunglasses resting atop his stylish hair to his overpriced shirt, pants, and shoes, the young man exuded wealth, reminding Sandeep of some social-media influencer douchebag. With the slightest of smirks, he said, "Wassup?"

"Who are you?" Sandeep snapped, storming close to the clear wall.

"I'm Devlin Varney. Alistair's son."

"Your father's an asshole."

"Nah. He's a good guy, just trying to do what he believes is right."

"Then you're an asshole."

Devlin laughed. "So, you must be one of my million Instasnapbook followers."

"Most assuredly not."

"If you can do what everyone says you can, I'd be one of your Instasnapbook followers."

"Is that why you're here? To get me to act like some kind of fucking circus animal for you to record and post on social media?"

Devlin slid his hands into his pockets and slouched. His eyes held a certain kindness, pity. "Look, you don't like being in there. No one would. I understand. I know about being in a prison."

Sandeep just glared at the young man; a million angry statements crammed into one fiery gaze.

"Not a prison like this one," Devlin continued. "One shaped like a shitty run-down house in a shitty run-down town with an abusive, alcoholic father who liked to punctuate his sentences with cigarette burns. My prison sentence was fourteen years, from the day I was born until Alistair adopted me."

It worked. Devlin's efforts to humanize himself in Sandeep's eyes worked. He could be lying, but there was an earnestness in his voice that Sandeep couldn't deny. He softened his expression and relaxed his stance in an effort to try the same thing. "If you know about prisons, then get me out of this one."

"You can get yourself out of this one. It's very easy to get out of. All you need is one simple word."

The word was "Yes" to Alistair's offer. As the senator had explained, Sandeep was an enemy of the state, possessing unchecked power. If he were an America-loving citizen, he'd become a member of the task force, allow them to study him, and use his talents to assist the government with other enemies of the state. It would have seemed like a good deal if he hadn't recently gotten out of a similar situation with Marvin Carver. "Not going to happen."

Devlin looked over his shoulder and took a step closer, looking more like a co-conspirator than a jailer. "Hey, I know you don't like my dad. You know what? I don't always agree with him. He isn't perfect, but who is?"

"He's asking me to do things that I don't agree with."

"That's never happened to you before? Every job you've ever had was perfect in your eyes? Your job descriptions were one hundred percent within your moral tolerance? There's no way the man you see in the mirror hasn't done things that you don't agree with. For what? A paycheck? Career advancement? Doing whatever it took to achieve your goals? Dude, I don't do much in life other than take great pics for Instasnapbook, but I do know you can't achieve your goals in prison."

Sandeep didn't know what to make of this kid. For days, members of the task force tried to convince him to join, but he resisted, not falling for their pseudo-psychological motivations. They even used his family. His parents had been emotionally manipulative, ultimately cutting him out of their lives because they deemed him a failure. Phrases like, "You're being the person they're accusing you of being," and "Don't you want to prove them wrong?" came from the task force. They tried to use his love of money against him. They dangled freedom in front of his face like the metaphorical carrot. Nothing worked on Sandeep, because it was so predictable that he steeled himself against their words, hid away the emotions that they were trying to tap into. But this kid made an excellent point—the task force wasn't asking him to do anything he hadn't already done.

Sandeep didn't reply, didn't want to give away any of his thoughts, but something in his face must have betrayed him. Devlin smiled as if he had accomplished what he set out to do and backed away from the cage. With a twinkle in his eye, he looked at Sandeep's hands and nodded. "C'mon, wizard, show me a fireball. Just one."

Sandeep thought about being obstinate and denying the kid's request, but of all the people involved in his capture and containment, Devlin had been the most honest. Making sure there was nothing flammable within his path, Sandeep extended his arm. A spot at the base of his skull began to warm, then buzzed with electricity. The sensation flowed down his neck and along his outstretched arm, growing hotter along the journey, uncomfortable by the time it reached his fingertips. Release. A melon-sized ball of flame burst a foot in front of Sandeep's hand, appearing and swirling away so quickly that it couldn't have set paper on fire.

Devlin bit his bottom lip and nodded. "Fuck, that is so cool. God, I wish I could do that."

No, you don't, Sandeep thought, the memories of accidentally setting himself on fire fresh in his mind, phantom scars making his skin itch.

Devlin opened his mouth, but before he could say anything, he looked down the hallway. Someone else was coming to see Sandeep. "Oh, hey."

Linda. Never once looking away from Sandeep, she addressed Devlin, "A little surprised to see you here. So, how's our guest doing today?"

"He's cool. Doesn't like my dad very much."

"So few people do."

Devlin's mood darkened as if something cast a shadow upon his face. After an ominous glance at Linda, he looked back at Sandeep and said, "I can understand why you don't want to be around these people." Hands in his pockets, he left.

"Spoiled, entitled little rich bitch-boy," Linda mumbled before presenting a beaming smile to Sandeep. "So, what shall we talk about today?"

Sandeep went back to glaring.

"Tsk, tsk, tsk. You shouldn't be so angry all the time, Sandeep. It isn't good for your health."

Normally he'd let her prattle on and on as she searched for the right trigger words to get through to him. Parents. Money. Power. Shame. Fear. After a few hours of listening to his silence, she'd leave. With Devlin's words still fresh in his mind, he asked, "What is it, exactly, you want from me?"

Linda's eyes widened as her jaw dropped, looking as happy as if walking into a surprise party. "Oh wow! We're actually talking today. That is some really great news. What a coincidence, too. I brought along a special guest to talk to you, so I guess I can just have him explain to you what we have to offer."

Stepping aside, Linda beckoned for someone to join her. A bald man, a little shorter than Sandeep. His basset hound eyes contained a sadness that held back a rage desperate to escape. Hands in his pockets, he had the relaxed slouch of a man ready to walk into a bar for a pint of beer or a brawl, or both. With the boredom of engaging in trite water cooler talk, he said, "Hey, Sandeep."

Jonathan.

CHAPTER
14

Pittsburgh, Pennsylvania

Michael hated millennials. Claire often chided him any time he made a disparaging comment about them, pointing out that he had plenty of good students in his class. His only retort was, "Not all kids in that generation are millennials. I know the difference between a good student and a millennial." He always stood by that statement just so he could lump all of his anger and frustration with the generation behind him into one compartmentalized word. And right now was no exception.

He didn't know Bree's age, nor did he care. If she acted like a millennial, then she was a millennial. Running up to a strange house filled with unfathomable terror and knocking on the door without considering anyone else's feelings or hypothesizing the potential consequences was myopic, selfish, and entitled. Bree was definitely a millennial. He whispered to himself, "Callow. Adjective. Immature and inexperienced."

"Bree! Get back here!" Edward tried to whisper but needed to be loud enough to get his voice across the lawn. A cartoonish mockery unbefitting the situation.

"My girlfriend isn't a child," Thelma snapped.

"She's certainly acting like one."

Michael didn't like Edward either, a man from his father's *I-know-best* generation, but on this issue, they agreed. If she was acting like a child, then she was a child.

"She's taking charge of the situation. I prefer that to standing about and dithering around. Or worse, what we're all doing right now, which is nothing," Thelma said.

"That is not entirely true," Michael said. He thought about using his ability to push Bree away from the door but doubted his actions would go according to plan, reality so rarely imitating the mental scenarios. The only other person capable of peacefully extricating Bree from this inflammatory situation was Claire. A simple thought from her and Bree would float away from the door all the way back to the cars. But one of the many reasons Michael loved his wife was her unyielding grip on the fibers of her staunch morality. That action would be too aggressive in her eyes, just as forceful as if she walked up to Bree and flung her over her shoulder. The point became moot when she shouted to everyone, "Hey, guys! The door's open!"

Michael glowered. He did not wish to do this. A walk through that house was a walk through Hell, Satan being a fat man with no sense of humanity. "We have to stop her."

"I think we should join her," Thelma said as she started to cross the street. Emma put a hand on her shoulder.

"You're not going in there," Emma said. "And neither is Edward."

"What?" Edward started. "Emma, I may not have abilities, but I can—"

Shaking her head, Emma cut him off, "Edward, please. If there were regular people in that house, then, yes, you're more than capable of handling yourself. But it's far too dangerous for you and Thelma to be involved. Michael and I have had interactions with the two individuals who might be in there. Claire and Sister Angela can join us if they'd like, but I don't believe Sister Angela's abilities would be useful."

Michael rolled his mental eyes. *Typical Bible beater*, he thought. *Facts are nothing more than dough to knead and stretch.* Michael knew he annoyed the others, but he called things what they were. The two "individuals" potentially in that house weren't people but monsters. He and Emma didn't have "interactions" with those monsters; they had to fight them for their lives. Even if Emma refused to remember the events as they had happened, Michael felt better prepared for what might be in store for them. He wished Claire wasn't joining them, though.

Sister Angela heeded Emma's flimsy warning and stayed behind while Michael, Claire, and Emma ran across the street. Michael had told Claire all of the stories, sparing no horrific detail. She knew what to expect even if she didn't have the experience.

The trio rushed through the opened door and stopped in their tracks when a bright light greeted them. The familiar tingle rushed from Michael's head and along his shoulders, a rushing river of energy. Michael dammed the flow when Bree moved the ersatz flashlight of her phone away from his eyes and shined it around the living room. She whispered, "It's so dark in here."

"No kidding," Michael whispered back. "Now let's get out of here."

"No. We came here for a reason—to stop two psychos."

"We don't know if they're here, we don't know what they're up to, and we aren't the ones to stop them. That's what the authorities are for."

Frustration burned within Bree's hot and hurried words. "We've been over this same circular argument a million times. The authorities aren't equipped to handle this."

"Neither are we," Emma said. A burst of hope bloomed within Michael's chest from the idea that Emma was starting to see things his way but fizzled away as she continued. "Without information. We need to take our time with this to understand what they're trying to do, if anything."

"Take our time?" Michael asked. "To what? Gather information? Set up around-the-clock surveillance for the next two weeks?"

"I think our discussion about what to do next should be done outside," Claire suggested.

"Claire, I think you're amazing and I usually agree with you, but not this time. I've listened to the stories Michael and Emma told. These two are *evil*," Bree argued.

"We can't—" Michael cut himself short when he heard a scraping noise from the far corner of the room.

The front door opened into the living room, a small dining room off to the left. Old newspapers covered the windows and blocked even a sliver of moonlight from entering the house. The only light came from Bree's phone, just enough to cast their faces in eerie shadows and hint at the location of the furniture. Michael was almost inaudible to his own ears as he whispered, "Did anyone else hear that?"

"What?" Bree asked, sweeping her phone from one side of the room to the other, too fast for Michael to register any details beyond the hoarder-level worth of boxes in the dining room and the living room furniture that was outdated by decades. Claire pulled out her phone and added light to the room but used slower strokes. A ghostly figure emerged from the back corner of the room. A woman. A naked woman.

Eyes wide with a charming smile unbefitting the nightmarish setting, she moved like a marionette, strings pulled by a drunken puppet master. Tone welcoming, she said, "My master knows you're here."

Michael approached slowly, with his hands up, the feelings of electricity coursing along his arms. The closer he got, the more he realized she was no longer human. Her arms and legs were held together by metal joints, a black tube and wires extended from the base of her spine and led into the darkness. She was just an advanced automaton like that thing in Thelma's building. Not real. Michael humored her anyway. "Who are you? Who's your master?"

"My name is Debra, and my master is Kevin." The fake woman took a few more jerky steps to move closer.

The lighting was terrible, but something about this woman seemed familiar. The last time he was here, a woman was on a table. Was that woman the inspiration for this machine? Is this . . . thing . . . that woman? There had been bodies in the basement. Cut up. Dissected. Michael remembered never to go into the basement, no matter what happened next. "Kevin is your master? Is . . . is he home?"

A few more steps. Her skin looked so real, the pain and fear in her eyes palpable. With the quiver of impending tears tugging at her chin, she mouthed the words, "Behind you."

With the twin lights of the phones glaring at him, Michael spun around. The darkness behind the phones moved, twisted, undulated as if Hell itself were giving birth to a pair of hands. "Emma!"

Standing between Bree and Claire, Emma reacted to Michael's warning and pushed both women out of the way while ducking under the reaching hands. The lights bounced around the room as Claire and Bree fought to steady themselves. Emma continued to move, dodging or swatting at something in the darkness. Finally getting themselves oriented, Claire and Bree focused their phone lights on Emma, on what she was fighting.

Stone.

"Bitch!" he yelled as he swung at air. Emma seemed to move faster than the light could keep up with. None of his punches connected while her attacks were furious—fingers to his eyes, chops to his throat, kicks to his crotch and kidneys. No effect.

Michael had fought this man before with Emma's help, a moment in time he tried to forget but now needed to recall. He remembered that his name was Stone. What else? They had fought in a hospital. Stone was yelling, screaming, threatening doctors. What was he saying? His skin! His skin was impervious to harm. "Emma! Take out his legs and move away."

As smoothly as a fish swimming through water, Emma darted behind Stone and kicked the backs of both knees, dropping him to the ground. A few back-flips and she was away from Michael's target.

It had been six months since Michael attempted a push this strong. At first, he was concerned about forgetting how to produce that kind of power, but he felt the electricity course through his entire body and let his emotions add to the process. His love for Claire and Sarah. His fear for his wife's safety. His anger for being put into this situation. Planting his feet shoulder-width apart, he extended his arms. A massive burst of energy released itself from his chest, neck, and shoulders, leaving behind an amazing sense of relief in its wake. The force of the invisible impact blew Stone through the wall.

Michael wasn't sure if getting Stone outside was a good strategy, but it could offer an opportunity to escape from the house. He turned to the mysterious woman, still not sure if she were real or not, and said, "Thank you."

"Kill me," she replied and then suddenly disappeared into the darkness, yanked away.

Before Michael could register what just happened, the ground shook. No, the whole house shook.

"What the hell is happening?" Bree yelled.

The center of the floor split open to expose the basement, and a dozen human hands clawed their way forth. Bree was extremely accurate. Hell was what was happening.

CHAPTER
15

Outside Atlanta, Georgia

"Ten thousand dollars is a lot of money," Mother said.

"It is. This is something you and I agree upon," Father said, "but we need to be smart about this."

"We are, Rutherford. It's the young man, his brother, and his father—no one else. We're gonna have Mr. Seltzer hold onto their phones."

"But we don't know if this will work."

"That's why we won't take the money until Horatio heals the young man. They can't get mad at us if we don't take their money."

"They can. They can walk right on out to the crowd on the other side of that curtain and tell them we don't deliver on our promises."

Mother waved her hand at Father hard enough to jiggle her arm. "We'll have Mr. Seltzer and his helpers escort them out the back. Even if they somehow try to disrupt your sermon, we'll let the congregation know that these individuals don't believe enough."

"Dang it, Belle, we're talking about giving a young man his hand back." Father looked worried. He should be. Horatio had never tried this before.

Mother and Father had always been selective of which parishioners Horatio laid hands upon. Gifting movement to the infirm was one thing, and removing ailments was their bread and butter, but they never allowed amputees near Horatio. They created all kinds of excuses, taking precautions to avoid being exposed as frauds before they could gain a following. Horatio's gift had no value unless it could be exploited.

"A year ago, he didn't have God's touch, and now he does. If his gift extends to helping those regain what they lost, then we can take our church national." Mother growled the last word.

Father ran his hand through his hair but forgot it had been properly coiffed, so he quickly did his best to fix it. He did a pretty good job considering he forwent a mirror, then approached Horatio. "What do you think, son?"

Horatio didn't care. All he could think about was last Sunday's sermon, about Molly, about being a normal teenager. He didn't care about his parents' fake congregation, nor did he relish the idea of taking this dog-and-pony show to a national stage. The hope of not being able to help popped into his mind. Maybe he'd withhold his gift to ruin his mother's designs? Oh, that thought tickled him so. Too much, because he had a slight smile when he mumbled, "Whatever."

Father put a hand on Horatio's shoulder and leaned in. "I'm sorry, son. I know this is difficult, but if this works, think of all the people you'll be able to help."

There it was, the reason he wouldn't try to hold back his ability, not even to thwart his mother. To help people. That was all he wanted to do, and if he'd have to be the sad marionette, then so be it. But he desperately wanted to be a teenager again.

Father took Horatio's silence as acceptance and gave his shoulder a supportive squeeze. Mother beckoned Father away and ordered him to revisit the stylist. Once Father's hair was in more capable hands, Mother waddled her way to Horatio, struggling with every step. It was unbefitting to tread through a house of God in flats, even if it was a tent set up in the middle of the field. Where else could she wear her three-hundred-dollar heels?

Horatio tuned her out as soon as she started talking; her words about his obligation to use his gift to honor God made his stomach churn. Thoughts of video games and social media offered a calming alternative to Mother's pleonasms about grace, honor, and duty. Molly slipped her way into his mind again, coaxing him to sneak away and find her. Sneak away. Escape. That would be easy, neither Mother nor Father paying him much mind until it was time to perform. Money would be no problem. People would be willing to pay, whether they were believers or not. He could travel the county, easily making enough to live a life in nicer hotels by visiting a local hospital and curing patients for the price of whatever cash was in the pockets of their loved ones. It'd be so easy. It was also just a fanciful daydream, his mother's scolding a harsh reminder. "Are you even listening to me? Now, sit up straight and smile. Our guests are arriving."

Three men came backstage: a frowning man with gray hair and two others, less than a decade older than Horatio, both of whom looked like younger versions of the gray-haired man. The one with the missing hand—Tanner, if Horatio had overheard his parents correctly—had a faint frown, unimpressed. Clearly not buying what Horatio's parents were selling. Tanner's brother confused Horatio. He dressed in clean blue jeans and a long-sleeved button-down shirt, just like his brother and their father, but he also wore black glasses with thick frames and looked all around the backstage area, even the underside of the tent and the ground. The area was nothing more than a few chairs and a couple of tables—one for paperwork, one for food and drinks. His lips moved as if conversing, but neither his brother nor father reacted to his words. Was he touched in the mind? Horatio wondered if he could heal those illnesses as well. Again, his parents never let him try, eschewing every check written by parents of children "touched by God's finger," as Mother would put it.

Tanner's father shook Rutherford's hand, his expression softening but not matching the smile that greeted him. With grand gestures, Rutherford led the trio to Horatio.

Mother stood behind Horatio and clutched his shoulders as if she were preparing to thwart an escape attempt. "Say the lines exactly how I gave them to you, and no lip about it, young man," she whispered into his ear while maintaining a cheerful smile. Horatio rolled his eyes and didn't care if anyone saw.

She took a few steps back and set the perimeter, everyone stopping at the same distance except for Tanner. He stood before Horatio and, with forced politeness, said, "Howdy."

From behind Tanner, his father cleared his throat. Tanner sighed and knelt. Horatio empathized, knowing the indignation of following a parent's command.

"By the grace of our one God, I have been gifted the ability to heal His children who worship under His name," Horatio said as he held out his hand. Tanner sighed again and put his hand in Horatio's. "Do you accept Jesus as your Lord and Savior?"

"Sure," Tanner muttered.

"Do you accept God, and only God, into your heart?"

"Yes." The word came out terse and fast, a sign of impatience.

Two more questions were supposed to follow, but Horatio decided the theatrics would do more harm than good. He opted not to ask them, ensuring a fight with his mother later should this not work, and put his other hand on top of Tanner's to complete the circuit. A buzz flowed from the back of his head through his left arm. After a few heartbeats, the fingertips on his right hand tingled, and then the buzz continued along up his arm, back to his head. This felt like every other time he laid hands and healed someone. Was this working?

Tanner gasped, his eyes widening, and gawped at the end of his forearm. An accident with a farming machine had mangled his hand, so the doctors removed it at the wrist. His skin stretched from something trying to poke through the blunt cap of skin.

Tanner squeezed Horatio's hand and stayed on his knees. He twisted his body and clenched his teeth but didn't close his eyes, didn't stop watching as his skin continued to stretch.

"Holy shit," Tanner's brother said. "Holy shit! This is real. This is really *real*."

Horatio's hand throbbed from Tanner's tightening grip. The flow of electricity didn't stop, didn't break the circuit. What Horatio felt was nothing compared to what Tanner had experienced with the accident, his hand ground to a stringy pulp caught between the gears of a cold machine, or what he was going through right now. Was it too much?

As five nubs sprouted from the expanding fleshy growth, Tanner started to shake and make a throaty noise akin to a trapped scream in a nightmare.

"Son?" Tanner's father said as he stepped forward.

Mother placed a hand on his arm and said, "Don't you worry none about your son. He's a strong young man, and this is all part of the process."

Lying bitch, Horatio thought. She didn't know what was normal and what wasn't. Swindling people was her version of normal. So caught up in her own world, she never once stopped to think about how abnormal it was to heal people simply by touching him. It wasn't normal to grow back other people's body parts, yet that was exactly what Horatio finished doing.

Tanner fell back when Horatio let go. Panting, Tanner sat up, sweat rolling along his face. He curled the fingers on his new hand. His father and brother rushed to him and helped him to his feet. His brother asked, "How does it feel?"

"Good," Tanner whispered. Rotating his wrist back and forth, he made and unclenched a fist. His voice warbled, either from the start of tears or a chuckle. "Real good. Strong. Like it did before."

Not one to let an opportunity slip away, Mother interjected herself into the family's happiness and escorted them away, but not before graciously accepting an envelope of cash from Tanner's father.

"I'm proud of you, son," Father said. He meant well, delivering the words while looking Horatio in the eye, but his message was misguided. Horatio did nothing to be proud of; he simply used a gift that God had given to him. "Let's get on with our celebration of the good word, shall we?"

Father slipped through the curtain to the stage and immediately launched into his pontifications. Mother and Mr. Seltzer continued conversing with Tanner and his family, leading them to the far end of the tent so they could slip from backstage into the audience without being disruptive. The other staff gathered close to the curtain to hear what Father had to say. Horatio was alone and looked at the back of the tent.

Ten thousand dollars to grow a hand back. That could last him quite a while, even if he stayed at the best hotels and ate in fancy restaurants every night. But he didn't want that. A humble apartment and sensible meals would suit him just fine. Where he wanted to go didn't matter. The priority was where he wanted to get away from. So caught up in his fantasies, he hadn't realized he had walked to the back of the tent until he was close enough to touch it.

The clapping of the crowd broke him from his reverie. He turned around and saw his father on stage, the curtain flaps held open by a few staff. Grace. Honor. Duty. Horatio sighed and walked away from his dream of escape. For now.

Horatio took to the stage and offered the crowd a nice smile, noticeable but not too wide. Like a trained circus animal, he sat in the chair at one end of the stage, ready to perform for the promise of scraps. He held his smile as Father reminded the audience that the laying of hands would go smoothly as long as everyone lined up in an orderly fashion when the time came. There were familiar faces, most notably the homeless-looking woman from last week, standing in the back. He wondered if she'd cause a fuss like she did last service, but he noticed a few new faces that seemed out of place.

Scattered throughout the crowd were three men in suits. There were plenty of upstanding gentlemen dressed in their nicest, but these three were different. They were neither farmers in their finest nor suburbanites dressing to impress. They were nondescript men in black suits and ties, all the same plain shade. And all three wore sunglasses.

While everyone else clapped in unison, their attention on the stage, these men simply sat, watching, but not the stage. Their gazes locked on the area beside the stage, where Mother escorted Tanner and his family from backstage into the audience. The three men in black suits stood and walked to the back of the tent. They conversed with the homeless woman and then left. She looked at Horatio and smiled, a wicked cut across her face exposing missing teeth.

Horatio didn't know what he had witnessed, but he knew enough about the world to know he would have to pay for his parents' sins.

CHAPTER
16

Pittsburgh, Pennsylvania

"Run!" Michael yelled.

Emma dove through the newly formed hole in the wall while Bree and Claire ran through the door. Michael tried to follow but fell, tripping over something. He tried to get back up, but something pulled at his feet, ankles, legs. He rolled over to assess the situation. The hands! The hands crawled from the newly formed canyon in the floor and grabbed his ankles. He kicked at them, but for every one he knocked away, two others took its place. And none of them were connected to arms.

As the fingers moved like fleshy spider legs, the hands scuttled across the floor and latched onto his legs. Four, five, six hands, with more crawling out of the hole in the floor. Light emanated from the basement, flickering and flashing like flames from the netherworld. Wires and tubes ran from the severed wrists to the basement. Some hands pulled while other hands braced themselves to support a larger body. *What kind of body needed so many hands?* Michael immediately regretted that thought.

A mythical creature concocted by a nightmare emerged from the pit of terror. Human arms segmented by more tubes and wires, connected to shoulders and chests, split and separated to support the mass of entrails caged within great tangles of metal. Legs and feet followed, divided like the hands and arms. What truly unnerved Michael were the heads.

More than a dozen heads snaked up from the hole, like eyestalks attached to a primordial deep-sea creature that time forgot. Skin slack, hair limp, the faces had no life to them other than their eyes, all looking right at Michael. Their lips. The lips on each face moved, whispering in varied volumes and drawls, no one voice syncing up with another, but they all repeated the same phrase, "Kill me."

"No!" Michael answered. "I can't! I won't!"

The house shuddered harder, and the crack widened, splitting the floorboards all the way to the door. Michael kicked at the hands again as he scrabbled away from the horror emerging from the basement. The house shook even more and moved.

The crack split the house in half. As the halves moved away from each other, the floor tilted. Michael reached for anything to keep from sliding into the pit below, but nothing was affixed to the floor. A lamp, the couch, the coffee table slid past him as he clawed at the floorboards. He couldn't find purchase, couldn't stop himself. He couldn't stop himself from looking into the basement as it opened up to swallow him.

The chimera of flesh and wiring flowed from below, a flower of gore blooming into a writhing mass of limbs and organs. Michael wanted to use his pushing ability, but toward what? Would it even help?

The floor continued to tilt, and he slid faster, grasping at any jagged piece of floorboard. Nothing. Suddenly, he stopped falling.

Claire.

The house had separated far enough to expose the outside. Everyone was yelling, pointing, moving, except for Claire. The cacophony of wood breaking mixed with whining machine parts turned their words into one screaming voice. After all, they were trying to deal with a moving house. But not Claire. A stolid fixture in the center of a maelstrom. His wife, arms extended, reaching for him. She used her telekinesis to pull him away from the moving house, but half a dozen hands still held on to him.

Claire amazed Michael in a hundred different ways every day before lunch, and this time was no exception. While trying to pull him away from the house, she used her ability to throw anything available at the abomination holding onto him. Furniture, lawn ornaments, a grill, mailboxes. Did her power have limits? At the moment, Michael didn't care. A lawnmower hit the wires connected to the hands pulling at Michael, yanking them away from his leg.

The release was sudden, and he flew away from the house. Claire's pulling turned into a pushing effort to soften his landing. It helped, but Michael still hit the ground hard and rolled. Pain exploded in his shoulder and radiated through his chest and back. His father's voice infiltrated his brain, telling him to suck it up. He listened. As soon as he got to his feet, Claire was in his arms, squeezing him. "Michael!"

"I love you. You're the best wife ever."

"I love you, too, and you're damn right I am. What do we do now?"

The worst questions had no answers. His first instinct was to run, but they had come all this way to find out if Stone had found Kevin. He did and they were clearly concocting a nefarious plan involving a beast made of more than a dozen humans. Now Stone was outside with no intention of peacefully going away, and Kevin turned his whole house into a machine.

The house split into four sections; each floor cut in half. The first floor split, and each half moved outward; the second floor also split in half but then rotated forward. It looked as if the house was trying to transform like the CGI robots in those insipid action movies Michael always rolled his eyes at. Right in the middle of the moving pieces was the monster, all the different sets of eyes still watching Michael.

"It's Mills Hook all over again," he whispered. The eyes. So many eyes. The air grew thick, clogged by the dirt and dust of buildings exploding and crumbling around. Hard to breathe. Hard to move. Hands grabbing at him, at Claire. Dozens of hands, hundreds. Bodies flowing like a river of death, the current heavy, crushing.

"Michael." Claire's voice. Where? Where was she? The debris cloud was too thick. Too many bodies around him. "*Michael!*"

No! That wasn't happening *now*. That happened *then*. Claire was here, with him, holding his hand and shaking his shoulder. She was here, right in front of him. "I'm here, Claire. I'm here. It's just . . . just . . ."

"I know. It's PTSD. We're in Pittsburgh, not Mills Hook. And we have to go. Let's get everyone in the cars and get out of here."

Michael believed that uneducated philistines claimed sole ownership of superstitions and wish-making; however, the thought of investing in those concepts crossed his mind when the house collapsed.

All four pieces stopped moving and fell, crushing the unnatural creation. He didn't know how or why; his sole hope was that it crushed Kevin. Two birds, one stone. Stone. The psychopath was still around and made himself known by rushing toward the group, screaming, "You fuckers! You killed him! You took away my last chance!"

Bree had her arms wrapped around Thelma, shielding her from the runaway locomotive. Emma struck before Stone could get to them, launching herself at his legs and tripping him. Ed held a broken board like a bat and hit Stone in the back of the knees to keep him from standing up. His next swing was at Stone's head, but the board broke upon contact. Emma tackled Ed to save him from Stone's punch. She was back on her feet in a blink, delivering a flurry of jabs at Stone's eyes. While Stone was distracted by Emma, Sister Angela crept up behind him, her outstretched hand reaching for Stone's head.

"No!" A tingle formed at the base of Michael's skull, a buildup of electricity. He extended his arm to create a pathway for the invisible lightning storm. As infrequently as he used his ability, he was surprised at his accuracy. The slightest ripple of air extended from his fingertips to Sister Angela's hand, pushing it away from Stone.

Stone turned and reached for her, obvious that her being a nun had no impact on his desire to kill her. Another buzz of electricity formed, and Michael released it via his other arm, this one bigger than before. This push was strong enough to knock Stone off his feet as if Michael had hit him in the chest with a sledgehammer.

"What the fuck is wrong with you, man?" Bree yelled. "She could have ended this! Turned him into a functioning member of society."

"Changing who he is would be the same as killing him."

"You've killed people before."

Bree struck a nerve. In Mills Hook, he fought and killed men. He didn't dare reflect upon that, even when he was alone; hence he had no idea what the final tally might have been. Whenever his mind refused to turn away from traipsing down dark alleys, he'd admit to himself that he had taken human life; on more optimistic—or argumentative—days, he'd debate if they were indeed human. They were all the same man. An entire town with a population of the same man. Had they been clones? Robots? Or some other inconceivable experiment that went against nature? If any of those were the case, he might have been doing God's work. Whatever the cause behind the Mills Hook happenings, Bree's statement wasn't entirely accurate. "That was different. There was no other choice. We can stop Stone, make sure he's brought to justice."

Michael positioned himself so that a portion of the collapsed roof was between him and Stone, who was now getting back to his feet. "Claire! Help!"

As Stone got back to his feet, Michael released another push, strong enough to send a quarter of the roof at Stone. Claire stood beside Michael, as she had always done throughout their lives together, and guided him. Hundreds of pounds of lumber and roof tiles crashed into Stone.

It wasn't enough.

The large man fought with the material on top of him, screaming as he moved the debris off of himself.

"We need to hit him again," Claire said as she moved behind another section of broken house.

Michael was exhausted and in pain, but he readied himself to throw more debris. Stone didn't attack, though. Panting, he glared at Michael and Claire one last time, then ran to the sanctuary of darkness within the neighboring forest.

Everyone ran to Michael and Claire, speaking or yelling all at once, voices blending together. Everyone was mad at Michael. Claire might have been as well, but she defended him and calmed everyone enough to curtail the conversation. Michael was too weary to catch the details, but Claire said it was late and they should stay at a hotel for the night.

"Guys!" Bree called out from within one of the SUVs. "Sirens! The cops are coming! We have to go!"

Seven people hurried into two vehicles and sped away, Michael wondering if he had done the right thing.

CHAPTER
17

Pittsburgh, Pennsylvania

"There. Turn there!" Laney yelled.

"Do you want to drive?" Clicked yelled back.

"If I were driving, we wouldn't have lost them."

"If you were driving, you'd be up their asses, and I think they'd notice a white creeper van trying to get their car pregnant no matter how dark it is."

Click was right. He usually was, no matter how often Laney tried to deny it. God bless him for being her oft-abused punching bag and sometimes-therapist. But God damn Pittsburgh's roads. Laney had never been to a city where she needed to think in three dimensions to drive or where four left turns would never make a square. "I just don't understand how we could have lost a car that's bugged."

Click huffed and took his phone from his lap, tossing it to Laney. The screen was black except for a red dot in the center, a blue triangle on the side, and white numbers indicating real-world distance between the two shapes. "It's a shitty transponder."

"I'll make Dean give you a raise to buy a better transponder."

"Yeah, yeah, yeah. Heard that all before. So, smart guy, where are we going?"

"We need to make a left."

"There are no lefts."

God damn Pittsburgh streets. Laney pulled out her phone and tapped her GPS app. The two-dimensional map added very little help in guiding them to the "X" on the treasure map while riding around the side of a mountain at night. But it might have helped enough. Holding the phones side by side, Laney scrolled through the map, following one particular road as it curved. Hoping it was the one, she said, "Make the next right."

86 BRIAN KOSCIENSKI & CHRIS PISANO

"You just said left."

"We're on the side of a mountain. You need to make a right to go left."

"That doesn't make any sense," Click mumbled but made the turn anyway.

"It's advanced geometry. You failed that in high school." Laney knew being mean to him in stressful situations was a terrible coping mechanism. She projected her shortcomings onto him to verbalize what she hated about herself and then used how Click dealt with her meanness as a form of affirmation. She needed psychological help. First, she needed this story.

The road curved as she had hoped, up the mountain and then back down. Yes! The blue triangle now moved closer to the red circle while the numbers went down. They were getting closer! Almost there.

"Holy fuck!" Click yelled as he slammed the brakes.

Both phones flew from Laney's hands as her head whipped forward. "Christ, Click!"

He didn't reply; instead, he slammed the van into park and rushed to the back. Laney looked up, her anger melting away into awe. The road sloped downward, houses on one side with long, unkempt lawns spacing them apart. Only one house had lights on—the one that was moving.

"Holy fuck," Laney whispered.

"I know!" Click yelled from the back of the van. He hurried back to the front and dropped a large camera on Laney's lap. Flopping into the driver's seat, he put the van back into drive and started back down the hill after turning off the headlights.

Laney's skill level with a video camera was nowhere near Click's, but she knew how to press "record" and point it at the action. In this instance, a two-story moving house had split into four separate pieces. The second-floor split from the ground floor, and then each floor divided into two. The two parts of the second floor moved away from each other and then lowered to the ground on either side of the first floor while the first floor lifted itself from the ground. There were squeals of metal against metal, accented by the sounds of cracking wood. The way it shifted made it look as if it were going to attack the people standing in front of it. *Are . . . are there* people *dangling from it?* Laney didn't know where the zoom functions were and cussed when the curvature of the road put a grouping of trees between her and the house.

She kept quiet, knowing Click couldn't go faster or they might wreck—they couldn't risk announcing their presence by turning on the headlights. But she wanted to curse to the point of inventing new words when the view cleared up. The house was no longer moving, just broken debris on the ground. The people were running in circles, but her view was blurry. Click stopped the van.

Sirens pierced the night air now that the noises of the moving house had ceased. The people on the lawn ran to the shelter of the SUVs like startled cockroaches. Within seconds, both vehicles were speeding down the hill. Laney jumped out of the van. "Come on, let's go."

"You can't be serious right now."

"As serious as a sideways colonoscopy."

"What? Ew! Your metaphors are terrifying."

"Click, get out of the van."

"Laney, get back in the van."

"Now who's the one not being serious?"

"The cops are coming up the mountain. We need to go."

"We're the fucking media! They can't tell us not to be here."

"But they sure as fuck can arrest us for being persons of interest. Think about it. We're here before they get here. We're the *only ones* here before they get here. No neighbors came out of their houses. No lights came on in any of the houses. Hell, all of the streetlights are out on this street."

Laney looked around. She had been so focused on the uncanny that she missed the obvious. "How is that possible?"

"That's a great question I have no answer to. That's such a great question that I'm sure the cops will ask us the same question, along with a million others I don't have an answer for. Oh, and super double bonus—if this has anything to do with people with special abilities, there's a good chance they'll hand us right to Senator Varney's task force. Bye-bye rights, and probably bye-bye our lives."

"Hmmm, interviewing Senator Varney is a really good idea. Maybe after this—"

Click laid on the horn to derail her train of thought. "Get in the fucking van!"

It was rare for Click to be this emotional, so Laney decided not to press the issue and got back in the van. As they drove away, she mumbled, "We're gonna get scooped."

"Jesus, Laney, what's with all the scooping? This isn't the thirties. There are four billion media outlets, and none of them are ever first to a story."

"People click on the first link they see regarding a story. We need to be that first link. There are probably a dozen news crews following those sirens."

"There will be zero news crews following those sirens because they have no idea where those sirens are going or coming from or why. And if by some miracle there are any news crews, they'll be local. Dean is national. We'll recapture any lost mouse clicks from the locals and then some. Let's just grab a coffee at the diner down the hill, and we'll come back in twenty minutes."

It was a long twenty minutes for Laney, her impatience fueled by bad coffee. She sat alone in a small booth scrolling through every local news website on her phone to make sure no one had reported the happenings on the mountain yet, while Click sat at the counter next to some blonde a decade past her prime. Ten minutes ago, he said he would ask around about the neighborhood on the mountain, but it was clear the blonde's cleavage took priority.

Just as Laney slipped her phone into her pocket and put a ten-dollar bill on the table, Click slid into the booth. "So, I got some information."

"Her digits? Her proclivities? What she wants you to cook her for breakfast tomorrow?"

"What? No. She was telling me about how a few of the regulars here live up the mountain, and they haven't been seen for a couple weeks."

"Then you got her digits?"

"Why are you being such a cunt?"

Laney suddenly felt the need to fight "the vapors" like an antebellum aristocrat. Too shocked to be offended, she couldn't believe Click had said that word let alone directed it at her. Not knowing what else to say, "How dare you?" fell from her mouth as did, "I should take you to HR."

"Is that before or after I take you to HR for creating a hostile work environment by your nastiness."

"But . . . but . . . that's what we do."

"No. We do the uptight older sister, whimsical little brother routine. It's weird because I'm a year older than you, but, hey, it works. At least it did up until this assignment. Why have you gone off the deep end with this? There seems to be more going on than just memories of LaKeisha messing with our minds."

Laney slouched back into the booth's seat, defeated. She looked out the window, past the streetlight changing from green to yellow, past the road that would take her back to the mountain, past the mountain itself. She looked at her future and how her decisions dictated what she saw. "I don't want to be irrelevant."

"No one does."

"When I was a full-time pageant contestant, that's how I felt. The feeling didn't go away when I made a feeble attempt to be an actress. Then I wanted to be a reporter, to be a part of something bigger. Of course, being a part of something bigger means being just another cog in the machine. Opportunities to be something bigger in that machine don't come along that often, and I don't want to miss or waste the opportunity with this story."

"We're not going to miss this opportunity."

Laney looked back at Click. It wasn't often that she cried, and when she did, it was because she was mad at herself. Thin streams flowed over her cheeks. "That's easy for you to say. I've been so focused on this that I have no other life. I have no boyfriend, no pets, no hobbies. Hell, the only marketable skill I have is a pretty face, and you know what? Time is slowly taking that from me while a million other pretty faces line up to take my spot. So, I guess the reason I've been so nasty to you is because I'm jealous. You've been having fun throughout this whole ordeal, and if this assignment falls apart, there's always another one. You're great at what you do, both as a videographer and a photographer. And you're way more likable than I am."

Click sat back and regarded Laney with his dark eyes, more like a disappointed father than a "whimsical little brother," as he put it. The frown went away, and his expression softened, almost to the point of pity. "See. What you did right now was open and honest communication. We should do that more often."

"Sorry." Laney didn't know what else to say.

"Apology accepted. Look at us being adults. Even though I think it's wildly crazy that you're jealous of me, I do hear you and understand what you're saying, but you need to remember two things. One, we're partners in this. I want this just as badly as you do, even though I go about things differently. You *need* to *trust me* when it comes to the story. And two, you'll never be more likable than me. I'm like a teddy bear version of Jesus. You just can't compete with that."

Laney chuckled as she wiped away her tears. "Okay, we're adults. Can we go now before you try to get me to sing Kumbaya?"

From the diner to the van, Click sang to the tune of Kumbaya, "Let's go up the hill. In my van."

"You did refer to yourself as a bratty younger brother."

"I did. I absolutely did."

Laney considered herself lucky to have a friend like Click. Everyone before him accepted her for how she looked. Click accepted her for who she was. At times she could be quite terrible, but Click helped her work through it. Someday she would return the favor.

They made their way back up the mountain, Click remembering the route. The road leading to the house that moved was blocked, which Laney expected. What she didn't expect was the construction equipment scooping up the debris and dumping it into trailer-sized dump trucks. "How did they get all that here so quickly?"

"I don't know," Click whispered. He pulled off to the berm and grabbed the video camera Laney had used earlier. Laney led the way to the two officers standing by temporary barricades, excited that no other news crews were there. She flashed a smile, but it had no effect as one of the officers said, "Sorry, ma'am, but you'll have to get back in your vehicle and move on."

Laney didn't like his tone and found it odd that he and his partner didn't look like regular officers. These two were decked out entirely in black with black helmets and visors, exposing only their mouths. She frowned and snapped, "My name is Laney Pederson, and I'm a journalist from—"

"No one is allowed beyond this point, ma'am. Not even the press."

"This is bullshit! This is America, and as a member of the press, I have the right to report what's happening on this road."

Both officers took a step closer to her. "Not tonight, ma'am."

Click grabbed her arm and said, "Sorry, officers, for any confusion. Have a nice night."

Laney tensed, readying to yank her arm free from his grip, but he squeezed and whispered, "What did we *just* talk about in the diner?"

Trust him. He had a plan.

They walked in silence back to the van. As soon as she shut the door, she said, "I know we're doing this adult thing now, so I'm *reeeeeeeally* forcing myself not to yell."

Hands shaking hard enough to jangle the keys, Click started the van and drove away fast enough to drive Laney back into her seat. "Click?"

"Do you remember Mills Hook?"

"Of course, I do!"

"Do you remember the frightening soldiers in black uniforms that killed all the people in town and then leveled it with heavy ordnance?"

"Yes, very much so. I still have nightmares about that day."

"Me too, which is why I recognized those uniforms. Laney, the guys cleaning up this mess are wearing the same uniforms."

CHAPTER
18

Pittsburgh, Pennsylvania

Carol fumed. She was a planner, a scheduler. She was always—*always*—the one in control. She had a plan, one that benefitted her greatly. A simple one, too. Run down to Georgia, grab the "miracle" kid, make him cure her cancer, then sell him to the highest bidder. Easy-peasy-dirty-kneesy. But no, the numbnuts she was working with messed it up. Men always messed up her plans! Now she was tromping through a forest in Pittsburgh at night.

She huffed and tucked a lock of hair behind her ear, tired of it falling in front of her night vision goggles. It wasn't entirely the men's fault, and the change in plan made sense. An opportunity presented itself, one that she'd be a fool to pass up. Edward had sent a text stating that he and his girlfriend's crew of misfits were looking for Kevin, the creepy robot-control man. The next text was an address. She and Conner came running, and now their new plan was to strap on some goggles and walk through the forest at night to Kevin's house.

"This looks like a good spot to stop," Conner said as he crossed his arms and leaned against a tree.

Waiting wasn't at the top of Carol's list of skills. If there were a list of unskills, then waiting would be there. Hands in her pants pockets, she paced in small circles. She wanted a smoke, a drink, and someone to go down on her, something—anything—to calm the nerves vibrating under her skin. Her smokes were back in the car, she didn't like to drink on assignment, and she was stuck with this asshole.

"Someone's gonna see you if you don't stop pacing," the asshole said.

With plenty of forest between her and the lawn, she could barely see the house in question. "No one's going to see me. We should move closer."

"Not until Eddie says so."

Carol chuckled. "I'm the one who fucks him, yet you're the one who acts like his bitch."

"Yeah? Well, at least I take this mission seriously enough to prepare for it. You look stupid."

Sure, a pantsuit with a plunging neckline blouse that exposed a ridiculous amount of cleavage, the deadliest weapon she possessed, wasn't tactical for this type of mission, but Carol was at least wearing a pair of sensible boots to trek around in the forest. She put little value in the words of a man wearing head-to-toe black with more knives and guns than a sporting goods store to compensate for oh-so-many shortcomings. "At least I don't look like an extra for a German dungeon porn movie with a ten-dollar budget. And if I look so stupid, why are you staring at my tits?"

Carol could tell he was scowling under his black mask and night vision goggles—she could almost feel it. He shifted topics by pulling his phone from one of the too many pockets. "Eddie says his girlfriend and a few others went inside."

They moved in closer but came to a halt at the edge of the forest. Carol was a city girl. Or a beach girl. Snow was acceptable, but only if at a resort. Pittsburgh had a downtown and plenty of ways to get laid, but it also had these pockets of hillbilly. The border between woods and backyard was barely discernible as she approached it. This and the neighboring lawns were all over-grown. No lights came from any house other than their target's. No streetlights either. Not much made her skin crawl, but this did. As did the target. But of all the potential merchandise available, he was the best choice.

They needed someone with an impressive ability, one that would make future bidders salivate, and for now, they needed merchandise willing to work with the buyer. From her meetings with Marvin Carver back when she sold information to him, he had told her about Kevin, the weird shit he was into and what he'd be willing to do as long as he had plenty of toys to play with. After Marvin disappeared, so did Kevin. No one thought to check his home, because no one thought he'd be stupid enough to return. Once Big Ed learned that was where the super friends were heading, creepy machine guy trumped kid Jesus.

"Holy shit, they're fucking noisy," Conner muttered.

He wasn't wrong. Two vehicles worth of people bickering about what to do. It was a four-hour drive from where they came from, and they still had no plan? No, Carol could never be friends with any of them. Maybe Bree. Just the right combination of cute and edgy. And Thelma looked like she was created straight from God's libido. But that weird thing that Bree did, curing people's addictions? No way! Carol loved her addictions right where they were.

In Carol's mind, they were all targets. After she, Edward, and Conner established themselves as the new world order of weapons moguls, they could work on the ol' snatch-n-grab-n-sell with the other ones. Sell them to people who would "persuade" them to use their abilities for whatever reasons the buyers had. It all hinged on Kevin.

"Do you think they know what they're getting into?" Conner asked.

"They must know something, or they wouldn't be here, right?"

"If they knew something, they wouldn't be walking right into the guy's house."

"I'm sure they know what to expect."

A few more minutes of silence. Carol hated silence; it was up there at the top of her unskill list with waiting. The nothingness of events led to the outside world going quiet. The inside world consisted of her brain asking for cigarettes, whiskey, and sex, the increasing volume of her heartbeat, and the wet, sloppy noises of cancer chewing away at her. The last one might have been her brain as well. Sometimes her brain wasn't nice to her, usually needing a distraction from the quiet, like a house splitting in half.

"You think they expected that?" Conner asked, his tone condescending. What an asshole.

No, they didn't expect that, judging by the way they were running around. But she did. Not specifically the house splitting into four separate pieces, but why. It was misdirection.

"They're going to get their asses kicked," Conner continued, a hint of excitement in his voice. He wanted bloodshed.

"No, they're not." Carol no longer watched the moving house but rather behind it.

"Are you daft? It's a mechanical house attacking people."

Kevin had plenty of time to modify the house, yet all it did was move around a bit. No attacking. He hadn't created a weapon; he created a distraction. The only reason he'd do that was for the sole purpose of escape. Carol ignored Conner and moved along the forest's edge. Timing her interception perfectly, she stepped in front of Kevin as he emerged from the overgrown grasses. "There you are, Chubby!"

Kevin stopped. Not so much that he stopped, but rather his chariot stopped—a padded chair on six metal legs with wires attached to various parts of his naked body. Carol's world was shades of green, yet his ghastly white body shimmered from a sheen of natural, unshowered body grease. Eyes wide, he remained petrified, a prey animal waiting for the predator to pounce before he attempted to flee.

Assuming a relaxed stance, Carol slid her hands into the pockets of her pants. "Running away?"

"I was attacked." His words were pure, like a child giving simple facts.

"So, through the woods to the nearest parking lot full of cars, right?"

"Yes."

"Sorry. I'm not going to let you do that."

Lips going tight, he squinted and furrowed his brow. The biggest surprise for Carol tonight was that he still had human emotions. The mechanical chair shifted, taking the weight on three legs. The other three changed, splitting apart to form claws, opened and ready to slice Carol to ribbons. She giggled.

Before Kevin could use his machination to shred through Carol, she removed a device from her pocket that resembled a gun handle with a lone red button and pushed it.

The mechanical arms went limp. The chair's legs gave out. Kevin's confused expression looked so pitiful as he started to pass out. Carol almost felt sorry for him. No, not really. Right as his eyes rolled up in his head, she punched him.

Rubbing her knuckles, she addressed Conner in his stupid black combat gear while he was standing around like a useless asshole. "What were you saying about being prepared for this mission?"

Conner stood in silence.

"That's what I thought," Carol said, pointing to the body on the ground. "Now call in the cleaning crew. I'm going into town to get drunk, high, and laid. If I hear from you before noon tomorrow, I'll find a way to do to you what I did to Kevin."

Conner pulled out his phone and called the cleaning crew, sirens splitting the night air by the time she got back to her car.

CHAPTER
19

Pittsburgh, Pennsylvania

"Not a word. Not a single fucking word from anyone." Claire was pissed, and her demands were directed not only at her husband and Bree, but at herself as she drove to the nearest motel. In the courtroom, she needed to be as levelheaded as possible at all times, even when there were surprises, so she had plenty of techniques to center herself. Right now, after barely surviving a situation Bree had put them in, and Michael could have stopped, she needed silence to collect her thoughts.

For a car full of hotheads, they listened well. Not a peep from any of them, just seething silence for ten minutes until she found a rat-trap motel far enough away from the sirens. Ten rooms total, Claire requested and paid for the two rooms at the far end.

"What the fuck, man?" Bree yelled at Michael as soon as they got through the door.

"Bree!" Claire snapped. With a mere thought, Claire used her ability to levitate the young woman a few inches off the ground. "We will treat this like any other meeting. That means being respectful."

"I know he's your husband, but he put our lives at risk by stopping Sister Angela from touching that psycho!"

"First of all, he wasn't the one who ran into a stranger's house before we had a plan. Just because it was taking longer to formulate a plan than you cared to wait doesn't give you the right to choose for everybody. Second of all, we don't know if Sister Angela's touch would have worked on Stone. His skin is impervious to harm, so it would be reasonable to assume that Sister Angela's abilities might not have worked on him. Let's not forget—you told us that when Marvin touched *you*, his abilities had no effect. If that were the case, Sister Angela might be hurt right now, or worse."

Bree hung her head and slumped her shoulders yet frowned and scowled. She looked like an angry ragdoll floating in the air. Claire set her down softly. Thelma put her arm around her girlfriend's shoulders to comfort her, but she exchanged a look with Claire letting her know that she agreed.

Michael also exchanged a look with Claire, but it was the secret, unspoken language they had developed over the years as a married couple. He disapproved of her using her powers to begin with, let alone in the manner she had just used them. In his mind, what she did to Bree was no different than slamming her against the wall and threatening her with a raised fist. Claire made sure to tell him with a biting expression that even though she defended his actions, she didn't agree with them. He sighed and looked away.

It didn't matter if anyone believed they were right—Claire's actions had the desired effect. Everyone's expressions softened; their anger muted. She created order from chaos with one simple act.

A sloppy circle had formed: Sister Angela sat on the bed while the three couples stood with their partners along the other three walls. Emma stepped forward and said, "Bree isn't wrong about what she said, Michael. Sister Angela's touch might not have worked, but you took that decision from her. She wanted to try to stop evil."

Michael frowned but didn't raise his voice. "She wanted to strip away who he was."

"Why is stripping away evil wrong?"

"Your religion's definition of evil is so broad and encapsulating that it would include everyone in this room."

"Don't you dare try to say that you did what you did because of my religious beliefs. And don't you dare try to defend him or compare him to any of us. The last time you and I faced him, he threatened to harm children. Only a true monster would do that."

"I am absolutely not defending him. I'm defending humanity's right not to have their mind twisted or have their personality changed by the touch of a hand by someone who believes in playing judge, jury, and executioner. That's downright cowardly."

"Cowardly is not taking a chance to stop an evil man," Bree said.

Michael rolled his eyes and moaned, "God, I wish Colton came along. At least it'd be a different voice in this circular conversation."

Bree snorted and shook her head. "Yeah, he'd be a huge help with his 'we shouldn't be using our powers' diatribe that he's spewed about a billion times."

"But he's *right*. Yes, he's said it a billion times, but that's because no one has shown the slightest indication that they're listening. Since no one is listening, I guess it's my turn to say it a billion times. These abilities are wrong, and we should not be using them."

"How can you say these abilities are wrong?" Emma asked. "Your wife saved you by using hers."

"She *had* to use them. If no one had these abilities, then we wouldn't have been in a predicament where she needed to use them. Using these abilities is wrong."

"Why do you get to decide?"

"I don't get to decide. The law gets to decide."

"I found God in Mexico," Sister Angela said. Michael opened his mouth, clearly ready to ask what that had to do with his statement but decided to shut it and listen. Everyone listened as she continued. "I lived with *mi madre*, and I never knew who my father was. She worked when she could, where she could. Our town had many *laws*, depending on which block you lived on, sometimes even which building you lived in. These *laws* taught me to keep my head down and walk fast. One night, my mother came home bruised, bleeding, her skirt ripped, and what little money she had on her stolen. She cried. She cried for hours. She cried not for herself, though, but for me. One week later, she introduced me to a man who told her that he could get me into America. I argued with her, told her I didn't want to go, told her that she was being naïve, and men break promises, men lie. I told her that he would make me do things or work in an awful place to pay off imaginary debts for his help. She told me that even if he did, it would be better than not leaving. But this man did none of those things. He helped me because he thought it was the right thing to do. That was my calling, because I had witnessed a true *miracle*. A man who wanted no money from me, no service, nothing that men with power want from women with no power. Such a thing does not exist."

Sister Angela looked at Michael. "Laws from the government didn't protect me from the laws of my neighborhood. I found God, I found salvation, and I found a life by avoiding laws."

"You're a U.S. citizen now, so you followed the law to become one," Michael countered.

"Wow," Bree moaned. "Didn't listen to a word of the story and completely missed the point."

"I didn't miss her point. Just because some laws failed her doesn't mean all laws are bad. She escaped from a place where the laws didn't work to a place where the laws do work."

Bree laughed and threw her hands in the air, exasperated. "The laws of this country don't work."

Thelma stepped in, addressing both Bree and Michael. "You're both right, and that's demonstrated by the laws of this country evolving. As I'm sure Claire can tell you, the law is changing all the time, especially when the law doesn't equal morality. Let's not forget that burning witches at the stake was perfectly legal, as was enslaving people."

"How many people had to die before those laws were changed?" Michael asked. "I apologize for sounding elitist, but Claire and I have a daughter, an eight-year-old girl. We have careers, a house, retirement plans. Yes, all of you have priorities and value in your lives, but Claire and I can't risk what we have to become revolutionaries."

"We're not talking about becoming revolutionaries, Michael," Claire said. She loved his intelligence, but it frustrated her that it came with close-mindedness.

"Then what are we talking about? We have these circular arguments every meeting and nothing gets solved. We talk about rules, yet we have none. We talk about community, but not a single one of us agrees wholeheartedly with another."

"Would you consider the church a community?" Sister Angela asked.

Michael rolled his eyes. "I can only imagine where you're going with this, but sure, I'll play along. Of course your church is a community, one with like-minded people congregating to celebrate one religion's beliefs."

"You are right that it is a community, but you are wrong that it's one religion. My congregation is five hundred people. That means five hundred different religions. No two people believe in exactly the same thing. There are lots of similarities but many, many differences that are overlooked, forgiven, or worked through in the name of those similarities. There are different people in that community with different ideals, different priorities, different goals. Some people are always there in the community, some show up when needed, some show up when in need. There are five hundred different views, but we are still one community."

"So . . . what are you saying?"

"We do what we've been doing. We meet. We talk. We look for others to join our community. Just because we found no answers tonight doesn't mean we won't find them."

"To find more people to argue with Colton and me about using their abilities?"

Sister Angela smirked. "Maybe find more who agree with you. Who will help you get us to change our minds."

"Such a bad idea."

"It's a very good idea," Emma said. "After Mills Hook, I didn't want to participate in whatever was going on. I was going to use my abilities to better things for the people in my life, if there was any way to use them to help. But now . . . now I want a voice. An opinion. She's right—whether I like it or not, whether *you* like it or not, we are all a part of the same community. It doesn't matter if we argue with each other until we're blue in the face—I want to express my voice. Don't you want a voice, Michael?"

"Not at the expense of my family. I do *not* want to put them in jeopardy."

Claire moved next to her husband and took his hand in hers. "That's the whole point of these meetings. To find ways to exist without putting anyone in jeopardy, find ways to exist within the current legal landscape while influencing the powers that be as we move forward."

"But we know very little about what's going on. Every medical practice that put these nanobots in our brains has disappeared. We don't know their motivations or if they're still operational. We don't know who was behind the Mills Hook slaughter. We don't know how many more people like us there are."

"We find them," Sister Angela blurted out. "We keep finding those like us. We *build* our community."

"I'm down with that," Bree said.

"You know I think it's a good idea," Emma said.

"I know you don't care about my opinion, Michael," Ed started as he stepped forward, "but, as I'm sure Thelma would agree, we're a part of this, too. We don't have abilities, but we love people who do. We don't want to see outsiders make decisions for you. We're here to support and help in any way we can."

"He's right," Thelma said. She squeezed Bree's hand, the message of solidarity and unity. "I'll do everything within my power to help in any way I can."

"The only community we should be a part of is normal people," Michael mumbled. He turned to Claire and looked deeply into her eyes. Faith was a mixture of fear and trust, and he had faith in her. "But . . . at least we can try to find like-minded people."

Claire had mixed feelings. She appreciated that Michael would continue to help everyone in the room with this burgeoning community. However, he only acquiesced so he could find more people who shared his mindset rather than actually helped build community. She didn't like Colton, but without him or others like him, Michael was now the sole dissident, the only voice offering a counterpoint to everyone else's opinions, making him the target for aspersions. She hated to see him in that role. But how many others out there agreed with him?

CHAPTER
20

Charlotte, North Carolina

"Nice place," Carol said as she sat at the table with Conner, an empty pint glass in front of him, a half-empty one in his hand. The restaurant was a wide-open space, lots of windows, lots of round tables covered in white cloth. The soft murmur of the polite conversations throughout the restaurant soothed Carol's pounding head from her hangover. She viewed most of her hangovers as trophies, a reward for a special night of carnality. This one was different, one that came after a long night of drinking by herself in her hotel room, wandering down the dark and lonely alleys of a town she had never visited before called Self-Pity. She didn't like it there, but the only way to get out of it was to get her plan back on track and get the two idiots she worked with to pick up the healer kid. "What'd you fuck up?"

Wiping his mouth with the back of his hand, Conner set the glass down and chuckled. "Why do you always have to be like that?"

"Because you're the way you are."

"So, you're a bitch because I'm charming, witty, and intelligent?"

"No, I'm a bitch because you have no concept of reality, and it makes me wonder how you got to become in charge of your own shop."

"I may be an asshole, but you, my dear, are *waaaay* more psycho than the devil himself, and you got your own shop."

Carol shrugged a shoulder. "Apparently the company promoted its assholes and psychos."

"Could be one of the reasons the company fell apart."

"I still blame Matthew Matthews for that. It was his shop that started this mess."

"Another psycho. Order a drink and we'll toast his untimely demise."

"His untimely demise came from him fucking up and putting us in this shit storm. I'm not drinking with you, and I'm not toasting a fuck-up dead man."

"Rumor has it you were the one who suggested he flip the switch for all the test subjects that came through his shop and started this shit storm. Come on, have a drink."

"Rumors are called rumors and not facts for a reason. I might be more inclined to order a drink you are so obviously desperate to roofie if you tell me why we're meeting here. Is this about the auction that you're setting up?"

Conner smirked. Carol hated that cat-catching-the-canary grin of his. "No peeking behind the curtains. I don't like to repeat myself, so we're just going to wait for Eddie. So, why don't you want to drink with me? You pregnant or something?"

"Not even close. I'm just not in the mood to be drugged and molested tonight. Especially not by you. I just can't deal with thinking about your tiny little garden gnome hands with your tiny little fingers all over my body. I feel like I'd wake up tomorrow with the taste of leprechaun in my mouth."

"What?" Conner squeaked and wiggled all ten fingers in front of his face. "Did you just say I have small hands? There is nothing small about them. What the hell are you talking about?"

"You're disputing my claim that you have small hands, but not my claim that you're trying to roofie me."

Conner wrapped his hands around his pint glass, knuckles white from throttling it. "I am not trying to drug you. My hands are not small. I'm just trying to connect with you."

"Not gonna happen."

Just as Conner crossed his arms over his chest and looked away, Edward arrived and sat down. "Did you compare him to a leprechaun again?"

"I did."

"He doesn't like that."

"I know."

"You should apologize so he tells us why he called this meeting."

Rolling her eyes, she moaned, "Fine. I'm sorry I called you a tiny, little, insignificant, embarrassingly small, micro-penis, good for nothing, miniscule, creepy leprechaun garden gnome. Will you pretty, pretty, pretty please tell us why we're here?"

Conner shook his head and laughed. Grabbing his pint, he said, "You are certainly an other-worldly character, you know that? Well, I'm a different kind of character. One that gets the job done. I sold our product."

"I gotta say, Conner, I'm impressed." Carol was actually sincere.

"I would agree with Carol on this matter," Edward added. "You set up, ran, and completed an auction in such a short time."

"No auction needed," Conner chuckled as he took a swig from his pint.

Carol and Edward sat straighter in their chairs. She wanted to rip the pint out of his hand, shove it up his ass, and yell, "What the fuck does that mean?" Instead, she decided to let the far suaver Edward field this question.

With the sternness of a father growing impatient, he asked, "What exactly do you mean?"

Conner set his pint back on the table and smirked, a twist of his lips that implied he wasn't sure if they were joking or not with their earnestness. "I mean I skipped setting up an auction and went straight to a buyer with a price and they accepted it."

Carol put her hands in front of her face at just the right distance to obscure Conner's head and then curled her fingers, symbolically crushing his brains. "Why the fucky-fucks of all great and mighty fucks would you do that?"

Squirming in his seat, Conner answered, "To be quick and efficient. The whole point of an auction is to get the most money, right? We knew we'd get ten million easy with a ceiling of about fifteen. Well, when I started making some inquiries, I found a buyer who accepted *twenty*. So, what's the point of wasting all that time and energy to create a hurry-up-and-wait situation."

Carol threw herself back in her chair and ran both hands through her hair now that she denied her fingers the satisfaction of choking, crushing, or gouging Conner. "Fuck, I hate when he makes a good point."

"It would be a good point if it weren't so short-sighted," Edward contradicted. "The idea behind this auction was to create interest and generate recognition and demand for our product. It wouldn't have mattered if someone bought Kevin for a million dollars or ten million; what matters is if Kevin gave them success. If a tech company used him to generate billions in new products of their own, then the next auction we hold could generate bids in the tens of millions, if not hundreds."

"Fuck, I hate when he tries to think for himself," Carol mumbled.

Conner shrugged and finished his pint. "Hey, twenty mil is twenty mil. Plenty to keep our shops running and get the next name on our list."

"The Georgia kid, right?"

"Yeah, him."

"Idiot," Edward growled.

"Well, this is what happens when you're too busy to participate because you're putting your fingers in gray pie," Carol snapped at Edward.

"I'm not the only one who left him unsupervised. It was your turn to watch him, so where the hell were you?"

She had spent the last week monitoring Horatio, tracking his every move and deep-diving into every social media outlet about peoples' sentiments. A new video leaked showing him healing some farm boy's hand, actually growing it back. People thought it was faked, a bit of special effects trickery to get more people into his parents' sham church. But there was a drastic uptick in those who believed it was real, with more than a few suggestions that Senator Varney's task force should investigate. She was so blinded by getting to Horatio first that she forwent asking pertinent questions. Until this second, she was happy to get the transaction over with, not how it came to be. "You know I'm not mature enough for this level of babysitting! Anyway, I was keeping an eye on our next target, making sure Varney hasn't snatched him yet."

Conner chuckled again. "Interesting you mentioned Varney . . ."

"No. For Christ's sake, Conner, how fucking stupid are you?" Carol said.

Conner leaned forward and scowled. "Look, you purple-haired bitch, my job was to find the players with the deepest pockets, and as sure as God made little green apples, no one has deeper pockets than the United States government, especially when it comes to the topic of xenophobia. They'll pay *anything* to spin a story that keeps the citizens shittin' their britches when they see their own shadow."

"You are such a fuck noodle, Conner."

"Fuck you."

Edward leaned forward and said, "Despite the lack of color in my language, I have to agree with Carol. Varney is our *competition*. He is going after the same products we are. The products *we* created."

"Which is something we should be taking advantage of. Like it or not, competition or not, he's currently our buyer and entering the restaurant as we speak."

Despite the fact that it wasn't his birth name, Carol wanted to do such unspeakable things to Conner that everyone with the "O'Conner" surname would rush to the nearest government office to change their name. But it was game-face time. Sending metaphorical daggers across the table to that colossal failure wouldn't help the negotiation process. Instead, she politely smiled when the silver fox came over to the table and said, "Good afternoon, lady and gentlemen. The rules of decorum state I should introduce myself before we get down to business. I'm Senator Alistair Varney, director of a special task force assigned to me by the President of the United States himself."

Carol didn't like the way he used his words as weapons, added by the fire-power of four humorless men in black suits standing behind him. She stood and shook his hand, ignoring the curious eyes of the other customers or the excited murmurs they exchanged about seeing a political celebrity. She made sure to add extra sugar to her words. "Pleased to meet you, sir. My name is Carol. This is Eddie and that's Conner. I'll be the one speaking for the group today, because I cut their tongues out and fed them to my pet Venus flytrap. His name is Matilda, and I'm teaching him how to fetch using human body parts."

No point in camouflaging the crazy. People's reactions to what she said gave her plenty of insight into who she was dealing with. Varney barely flinched and took his sweet time withdrawing his hand from hers. Smile widening, he said, "I do prefer negotiating with one person rather than a group. Saves time and energy, don't you think?"

"I do. I really do." Carol sat at the same time as Varney, never breaking eye contact. No reaction to her opening statements meant her words held no weight. If she threatened to cut his balls off, he'd laugh because he didn't respect her enough to think of her as a threat. Probably because she was a woman. This rankled her. She wanted to fuck him over in the name of feminism.

The four goons all took one step closer as Varney made himself comfortable. After a slow sip of the complimentary water, he opened with, "It's clear that you don't wish to waste any time with conversational filler about my travels here or the weather, so I'll skip past the appetizers and get right to the meal. Your colleague Mr. O'Conner and I have come to a mutually beneficial agreement. Is this still the case?"

Carol wanted to pull the plug, but that would damage their reputation and make an enemy out of a very powerful entity. Plus, Conner was right about one thing—twenty million was a good offer. The resources needed to track down products, kidnap them, and clean up afterward were *not* cheap! "As long as you still got the money."

"Oh, Carol, I work for the government. Of course, I have the money."

"Okay. Prove it." Carol slid her phone to him, ready to make the transfer after he filled in the pertinent fields.

"I need more than just the twinkle in your eye to transfer twenty million dollars."

Carol looked at Conner with an angel's smile and the devil's eyes. He tossed a set of car keys to Varney.

Smile never wavering, he asked, "These are for . . . ?"

"Windowless van in the alley," Carol answered. Once she realized that Conner had brought the product along, she knew exactly how he had been delivered. "Your boy is naked, blindfolded, and wrapped in plastic. I don't know how his abilities work, but I'm thinking he needs to touch the machine to control it, so we didn't want to take any chances. Can't guarantee he didn't piss himself, so hold your breath when you open the doors."

Holding the keys as if they were what had been urinated on, Varney handed them to a member of his entourage and then picked up Carol's phone. "While my assistant double-checks to make sure nothing untoward has happened to the van, I can get started on setting up the transaction. This also provides plenty of time to talk about our next business arrangement."

"Let's finish this one first, shall we?"

"Oh, you are a pragmatic one, aren't you?"

"I are. I really are."

Varney remained unflinching as Carol stared at him. This almost unnerved her. What kind of man showed zero concern about a psychotic bitch staring him down? Finally, his watch buzzed to display a message that the van and merchandise were intact. Varney tapped the send button, and Carol watched twenty million dollars electronically slide into her bank account. "There. Now that—"

Time for a power play. Carol snatched her phone from his hand and said, "No."

Varney chuckled. "No? You didn't even give me a chance to finish my statement."

"I don't give a fuck about that statement, just the one before that, unless the statement you were about to make was referencing your prior statement, then, in that case, the answer is, 'No.'"

Varney leaned forward and placed his elbows on the table, fingers interlaced. "It appears that you don't know who you're dealing with. I have the full backing of—"

Carol cut him off by reaching into her jacket pocket and pulling out her magic trigger, the device shaped like a gun grip with a large, red button on top. She placed it on the table in front of her. For the first time since meeting him, Varney stopped smiling. He shifted his hands, placing them on the table as if ready to push himself away, and asked, "What is that?"

"If you have to ask, you don't know who *you're* dealing with, so I'll tell you. We're the people who made the fucking products. We know how they tick; we know how to make more, and most importantly, we know how to *stop* them.

This little button does just that. Trust me, all the ones running around right now are just experiments."

Varney addressed Carol but stared at the device as if it had joined the conversation. "Experiments take place in a laboratory, under scrutiny and—"

"Sorry, Senator, but nature doesn't give a shit about laboratories. How people with these special abilities act under laboratory conditions are completely different than how they would act in the real world. Instead of keeping our shit in labs, we decided to say, 'fuck it, let's see what the real world has to say.'"

As if it took a great deal of effort, Varney pulled his eyes away from the device and looked directly into Carol's eyes. She could tell that he had a hundred things to say but chose, "Who do you work for?"

No one. She, Conner, and Edward no longer had to answer to anyone. The faceless power brokers who had control cut ties with their shops and disappeared after the Matthew Matthews shit storm. Instead of the truth, Carol went with, "A super top-secret organization that is so super top-secret that the government doesn't know about us. Or maybe they do? Maybe you and I will see each other at the office Christmas party this year. Get drunk together. Photocopy our genitalia and email the images to our boss."

"I will find you."

Carol picked up the device and lasciviously ran her index finger over the button. "No, you won't."

Varney stared at her as if she were playing with a cobra. With one final glance at the red button device, he stood and left, his goons in tow.

The trio sat in silence until all eyes and quiet conversations in the restaurant were on something other than Senator Varney. Edward said, "I understand not working with him, but did we need to make an enemy out of him?"

"No? Then why'd you and Chuckles keep your mouths shut? You know my brain is a bag of weasels, yet you let me run the entire transaction. Why? I'll tell you—it's because you know I'm right."

"Despite what your over-inflated ego is telling you, it's not a good idea to make an enemy of him."

Carol stood and slid the mechanism into her pocket. "I don't give a shit about him. I do give a shit about the holy-heal-all kid, so we're gonna prep to get him. Now."

Edward and Conner followed her as she strode out of the restaurant. She wanted to take the lead so the other two couldn't see her ear-to-ear smile from what she had just learned—Senator Alistair Varney had special abilities.

CHAPTER
21

Camp Hill, Pennsylvania

Michael studied the Jenga stack, specifically the only layer left with three blocks. The block in the middle was his only logical choice. *Deep breath and hold.* Steadily, he pushed the block with his index finger, the tower too tall for the tapping method. A bead of sweat tickled its way down his face and along his ear. In the zone. Too focused. Intensity on high. Success! The placement of the block took less time and effort than the removal. *Let's see what my opponent does with this!*

Sarah snatched a side block halfway down the tower and plunked it next to the one Michael had just placed. "Your turn, Dad."

Back to studying the stack.

Claire entered the kitchen and smiled at the game that pitted father against daughter in a challenge of wits and dexterity. "I see Sarah's winning."

Michael stood and leaned over the butcher block island to get a better view of what he had to work with. With a surgeon's touch, he removed a side block from close to the top of the tower and gently finished creating a new layer on the top. "This is Jenga, Claire. There is no position of winning or losing, just a winner and a loser."

Sarah snatched another block close to the bottom to create another single block layer and dropped it onto the top of the stack.

"Okay, so maybe at first glance, it appears that my opponent has the slightest of advantages, but lest you forget, appearances can be deceiving," Michael said as he went to work on another side piece. It was tighter than he would have liked, but the last block in the row seemed capable enough to shoulder the remaining load.

"I love your optimistic view of the situation," Claire said as she opened the refrigerator door. "Would anyone like a snack?"

"Ooooooh! Me, please!" Sarah shouted. "Double cheeseburger, lettuce, double pickle, onion, relish, tomato, and another pickle."

Claire rubbed her chin with exaggerated movements while she examined the refrigerator's contents. "Hmmm. All out of that. How about some grapes?"

"Ooooooh! Yes, please!"

Michael stopped pushing on his targeted block and withdrew his hand to say, "I'd like some too, please."

"Fresh grapes coming right up." Claire scrutinized the batch and went to the sink. "Wow, these are dirty."

Holding his breath, Michael removed the block and placed it on top of the stack. "Whew. Did you know 'Dirty Grapes' was my nickname in high school?"

Sarah snatched a block from the row toward the bottom and dropped it on the top.

"Really?" Claire asked with a chuckle. "Why was that?"

Tone soft with minimal fluctuation to distract from scrutinizing the tower, he answered, "It was the summer between junior and senior year when I worked at the winery next to the coal depot. So much coal dust. One of my responsibilities was to take a mister and clean off the dirty grapes, and that's why my friends gave me that nickname."

"Your friends from the winery you worked at? Your work winery friends?"

"Yep. An exchange student named Terry Tamaguchi and a swarthy fellow from Italy who only went by Marco."

"Tamaguchi? And he was from Japan?"

"Switzerland. Don't make assumptions."

"My apologies to Mister Tamaguchi, if he indeed self-identified as a 'he.' So, you three spent a summer washing grapes?"

As he slid a block free at an excoriatingly slow pace, Michael continued, "I'm sure he accepts your apology wherever he may be. Those halcyon days were filled with more than just keeping the pristine quality of future wine ingredients. We helped nurture the nature by reading poetry and subsequently analyzing the works, or comparing the high baroque grand painters to the pre-industrial revolution musical composers, or hypothesizing how it's possible to use wormholes to slingshot around black holes so one may travel back in time to stop the events that led to the World Wars and then debated if we even should since these events helped shape the world we're currently in. That was how we spent our days, but by the cover of night . . . well, that's when things really got interesting—we'd wash the cars of senior citizens for free. We each had matching mustaches, thick and to the corners of our mouths, as was the style of the time." To punctuate the end of his story, he gently placed the block atop the stack.

Sarah grabbed a block from the middle and slapped it next to the one her father just placed. "Did you really do all that?"

Laughing, Claire used a paper towel to dab the moisture from the grapes. "No, sweetie, he did literally none of those things. It was just a silly story."

Michael wanted to defend himself, but he was knuckle-deep in removing the perfect piece.

"Why was he telling those silly stories, then?" Sarah asked.

"Well, Daddy is being silly to get me to laugh, which is his silly way of flirting with me."

"Oooooooh. Are you two gonna do it?"

The tower crashed around Michael's hand, blocks cascading to the floor.

"Whoa!" both parents exclaimed in unison.

Too upset about losing the game, Michael let Claire take the lead with the necessary line of questioning. "Do you know what that phrase means?"

Sarah looked down and shrugged her shoulders.

"That's okay, sweetie. So, where did you hear that phrase?"

Sarah glanced up and to the right as she said, "School?"

"I don't think so. Want to try again?"

Another glance up and right. "Internet?"

"Still sounds like the wrong answer. We need the truth now."

With a body deflating sigh, she moaned, "Grandpa."

Michael tensed; his whole body turned into a fist. As a child he was subjected to his father's distorted view of manhood, decades before the term "toxic masculinity" became *en vogue*. In a misguided attempt to make Michael be a man—along with signing him up for sports he didn't know how to play and disallowing him to take dance classes—Buck Roseman would talk the same way around his son as he would his old marine buddies.

The muscles along Michael's forehead tightened, and his clenched jaw started to hurt. Aches and pains were often his companions during his trips down his childhood memory lane. Claire took one look at him and handed the grapes to Sarah. "Here you go, sweetie. Why don't you take these and play in your room?"

"Are you two mad at me?"

"Absolutely not. We never want you to stop asking questions."

"Okay," Sarah said as she snatched the grapes from Claire and raced to the stairs. Despite the stairs to the second floor being carpeted, every footfall from the kitchen to her bedroom rattled the house.

"Well, we're going to fire the babysitter," Michael said as he picked up the blocks from the floor.

"Michael . . ."

"I'm serious, Claire. His language around her is unacceptable. I'm not going to allow my father to turn our daughter into the son he wished he had."

"We don't know what happened. It might have been an accidental slip. He might have been talking on the phone, thinking he was alone, and Sarah was listening. You know how she's always snooping around."

Michael liked putting this game away. All the pieces fit precisely into the box they came in, lying side by side in perfect harmony. Life should be that way. "You're right and I know there are numerous ways she could have heard the phrase. That doesn't mean he's not acting like he did when I was a child. He can be so infuriating."

"I know. But he's all too happy to be a grandfather and take an active role in our daughter's life. And we need him."

"I know we need him. He and Mom are wonderful—and free—babysitters."

"Actually, I meant we'll be needing him soon."

"Why would we be—?" Claire was holding her phone, sympathy playing across her face. "Oh, dear God, now what?"

Claire tapped away at her phone. "Do you remember Horatio? The teenager who might be a faith healer?"

"Whose parents should be locked up for abusing their underage child by making him a participant in their scam religion to bilk money from the pockets of the undereducated? I do. I do remember him."

"Then you need to see this."

The video started with the image of a younger man, mid-twenties, looking agitated. Behind him was an older man, both dressed in flannel shirts tucked into their jeans and wearing Stetsons. The narrator's voice was barely above a whisper and held the tone and accent of a younger man from the south. "Okay, I just turned my glasses on. I got these yesterday, so I'm not sure what all they can do. Anyway, we're on our way to meet Horatio Jackson, that kid with the videos of him healin' people. I know it's all fake, and y'all know it's all fake, but then the damnedest thing happened, and I now find myself in a position to expose him and his parents for the frauds they are."

The narrator's hand popped up on screen and extended away from the viewer, grabbing the arm of the young man in view to get his attention. "This is my older brother, Tanner. He lost his hand in an accident on our farm."

"Whatever, Parker," Tanner mumbled as he rolled his eyes and turned his back on his brother. They continued to follow their father across a grassy field to a large tent.

Parker continued, "A week ago, Pa received ten thousand dollars cash and a set of instructions. The mysterious donor got Tanner an appointment to meet with Horatio. We give the money to his parents if Horatio heals Tanner. If Tanner don't get healed, then we keep the cash. Of course, this fake church won't allow phones or cameras, so that's why I bought these glasses, to record these bastards tryin' to scam us out of money. These things cost me a pretty penny, but real soon, the three of us are gonna be ten thousand dollars richer."

A hot poker skewered Michael's stomach. He knew where this was going, knew that Parker's family would not keep the ten thousand dollars. The fire in his gut grew hotter as introductions were made, and Tanner knelt in front of Horatio. A few beads of sweat rolled down Michael's face when Tanner's brother yelled, "Holy shit! This is real. This is really *real*!"

Michael handed the phone back to Claire and ran his hands over his face. "He can do what Marvin was able to do. Do we have another Marvin? Do you think he can absorb other people's abilities like Marvin could? This is a nightmare. Another Marvin."

Michael's world blurred. Why hadn't he thought of there being another Marvin before? After all, Colton had the exact same ability as he did, and they shared similar attitudes toward it. Maybe this kid was just as megalomaniacal as Marvin? The idea of facing another psychopath who could manipulate people's biology was too daunting, too oppressive. Claire saved him before he could spin too far out of control.

"We don't know what he can do." Claire placed her hand on Michael's cheek. That always worked. The softness of her touch. The warmth of her fingers. This reminded him that they were partners, and he would never have to face the world alone. "We don't even know if it's for real. Many of the comments are from people who don't believe it's true. Someone recently posted a video of a man levitating three cars, but it was quickly exposed as an elaborate hoax by a few wannabe filmmakers showing off their special effects skills. Thanks to social media completely roasting them, more and more people are quick not to believe these things."

"I feel like there is a 'however' looming nearby."

"*However*, there are well over a million views. This video has to have garnered the attention of Senator Varney's task force."

"How do we know the task force hasn't gotten to him already?"

"He's a minor celebrity. It would be in the news somewhere, and I've been checking. The church's website shows no appearance cancellations."

"Do I even want to know where their next appearance will be?"

"Georgia. This Sunday."

"Of course, it is. So, we need my parents."

"We need your parents."

Michael sighed. "Okay. I'll call my parents and then Colton. You call everyone else."

"Colton? He told us not to call him."

"Well, everyone keeps shoving the idea of community down my throat. Colton is a part of the community, so no matter how much everyone else doesn't like him, he still deserves to know what's going on in it."

Claire sighed. "Fine, as long as you realize everyone will be mad at you."

Michael shrugged. "I'm going to enact my right to be a conscientious dissenter, so everyone will be mad at me anyway." And he was going to be damned if he would spend an entire drive to Georgia being the only person who didn't want to go.

CHAPTER
22

Field outside Augusta, Georgia

Ants crawled under Emma's skin. The pews in her church were hardly considered comfortable, but they were infinitely more acceptable than the rickety slats of wood she sat on, held together by the prayers of the people who sat on them. And her church was a real church, not this farcical tent of deception.

She had no objections to sitting in a chair on the grass for a church service, often finding open-air Mass refreshing and beautiful, a delightful way to get closer to God. But this? This blasphemy of shoving too many people under a ratty tent, stuffy and smelly from the trapped heat, to sell them a false idol? Both of her legs bounced with nervous energy.

"Pssst." Michael leaned over and whispered across Sister Angela. "Feel like drawing more attention to us?"

Edward sat on her left and placed a comforting hand on her leg. She took a long breath and put her hands on his, gaining strength from his strength. As a good Christian, she should have more patience. On the flip side, as a good Christian, she should tear down this false temple.

A burst of ice bloomed within her chest at that thought. That was zealot thinking, an idea only radicals would have. She didn't think like that. Usually. It was difficult for her not to be angry while sitting here. Angry at the hucksters running this "church" and lying to people for profit. But if these people around her didn't believe the egregious lies, then these charlatans wouldn't be up there spewing their filth. Did she have the right to be so judgmental? Sister Angela didn't seem as offended, and she gave her entire life to the church. Sitting in a mockery of everything she devoted herself to, the nun smiled. Why?

Sitting next to Sister Angela, Emma leaned close and whispered, "What do you think of this?"

Sister Angela looked around, then replied, "I think the priest at my church would have the most difficult time fighting off the sin of jealousy if he saw this many worshipers."

"But they're worshiping a false idol."

"Are they? I see more Bibles and crucifixes here than any other church I've been to."

"I can't imagine God approving of this."

"No?"

Emma appreciated the sacrifice necessary to be a nun, but right now, Sister Angela was infuriating. "So, you're a 'God works in mysterious ways' type of person."

"He has yet to provide anyone with a rulebook. The closest thing we have is the Bible, and that is interpreted differently by different—"

"I know. I remember the speech you gave in the hotel room."

Sister Angela sighed. "I understand your frustration, and I'm hearing what you're saying. However, everyone is here in God's name. That is never bad. If Horatio is one of us, then he's truly miraculously healing the sick. He's giving of himself to others, in God's name. If his parents are forcing him to do this, or if they are using God's name for profit, then I have full faith that they *will* be judged. In the meantime, there are a lot of people here worshiping."

Were they? Hunger brightened the eyes of every attendee. They were all but salivating. Yes, they had Bibles and crucifixes in hand, but they held these items as if they were tickets to exchange for their selfish needs. This wasn't religion for them—this was a transaction.

"Are you okay?" Edward asked. Emma's leg had started to bounce again. "If this is too uncomfortable for you, we can step outside."

Emma placed her hands on her lap, a conscious effort to keep her legs under control. Yesterday, Michael and Claire shared a video with her that explained why they were coming to Georgia to investigate. Of course, she and Edward insisted on joining them. So did Thelma, Bree, and Sister Angela. Colton declined the invitation to join, and for that, Emma promised to put a little extra in her congregation's collection plate. Clearly, she didn't give enough thought to what she was walking into. Was she okay? No. And she didn't know why. This was blasphemy but nothing she hadn't witnessed before. Greedy people starting their own churches, sometimes their own religions, to bilk the innocent out of their money. How many televangelists have risen and fallen because of their corruption? Yet, people still flock to them with their wallets wide open. All those fake churches and false messages had upset her, but she never did anything more than throw away pamphlets handed to her or change the channel when a charlatan came on screen. "I am uncomfortable, but I don't need to step outside."

"Are you sure?"

She wasn't sure. Lately she had been more irritable, quick to have unsettling thoughts and slow to be Christian about them. Were her abilities making her feel this way? She had always wondered about them, wondered why she had them. All of the special people she had met had abilities that matched their personalities. Except for her. Her devotion to the church had been a part of her life even before memory, so why did she have the speed of a professional fighter and the accuracy of a top marksman? Why was an advocate of peace such a perfect killing machine? Whenever her irritability grew too intense, she would spend time at her fitness center to burn it away through exercise. The irritability had been coming faster lately, and the exercise took longer to burn away those feelings. Was her ability turning her into this angry person? Or had the anger always been inside her and her abilities truly matched her personality?

Calm. Sister Angela was right. The people here worshiped. Those who ran the church would get judged—*harshly*—later. Emma forced herself to believe that. "I'm sorry to be a distraction. Places like this do make me uncomfortable. The people running this are users. Using my faith, using their son, using those who don't have the proper faculties to know they're being used. I don't know if it's my abilities, but I feel a little more agitated than usual."

Edward squeezed her hand, his way of expressing his love. Retired Army, he was a hard man with a hard face and cold, slate-gray eyes. He had never once raised his voice, and he always expressed himself well. He was a good man, almost as good as her late husband. However, Edward had certain skills that her late husband never had, nor needed, such as observing hidden dangers others missed. "Well, unfortunately, you may need to use them sooner than later."

"Why do you think that?"

"The men and women by themselves, most of them in black suits. I believe they're agents for Senator Varney's task force. Judging by how many of them there are, I think they're going to go after Horatio when this is over."

Emma had been so focused on the people she expected to see here that she missed all the ones who looked like they shouldn't be here. A dozen on the left side of the tent. She couldn't get a count on how many there were on the right side because everyone suddenly stood at once. "What's happening?"

Edward stood as well and held Emma's hand to guide her to her feet. "Everyone is lining up for Horatio to heal them."

Emma hadn't been paying attention. She and the others sat toward the back of the tent, but those behind them bustled past, common courtesy be damned, shoving their way into the packed throng of people. Emma groused until she realized Michael was just as vocal about the rudeness.

"I think it would be best if Emma and Michael go to the rental," Edward said.

"What? Why?" Michael asked, making a face at a man who shouldered past him to get closer to the line.

Edward guided Emma and their companions to the back of the line, squirming as if it were a discontent snake. "Because you and Emma are both agitated by being here. I believe Varney's task force is here, and I also believe they're going to try to capture Horatio. If that happens, we need to be ready. Emma and Michael will go back to the rental and have it running. The five of us will stay in the tent and follow the crowd. We'll try to get as close as we can without raising any suspicion while keeping an eye on the potential agents. I suspect the task force doesn't want to create a big scene, so they'll wait until after the parishioners leave, flash their badges, and take Horatio."

"And then what? We're going to chase them in the huge rental SUV? You can't be serious."

"That's a possibility. There's a possibility I'm completely wrong about the situation, but if I'm not wrong, we need to be prepared."

"Unbelievable. You're actually suggesting we fight the American government. We'd be labeled terrorists. Our lives would be over. Sarah would lose her parents. Claire, you can't think this is a good idea."

"This is why we need to remove you from this situation," Edward said.

"We need to stand up for ourselves and fight for our rights, if necessary," Bree snarled.

"Rights? We're not a band of revolutionaries trying to overthrow a government. We're a handful of people who have no idea what's going on."

"All revolutions start with a handful of people," Bree replied.

Emma admired Claire's ability to deescalate a situation. She took her husband's hand and calmed him down. "You're right, Michael, we don't know what's going on. That's what we're trying to do, figure out what's going on. We need to remember that this boy is only four or five years older than Sarah. If Edward's right about the task force being here, we need to make sure they handle the situation properly."

"I don't like this. I don't like this one bit. I barely agreed to finding out if this kid has abilities, and now everyone's talking about fighting the United States government. We have a daughter to think about."

"I *am* thinking about her. What happens to her if Varney shows up at our house and takes *us* away?"

Michael's jaw muscle rippled like ocean waves, his eyes the color of storm clouds. He simply said, "Okay," and turned to leave the tent.

Edward wasted no time sharing his plan while tapping away on his phone. "We'll split up. Try to blend in. Interact with people only if you have to. I've started a text chain so we can share information. Emma, keep the SUV running just in case, and text if you see anything suspicious happening outside."

"I will," she replied. They exchanged a brief kiss, and she chased after Michael.

The parking outside was more organized than the chaos inside. The grass of the field was flattened from the dozens of cars driving on it, but there were no dirt patches or gullies from overuse. Three rows of cars, thirty to forty in each row. By the time Michael and Emma reached the rental, a family of three had made their way to their car, crying tears of joy. Emma got in the driver's seat while Michael got in the back seat. "Claire's right, you know."

"Of course, she's right," Michael huffed. "She's intelligent and forward-thinking, which are a couple of reasons I married her. I'd follow her through Hell, which is exactly where it seems like we're going. I just wasn't prepared to fight the government today."

"Doing the right thing is rarely easy."

Michael snorted. "Easy for you to say. I'm an English professor, Emma, not God's hyper ninja like you."

Emma opted not to respond. His words cut deep to the secret place inside her where she stored the concerns about her abilities. A tear rolled down her cheek as more happy families left the tent.

CHAPTER
23

Field outside Augusta, Georgia

Mother is so stupid, Horatio thought.

Both Father and Mr. Seltzer continued to express concern that Tanner's video would go viral, as they had every day since it was posted. Their concerns were repeated—too much attention too quickly could cause too many problems. Father brought it up again today as he shifted the curtain just enough to watch the seats fill. "It's standing room only already. This is too many people. We need to find Tanner's father and ask him to take that video down."

"Don't be absurd, Rutherford. That video is the best thing that happened to us. That video is free advertising, and free advertising is good business." Mother tugged the bottom of her ill-fitting suit jacket as if it were a reasonable substitute for a college degree.

"We need a bigger space."

"We'll get one real soon; don't you worry none. Thanks to that video, we have over a dozen people scheduled to meet with Horatio next week, and we're asking for a fifteen-thousand-dollar donation for each request to lay hands. That will be enough to help us start our search for a more permanent address. No more fire halls and farmers' fields."

A permanent address didn't mean a more consistent lifestyle. The bars of a cage looked the same to a zoo animal as they did to a circus animal. Horatio moved the curtain back an inch to peek at the crowd. Father was right. Standing room only. No sign of anyone interesting like Molly. Just the perfect representation of the seven deadly sins. However, something looked a little different about this crowd than past ones. There were men in black suits scattered throughout. There were plenty of nicely dressed fellows in the crowd, quite a few in suits even, but these men were alone. And their suits looked alike. "Dad? Do you see the men in black suits?"

"I do, son," Father said, looking at the crowd from behind the curtain.

"Don't they seem a might suspicious sitting by themselves?"

"They do, son."

"Nonsense," Mother snapped as she pulled Horatio away with one hand and closed the gap in the curtain with the other. "This church is open to everyone. Even single men who dress nicely. Now, quit gawking, Rutherford, and get ready to get out there."

At first, Horatio was concerned about the men in black, wondering if they had anything to do with that senator he had seen online with his task force to track down people with special abilities. Mother said that if there were people with special abilities, they were freaks and received their powers through unholy contrivances or worse—through science. Father thought that if there were people with special abilities, Horatio would be exempt from the government's scrutinous eye based on religious immunity since he received his gifts from God—no other explanation was feasible. Watching Mother boss everyone around, Horatio changed his mind and prayed that those men were from the government, here to take him away.

What life would he have if the men in black swooped in and spirited him away? A better one than this, without a doubt. Capture would be his way to freedom. The government would be stupid if they dissected him like the paranoid media would have everyone believe. Horatio had a gift, a valuable gift. Sure, the government would keep him squirreled away and study him, but they couldn't *make* him use his abilities. They would need to bargain with him, which was a better position than where he found himself now.

Time passed quickly as he fantasized about a new life. On autopilot, he stepped onto the stage, waved to the crowd, said a few words, and sat in his chair to be groped by hundreds of hands. Yes, being property of the United States government with other people like him was preferable to this. *Other people like him.* Were there other people like him? There must be, or else a task force wouldn't be needed. Oh, the thoughts of meeting more people like him!

This new fantasy blurred time, turning his indentured servitude from excruciating to almost whimsical. He needed no active thoughts to ask the scripted questions and smile as if he cared about those words. The only change in routine was the occasional need to say, "You're welcome," to a "Thank you," but those moments were rare. All his brainpower went to daydreaming about finding others like himself. He thought the superheroes of comic books and movies were too farfetched, but if there were others like him, they could do a lot of good for the world. What abilities would they have? Would they try to remain hidden, or would they let the world know they were trying to save it? How would he fit in with their grand scheme? Most importantly, were there any his age? Before his fantasies could take him any farther, there were no more people to heal.

"You did well, son," Father said as he helped him from his chair and finished with a hug.

"Thank you," Horatio whispered, not because of the compliment but for the attempt at being a father. If Mother could only put in a fraction of the effort. A half-hearted compliment to him as opposed to a full-on bitch-session to Mr. Seltzer and their ushers.

"Belle? What seems to be the fuss?" Father asked as soon as he and Horatio got backstage.

Horatio froze.

The men in black suits. Four of them talking to Mother and Mr. Seltzer.

"These men wish to meet with Horatio. I'm trying to tell them that Mass is over for today, and they'll need to come back next week. Of course, if they're willing to make a donation . . ."

"Ma'am, we're with the special task force appointed to Senator Alistair Varney from the United States government to investigate all incidences of individuals displaying abilities that far exceed the capabilities of—"

"I know about your task force," Mother cut him off. "If there are blasphemous freaks out there like you believe, then my son isn't one of them. His are the gifts from God Himself."

"It doesn't matter where his abilities come from; it's our duty to bring him to our facility in Virginia so we may study him—"

"Now hold on a minute," Father said in a stern voice Horatio had rarely heard.

"You are absolutely not studying him!" Mother shrieked in a pitch Horatio had heard at least once a day.

It was happening! What Horatio had been daydreaming about was coming true. The men in the suits were exactly who he thought they were. Fear and excitement tickled his insides, the uncertainty of the situation blending with the endless possibilities of a positive outcome, like working up the courage to introduce himself to a cute girl. Which was why he didn't move a muscle when his mother yelled at him, "Horatio! Come here!"

"Son?" Father asked. "It's okay. Come here and we'll make sure that they won't take you away."

"Sir," the agent said, voice louder, more impatient. "We are here to bring him back to our—"

"You will do no such thing!" Mother screamed.

Two more men in black suits approached Horatio, each grabbing an arm. Their grips were tight but not uncomfortable. One of them said, "You have to come with us. Please don't struggle."

Horatio did as he was told, not because a government agent told him to, but because he wanted to. He walked willingly between the two men as they led him through the backstage area. The look of anger upon his mother's face, her chubby cheeks and full lips twisting like balloons making a cartoonish animal, was an image he would never forget. Her golden goose was being taken from her, walking out of his own free will. However, no troll released its gold without a fight.

Mother shoved one of the agents hard enough to knock him off balance. "You will let go of my son, and you will let go of him *now*!"

The other three agents drew their guns.

Mr. Seltzer and the ushers stood around and looked from Mother to the agents, unsure what to do.

"Everyone, remain calm," one of the agents shouted.

Fists clenched, Mother continued storming toward Horatio, gait unsteady from maneuvering in high heels across the grass.

One of the agents pointed his gun at Mother.

Horatio wished to get away from her but not like this. Not with a man ready to kill her.

"No!" the agent she had pushed shouted to the one holding the gun. "You and Morris keep an eye on the ushers. Foster, help me with the parents."

Agent Foster holstered his gun and stepped in front of Father, all he needed to do to stop him from advancing any farther. The other agent had his hands full with Mother but kept her contained as Horatio left the backstage area with the agents.

The tent area was almost empty, with a few small groups of people socializing or hoping to talk to Horatio, groupies waiting to be blessed by the superstar idol. Another half-dozen agents shooed them away by waving badges and pointing to the exits. The stragglers complied, but not before sneaking last-second peeks over their shoulders on their way out. The last group of people had a nun and a girl with blue hair. They struck Horatio as odd since it wasn't often people like that attended Masses like this one. It didn't matter, though, as a few agents escorted those people out the left exit while those with Horatio led him toward the right exit.

Something wasn't right. The agents escorting the group with the nun raised their voices. One of them collapsed, and the other two left the ground as if tossed in the air. They crashed into the last few rows of chairs. The two with Horatio walked faster, forcing him to do the same, but the one on his right got plucked away like a flower and tossed into the chairs as well.

They were under attack! By whom? Someone who attended service? Someone he healed? Too afraid to turn around, Horatio ran side by side with the remaining agent. Outside the tent, black SUVs were waiting with their doors open. More men inside, waving and gesturing for Horatio and the other agent to hurry. Horatio jumped into the backseat just as the agent who had helped him got yanked away by an invisible hand.

The door slammed shut, and a plume of grass and dirt arced behind the SUV as the driver hit the gas pedal. Crackling voices came from the radio as the men in black suits yelled questions to each other. They sped through the field with an SUV on either side and one behind them. However, the one behind them wasn't theirs.

It wasn't fair. Horatio finally escaped from his parents, and now someone was trying to kill him.

CHAPTER
24

Field outside Augusta, Georgia

Michael hoped beyond hope that the next person to exit the tent would be Claire. Nope. There was a dark coincidence to the notion that everyone else was getting their prayers answered except for him. The next group of people? Nope. *Maybe if I believed as much as they do? Okay, God, I believe now, so let's grab Claire and get out of here.* More people, but no Claire.

"It doesn't work that way," Emma said from the front seat, her words tired.

"Excuse me?" Michael replied.

"Believing in God is more than an offhanded prayer in the backseat of a rental vehicle."

Is mind reading one of her new abilities? "Why would you think I believe that?"

"You didn't use your thinking voice; you used your real voice."

Damn it! "Well, that's embarrassing."

"No. Just sad."

"Sad that I don't want to put the lives of my daughter's parents in peril?"

"No. Sad that you don't know the difference between God and a genie."

Michael huffed. He knew it was immature, but he couldn't stop himself. Emma didn't have children, so she'd never be able to understand. There was no point in attempting any discussion with her. "A lot of people have left, so they should be coming out soon."

"Unfortunately, none of the men in black suits exited yet."

She was wrong about many things, but she was certainly right about that observation. Sliding across the backseat, Michael got a better view of the parking area to see if there was anything unusual. Not many other cars remained. A couple sedans. A handful of pickup trucks. A creepy white windowless van.

A few black SUVs. A couple of families made their way to their vehicles. A small group of people conversed in between a pickup and a car. Lots of crying and hugging. The white van was running, but the windows were tinted. Weird, but nothing noteworthy. Until the three black SUVs started simultaneously and drove to one side of the tent in tight formation. "Emma? We might have trouble."

"I agree," she said and pushed the ignition button.

As she guided the rental along the field toward the trio of black SUVs, Ed exited the tent, frowning and gesturing. Thelma and Bree followed. Michael couldn't hear anything they were saying, but their mouths were moving. Sister Angela and Claire exited as well, but they both stumbled as if pushed. Claire turned around and went back inside.

"Go! Drive!" Michael yelled.

Emma hit the gas and changed direction, aiming for their companions.

"Oh, shit," Michael mumbled when a man in a black suit exited the tent from the opposite end, running with Horatio toward the trio of SUVs. The man suddenly went airborne as Horatio jumped into the middle vehicle. All three vehicles sped away in unison.

Close enough, Emma slammed the brakes and threw the rental into park. She opened the driver's door, then slid into the passenger seat. Ed jumped into the driver's seat as the others piled in the back. They tore after the black SUVs before the doors were closed.

Michael squeezed Claire's hand. "What happened in there?"

She returned the gesture but kept her gaze on what was happening in front of them. "Ed was right. The men in the black suits grabbed Horatio right after the service. Sister Angela and I tried to stop them."

"Sister Angela?"

"She touched one of the men and he collapsed."

Michael leaned forward to get an explanation about this new ability of hers, but she was looking out the windshield as well. An exceptionally large bump made him smack his head against the back of the passenger seat. "Damn it!"

They were only doing forty, but it felt like a hundred. Every imperfection of the grassy field shook the vehicle like an unbalanced washing machine. Michael clutched Claire with one hand and grabbed the shoulder of the passenger seat with the other. He wanted them to stop but knew his request would go unheeded, and Claire would say something like, "Think about Sarah. What if someone took her from us and we couldn't stop them, but someone else could?" Well, he *was* thinking about Sarah! Thinking about how dangerous and stupid this situation was, about the hundred ways he and Claire could get arrested by the federal government, and another hundred ways they could die. And they'd be leaving that poor girl with his father. "We have to stop this."

"Then do something!" Bree yelled from the seat behind Michael. "Use your ability to stop them!"

That wasn't what he had meant. "Me? Why me?"

"Because you're the only one with an ability capable of stopping them."

"What about Emma? Super Ed can pull up to one of the SUVs, and Emma can ninja her way into it and stop them."

"Be serious!"

He was serious.

"What about you, Claire?" Thelma asked from next to Bree. "Do you think you'd be able to do anything?"

"I don't know," Claire answered. "I've never tried to move anything so heavy. And they're moving. And so are we."

But she was going to try anyway unless Michael stepped in. "I'll do it."

"Are you sure?" Bree asked. "You might break a nail."

Michael glared at her in response.

"You don't have to do this," Claire said.

"I can try. However, I push things. I don't see what good pushing something farther from us is when we're trying to catch it, so I'm up for suggestions."

"We'll try a pit maneuver," Ed said. They had been behind the middle SUV, but he guided the rental to move behind the left one.

"A what?" Michael asked.

Ed drifted a little more to the left and accelerated. He was getting closer, but they would run out of field long before catching up. "It's a pursuit tactic employed by police to bring an end to a chase. Aim for the spot above the driver-side rear tire and focus your push there."

The window came down and Michael adjusted himself. Right knee on the seat, he did his best to find a comfortable spot for his left foot to add stability as he leaned out the window. He learned there wasn't one as pain flared up his ankle and knee. Claire grabbed his shirt and belt. With every bump, the car door punched him in his ribs and nonexistent abs. The wind stung his cheeks and made his eyes water. The SUVs were speeding up, so it was now or never.

Using his hands to help aim, he pointed at the spot on the vehicle he wanted to hit. The usual tingle started at the base of his skull and ran along his shoulders and through his arms. A column of air disrupted the flying dirt and grass all the way from his fingertips to the spot he was aiming for. The disruption lasted for a fraction of a second, quickly consumed by the detritus of SUVs chasing each other over a field, but it surprised Michael. He had never seen his "push" before.

The SUV wobbled, but nothing substantial happened. He had one more chance, but his effort needed to be bigger. He knew little about his abilities, but anger helped. And there was plenty to be angry about.

This whole situation was miserable. He was in pain and here against his will, sticking his nose in other people's business, chasing after a government task force—a *federal* government task force—in some field in a hot and humid state he hated instead of spending time with his daughter who was now with his mother and father, the same man who made Michael feel inadequate for every stage of his life, including this one. The feeling at the base of his skull grew way beyond a tingle, now a jagged ball of burning electricity. Michael surprised himself again by screaming as he released the energy. Another disruption in the swirls of dirt and grass. The driver-side tires left the ground, and the driver had to fight to keep the vehicle from spinning out, but the SUV didn't flip or spin out. Instead, it and the other two sped up and pulled away from their pursuers.

"Damn it!" Michael yelled as he twisted himself back inside.

"Can we go any faster?" Bree asked.

"Not without flipping us," Ed replied.

"Are you okay?" Claire asked Michael, her hands on his face.

"Yes, thank you. I'm just happy I didn't get shot. Wait . . . why aren't they shooting at us?"

"He's right," Bree said. "Shouldn't they have tried to take out our tires or something?"

In unison, the three SUVs braked and turned ninety degrees as they all slid to a stop, forming a blockade. Ed slammed the brakes in kind, throwing everyone behind him into the seats in front of them.

By the time Michael reoriented himself, eight men in black suits stood outside the vehicles with guns drawn. He sighed and said, "Or they could be waiting to see if any of us had special abilities and then set a trap."

All eight approached and formed a semi-circle around the rental. One of them yelled, "Out of the vehicle and on the ground!"

"Their guns," Emma started. "They don't look like regular guns."

"They're not," Ed replied. "They're stun guns."

As if Ed's words flipped a switch within Emma, she flung the door open and bolted out of the vehicle. The four closest black suits shot. Emma dodged the buzzing prongs of all four stun guns. Smaller than all the men, Emma focused on speed and weak points. She dropped the man closest to her with two kicks to the backs of his knees, a backhand chop to his throat, and then jumped to funnel her weight through her elbow to his nose. Before he crumbled into a heap, she grabbed his weapon and threw it at the man behind him. As it bounced off his head, she leaped into the air and hooked her leg around his neck, her momentum enough to bring him to the ground. Hitting him a few times with his own weapon rendered him unconscious.

"Jesus, Emma! A little warning would be nice," Michael yelled as he opened the door. By the time he and Claire exited, Emma was sliding across the hood to the other two black suits who had shot at her. Maneuvering between them, she had to do little more than dodge their attacks, causing them to punch each other.

The other four agents approached, prepared to discharge their weapons. Michael built up a charge and pushed the first one he looked at, sending him tumbling along the ground. Claire lifted the man next to him and tossed him into a third. Ed took advantage of the distraction and jumped from the car fast enough to disarm the fourth black suit.

A few men were unconscious, but the others were frantically talking, describing the situation. Michael assumed they were wearing earpieces, the lone bright spot about this mess. If they had to relay the action verbally, then no one was wearing a bodycam.

Thelma and Bree exited the rental behind Sister Angela. Michael said, "You three, go get the kid."

"Why us?" Bree snapped.

"Because Sister Angela is a nun, Thelma is disarming, and you're young and hip. At least one of you can get him to trust us. And before you jump on your feminist high horse, let's not forget that you three have yet to beat the shit out of anyone or throw people around with your mind, which could be scary for a kid in his early teens to witness."

"Fine! You don't have to be a dick about it."

"Dear God in Heaven," Michael mumbled as the women ran toward the vehicle with Horatio.

The hairs on his arm stood on end. Wisps of Claire's hair stood away from her head. The air crackled.

"Michael?" Claire asked, looking around. "What's happening?"

"I don't know." The men in suits looked confused as well. He slowly turned, looking for anything out of the ordinary. "There! Claire over there."

A pinpoint of light floated in the air, then grew. By the time it became the size of a basketball, Michael had estimated it to be about thirty feet away. As it continued growing in size, the circle stopped being solid, the edges pulling away from the middle, creating a hoop of expanding light. Larger, wider, it grew. It wasn't just a hoop of light but a hole in the air. When it hit ten feet in diameter, it stopped getting bigger, now large enough to display a room within the shining white perimeter. There was movement inside. A person. A man. He stepped out of the room right onto the grassy field.

Senator Alistair Varney.

CHAPTER
25

Field outside Augusta, Georgia

Senator Alistair Varney just stepped out of a hole in the air.

Claire thought her brain was rebelling against her, reacting to the insanity of the last five minutes. The car chase. Michael willingly using his abilities. Engaging Varney's task force. Emma taking out half of it by herself. This was dangerous for so many reasons. Michael wasn't wrong about that. But she just couldn't let the government take a fourteen-year-old boy from the arms of his parents, no matter the reason. At first, she thought it wouldn't be too difficult—just use their combined abilities to fend off the task force while Horatio's parents took him to safety. After things cooled down, she and the others would explain to Horatio's parents about the community they were building and allow them unfettered access to it. That was not at all what had happened; now she was facing madness.

Alistair strolled from the hole as naturally as walking out of an office. Three men followed behind him, and the hole winked out of existence like a soap bubble popping. The three men standing behind Varney were clad in thick black material, including boots and gloves. Black helmets and full-face visors covered their heads. A pang of familiarity stabbed at Claire; she felt like she had seen these three before. Two of them were in good shape, the shorter one a bit more muscular. But the third . . . the third man was obese and sitting on a mobile chair, one with six silver legs like he was riding a metal insect. It moved without the man so much as lifting a finger. Claire had never seen this man before, but there was only one person this could be.

"Kevin!" Claire said. "I think that's Kevin."

"What?" Michael and Bree snapped.

"How?" Emma asked, a warble in her voice. "How is that possible?"

"We never saw what happened to him after his house collapsed," Claire said. "We assumed he was still inside."

Claire and her companions huddled closer. The men in black suits stopped attacking; instead, those standing tended to the fallen. Claire worried about what Emma would do. Everyone's tension was palpable, crashing about like ocean waves. The way Emma had dashed from the rental and attacked the task force suits seemed like a reflex, almost as if she had no control over it. As usual, her performance was devastating and impressive, but now wouldn't be the best time for her skills, possibly causing more harm than good. As long as there were no sudden movements, there shouldn't be a need for Emma to freak out. But that all depended on what the newcomers did.

Alistair was the consummate politician: fake smile, perfect posture, hair as if a crew of stylists had worked on it before his big entrance. He strode closer to the group, his hands behind his back as if ready to critique art in a museum. "I don't believe I need to introduce myself, do I? Obviously, we all know why I'm here. However, I'm more than a little surprised by this recent development. When I awoke this morning, I thought I would meet young Horatio and help him understand what's happening to him."

Eyes wide, Horatio poked his head out from the backseat of the SUV.

Arms outstretched as if ready to greet an old friend, Alistair gestured to Horatio. "Ah! There he is! Come on out, son. I'm here to help you. In fact, I'm probably the only one who can."

As timid as a fawn leaving the forest for the first time, Horatio stepped out of the SUV and glanced at the men in suits. Then he looked at the over-weight man on the moving, six-legged chair. Staring at Kevin, he walked toward Alistair.

"Horatio!" Claire called to him. "Horatio, please stop. Don't go to him. He just wants to study you, to use you. I know you don't know us, but we're here to help you. Some of us are special, like you. We can help. Senator Varney wants to turn you into a prisoner. Come with us and we can help you get back to your parents."

Horatio's round-eyed uncertainty disappeared into a frown of disgust at the mention of his parents. Claire's gut knotted—this boy would rather go with a stranger than back to his parents. This made Alistair smile. "Of course, we wish to study you, Horatio. You have an amazing talent. Unfortunately, it doesn't seem like the people in your life appreciate your gift, but I sure do. Yes, we'll study you, but you'll live in the lap of luxury while helping the United States government. Don't you want to help your country, son?"

"Horatio, please," Claire tried again. "These men kidnapped you. They aren't following the law."

"We're the United States government, son. We're the ones who wrote the law. And since these nice individuals decided to show up and give us a demonstration of what they can do and spout off about the importance of following the law, it's obvious they wish to join us."

"Your laws are bullshit!" Bree yelled. "You can go fuck yourself if you think we're coming with you."

Claire appreciated Bree's passion, but the young woman was impetuous. There was something about the way Alistair looked at her. His smile faded and he squinted slightly, as if he recognized her but wasn't certain where from. "Whether you like it or not, young lady, the law applies to all Americans, even special ones such as yourself. Speaking of . . . would you care to explain what your abilities are? Or better yet, show us?"

Bree gritted her teeth and clenched her fists but slouched and stepped back. Claire suspected Alistair knew who she was. If he knew her, it was safe to assume he knew everyone else. If he did, then why hadn't he shown up at their houses yet?

"So, you've suddenly become shy," Alistair continued. "No need to be coy. You'll have to show us eventually when we take you into custody."

"Not gonna happen, asshole," Bree snarled.

"Oh, don't be so sure about that."

The three men with him approached and fanned out. On his creepy chair, Kevin skittered closer to the black SUVs, closer to Horatio. Wires snaked from the back of the chair and sank into the closest vehicle's taillights. The back door flung open, and a dozen wires shot out, wrapping themselves around Horatio's arms and chest. Eyes wide, the young man pulled against them but could do nothing to stop them from dragging him to the backseat.

But Claire could.

She reached out with her mind—she could describe the sensation no other way—and grabbed ahold of him as if she did so with her hands. She tried to pull Horatio to her, but the wires had a tighter grip than she expected. She said to Michael, "I need a little help. See if you can distract Kevin."

"I can be very distracting," he replied.

Before Michael could help, the other two men clad in black moved closer. The shorter of the two held out his hands and said, "Stop what you're doing and come with us. It ain't as bad as you think."

Claire knew that voice. She knew this man.

Michael extended his hand and pushed the man away, nothing too strong, just enough to knock him off his feet and send him heels over head a few times. The taller of the black-clad men stepped forward and extended both hands. A plume of fire shot forth, a sideways geyser of flame.

Claire thanked God for Michael's reflexes. He took a step and leaned forward, looking as if he were pushing against an invisible wall with both hands. It worked! The fire wrapped around him and Claire, dissipating harmlessly behind them. The heat was intense.

Sandeep! If this was Sandeep, that meant . . . "It's Jonathan and Sandeep!"

"Edward, take care of the short one," Emma said. "He can see through other people's eyes. He's a bruiser, so don't underestimate him."

Like a prizefighter stepping into the ring, Edward clenched his fists and stalked toward Jonathan. A half-foot shorter, Jonathan stood straight and kept his elbows high as he poked at Edward with a few jabs. Edward rolled his shoulders forward and came at Jonathan with his hands tight to his face. When he moved in close enough, he went for the exposed gut throwing a left. Jonathan cocked his right fist back and swung hard. It would have been devastating if Edward had fallen for the trap. Instead, the older man spun and gave Jonathan nothing more than the muscles between his shoulder blades to strike. Left foot as a pivot point, Edward continued to spin and converted his momentum into a kick to Jonathan's chest. Claire almost felt bad for Jonathan as he flew off his feet but was happy—and impressed—that Edward could take care of himself.

Emma launched herself at Sandeep. He kept her from getting too close with his mastery of flame, sending it at her in waves and streaks and bursts. Even though she couldn't get too close to Sandeep, she kept him engaged. But that meant she had to turn her attention away from the men in black suits.

Their stun guns were single shot, but even unarmed, seven men were more than enough to apprehend Bree, Thelma, and Sister Angela. Bree's ability to remove a person's addiction did her little good in this situation, but that didn't stop her from clocking the jaw of the first black suit to approach. Thelma had been taking self-defense classes and it showed, but she was effective only when helping Bree. As soon as she tried to fend off an attacker by herself, he outmaneuvered her with ease and quickly pinned her arms behind her back. Claire couldn't help, too focused on extricating Horatio from Kevin's grip of wire fingers. Then Sister Angela surprised her.

Rushing to the man who pinned Thelma's arms behind her back, Sister Angela touched his neck. He collapsed. Claire assumed he was still alive, given a nun's traditional stance on killing, but she wondered if he would still be the same person he was when he woke up this morning. The other agents now focused on Sister Angela, aware of the nun's trick. Suddenly three of the men flew backward. Michael!

"You get Horatio," he said. "I'll help after I finish with these guys."

Michael suddenly flew backward and slammed into the rental SUV as if the vehicle had reached out and grabbed him. The rear door was still open. Face twisted in pain, he fought against whatever force was pulling him inside. But he lost the battle, getting sucked into the backseat. All the doors slammed shut.

Someone did that. Who? Sandeep and Jonathan didn't have those capabilities, and if any of the men that Thelma, Bree, and Sister Angela fought against were able to do that, they would have done it sooner. It must have been either Alistair or Kevin.

Alistair looked bored. Arms crossed over his chest, he seemed content to watch the chaos unfold around him. As a politician it was unlikely he'd get his hands dirty. It was more likely Kevin had gained control of the rental and commanded it to capture Michael. Just in case it was Alistair, Claire decided she'd take a two-birds-one-stone approach and toss Kevin into Alistair.

Claire held out her left hand toward Horatio and extended her right arm, fingers pointing at Kevin. She wasn't sure if this action was superfluous or not, but it helped her focus, especially when trying to move more than one object. A tingle flowed along her arm and jumped from her hand as if her fingers extended all the way to Kevin. Got him! He slowly started to float off his six-legged apparatus.

Kevin flailed his arms and kicked his legs like a beetle on its back as Claire lifted him higher. Panicked, he looked around and reached for the chair as he floated away. A wire shot from his wrist and made contact with the mobile chair. That was all he needed.

The wires holding Horatio retreated into the SUV, and Claire could guide the teenager to her, his eyes wide as he floated through the air. She set him down next to her and grabbed his arm, just in case the experience left him too weak in the knees to stand on his own. "Horatio? My name is Claire. My friends and I are here to help you, to protect you. There's a lot going on and you have a lot of questions, but I promise that when this is all over, we'll get everything sorted out and get you back to your parents."

Through the chaos of events swirling around them, the fighting, the wires that moved on their own, the fire erupting in controlled bursts, Horatio grabbed Claire's arm with both hands and looked her in the eye while his lips quivered. "Please don't send me back to my parents."

Claire wanted to ask why, wanted to understand what his circumstances were, but the squeal of moving metal filled the air. The wires had released Horatio only because they were needed elsewhere. Wires shot from the front and back of the SUV, weaving their way into the other two matching vehicles. All three machines rattled and shifted. The doors opened and the hoods of all three vehicles blew off. Windows exploded into kernels of glass as the vehicle frames twisted. The engines came to life as the SUVs broke apart and reformed.

Everyone stopped what they were doing to watch Kevin's creation. Instinctively, Claire put herself between Horatio and the mechanical nightmare.

The center vehicle and parts of the other two formed a protective shell around Kevin, his mechanized chair settling on top of a chassis with the twelve tires on the underside. Two engines protruded from either side and extended forward like deadly hands, the fans spinning at blinding speeds. The giant machine kept transforming as it rolled forward, making accommodations for the third engine.

Claire had enough.

This situation was too much to handle. Kevin's power was deadly and seemingly limitless. A United States politician permitted that monster to abuse his abilities freely in an effort to capture a teenage boy. There were agents of this new task force willingly working for a man who thought this course of action was acceptable. Then there were Jonathan and Sandeep, two individuals she met while researching how she received these abilities. She had spent time with them, learned about their lives. Now they were here, hunting down their own kind.

This had to stop.

Now.

Claire extended her hands, reaching for the approaching vehicle. The men in black suits ran toward Alistair to get out of the machine's way while Bree, Thelma, and Sister Angela ran in the opposite direction. Jonathan and Sandeep disengaged from their efforts against Edward and Emma; they too moved closer to Alistair as if he were a shield.

Claire did not move.

All three engines of Kevin's machine revved harder as it rolled faster toward Claire.

"Claire!" Michael shouted; his voice muffled as he pounded on the rental's windows. "Claire! Run!"

Claire didn't run. She planted her feet and stood firm. The electricity flowed from the base of her skull and rushed to her fingertips. But she didn't release it. The sensation built up, growing stronger. She reached out with her mind, touching every part of the machine she could see.

"Claire!"

The engines hummed and the body of the death machine squealed as it rolled closer.

Claire's fingers curled as if grabbing every piece of the machine. The force of her heartbeat thumped through her entire body, throbbing energy ran along her arms. She released every bit of power while throwing her hands apart.

In a silent explosion, Claire disassembled Kevin's machine, hundreds of parts twirling through the air like a puffed dandelion. The engines hit the ground first, a hundred feet away in either direction. Components and chunks of frame rained upon the field while some of the fiberglass sidings fluttered down. The tires blew away in all directions, leaving Kevin to flop onto the ground.

Kevin got to his feet as fast as his body would allow and waddled to Alistair. When he stood next to the politician, he tapped away at his wrist. The hole in the air opened again. He started to step inside but stopped as if he needed approval first.

Alistair frowned, his fists clenched from frustration, no longer in control. Claire was exhausted, her belly empty as she fought to keep from trembling. She wanted to collapse, but assholes like Alistair only responded to displays of strength, and he wasn't moving. Digging deep and flexing her muscles to control herself, she needed one more show of power.

Claire spread her fingers wide and called upon another burst of electricity to flow along her arms, through her hands, across her fingers. Ten fingers, ten items. Reaching out to the debris on the ground, Claire lifted ten items, lighter pieces with jagged edges, and moved them through the air toward those who supported Alistair. Everyone tightened their ranks, huddling closer together. Finally, Kevin no longer waited for permission and scurried the rest of the way through the hole. The others followed quickly. Once they all fled, Claire dropped the items and glared at Alistair. The senator frowned and snorted but stepped through the hole as well.

The hole disappeared and Claire dropped to her knees.

Horatio tried to help her to her feet while everyone rushed in. No longer trapped in the rental, Michael jumped out and dropped to his knees beside her. Hugging his wife, he said, "Claire, oh God, are you okay?"

"Yeah," she panted. "Just weak."

"I can imagine. Want to try to stand?"

"Yeah, I feel better."

By the time she got to her feet, the rest of her companions were around her, most of their eyes wide from surprise, except for Bree. She was smiling. "Holy shit, Claire! That was fucking *amazing*! You *literally* tore apart three SUVs!"

"I don't think that's what we need to focus on right now," Michael snarled.

Bree huffed and rolled her eyes. "Of course not. God forbid you take a moment to recognize how incredible your wife is."

"I know she's incredible, and I tell her that every day, but that's not the point. We just moved up the United States government's shit list to number one."

"They don't know who we are."

"Don't be so naïve! They probably have our names and faces and addresses on wanted posters in the post office right now."

"There were no cameras. The task force agents were all wearing suits, so there were no bodycams. They thought they had a simple in-and-out snatch-and-grab, so that's what they prepared for. They weren't expecting us. I'm sure they'll start looking, but they have no pictures of us, so they'll have to go by memories and sketch artists."

"Alistair knows who we are," Thelma said, her voice soft but raspy as if she had been crying. She wasn't with the rest of the group. Instead, she stood alone and stared at the spot where Alistair had arrived and departed.

"Why do you say that?" Ed asked.

"Because . . ." Thelma turned around to face everyone, two streams of tears flowing over her face. "He's my husband. Senator Alistair Varney is Marvin Carver."

CHAPTER
26

Forest outside Augusta, Georgia

"Please tell me you got that," Laney said.

"I got that," Click replied.

"Are you sure?"

"Jesus Christ, Laney! When you interview someone, do I barrage you with, 'Did you ask the question? The important question? Did you ask it?' I got the shot."

Laney glanced at the camera on Click's shoulder, double-checking to make sure the lens cap was off. The red light was on, and she heard the soft whirs of the internal mechanisms. He was indeed recording. But what? "Can you zoom in on Senator Varney?"

"I doubt we'll be able to get a clear shot of anyone's faces. We're too far away. And we don't know it's Varney."

Laney went back to watching the action play out on her tablet, thanks to its wireless connection to Click's camera. Click was right; they were too far away. They had followed these people from Pennsylvania to Georgia, too many hours stewing in the funk of body odor in the van, and she was finally getting rewarded for her determination and patience. When the old lady and friends chose to make the tent-covered sermon of the internet-famous faith healer their first stop, Laney knew something would happen. Something big. She didn't expect Senator Varney's task force to raid the place, kidnap the healer kid, and lead a chase through a field.

She and Click found a utility road that cut through the surrounding forest, paralleling the car chase. They were too busy trying to keep from losing control of the van to get good chase footage. But when the chase was over . . . things got interesting.

As soon as the three black SUVs stopped, so did they. Grabbing the camera and tablet, they ran through the forest to the field. The edge of the woods was close enough—any closer risked exposure. Too far away, though, for clear shots. No time or opportunity to get back in the van to get closer—this would have to be good enough. Laney cursed her luck, but she got excited when her tablet came alive with what the camera saw.

Click kept the angle wide. He sacrificed some details, but he captured all the action, including when the old lady went hyper ninja on half the men in suits. And did the one guy go flying backward without being touched? One of the men was floating!

Laney almost told Click to zoom in so they could figure out what was happening but became glad that she didn't when Senator Varney and three others stepped out of a hole that appeared in the air. Click was right about not knowing it was Varney for a fact, but who else could it be?

People fighting, a man riding on a six-legged chair, bursts of fire from thin air, wires from one of the SUVs grabbing the healer kid. Laney's spine turned to ice when the three SUVs merged into one machine, and she almost lost control of her bladder when the one woman ripped it apart with the swipe of her hands. That was too impossible to believe, and she just witnessed it, watched it all with her own eyes. She wanted to see it again as soon as possible, which prompted her to ask Click if he was recording.

"I think it's worth the risk now to zoom in on Varney," Laney said.

"Fine."

Just as Click started to zoom, Varney disappeared, stepping back through the hole in the air. After a few minutes, everyone in the field hopped into the remaining SUV and drove away. Click stopped recording and they hurried through the woods to the van. "Should we follow them?"

"No," Laney said. "We finally got some amazing footage. If we need something more, we know where the old lady lives."

"Okay. Let's take a beat, find a hotel, and go over what we captured."

"I can't wait to show this to Dean and get it posted."

"It won't do any good," a voice interrupted their conversation. A woman with purple hair.

Laney and Click got back to the van and were greeted by two people leaning against it. The woman with purple hair wore a pantsuit with her blouse unbuttoned to expose an inappropriate amount of cleavage. The man next to her had flame-red hair and dressed as if ready to rob a museum at night—black pants, boots, and turtleneck. Laney didn't like surprises, but she had been in worse situations before. Parked behind Click's white van was a black one.

Laney played it cool to assess the threat level of these two and see if there were any more unknown variables she could ferret out. Showing no reaction to the surprise, she asked in a conversational tone, "Why is that?"

The purple-haired woman took a long drag from a vape stick. She exhaled; two white columns plumed from her nostrils, like a dragon preparing to eat a daring adventurer. "Because no one will believe it."

"Why would you think that?"

"Because no one believed your footage from Mills Hook."

This woman had control of the situation, and it was becoming harder for Laney to act like it didn't bother her. "There were plenty of people who did."

The mystery woman smiled, a sinister action where her lips oozed away to reveal vicious teeth. If it came out later that she ate the hearts of babies, Laney would believe it. "Dumb ones who think they're smart by jumping from one conspiracy to the next. I've read the comments attached to your 'coverage' of the Mills Hook incident. Hell, I personally left a hundred of them. Not very flattering."

"Who are you?"

"I'm Carol and this racially insensitive portrayal of an Irish person is Conner. And you are Laney Pederson, ex-model and failed-actress-turned-journalist with your cute sidekick cameraman Charles Lickman." After another drag, Carol looked at Click and said, "God, I bet your last name alone gets you three dates a week."

"Is . . . is that my vape stick?" Click asked.

Carol slinked toward Click, stopping inches in front of him. She ran her tongue over the tip of the vape stick, then slid it in and out of her puckered lips. "Cinnamon. Yummy. Do you want me to put it back where I found it?"

Click audibly gulped. "No. You can keep it as *looooong* as you want."

"Jesus Christ, Click," Laney blurted.

Carol glanced over her shoulder with a look of hunger in her eyes, those of a predator. Laney had seen this look a million times before, from men in bars, men in suits behind desks, men who thought she owed them. Men who thought they had power over her. Carol had power and knew how to abuse it. "A little jealousy there, Laney? Have you taken time away from being in front of the camera to sneak behind it?"

Laney crossed her arms over her chest. "What do you want?"

"I thought I was being uncomfortably obvious. I want you and me to use his dad bod as the meat in our love sandwich."

Click audibly gulped again.

"Don't get too worked up, Chubby," Conner said, still leaning against the van with his hands in his pockets. "She uses the promise of sex to get people to do whatever she wants."

Carol smirked as she took another hit from the vape stick. Swirls of white curled from her mouth as she winked at Laney and said, "Conner uses his caricature of 1980s machismo as a defense mechanism, because never once have I ever promised him even the slightest morsel of sexual favor, yet he still does everything I want him to. Now for you, I'd promise anything you want for a good hard pounding."

Laney cocked her head and squinted, an overt signal that she was bored by Carol's antics. "Unless you give me a more compelling reason than your tits in order to not release the footage we got, then take your leprechaun to find his pot of gold and get the fuck out of our way."

Conner scowled. "Leprechaun? I'm just standing here minding my own business, lady! What the fuck I do to you to deserve such name-calling?"

"Shut up, Conner," Carol laughed. She held the vape stick in her mouth while fishing out her phone from her pants pocket. Using both thumbs, she tapped away at the screen. She winked again at Laney, then looked at the tree-tops. A buzzing noise, faint at first, but it got louder until three drones hovered overhead. A few more taps on her screen and Carol landed the drones right in front of Conner. "There's your gold, leprechaun. Now load it all into the van."

Conner replied with two middle fingers but did as he was told.

"See? Everything I tell him to." Carol laughed again.

After a few more taps, she took the vape stick out of her mouth and turned her phone so Laney could see it. Click moved closer but awkwardly made sure no part of him touched any part of Laney. The video played out similarly to what Click had captured, except in higher resolution. "Fuck," Click whispered. "I need some drones."

Laney watched, seething in silence. She didn't know who Carol and Conner worked for, but she knew one thing—she was getting scooped. The last segment of the video was a crystal-clear image of Senator Varney stepping through the hole in the air. Laney asked, "So, you're going to post this on the internet?"

"Only if you post your little amateur-hour nonsense."

Click slouched and looked at his shoes.

"Don't worry, cutie," Carol said. "I'll make it up to you later."

"So, why don't you want us to post what we have if you're not posting what you have?" Laney asked.

"Because the story's not big enough."

Click's eyes went wide. "Not big enough? What do you mean not big enough? There was a dude who made and controlled fire, a guy who made a robot out of three SUVs, a woman who tore apart said robot and—oh yeah—people coming out of and back into a hole in the fucking air. And you're saying the story's not big enough?"

Carol shrugged her shoulders. "Umm, yeah, I'm pretty sure that is *exactly* what I said."

Laney said, "I think he's trying to ask, if what we just witnessed isn't the story, then what is?"

"Senator Varney is lying to the American people. It's pretty obvious he has people with special abilities on his payroll. He stated that his task force was needed to protect the public from people with special abilities, not recruit them for his own nefarious means. We'd like you two to go undercover into his organization and expose him."

"Whoa," Click said, taking a step back. "Whoa, whoa, whoa. That's pretty hardcore. We're talking about trying to find a secret government institution and then trying to find a way to sneak in."

"We got that taken care of," Carol said. "We can get you inside as soon as tomorrow."

"How is that possible?"

"We're part of a super-secret-so-secret-that-the-government-doesn't-know-we-exist organization. We have means."

"Then why don't you do it?"

"Oh, we've had recent dealings with the senator, so we wouldn't be able to get too far. And before you ask about using any of our employees, they're all science nerds or men in black suits like you saw earlier. None of them have a penchant for digging around and putting their noses where they don't belong."

Laney didn't know what to make of this. This strange woman—in many meanings of the word—had offered her a blank check. If what she said was true, this could be the story of the century. If. "Why? Why do you want to do this? What's in it for you?"

"Let's just say we view Varney as competition."

"Do you think that if we expose him, that will be enough to take him down? I've read the comments about his speeches. More people think he's full of shit than believe what he's saying."

"You've been a journalist long enough to know that one story can change those percentages. Look, half of the industries in America exist because of the country's inability to move past its xenophobia. People don't give a shit if there are little green men beyond the stars; they just want them dead."

"How do we know you're not going to kill us after this is all over?" Click asked.

"Seriously?" Carol laughed. "First of all, we're telling you to post everything you find to the interwebs. We'd be pretty fucking stupid to kill you after millions of people learn your names. Second of all, what the hell, man? We haven't done anything remotely threatening. In fact, I've been trying to slide between Laney's legs the way I slid into your DMs."

Frowning, Click pulled out his phone and swiped the screen a few times. "You sent me like a dozen dick pics."

"You haven't looked at my tits even once, so I don't know what you're into."

"I haven't looked because my parents raised me to be a gentleman!"

"Sure thing, Casanova." Carol shook her head as she strolled to the black van. She gestured to it as if she were a showroom model. "So, kids, are you gonna be sissies or take the candy and get into the windowless van?"

Laney and Click exchanged one final glance. Click's eyebrows were raised, his jaw clenched. He was terrified. Laney was as well, but she hid it better. Without needing to debate the pros and cons, they walked to the black van.

CHAPTER
27

I-81 North, Pennsylvania

Horatio smiled. He knew he shouldn't be smiling, but he couldn't help it. He was away from his parents, his church—if it could even be called that—and it felt wonderful. He had no plans of going back anytime soon, even though he lied and told his mother the opposite.

"Mother, I'm okay," he had said into the phone. The people he was with argued a lot. One of two things everyone agreed on was that he should call his parents. The other thing they all agreed on was the fastest route to get back to Pennsylvania, and that was only because the GPS gave them that information. "I'm with people like me."

"There is *no one* like you, Horatio! You are God's one and only!" Mother replied, more upset by a proclamation against her belief system than the fact that the government attempted to kidnap her son.

"Mother, please listen to me. Do you remember the bicycle accident I got in two years ago?"

"Of course, I do, Horatio. How could I possibly forget such a tragedy?"

Horatio rarely agreed with his mother's overblown description of events, but he agreed that "tragedy" was the correct word to use. He had been playing video games at a friend's house and lost track of time. The fastest way home was a treacherous dirt road pockmarked with holes and coated in loose gravel. And steeper than he could negotiate. As it so often did, the fear of getting into trouble led to panic, panic led to recklessness, recklessness led to hitting the ground face first. The impact broke his upper jaw and the bones of his right cheek. The intensity of the pain brought forth waves of nausea and bouts of tunnel vision. He had to stop often as he spent an hour stumbling home. That was when Mother clamped down on his decisions. Waking up one day with

God's touch just made her totalitarianism worse. "The clinic that performed the surgery to repair my jaw and cheek. That's where it happened."

"Where what happened?"

"Where they put nanobots in me."

"Where *what*? Horatio, you are making no sense. Now, you tell the people you're with to bring you home *right now*."

"Mother, you're not listening. A group of people, bad people, put these tiny robots in me, in my brain, as an experiment. Some of the people I'm with have these little robots, nanobots, in their brains like I do. They can do things, too. Not heal people like I do . . . well, the one girl can cure people of their addictions, so that's a little like what I can do. She has blue hair and is really cool." Horatio stopped short of mentioning that Bree was a lesbian. Unless Bree had a checkbook in hand, Mother would not approve. Bree would automatically be one of "Them." He wanted to humanize the people he was with as best he could. They weren't nameless or faceless—they were real and had something in common with him.

"Horatio, they're trying to fill your head with nonsense and lies. Now, you tell them to bring you right back or your father and I have no choice but to call the police."

Horatio sighed, disappointed for thinking his mother might make an effort to understand. How foolish. "If you do that, then the men in black suits—the men who work for the federal government—who took me from you and Father will get involved. Those men will probably contact you and Father soon anyway."

"Then, if we must work with them to get you back, that's what we'll have to do."

"There is no getting me back, Mother, if the men in black suits get me. Don't you understand? They put me in an SUV and forcibly *took me from you*. If the government gets me, *you will never see me again*. It's not a threat, it's not meant to scare you—it's the truth. Think about all the times you and Father and Mr. Seltzer and the others who help run the church complain about the government. How the government is out to hurt you and the church. Well, it's now real, Mother. The government wants to take me away from you. The people I'm with are actually protecting me from the government. They will keep me safe until Senator Varney stops hunting people like us. They want me to be with you and Father, and they will bring me back when it's safe."

The other end of the call would have been quiet if not for the soft sobbing. He didn't want to be mean to his mother because, by extension, he'd be mean to his father. But he needed her to understand, to stop viewing every conversation as a way to improve the bottom line. If making her cry was the only way to that, then so be it.

"Okay," Mother sniffled. "Okay, but I want phone calls every day. More than one. Your father and I need to know that you're all right. And I want to talk to someone you're with right now!"

Horatio handed the phone to Claire. She seemed to be the most reasonable one of the group, and she was a lawyer. If anyone could use a lot of words to give away little information, it'd be her. Claire did just that, giving Mother as much assurance as possible by letting her know she was a mother herself. No, they couldn't give last names or specific locations, but yes, they'd make sure Horatio called her multiple times a day. That was that—Horatio was free. Or so he thought.

After Claire hung up the phone, Michael said, "You know, being vague and limiting information doesn't matter anyway if Varney is Marvin."

"We don't know that for sure," Emma said.

"We do," Thelma replied. Ever since they drove away, she had been staring out the window, crying. Not big gulping sobs but silent tears.

"How can you be so sure?" Bree asked.

"We've been married for decades. I know my husband when I see him, no matter how different he looks."

Bree crossed her arms and looked away, her eyes turning red from impending tears. She sat between Thelma and Sister Angela in the middle row of seats. Horatio sat with Michael and Claire in the back row of seats. Sister Angela looked at Bree with sadness in her eyes.

"Who's Marvin?" Horatio asked as softly as possible. He didn't want to make anyone else cry today—his mother was enough.

"A piece of fucking shit," Bree blurted out.

"He's the textbook definition of evil incarnate," Michael answered.

"It's rare when I agree with Michael," Emma said from the passenger seat. "This is one of those times."

Horatio heard what everyone said, but he waited for Thelma to answer. After all, she just professed that Marvin was her husband. After a few more minutes of silence, Thelma spoke as if she were reading from a book rather than her heart. "They're not wrong. We got married very young. He has abilities, similar to yours, Horatio, except he can do more than just heal people. He can change them, shape them like clay. I'm a perfect example of that. I can guarantee you that I'm older than your mother."

"Whoa." Horatio couldn't stop his reaction. Bree had blue hair, tattoos, and facial piercings, yet Horatio assumed she was older than Thelma. She *looked* older.

Thelma offered a sad chuckle to Horatio's reaction. Horatio could understand her wearisome response, one he had given many times himself when a parishioner would overreact to seeing his gifts firsthand.

"I know it's akin to a miracle to have the hands of my personal clock turned back," Thelma continued. "But he didn't ask me if I wanted him to—he just made me look the way he wanted me to look. And he did—" She swallowed down a sob. After exhaling to compose herself, she finished, "He did some truly horrific things. Not just to me, but others as well."

Horatio was too young to pick up on subtle conversational cues, so he wasn't sure if she had given one or not. Instead of erring on the side of caution, he asked, "What happened?"

The car was quiet, only muted highway noises. Thelma inhaled deeply and sighed, trying to pare down a lifetime of information into a succinct answer. "Life had taken hold of him by the time he got these abilities. He wasn't where he wanted to be. He wasn't who he thought he should have been. He wasn't happy, and he blamed everyone. When he had the ability to change his fate, it seemed like a miracle, a blessing. It was just delicious-tasting poison. He took out his frustrations on people who didn't deserve it in his quest to get to where he thought he should be. As it is so often with power, it wasn't enough. He wanted more and more and more until I had no other choice than . . . than to kill him."

"Whoa," Horatio muttered again.

"Well, obviously, it didn't take," Michael said.

"How is that possible?" Bree asked. "Other than Sister Angela, we were all there. We saw what Thelma did."

"Derrick," Emma whispered. It seemed like it hurt her to say his name.

"Of course," Michael said. "That makes sense."

Claire must have sensed Horatio's confusion, because she answered his question before he asked it. Good mothers did that. Placing her hand on his, she said, "Derrick was a young man that Michael and Emma had met when their abilities first appeared. He had the ability to make people see things that weren't there. If Marvin touches someone who has special abilities, he can mimic them, so it's possible he used Derrick's ability to make us think he's dead."

Horatio deduced that Derrick was dead since he wasn't with them now and also from the way Emma became even sadder than usual and Michael's jaw muscles rippled.

More silence. Horatio could tell the memories of Marvin weighed heavily on everyone's minds. For hours. His mind didn't have the same encumbrances; instead, it ran free, traipsing through the happier notions and possibilities of the future. And he smiled. He knew he shouldn't be smiling, but he couldn't help it.

"If Varney is Marvin—" Bree broke the silence.

"He *is* Marvin," Thelma interjected.

"Then why hasn't he come after us yet?"

For a brief moment, the weight had been lifted. Maybe Thelma was wrong? Maybe Varney wasn't this Marvin person after all?

"I don't know," Thelma said. "But it's him. I'd bet my life on it."

"You're betting all of our lives on it," Michael said.

"No, she's not," Bree snapped. Even though it was obvious Bree had been hurt by Thelma, she still defended her. "Marvin or not, Varney is the problem."

"Right," Michael said. "A problem, Marvin or not. A problem we need to figure out. We can't assume that, if Varney is Marvin, he'll leave us alone now just because he's left us alone thus far."

"Why not?"

"We just kicked his ass and ran off with who he was trying to recruit. He might not have cared about us before, but I'm pretty sure we just painted a gigantic target on our backs. And now that he has the full backing of the United States government, who knows what he's doing right now. Tapping our phones. Dispensing fake news about us. Jesus, he could be draining all of our bank accounts and deleting our lives right now!"

"Michael, please calm down," Claire said. "I'm sure that hasn't happened. Let's not forget that the attempted kidnapping started with the traditional men in black suits and only escalated when we intervened. They did their best to clear out the church before they moved on Horatio. I have a feeling Varney . . . Marvin . . . only got involved because we were in the middle of nowhere. We're getting close to your parents' house, so let's get Sarah and head home. We'll all just head home and take a breath; get a good night's sleep, and we'll talk tomorrow."

Everyone agreed, although Michael just grunted and went back to looking out the window in furrowed-brow silence. Claire gave directions to Edward, guiding the SUV off the highway and onto uphill forest-lined back roads. As the tree density increased, the number of houses decreased. The driveways were long, and from what Horatio could see of the houses hiding behind the trees, they looked large and expensive. He wondered if he'd ever live in a house like this someday. Then a thought struck him about a more immediate concern— where would he live *now*?

The obvious choice was with Michael and Claire. Michael made him nervous with his seemingly random outbursts of irrational negativity, but Claire was a calming factor. Horatio liked Claire—smart and kind. Sister Angela was not an option. He didn't think people as old as Edward and Emma would want a teenager living with them. He'd love to hang out with Bree and Thelma, but he didn't know if they lived together or not. He was about to ask, but Michael delivered another of his random outbursts and said, "Something doesn't seem right."

Edward guided the SUV along the gravel-lined driveway. The house was large and wood-sided with an asymmetrical roof, huge windows, and a porch that went all the way around the front and sides. The curtains were open, and someone was standing in front of the biggest window.

An angry-looking bald man.

CHAPTER
28

Arlington, Virginia

"You still with me?" Sandeep asked.

Jonathan's eyes weren't focused on Sandeep. At first glance it seemed as if Jonathan were watching something an inch to Sandeep's left, but in reality, he was miles away, maybe even hundreds of miles away—wherever Claire was. Sandeep never asked Jonathan about the range of his abilities, but he didn't seem to have any difficulty watching Claire now. Jonathan shifted his gaze to look Sandeep in the eye. "Yeah, I'm here."

"No, you're not. It's her, isn't it?"

The slightest of smirks tugged at the right corner of Jonathan's mouth. "Yeah. Haven't seen her since Mills Hook."

"I understand. Do you want to talk about it?"

"How about over a beer?"

Sandeep smiled and gestured to his living quarters. "Sure. Grab a six-pack and come on in."

Jonathan frowned. A stooped brow was his default facial expression, but Sandeep had spent enough time with him to differentiate between that and a frown. "C'mon, man. You know you could get out of there."

Sandeep put his hands in his pockets and leaned against the plexiglass barrier while looking around his cell. "Maybe. But I don't want to mess this gig up. I'm just going to follow the rules this time."

"Bullshit."

"I'm serious. This is a different situation than when I worked for Carver. I want to be a different person."

"Man, I don't know about working for Carver, but this is a good gig. We use our abilities to fight other people with abilities. We live like kings until it's time to move on."

"That's the difference—we won't be moving on. This is the government; Carver was a small-minded businessman. Of the few Americans who even know this task force exists, most think it's nonsensical, like most committees and task forces and special projects run by the government. However, the reason *this* task force exists is real. There are many more people like us out there, and when the general public learns about it, we don't want to be out there with them. We want the safety this opportunity provides. So, I'll stay in my cage until I get the official word to leave."

"Official word? C'mon, man. This isn't—" Jonathan's eyes shifted the tiniest bit left, watching something other than Sandeep. After a few heartbeats, his eyes widened, his breathing increased. He suddenly sprinted away from Sandeep's cell. "Fuck!"

"What was that all about?" came from down the hallway before Sandeep could ask himself that same question. Linda. Hair down, large rimmed glasses on her face, she strolled through the hallway with her hands in her white lab coat over a smart burgundy blouse and knee-length black skirt. Her stride in heels was as casual as if she were wearing loafers.

"I don't know," Sandeep answered once Linda sauntered to the plexiglass barrier. "He was watching Claire and then freaked out."

"Watching Claire?"

"You know his special ability is to see through other people's eyes, right?"

"Yes, I know this."

"Well, it only works if he knows where the person is or at least has a really good idea of where they are."

"I know this as well."

"Well, after Mills Hook, he lost contact with Claire."

"Okay. Who's Claire?"

Sandeep paused, not wanting to share secrets that weren't his, not wanting to put a target on someone else that had been painted on him. But he and his team had engaged with her. Varney must not know who they were yet, because it'd been about ten hours, and there had been no debriefing for Sandeep, Jonathan, and Kevin. "She's a woman Jonathan and I met when we first discovered our abilities. The three of us had spent some time uncovering the mystery of how we got them."

"A small outpatient surgery center specializing in sinuses which was just a cover for a secret organization experimenting on nanotechnology and the human brain."

"Correct. During our time together, Jonathan had become quite taken with her . . ."

"And he looks through her eyes? Well, that's creepy."

"Actually, he watches her through her husband's eyes."

"Ew! That's extra creepy. And you let him do this? What's wrong with you?"

Sandeep took a step back, offended by her making him responsible for Jonathan's actions. "I don't *let* him do anything."

"Well, you don't stop him either, which makes you an accomplice to his perversion. You're a perv by association."

Sandeep was getting mad now. He screwed up his life plenty on his own, and was currently trying to fix it, so he didn't need further assistance from misguided implications. "I assure you I'm no pervert. I expressed my distaste to Jonathan plenty of times. He acknowledges that it's wrong but says he can't stop himself."

"He's pleading addiction? That's so weak. I mean, how would you feel if someone did that to someone you loved?"

"I know! That's the very argument I used with him. He grunted something unintelligible about being unloved, and then we parted ways."

Linda pushed her glasses back up, having slid halfway down her nose while berating Sandeep. She pursed her lips as if preparing them to spit more acid, and Sandeep rocked back, uncertain the barrier between them would stop him from getting burned. Suddenly, shaking her head a few times, she blinked as if trying to guide her train of thought back on track. "So . . . you two parted ways. Then you found each other again when you each took jobs working with Marvin Carver."

"I worked for Carver and I tried to recruit Jonathan."

"Then you and Jonathan were involved with destroying the entire town of Mills Hook, West Virginia."

"We had nothing to do with that. We don't know what happened or who caused it. When the situation turned dangerous past the point of our control, we ran."

"Then you two decided to use Jonathan's ability to win poker tournaments throughout various casinos."

"And now I'm here in this cell."

"Which you can get out of any time you'd like."

"I prefer to get official word, preferably from Senator Varney himself, that I am free to move about the compound."

"Bullshit."

"Excuse me?"

"You heard me. I call bullshit on you wanting to follow orders. You were all but combative when you first arrived, and now you're toeing the line."

"I was combative because I was lied to, drugged, and kidnapped. You could have just asked me to come in."

"We couldn't have and you know it. You would have said, 'no,' even though you would want to say, 'yes,' which is why you keep yourself in this cell."

"I'm in this cell because I want to follow the rules."

"Oh, please. You're in this cell to shift blame. You're in this cell to make yourself feel better about doing what's asked of you. You're in this cell to lie to yourself about being a prisoner here and doing what you do because you were ordered to. You're in this cell so you don't have to admit to yourself that you like this gig, that it makes you feel special and valued."

Sandeep glared at her. She remained unflinching yet relaxed, as if apathetically discussing politics or religion. How could she be so wrong in her assessment? Or was she?

Surrendering to the staring contest, Sandeep looked away and ran his hand through his hair, hoping the act would miraculously organize his thoughts. It didn't and they were as muddled as ever. Before his abilities, he was an investments manager and exceptional at it. He liked what he did because he did it well. People gave him money to do what they couldn't. People gave him money because he was special and valued. People gave him money because he performed better than most other investment managers. He was a winner. But Varney wanted him to be a soldier, wanted him to follow orders. Did it matter?

Sandeep hated being used, hated the way Marvin Carver had viewed him as an asset, as property. But if he was being honest with himself, he had enjoyed the assignments. He enjoyed winning. The situation he was in now was similar. Instead of embracing the opportunity to be amazing, he wallowed in passive-aggressive self-pity. This opportunity came with a price, though. Was he willing to pay it?

His head hurt. Damn Linda for getting inside of it. "Is this why your bosses sent you down here? To point out that I *want* to be a part of the team and go on assignments?"

"My bosses don't know I'm here. Half of them don't give a shit about your motivations, and the other half don't give a rat's ass. They just want you to follow orders."

"Then why are you here?"

"Because I like you, dumbass. I wouldn't mind giving 'us' a chance. You know, getting to know each other enough to make a reasonable determination if there should be an 'us' or not. But I don't want to get involved with a guy who will be a bystander in his own life because the world threw a few variables at him that he doesn't want to deal with."

Sandeep slid his hands into his pockets and approached the barrier. His posture relaxed, and he scowled at Linda. "Why should I want to get involved with someone who hit on me at a bar to set me up for capture?"

"I was hitting on you at the bar because you're intelligent, quick, witty, and pretty. The fact that you have special abilities that my employer wants to use in the service of our great country is pure serendipity."

Sandeep regarded her in silence. More questions. Was she telling the truth? Could he trust her? Was she just using his desires to manipulate him? And then she asked one more question.

With a swipe of her keycard, she opened his door. Hands back in her pockets, she said, "The door is open. I have no authority to make this magical decision about giving you more leeway that you keep going on about. I have no authority to tell you what to do. I do, however, have access to all kinds of fun toys that can explore your abilities and focus them, possibly enhance them. Through this door is opportunity, Sandeep. Whether you walk through this door or stay in this cell, all your limitations are on you. So, I'm going to the compound's bar for a drink. Would you like to join me?"

Whatever her motivations, she challenged him. He didn't dislike it. It made him curious. He sighed.

And walked out the door.

CHAPTER
29

Near Michaux State Forest, Pennsylvania

It started to rain.

Every drop lingered in the air, a casual descent, each one wishing to be seen. The rain slowed for Claire, almost to the point of standstill. A maelstrom of horrific scenarios raged through her mind, ten, a hundred, a thousand per second, each worse than the last. The faster they got, the slower Claire's world moved. A raindrop hit Michael's hand and exploded into a dozen tinier droplets as he jumped out of the SUV. "No," he mumbled, the word a slow primal grunt of emotions. "No. No. No. No." Shards of loose gravel from the parking pad tumbled through the air as he ran to the house's front door, and Claire saw each and every one of them.

She jumped out after him, desperately telling her legs to move faster, wishing she had time to think and not just act. Noises and voices of everyone else getting out of the vehicle behind her were meaningless sounds. Her child was in the house with a monster.

"Sarah!" Michael shouted as he flung the door open hard enough to rattle the closest windows. "Sarah!"

Claire caught up with him, her whole body tingling and humming, her power building and screaming for release, an electric beast trapped in a cage.

The front door opened to a small foyer—only large enough to offer space for a few pairs of shoes beside a small coat closet—and the living room. This room was lived in with a small sectional couch and a desk built to hold scattered papers and a computer. No one was using it at the moment. A doorway at the other side of the room led to a small hallway. To the right, the bathroom and bedrooms; to the left, the kitchen and family room. In the hallway, Claire heard soft sobs coming from the left.

"Sarah!" Michael bolted through the kitchen and stopped dead at the doorway. After a moment to absorb what was happening in the living room, he stepped in. Claire joined him.

Directly in front of them was a set of sliding glass doors, condensation forming at the corners from the rain. They led to a rolling, well-manicured yard surrounded by the forest, three neighboring houses hidden within the trees. The family room took up the entire width of the house, a fireplace taking up most of the left wall. The entertainment center with a television large enough to use in a sports arena and a couch that could only be described as a cloud for the soul were also to the left. Michael's mother, Stella, sobbed and shook on the couch, holding Buck. Michael's father was a lot like Claire's—rough and tumble, burly and brawny—and she had never once seen Buck look small. Never seen him like this. Head on his wife's lap, he lay on the couch, clutching his side. Eyes closed, his face contorted on every exhale, his inhales whistled.

The right side of the room had a giant hutch with ornate scrollwork carved into the dark wood, used to display sports memorabilia from World Series baseballs to Super Bowl tickets to spark plugs from the earliest days of NASCAR. Along the right wall was a bar, the wood similar to the hutch, making it look comforting yet sophisticated. Four cushioned stools lined the front of the bar. Sitting on one of those stools was the source of Buck's pain, Stella's tears, Michael's and Claire's fears.

Stone.

Sarah was on the stool next to him. Her eyes widened, and she tried to jump off, but Stone's meaty hand clamped down on her shoulder. Tears flowed over her reddening cheeks. "Mommy! Daddy!" she sobbed, the only words her mouth could form.

"Sarah!" Michael yelled. "If you hurt her, I'll—"

"You'll what?" Stone barked. "You'll push me around with your mind? You try that and I'm taking your little girl with me."

Michael clenched his fists so hard Claire swore she heard his knuckles crack.

"Michael?" Stella shrieked; his name burst from her mouth as if it had just won its fight for release. "Who is he? What does he want?"

"Sarah?" Claire said. Her daughter squeezed her eyes shut and trembled. "Sarah, it'll be okay. I promise it'll be okay."

"What are you doing here?" Michael growled through clenched teeth.

"Well, you ruined my chance to become normal . . . did you know that? Did you know that was why I went to see Kevin? To be normal? I figured he controlled robots or made robots or talked to them or whatever the fuck. I figured we got little, tiny robots in our brains, right? I figured Kevin could, I don't know, kill mine or whatever. Then you fucks came along, especially you. You pushed me with your mind like you did in Harrisburg a couple years ago. You wore a mask, but that was you wasn't it . . ."

Stone paused while digging in his back pocket to pull out a card. He only took a glance and then flicked it toward Michael. Not a card; a driver's license. "Michael Roseman. I went to your house, and you weren't home. A simple internet search connected the dots from you to your folks."

"What's happening?" Stella shrieked again.

"What do you want?" Michael asked.

Claire released the energy building up within her. Like turning a faucet, she let it slowly flow from her, flow over everything in front of her. She felt the floor, the hutch, the pool table, the bar stools, then finally, her daughter. She hugged Sarah, enveloped her within the energy. And pulled.

Stone tightened his grip on Sarah's shoulder hard enough to make her cry out, keeping her on the stool next to him.

Michael started to step forward but stopped when Stone waggled the index finger on his other hand. "Ah, ah, ah. You stay where you are. And no more of that tricky shit from you, bitch, or I'll break every bone in her arms."

A hot poker of regret stabbed the back of Claire's throat, the fire spreading upward. She tried to be strong and not cry, to give her daughter hope and show no weakness in front of this monster, but the tears came anyway. She choked out, "We'll give you anything you want. Just, please, please let her go."

"What do you want?" Michael asked again.

"I want what you took from me!"

"What the fuck do you mean?"

"I want a cure. I want to get rid of the robots in my brain. I don't care how; I just want to be able to feel again."

Michael took a deep breath and extended his hands palms down. On his exhale, he took a small step forward and lowered his hand as if asking for silence. "Look . . . Stone, is it? We don't know how to do that. Trust me—if there were a way to extricate the nanobots from our brains, I'd be the first in line."

"Then you better figure something out."

"Stone, think about it. Coming here and threatening us, hurting our daughter, won't help you because we simply can't give you what you're asking for. You should go to a hospital."

"I did, remember? Then you threw me into the fucking river!"

Claire remembered that story. When Michael first told her that he, Derrick, and Emma went to the hospital Stone was terrorizing, she thought it was almost too fantastical to be true. Michael never displayed such levels of bravery, nor could she imagine him running around in a leather mask usually reserved for those who enjoyed a kinkier lifestyle. She couldn't fathom the consequences that came from his actions.

"That's because I didn't understand to the fullest capacity what was happening," Michael said, his empathetic tone softening. "Hell, I barely had any idea what was happening to me at that time, let alone what your motivations were. So now that I know what you need, I think the best course of action is to search for someone with more knowledge than a bunch of people ignorant of the sophisticated sciences involved with our uniqueness. Have you thought about contacting Senator Varney's task force? I'm sure they can help you more than we could."

Stone stood from his stool and grabbed Sarah, holding her with both hands, her arms pinned to her sides. He moved away from the bar, closer to Michael and Claire. "Yeah? Is that what you think? Turning myself into the cops is the best thing for me?"

Michael and Claire put their hands out, wordlessly begging Stone to release their daughter. The panic in his voice obvious, Michael started, "Stone—"

"That ain't gonna happen!" Stone cut him off. "*You* are the one who took away my other options, so *you* are gonna be the one to find me some new options! I ain't leaving here until you find me other options, and just remember, since I can't feel anything no more, I'm just guessing how tightly I'm squeezing."

Sarah cried out and kicked her feet, but her efforts had no effect on Stone's massive arms.

"Sarah!" Michael cried out.

"No!" Claire yelled.

Stella screamed and Buck moaned.

The lights flickered and a hum of electricity passed through the air.

"Stop! We can give you what you want!" came from behind Michael and Claire.

Sister Angela.

The room went quiet as she and Horatio entered, her hands on his shoulders for strength and support. Sister Angela said as they walked toward Stone, "We can help you. Our special abilities are for helping people."

"Stop!" Stone shouted. "Stop right fucking there. I saw you at Kevin's house, and you were trying to touch me. If you were trying to touch me, you weren't trying to heal me. I don't know what the fuck you can do, but you ain't touching me."

"I can heal you," Horatio said.

"You. You look familiar. Why do you look familiar?"

"My name is Horatio Jackson. My parents run a traveling church in Georgia, where I use my abilities to heal people. They often record the services and post them online."

"Yeah. I've seen a couple of those. I always thought they were asshole frauds."

"*They* are asshole frauds, stealing money from the innocent and the under-educated. I'm nothing like them."

Stone chuckled. "Okay, kid. I like you. Come on and let's see what you can do. But the nun doesn't come one step closer."

As Horatio approached Stone, Claire brought her hands to her mouth. She wanted to tell Horatio to stop, that Stone was too dangerous, that she didn't want him to put himself in harm's way. But the tears she cried were for Sarah. She looked so small, a ragdoll that Stone could throw away at any time. She prayed. She prayed that a fourteen-year-old boy could stop this madness.

Approaching Stone like he would a snarling dog, Horatio took one cautious step at a time, the fingers on his outstretched hand spread wide to indicate he meant no harm. The boy swallowed an audible gulp as he placed a hand on Stone's forearm. Claire had seen enough of his videos to know he usually asked the person he was healing if they believed in God. He said nothing to Stone, presumably because everyone in the room knew the answer.

Horatio placed his other hand on Stone's forearm and closed his eyes. Claire's heart smashed into her cracking ribs like a racecar piston. *Please work. Please work. Please . . .*

Horatio opened his eyes and worked his bottom lip with his teeth. He gulped again. Rolling his shoulders, he closed his eyes again but started to breathe faster. He adjusted his hands. He swallowed hard. He opened his eyes and looked at Claire.

This boy was a stranger to her, but she could read his face as if she had seen him every day of her life. The wide-eyed fear. The confusion. The unspoken request for help. It wasn't working.

"Horatio?" Michael asked. "It's okay. Go ahead and work your magic on him, buddy."

"It's not working," Horatio whispered.

"What do you mean it's not working?" Stone barked, causing Horatio to release his arm and jump backward. "You said you can cure me, so cure me."

"You're not sick. The way you are is the way you are. I can't fix what's not broken."

"You said you could cure me!" Stone roared, his eyes bulging as spittle flew from his mouth. "You said you could cure me!"

Sister Angela pulled Horatio close to her, wrapping her arms around him.

Stone roared again.

Claire's life might end in the next few minutes, or she could live to be a hundred. No matter when her death would fall on that scale, then and only then would she forget the sound of her daughter's bones breaking.

CHAPTER
30

Near Michaux State Forest, Pennsylvania

The most frustrating aspect of Michael's relationship with his father wasn't that they were so different; instead, it was how similar they were. The similarities magnified the differences. They both displayed near-obsessiveness regarding what entertained them: Buck with his sports, Michael with his literature. Both of them worked hard for their careers. Buck used blood, sweat, and tears to climb from construction worker to manager in the firm before retirement. At the same time, Michael read, studied, and analyzed books to the point of heart palpitations, yet Buck refused to refer to what Michael had done as work since he did it all from the comfort of a chair. Then there was their temper. Buck yelled and screamed, a blustery display for all to see whenever his agitation levels surpassed critical levels. That was how he calmed himself. On the other hand, Michael chose a much more civilized method of dealing with his anger—by suppressing it, ignoring it, or both. When it came time to confront his anger, it often overpowered him like a rabid jungle beast. And when it came to his family, his temper gave him permission to use any means necessary to protect them.

Michael's world turned into a series of clicking snapshots:
Click.
Stone's enraged face, eyes bulging and red.
Click.
Sarah's arms, straight one second, bent and mangled the next.
Click.
The pain on her face, her mouth opening.
Click.
More.

Click.

And more.

As soon as his daughter screamed, he pushed and Claire pulled. He hadn't released a massive buildup of energy since Mills Hook, and never had he concentrated it in such a tight focal point. The lights in the house flickered again as he blasted Stone through the glass doors and across the lawn—half a football field, as Buck would describe it.

Claire pulled Sarah away from Stone. She and Michael dropped to their knees and rested Sarah on their laps. They reached for her, hands desperate to offer comfort, but pulled away, uncertain how to touch her without making the pain worse. Michael did his best to cradle her bare feet, but she kicked and thrashed too hard.

Michael's tears blurred his vision, but he still saw a horror he could never imagine. His daughter's mouth stretched in impossible ways to release wails of agony that no longer sounded human. "Horatio!" Michael cried out between Sarah's screams. "Help!"

Unblinking, the boy knelt, his hands shaking as he reached for Sarah. "I don't . . . where . . . can she . . . ? I can't . . . where should I . . . ?"

"Anywhere!" Michael yelled. "Just fix her."

Horatio touched her left arm, bent at right angles in three different places, and she shrieked louder. He yanked his hands away and then reached for her feet. Sarah kicked his hands, his chest, Michael's arms. He then cupped her face with his hands. Screaming, she violently shook her head.

"Horatio!"

"I'm trying," he wept. "I'm trying!"

"Fix her!"

"Michael! He's just a boy," Claire cried.

Claire was right. Horatio wasn't much older than the little girl he was trying to save. His ability wasn't like Marvin's. If only that bastard were here, all he'd need is a single touch and he'd . . . "Claire! Claire, look into my eyes and tell Jonathan to get Marvin. Tell Jonathan we need Marvin here now!"

Claire's eyes were wide, unblinking, almost dazed from trying to make sense of what was happening around her. "Wha . . . What?"

"Claire, please!"

She blinked and shook her head, fighting through the murkiness of panic. Looking at Michael, she moved her lips and mouth in exaggerated annunciation. "Jonathan, we need your help. We need Marvin. Tell Marvin—" She paused, mulled over something for a few seconds, and then continued, "Varney.

Tell Senator Varney we need his help. Tell him we need him here. Tell him to get here like you did in the field—"

The bar rippled, then disappeared, replaced by a hole—a doorway. Senator Varney strode out while adjusting his tie, Jonathan right behind him. "So, what seems to be—"

"Skip the bullshit, Marvin," Michael yelled. "Help my daughter!"

Senator Varney reeled back as if insulted by Michael's accusation. "I'm sorry to disappoint you, but my name is Alistair Varn—"

"Marvin Carver!" Thelma screamed as she stormed into the room, Bree marching beside her. A butcher's knife clenched in her hand, she continued, "Do something *good* for once in your miserable life!"

At first, Varney's expression went slack-jawed. After a moment, it shifted to sternness as he looked at Michael. "What if there comes a time when I need a favor?"

"Jesus Christ, Marvin! Fine! Anything. Just help my daughter."

Varney swept his fingers across Sarah's forehead. The effects were immediate. The squishing noises of muscle moving to accommodate the scraping of shifting bones made Michael wince, but they were brief. Sarah's arms were back to normal, unbroken. However, she wasn't.

"Oh, Sarah," Claire said through gulping sobs. "You're okay now. You're okay."

Claire wrapped her arms around her daughter, but Sarah kept looking at her hands as if she had never seen them before. "My arms were hurt. The bad man hurt my arms. They weren't working right."

"I know, baby, I know, but they're better now."

Voice trembling from panic, Sarah shook her arms as if trying to air dry wet hands and cried, "My arms were hurt, Mommy! My arms weren't moving right!"

This was the real pain, Michael knew. Not being able to reconcile what had just happened. Hell, he barely understood what just happened. To Sarah, this was magic gone wrong, a nightmare she couldn't wake from. A memory that would never recede, never become less vibrant, no matter how many years separated her from this event. This moment would affect her for the rest of her life.

"Daddy? Mommy? What happened to my arms?"

That question would never be answered in a satisfying way, a way to justify the pain, the fear, the shock. The very existence of Hell was locked within that question, and there was no way he could condemn his daughter.

Michael twisted to look at Sister Angela. "Please. Please make her forget."

"Michael?" Claire asked. "Are . . . are you sure?"

Sister Angela approached as Michael turned back to Claire. "Just today. I just want her to forget today."

"But . . . about what you said about her abilities being too dangerous . . . ?"

"I was wrong. I was wrong about so, so many things." He looked from his daughter, still crying and shaking her hands, up to Sister Angela. "Please help her."

Sister Angela nodded. She knelt as Michael stood, taking his place. While Claire did her best to cradle her squirming daughter, Sister Angela placed her hands on Sarah's cheeks and closed her eyes. Sarah's flailing calmed to twitching, then finally, her eyelids fluttered, and she fell asleep.

Claire clutched Sarah and held her against her body. "Thank you, Sister. Thank you. Thank you."

"Interesting ability," Varney said as he approached Michael. "What exactly can she do?"

"Well, Marvin, she can call upon her ability of none of your fucking business."

Varney scowled and grumbled, "You should be more willing to cooperate and share information with someone to whom you owe your daughter's life."

It was Michael's turn to scowl. "I'll deal with you later."

Michael needed to thank Sister Angela, but Claire was doing that enough for the both of them. First, he needed to speak to Horatio. "I'm sorry. The situation was pure catastrophe, and I did not react well. I should have tried to help calm you instead of yelling at you."

Michael wasn't sure if the boy had heard him even though he talked directly to him. Horatio stared at his hands as if they had suddenly appeared at the ends of his wrists. "Have I lost the touch? Was it a gift from God and He took it from me?"

It was now Ed's and Emma's turn to participate, a much better choice to communicate with a shaken teenager than Michael. Ed put a hand on his shoulder while Emma said, "They may be gifts from God, but He didn't hand them to you. As we explained on the car ride here, there are nanobots in your brain. There was too much excitement, Horatio. You were afraid and Sarah was in too much pain to hear you let alone understand what was happening."

Ed nodded to Buck on the couch, his body quaking with every short, labored breath. "How about you try to help him, son. He looks like he could use it."

"Yeah?"

"Yes. You're calmer now than with the little girl, right?"

"Yeah. Yes."

Without further prodding, Horatio went to Buck and grabbed his forearm with both hands. When he was a petulant teenager, Michael had wished his father dead a few times, but now he hoped with every fiber of his being that Horatio could help him, save him. Had he opted to pray instead of merely hope, he might have mulled over the idea of becoming religious. Buck's tensed body eased, his breaths longer and slower. Relief and surprise replaced fear and pain. "What . . . ?" his voice dry and weak as he struggled to sit up. "What . . . the hell . . . is happening?"

"Ahh," Varney said with the smile of a salesman. "I see there's truth behind all those videos of you healing people. I'm a healer, too."

"No!" Thelma yelled. She stepped closer to Varney, pointing the knife at him. "Don't you dare say that. You are no healer. You are a destroyer! A monster!"

"Hello, Thelma," Varney said. He ran his hands over his suit jacket and then adjusted his tie. Minor but noticeable fidgeting. Was Marvin nervous? Could he still be in love with Thelma? "You still look amazing."

"I only look this way because you *made me* look this way. Just like you controlled *every* aspect of my life. You made me an addict. Made me addicted to you and kept me as a pet caged in our house. You gave me children and then *stole* them from me."

Varney looked genuinely confused. "Thelma, I—?"

"Carver?" A gruff question from outside. Stone stormed in through the door he had been blasted out of, acting as if everyone else in the room were insignificant. "Is that really fucking you? I need you to fix me. I need—"

Michael's anger returned, his rage flowing through his arm like a lightning bolt and into Stone's chest. He sent Stone tumbling over the lawn again, but this time he wasn't satisfied with just that. His temper told him to finish this.

"Michael?" Still on the floor cradling Sarah, Claire called to him as he walked toward the door. "Michael, what are you doing?"

"What's going on, son?" Buck asked as Michael walked past the couch.

The lights flickered again as Michael paused to address his father. "I'm going to scare the fucking devil, Dad."

Tiny blue sparks jumped from the nearby outlet toward him as he continued out the door, onto the lawn.

Stone was getting to his feet. It was raining harder. Michael didn't feel it, his rage was an ocean of flame, each wave a surge of heat throughout his body. He kept walking toward Stone.

"Oh, you're a big man now?" Stone yelled. "You think you're a big man because you tossed me outside?"

Michael kept walking toward Stone.

"Guess what, big man? I'm stronger than you are! I'm stronger than you will ever be! You throw me around all you want, but I'll keep coming. I'll keep coming for you, your family, your friends!"

Michael kept walking.

Stone stopped. With outstretched arms, he yelled, "You wanna throw me around again? Here you go. You think you can stop me? Go ahead and knock me down again and again and again. But there'll be a time when you can't knock me down, and you'll be a dead man! You hear me? Come on!"

Michael stopped, fifty feet of well-manicured lawn between him and Stone. Feet shoulder-width apart, left foot in front. He raised his fists, thumbs on the outside. Twisting at the waist, he reeled back with his right fist.

A hum filled the air, then a buzz. A crackle of electricity, the sizzle of water vaporizing.

Michael had been wrong about power, about his original thoughts that no one should have it. He had eschewed the ideals of his father that violence was needed in this world. Michael had once thought society could be further along if there were no wars. But there was Stone. And Marvin. And people like them. These people were a force of destruction, using power to seek power. Stone thought he had power, and he wanted more power. Michael was going to give it to him.

Michael didn't need to summon the tingle at the base of his skull; it was already there. And growing stronger. He threw the punch as if Stone were standing right in front of him. Power line transformers exploded into plumes of sparks as jagged bolts of lightning shot from the houses hidden by the trees, converging at the back of Michael's neck. Blue ribbons of electricity chased each other around the column of air speeding from Michael's fist, blasting through Stone's chest and destroying the first dozen trees in the forest behind the yard.

A wisp of smoke curled from behind Michael, carrying the smell of burnt skin.

Stone wobbled, a drunkard regaining his balance after hopping off a bar-stool. He looked down at his chest, then stuck his hand in the perfectly round hole. Eyelids fluttering, he pulled his hand out and examined it. Globs of a sticky substance oozed over his knuckles. Michael assumed that was his blood, or at least what it had been turned into.

Had Michael been a shallower person, he would have relished the look of utter disbelief on Stone's face. Instead, he found satisfaction in watching the man who hurt his daughter fall to his knees and ultimately collapse. There would be nightmares for years to come, the nausea of taking a life already roiling around in his gut. He had killed people before in Mills Hook, but he rationalized that they were all some sort of clones, freakish and unnatural things without a soul. Well, Stone didn't have a soul either—also freakish and unnatural. Unfortunately, that thought pulled at a stray thread from Michael's loosely knitted tapestry of sanity. He was just as freakish and unnatural. Did that mean he was bereft of soul?

Michael shook his head, hoping it would act as a reset switch, or at least a pause button. He couldn't think of his morals or the consequences of shredding them like out-of-date documents. He started to walk back to his parents' house, now darkened from loss of electricity, and was thankful he had been far enough away that no one could have seen the details of his actions. Then he heard commotion. Crying? Emma?

Michael ran back to the house.

CHAPTER
31

Near Michaux State Forest, Pennsylvania

Claire squeezed her daughter tighter when Stone re-entered the house. Her instinct was to reach out with her abilities and throw something at him. But what? What could she use to hurt a man who couldn't be hurt? Then Michael stepped in and pushed the intruder back out of the house. But he was going after him.

"Michael? Michael, what are you doing?"

"What's going on, son?" Buck asked as Michael walked past the couch.

The lights flickered again as Michael paused to address his father. "I'm going to scare the fucking devil, Dad."

Tiny blue sparks jumped from the nearby outlet toward him as he continued out the door, onto the lawn.

Claire couldn't let her husband face that monster alone. She stood and carried Sarah to her in-laws on the couch. Stella was still crying but smiled, happy that her husband had been saved while trapped in a chaotic situation that almost took him from her. She fussed over Buck, and he was so drained and confused that he let her. "Stella? Could you watch Sarah?"

"Oh, my precious," Stella sobbed with outstretched arms. Her tears flowed faster while her smile grew larger.

"I'll protect her this time. I'll be better this time," Buck muttered as if half asleep.

Claire stepped through the hole where the glass doors had been. Varney stood on the small patio, close enough to the house that the overhang protected him from the rain. Hands in his pockets, he chuckled. "I sure love when he gets angry."

Claire crossed her arms over her chest and glared at Marvin. Even though he looked like Senator Varney, she could now "see" Marvin. The way he stood. The smug look in his eye. The non-verbal cues. She thought Thelma was crazy when she had first mentioned it, but not anymore. This was absolutely Marvin who made a smartass comment about her husband, but refused to acknowledge his statement. She sure didn't like when Michael got angry. He had always controlled his temper, but she knew it was there, stirring deep within him, a mythical dragon whose lair was the heart of a volcano.

From this distance, she could hear Stone's voice but not his words. He gesticulated as he walked closer to Michael, then stopped and stretched out his arms. Michael stopped, too, then reeled his fist back as if he were going to punch Stone. But he was too far away to hit him. "What is he doing?" she muttered to herself.

Behind her, the flickering of the lights intensified, a switch being turned off and on. The buzz of static grew louder than the rain. As Michael threw the punch, arcs of white lightning jumped from behind her, from three other locations within the surrounding forest, and struck Michael. A disturbance tunneled through the rain between Michael and the trees at the end of the property, passing through Stone like a pencil poking through paper.

"Michael!" Claire started to move but stopped when she saw that her husband was still standing. He was unharmed, watching Stone as he collapsed in a heap.

"Holy shit," Marvin whispered.

That was certainly a succinct way of summing up Claire's feelings. Fear that her husband might be hurt. Wonder at how he did that. Sadness because she knew the pain and guilt he would go through after doing what he had to. Frustration that men like Stone forced Michael to take such drastic measures. And men like Marvin Carver.

It was not lost on Claire that she was standing next to the most dangerous man on the planet. His primary ability was manipulating biology with even the slightest touch. With that came the ability to absorb other special peoples' abilities and use them as his own. However, he could only use one ability at a time, and as of now, the only person immune to his touch was Bree. Those were his only two weaknesses, and now he had the backing of the United States' wallet and the technology to teleport. This was a problem. One that would have to wait as a scream came from the house.

Both Claire and Marvin rushed back inside; Claire immediately ran to Sarah and her in-laws; Marvin ran to Jonathan.

"What happened?" Claire asked.

"I don't know," Stella replied. "The lights went out. There was a commotion, and the gray-haired woman screamed."

Emma?

Enough predawn light made its way through the clouds outside for Claire to see Bree and Thelma assisting Sister Angela and Emma to their feet as if they had fallen.

"Edward?" Emma yelled, looking into the kitchen. She then ran. "Edward?"

Claire followed Emma as she continued calling Ed's name through the kitchen and into the living room. She reached Emma at the door to the outside just in time to see the SUV tear out of the driveway. "Emma? What happened?"

The older woman shook as she brought her hands to her face. "I don't know. I really don't know."

Claire put her arm around Emma's shoulders and led her back through the house. They made it back into the family room when Michael did from the other side. Water cascaded from his body as he stood in the doorway with his fists clenched, looking at Marvin. "What the fuck is happening in here?"

Marvin raised his hands, palms out, as a form of surrender. "It wasn't me."

"I smell bullshit, Marvin."

"Seriously, not me."

"It was Edward," Emma said, her voice limp. "Right after the lights went out, he pushed me into Sister Angela and then ran."

"See, Michael, not me," Marvin said. "Edward. It's weird he attacked the old lady and the nun, but everyone seems fine, except . . . where's Horatio?"

"Gone," Sister Angela said. "Mr. Edwards took him."

"Edward took Horatio?" Claire asked. "That makes no sense. Why would he do that?"

"What a minute," Marvin blurted. "Did I just hear that his name is Edward Edwards?"

"What does that have to do with anything?" Thelma asked.

Marvin scowled at Michael and snapped, "Jesus Christ, Roseman. Didn't his name give it away?"

Michael ran both hands through his hair, splashing water everywhere. "Why the hell would I know his last name? I haven't seen Emma for months, let alone asked her for a background check on the man she's dating!"

"Am I missing something?" Bree asked. "I feel like I'm missing something. What does his name have to do with anything?"

"When Marvin and I did some digging into how we got our abilities, we found the people responsible. The head of the organization's name was Matthew Matthews."

"You don't think it's just a coincidence? About the names?" Bree followed up. Claire shared her sentiment. Marvin was making a huge leap in logic. And why would it even matter? Matthew Matthews had died when Michael and Marvin destroyed the building and the corporation that created the nanobots. Claire assumed it was the same entity that implanted the nanobots within everyone's brains. Was there more to this story?

Michael looked at Marvin as a way to pass the question to him. Marvin knew it wasn't a coincidence. The way his facial features hardened, the way his jaw muscles flexed as if chewing on different scenarios to see which one tasted the best. He looked at Michael and said, "I need you to come with me."

"Excuse me? No. A madman intruded on my parents' lives and almost killed my daughter. And, by the way, now lies dead on the lawn outside. Unlike you, we're not adept at sweeping dead bodies under the rug. So, I think my time is better served here to help wade through the abundance of grief and come up with ways to deal with the authorities when they come to investigate the dead body on the lawn."

Marvin smirked the way an adult would at a child for giving outlandishly immature reasons why a bee was the deadliest creature on the planet. He gazed out the hole between the family room and the lawn. After a few seconds of silence, Stella gasped as Stone's corpse floated into the room. His impenetrable skin was a few shades closer to gray than it had been minutes ago, thanks to the hole where his heart had been. Claire took no pleasure in watching the body float across the room and into the hole where the bar had been, into a room that looked like a white-walled laboratory.

One ability at a time. This notion repeated itself in Claire's head. It was clear by the way Thelma wielded the butcher's knife, her body tense and ready to strike, that she was thinking the same thing. If Marvin was using telekinesis, he couldn't instantly heal himself should Thelma plunge the knife into his back. How long would it take to switch abilities? Thelma had killed him once already, and it seemed that it didn't work. In Mills Hook, she bludgeoned him to death, pulverizing his skull to jelly, yet here he stood as Senator Alistair Varney.

"There," Marvin said, the tone of accomplishment in his voice. "The murder scene has been scrubbed. The next time your old man mows the lawn, it'll be like it never happened."

Michael clenched his fists and gritted his teeth. "It was *not* murder."

Marvin flicked his hand dismissively. "Whatever you say. But I still need you to come with me."

"Not going to happen, Marvin."

"Have you forgotten already that you said you'd do anything to repay your debt to me for saving your daughter? Oh, I'm sure you'll be overly dramatic about it and make some Faustian reference to dealing with the devil, but it won't change the fact that my request is by no means a request."

The room grew quiet, and only the sounds of water dripping from Michael to the floor and Sarah's breathing, almost a soft snore, could be heard. Claire crossed the room to stand beside her husband. Whatever he chose to do, however he would react, she would stand by him, ready to use her abilities if she had to. Bree moved closer to Thelma, whose posture hadn't relaxed.

Marvin sighed and then continued, "I know who has Horatio, and I can help you get him back. I need Michael to come with me because it'll be easier to show him than try to explain it to everyone in the middle of a living room."

There was weariness in Michael's eyes. Claire knew what he wanted—an evening of playing with Sarah, then curling up on the couch together with a glass of sherry and a good book. She had been so determined to help foster a community that she had almost forgotten that was what she wanted as well. She grabbed his hand and squeezed. "I support whatever you choose to do."

"Thank you." His smile soft, his eyes loving. He looked at her as if memorizing every detail of her face, studying a piece of artwork he was afraid of never seeing again. He always looked at her like that. Always. "I think I have to go with him."

Claire was disappointed. She had hoped Michael would continue refusing until Marvin decided to leave. That was wishful thinking that bordered on whimsical.

"I knew you'd do the right thing," Marvin chuckled. "As whiny as you are, you at least try to do what's right. Come on, Jonathan. We're done here."

Claire tightened her grip on Michael's hand as Jonathan walked by her. She knew he had a crush on her, but she never knew he'd stalked her using her husband's eyes. Any time she had been around him when he used his abilities, the other person was fairly close. He saw her plea for help from miles away. How far was his limit? Did he have a limit?

"But first," Michael said as he looked pointedly at Jonathan. "I want to limit his power."

Jonathan stopped and scowled. Bald with a bent nose, he was shorter than Michael but had corded muscles that had been in more brawls than a soccer hooligan. When he frowned, he looked as if he could be capable of terrible things. "Excuse me? The fuck did you just say?"

"Claire doesn't like you looking at her through my eyes, or anyone else's, for that matter. The nun has an ability that will alter the way you think. She's going to use it on you so that you'll never want to spy on Claire again."

Jonathan stepped closer to Michael. A move like that would have made Michael take two steps back and start rambling, absently using his words until he found a few to get him out of confrontation. This time, he didn't move, even when Jonathan growled, "You're fucked in the head if you think I'll let you take my ability from me."

"Not me. The nun. Pay attention. And I'm not talking about your ability, just you using it to spy on my wife, you creeper."

"I don't trust you."

"Still not me. Still Sister Angela. And she's a fucking *nun*. If she's going to lie to you, she'll need to change professions. I promise that she'll promise only to alter your desire to spy on Claire."

"What if I refuse?"

"To coin a phrase I just recently heard, this request is by no means a request."

Jaw jutting out, Jonathan took one more step closer to Michael. Then flew across the room and slammed into the fireplace.

"Fuck! Cocksucker!" Jonathan yelled as he got to his feet. Then slammed into the fireplace again.

Again.

Again.

And again.

Every time Jonathan attempted to get to his feet, Michael pushed him. Harder and harder. Claire swore the last time she saw a little piece of brick fall away. Face scraped and blood flowing from his nose, Jonathan got to his hands and knees. He coughed and held out a hand as a form of surrender. "I need . . . to hear the nun promise."

Michael glanced at Sister Angela, and she hurried over to Jonathan. She placed her hands on his cheeks and said, "I promise." In less than a minute, she was done.

Jonathan got to his feet and walked directly to the hole in the air where the bar was while running his sleeve across his nose. No threats, no words, not even a single glance in Michael's direction.

"That's a very interesting ability she has," Marvin said.

"No one in this room will let you touch her," Michael replied.

Marvin rolled his eyes, then looked at Jonathan as he approached. Before he walked through the hole to the laboratory, Marvin stopped him. He whispered, but Claire overheard Marvin say, "Sandeep doesn't need to know who I really am."

"Secret's safe with me, boss," Jonathan replied and stepped into the laboratory.

Claire hugged Michael and whispered, "Thank you."

"Anything for you," he whispered back. "I'm sorry I'm leaving you to clean up this mess."

Claire chuckled—gallows humor. "Don't worry about it. You be careful."

It was Michael's turn to chuckle. "Just because I'm stepping through a hole ripped into the very fabric of space and time to follow a United States senator dedicated to hunting special people like us who is a special person like us who, also, should be dead while keeping in his employ another man whom I just thoroughly pissed off? Trust me, I'd rather deal with that than half my students during finals week."

Claire laughed, but it brought tears with it. "Fibber."

Michael shrugged. "Just take care of Sarah. And my parents."

"I will."

Michael let go of Claire and winked at her. Marvin stood at the portal's threshold to the laboratory and frowned as Michael approached. "Aren't you going to change first?"

"Nope. I have nothing to change into. This is my parents' house, not mine."

"Can't you at least dry off first? You're soaked."

Michael smiled and put his wet arm around Marvin's shoulders, water flowing over his suit jacket. "No worries. I'm sure you'll bilk the American taxpayers for your dry cleaning."

"Jonathan summed it up perfectly. You really are a cocksucker."

The two men walked through the rift, and it disappeared.

CHAPTER
32

Arlington, Virginia

You can catch more flies with honey than vinegar. Marvin Carver learned this too late when he was a businessman. When he figured out how to master his abilities, he used them in straightforward and rather Machiavellian ways. People became his puppets, and he forgot he still had to use charm when necessary. He learned from that mistake. And during his time as a politician, he learned that even though he caught more flies with honey, he could catch them all with bullshit. "I'm doing this for the good of the country."

"Bullshit, Marvin. I don't believe that for a second," Michael replied. "You're a soulless disciple of avarice whose very existence scoffs in the face of altruism. Everything you do is for the good of you."

Marvin chuckled and shook his head. Still in the guise of Senator Varney, he waited until the four individuals in lab coats attended to the dead man with the impenetrable skin on the metal table before he strode over to a thin, white closet. From within it, he grabbed two small towels and tossed them to Michael. "I'm a little surprised you can even see me *alllllll* the way up there on that high horse of yours. Even if what you think of me is true, the safety of this country is a beneficial consolation."

"I don't need to be on any kind of horse, be it high, low, or rocking, to know that hunting down and kidnapping a fourteen-year-old boy is wrong."

"How the hell would you describe what you and your merry band of misfits did?"

"Liberated a minor outside of social norms from the tyrannical reach of an oppressive government."

"Jesus Christ, you bleeding hearts are always so dramatic with your overblown and inaccurate assessment of the situation. With Horatio, there was no way to approach his parents about him first. You saw how they are. Name one thing about them that seemed in any way reasonable. We needed to rip the band-aid off quickly. Ask for forgiveness rather than permission—feel free to add your own cliché if you'd like, but no matter which one you use, it was the right thing to do. We absolutely would have contacted his parents and worked with them, but the priority was taking him off the stage."

Michael shoved one towel up his shirt, wiped around, then tossed it back to Marvin. He kept the other towel. After he dried his face, he draped it around his neck. Marvin threw the towel he had into the nearest trash can and led Michael out of the laboratory and into a carpeted, well-lit hallway. As they walked, Michael sneered and asked, "Stage? What stage?"

"The world's stage. He was garnering too much attention, especially after it was leaked online that he could actually regrow people's body parts."

"Did you see the comments, though? It sure didn't seem like a lot of people believed the video was real."

At the end of the hallway was a set of double doors. Access could only be gained via a palm scanner. The room they guarded was large, three-tiered in a semi-circle. A row of four monitors took up the wall that made the flat part of the half-circle. There was a line of twelve desks in front of the monitors. The next tier up was ten desks. Eight desks were on the next tier up in the back of the room. Each desk had three monitors, a desktop computer, a laptop, and an analyst in a comfortable chair to run them all. All the smaller screens were alive with motion, video upon video playing, while the four large screens at the front of the room remained black. "Of course we saw the comments. We see all of the comments. And analyze them, track them, and look for trends to mitigate the situation."

"You mean to find your next target." Michael looked around the room, obviously impressed with what he saw but not so distracted that he couldn't issue a snarky comment.

"Mitigate the situation," Marvin repeated. "To go back to your earlier question—yes, the comments on Horatio's video garnered a lot of skepticism and negative feedback, but it was the positive feedback that concerned us. There was a spike in responsiveness. Extrapolating the numbers to create a look-alike pool of viewers for that video to compare it to an aggregate of the viewers from Horatio's other videos, there were over three times as many people who believed the video was real compared to the number of people who believed his other videos were real. And that was when the video first came out. Because of it, there has been a retroactive sympathetic response to his previous videos, meaning that more people now believe those videos are true."

Michael squinted and Marvin felt him sizing him up, processing his words. "What does that matter to you? You're actively hunting people like us. You put out a very public call to arms."

That was to create fear and spread paranoia, to make neighbors turn on neighbors. "That was to weed out the crazies and set a measuring stick so we knew the percentage of the population who believe people like us exist. Thanks to Horatio, the number has increased. Hell, even the video of Mills Hook is starting to become part of the collective discussion again."

Michael smirked. Marvin hated that. "Speaking of Mills Hook . . . I saw you die there. Why aren't you still dead?"

As much as Marvin tried to rebrand the incidents in Mills Hook as necessary to start his journey down this new path, a better path, it still hurt to think his wife wanted to kill him. He tried to keep his tone relaxed and even, as if talking about events he had seen on a television show, but he wasn't sure how well he was doing. "I used Derrick's ability. I was able to make you all see what Thelma wanted to see. Apparently, she wanted to see me dead."

"She wasn't the only one."

"Before you go on some diatribe about good and evil, just remember—had she been successful in killing me, you and Claire and the rest of your crew would be dead as well."

Michael's posture shifted, becoming more rigid. "What exactly do you mean by that?"

Marvin paused to offer just the right amount of smugness. "So, you thought it was perfectly natural for a group of armed soldiers to walk right by you and your companions without acknowledging a handful of civilians stumbling through a small town they turned into a warzone?"

Michael went pale and Marvin savored it. "That . . . that was you?"

"Yes. As weird as Derrick's abilities are, they do come in handy."

"Why? Why did you help us?"

What made lies work was the truth. As long as the roots of the truth were deep, the branches of lies would be free to form thick canopies. The truth: "I was impressed with your resolve, with what you were willing to do to protect your wife."

Michael squinted, dubious. Whether he accepted that answer or not, Marvin couldn't tell. Instead of challenging that answer, Michael asked, "Why let everyone think you were dead? You used your abilities to amass wealth, and you just let it all go?"

Because I still love Thelma. He obviously had a lot of work to do to get back into her good graces, but he figured step one was to make sure she was comfortable financially. There was no way he'd share that with Michael. Instead, he went with, "To keep tabs on people with our abilities."

"So you can find them and absorb them, obviously."

The lie: "No, so I can keep track of them." The truth: "You've seen with your own eyes what happens if these people lose control. You have an ability you don't like or want to use, and that's fine. You can control it enough not to use it. There are people out there who can't control their abilities, or worse, like Stone, abuse them. And don't forget about those who no longer look human. You remember Robert, don't you?"

"The kid who was turned into a walking, talking rabbit? I do."

"I saved him. I turned him back into a human. I gave him an opportunity for a normal life as my son, Devlin."

"That justifies stealing the life of Senator Varney? That justifies you playing God with people like us?"

"I'm not playing God. I know about people like us, and this is the best way to use it not only to protect us from regular people, but to protect regular people from us. Here, I'll show you."

Marvin led Michael to the desk closest to them. The chubby young man with a beard sitting there looked up at Marvin and smiled, "Hey, boss. What can I do ya for?"

The young man seemed affable, his smile disarming. He didn't look familiar, but Marvin never paid much mind to the analysts, so they all looked the same to him. "Do you mind if I use your workspace?"

"No worries, boss. Angie over here needs my help anyway." The man finished with a wink and a finger gun, then rolled his chair next to the woman at the neighboring workstation.

As Marvin leaned over to take control of the mouse and keyboard, Michael whispered, "It doesn't seem like your employees are addicted to their work anymore."

The truth: "I don't do that anymore. It became exhausting to maintain the perfect addiction levels in everyone." The lie: "It's easier to treat them like human beings to get them to do what I want." The truth: "Plus, a big fat bonus check is also very motivating."

Michael grunted but didn't add anything more to the conversation. After a few keystrokes and mouse clicks, the four screens at the front of the room came to life. They each played videos, and a few had the quality of found footage. Except the first one. The image was crisp and clear, focused solely on one man. He had Asian features; his black hair was cropped short. He was sitting on a workout bench wearing only nylon shorts—his impossibly massive chest seemed too large for any shirt. Thrusting his hands forward, then back, the muscles in his shoulders, each one larger than his head, rippled as he readied himself. With a quick exhale, he lay back on the bench and positioned himself to where his head was under the weight bar. He lifted the bar in quick, controlled movements, and it bent from the number of metal plates on each end. Still, he bench pressed it five times. After setting it back, he sat up and exhaled again. White lettering popped up on the bottom of the screen: 1,035 pounds.

The second screen showed two women in flouncy skirts and tight tops walking along a macadam path bordered by trees, passing by the occasional lamppost designed for decoration rather than illumination efficiency. Suddenly, the one girl stopped and swatted her leg. Then smacked her arm. She flailed her arms while jumping around, her friend now swatting at her as well. The camera holder zoomed in, and the image blurred for a few seconds. Once the clarity adjusted, streams of spiders flowed along the pathway and up the girl's legs, so many that they coated her in undulating shades of brown, her face distended into a scream.

The third video was shorter, showing a humanoid creature trying to hide while moving through a thick patch of brush. What looked like a series of overlapping shells ran along the person's arms, legs, and torso. The analysts referred to this individual as "Armadillo Man," but Marvin kept that information to himself, not wanting a lecture from Michael about sensitivity.

The fourth video was the showstopper, the one that would sway Michael to do what Marvin needed him to do. The images were monochrome gray of a man walking along a small-town sidewalk, hands inside the pockets of his windbreaker and a baseball cap pulled low to obscure his face. Across the street, a car tried to navigate into a tight parking space but failed and hit the front of another car. It must have been louder than it looked, because the man in the ball cap with his head down quickly turned to look at the commotion, giving the camera a perfect shot of his face. The video stopped playing, the man's face frozen on the screen.

"No," Michael whispered. "No. It can't be."

Marvin stood straight and pointed to the first three video screens as he lied, "China. Columbia. Africa." He saved the truth for the fourth monitor. "Maine."

Marvin let Michael take in the images, all four now paused, and then continued, "Whether you agree with what I'm doing here or not is irrelevant. There are more and more of us popping up around the world. What do you think some of those governments would do if they got their hands on that kind of power? We need to know. We need to monitor people like us. I'm not going to 'bring in' you, your wife, or any of your merry little misfits, because I know who you are, where you are, and—other than our little misunderstanding with Horatio—you all are being responsible with your abilities." Marvin gestured to the first three monitors. "They are the ones I'm trying to find, monitor, and protect. Or stop them from abusing their abilities, maybe even stop their governments from finding and abusing them." He pointed to the fourth monitor. "Thanks to our efforts here, we've learned his name is Ethan Steiger. We haven't found him—or more accurately, 'them,' yet—but we're narrowing the search down."

Michael couldn't take his eyes off Ethan. The fire behind his arguments was no longer there as he mumbled, "But it just feels wrong to spy on people."

"They're dangerous people. Dangerous people that other governments could weaponize. Dangerous people that could take over whole countries. You remember Mills Hook, Michael. You remember Ethan Steiger at Mills Hook. Hell, Ethan was the entire population of Mills Hook. Our research has led us to believe that he somehow doubles every thirty days. Even if one Ethan made it out alive, do you know how many there could be right now? Six months later?"

Michael looked perplexed, then gazed at his hands, using his fingers in an attempt to solve the equation. "I don't know. Like a dozen?"

"Really?"

"I don't know! I'm an English professor, not a math professor!"

Marvin sighed. Knowing any other response would only cause more dissension, he said, "Sixty-four. In six more months, there'd be over four thousand. And that's if there was only one survivor. If four escaped alive, there could be over sixteen thousand in half a year. Ten survivors would equal forty thousand."

Michael ran his hand through his hair as he paced in a tight circle. "How? How is this possible? How are there so many people like us?"

"The people who destroyed the town of Mills Hook and bulldozed it, literally removing it from existence, are the same people who created us."

Michael took a step backward and held out his hands as if trying to stop Marvin's words from reaching him. "Whoa! They're gone. You and I found their facility in Hershey, and we were there when it was destroyed."

"Don't be so naïve, Roseman. That wasn't their headquarters. That was just one facility out of many."

Michael changed shades again, this time to green, as realization sunk in. "Jesus. How many other facilities are there?"

"Another thing we're trying to find out here. We know of at least three more, and each facility's head uses that stupid naming mechanic of their first names being the same as their last names, like Matthew Matthews."

"And Edward Edwards, Shit. Okay, so what do you want from me?"

"Simple. Get Horatio. And . . ." Marvin reached into his pocket and held out a thumb drive. "Insert this in any computer you find."

Michael's expression flattened, looking as if Marvin had thrown a glass of water at him for no reason. "You can't be serious."

"Very. Thanks to Kevin's portal technology, we can put you and your team right inside the building where Edward Edwards plans to take him."

"Then why in the name of all that is holy and unholy don't you go there yourself? You have people with abilities and men with guns."

"It's not that simple. We're still a government agency with all of the accompanying red tape. I don't know how large that mysterious organization is or if they have their claws in the bureaucratic pie, which they probably do. If we move on them, there could be Hell to pay. I'm assuming every computer there is on their network, so plugging this into any one of them will help me answer some questions."

"So, you want me, my wife, and my friends to risk life and limb."

"If you do this, you, your wife, and your friends will be erased from our database and never hear from us, as long as you live regular lives. Forget you have these abilities, and you'll never hear from me again."

Michael stared at the thumb drive. Marvin knew enough about Michael to know he didn't want his abilities, didn't want to be a part of this community. This was an opportunity, a tool to use against his companions to tell them they had to stop. Michael grumbled, "I thought you stopped using negative reinforcement to get what you want?"

"Do you want money? I'll give you money."

"Fuck you." Michael grabbed the flash drive and walked away toward the door they had come through.

Marvin chuckled, happy that his plan was in motion. He turned to the young man with the beard to let him know he could have his workstation back, but he was gone. And so was the woman he had been sitting with.

CHAPTER
33

Arlington, Virginia

Laney rolled her eyes as Click struck up a conversation with the security guard waving a wand over him. They had very different ways of getting through security.

The setup was exactly how Carol had described it. A small lobby just inviting enough for visitors—a smiling receptionist, a few comfortable chairs, a couple of plants in the sun-drenched corner—and a bank of lockers on one wall. All personal electronics needed to go into a locker, then Laney was subjected to an intensive purse search. The security guard didn't seem to care it was a mess; she rifled through it and then searched Laney for electronic devices via a handheld scanner. No interaction other than forced and polite smiles. Click opted for a different tactic.

While conversing with the male guard throughout the process, Click took three times longer to get through security than Laney. Not only was he jeopardizing their mission by creating opportunities to slip up, but she was beginning to feel uncomfortable just standing in a corridor while others who belonged in the building passed by. Someone was going to ask questions she didn't have answers for. A debate raged within her mind. Should she extricate him from the situation, or should she abandon him and go about this mission on her own? Every excuse to pull him away seemed lame, so she decided to go about this mission on her own. Where to start?

Carol hadn't been clear about what Laney and Click would do once they infiltrated the offices of Senator Varney's task force. All Carol had said was that the fake ID badges would get them through the security checkpoint in the lobby. Then she handed them each a pair of glasses. "Wear these. They'll record what you look at. Video only, no audio."

"Won't the electronics trip their sensors?"

Carol then handed them each a small bottle labeled as eye drops. "Nope, because there are no electronics in them. I don't know the technical wordies about the process because I don't care and that shit bores me, but the lenses are basically camera film protected by a thin coating. Before you put them on, put a couple drops on the left side of each lens. This activates bacteria that eat the coating, exposing the film. Right behind those bacteria are different bacteria that eat the first bacteria and leave behind a residue that keeps the 'film' from being overexposed."

"Is it safe to have live bacteria so close to our eyes?" Click asked.

Carol sighed and patted his cheek. "So cute, yet so clearly fell asleep in biology class."

Click looked at Laney and whispered, "What does she mean by that?"

"It means she thinks you're cute," Laney answered in a mock whisper.

"Okay. How about the other part?"

"The bacteria? We, literally, have more than a pound of bacteria in our bodies at all times."

"Nicely done, you," Carol said with a wink and a piranha smile. "I'll show you what you won later."

"I got a 'B' in biology, thank you very much," Click mumbled.

"Good, then this next part should be simple for you," Carol said as she reached into her pants pocket and pulled out a thumb drive. "If this is in your pocket or bag or backpack or shoe, it will get detected when you try to get past security. The glasses will add visuals to your story, but if you can get to a computer, you'll be able to get *a lot* of data onto this little thing."

"So . . . someone has to swallow it?" Click asked.

"Only if you're bulimic."

"Then how are we going to get it past security?"

Carol pulled a condom out of her pocket, unwrapped it, and unfurled it. She dropped the thumb drive into the condom.

Click looked at Laney and said, "Well, I guess this is going to be an uncomfortable mission for you."

Both Laney and Carol crossed their arms and cocked their hips, expressions of fire and venom sweeping over their faces. Laney said, "That is the most sexist thing I've heard you say, and let's not forget that you're a guy who can't even remember the name of the girl he hooks up with the very next morning half the time."

"But—"

"*Exactly!*" Carol said as she dangled it in front of his face. "Listen, sunshine. I have a literal pallet full of condoms back at my place. You can put them on anything you want and put that anything wherever you'd like, but I need to see you walk up a hill before you attempt to climb Everest. Men's room is out the doors, down the hall, and to the left."

The longer Click stared at the thumb drive in the latex pouch, the deeper he frowned. He finally snatched the thumb drive from Carol and growled, "This *sooooooo* better be worth it."

"I have a thumb drive in the shape of a unicorn if you prefer," Carol called out as he left.

Laney couldn't help but laugh. She never liked to see her friends suffer, but sometimes Click just deserved it. Of course, Click was her *only* friend, so in a moment of weakness, she said, "You shouldn't make promises you don't intend on keeping."

Carol prowled closer to Laney like a jungle cat ready to tear into its next meal. "What promises might those be?"

"Your overly overt sexual innuendos."

"If you're referring to what Conner said earlier, he's just a whiny little slime-bag. I never make promises I don't intend on keeping. Case in point—all of the innuendos I've been throwing your way."

"Sorry, I'm not interested."

"Are you sure? Because I can promise you pleasures that haven't even been invented yet."

Something stirred within Laney, a desire. Not the typical desire to want someone, but rather the desire to be wanted. Her attractiveness was both a blessing and a curse, which she learned early on in her life. It was a way to get what she wanted and why she had taken self-defense classes and carried pepper spray in her purse. She was used to people looking at her as if she were a trophy, a prize to be won. It had been way too long since anyone looked at her with such verve, as if Carol needed her for sustenance and might die without her.

Laney leaned close enough for her lips to brush over Carol's ear with every intention of telling the woman she was wasting her time but surprised herself when she whispered, "Now is neither the time nor the place."

Stunned by her words, Laney walked away from Carol, left the room, and waited for a red-faced Click to exit the men's room.

Now standing in the hallway of the task force's office building, she shooed away that memory and adjusted her glasses as she waited for Click to finish his interactions with the security guard.

"Hey," Click said, smile broad and simple. "Sorry about that. I told Stan my apartment needed some life and asked him if he knew where the building got the Ficus in the corner. He told me the plants came from the home and garden store in the plaza off eighty-three, where his son works. Super proud of his son, an all-state running back with some big-name colleges looking at him—"

"You can't be serious," Laney angry-whispered at him. "We're on a mission, and your talking Ficus and football with one of the people who could expose us by any little misstep. Let's walk around the building to see if we can figure out the best place we should be."

"Hey!" Stan called out to Click and then waved him back over.

"Fuck," Laney whispered to herself. "We're fucked."

After an exchange that ended in a handshake, Click rejoined Laney in the hallway. Wanting to get away from security, she started to walk. She didn't know where, just anywhere that didn't jeopardize the mission. "What was that all about?"

Click held up a card, plain white and the same size as their fake ID badges. "He said because I was so cool, he gave me a temporary badge for the day and put twenty dollars in cafeteria credits on it. I heard it was pretty impressive, so I can't wait for lunch now."

"I can't believe you're willing to jeopardize the mission for some fucking snacks. You know you don't *actually* work here, right?"

"I do today, and I might tomorrow after that comment. That's not the only thing about this badge. It will get us into the analytics room."

The fake IDs Carol had supplied granted access to the building, but nowhere more secure than that. Half of Laney's fear of getting caught stemmed from not being able to get into anywhere that gave them sufficient access to the data they needed. "How . . . ? What . . . ? Why . . . ?"

"Are all great questions a journalist should ask." Click reached into his pocket and pulled out the fake ID Carol had supplied, half-chewed and too gnarled for the magnetic strip to be used. "I just told my new friend Stan that my dog got ahold of my badge. Yesterday was my first day on the job in the analytics department and how I was nervous about missing time because of running to HR to fix a stupid mistake. He said he knew how intimidating this place could be, so he gave me a temp badge so I could get to my desk right away and then go to HR during lunch."

"That's . . . amazing."

"No. It's called being a decent human being and not treating others like they're invading your space. Your ice queen routine needs to change."

"Fine. I'll work on character growth later. We need to find the analytics room and . . . wait. Why is your badge chewed? You don't have a dog."

"I bit down on it while shoving a thumb drive up my ass, and then I got the idea for the dog-ate-my-homework story. So, before we look for the analytics room, I'm going to step in here first."

Laney hadn't realized they were standing next to the men's room until Click slipped inside. She mumbled as the door closed, "I've had worse go in there for less, you whiner."

While Click prepared for the next stage of the mission, Laney found a small map of the floor next to a stairwell. By the time Click joined her, she knew where to go.

The temporary badge worked with one swipe. The analytics room was dimly lit, the soft light easy on the eyes. It had one flat wall with four stadium-sized monitors on it. The room had only one other wall, curving to create a half-circle. The floor was tiered, the sections starting large at the front of the room with the monitors and shrinking with each of the large steps up to the back of the room. Minimalistic yet sturdy desks abutted each other, with two computers and three monitors.

"What do we do?" Click whispered.

The chairs were only filled to three-quarters capacity, and no one seemed to notice two new people entering the back of the room, both facts Laney viewed as good news. She whispered back, "I'm assuming the closer the employees are to the front of the room, the more important they are, so let's find two empty seats back here. There. Toward the other door—the two workstations next to each other."

They followed the curved wall across the back of the room, and Click whispered, "What do we do when those employees come back from wherever they are?"

"Then we just have to hurry."

Laney sat and moved the mouse; the black screens came to life. "Shit. I need a password."

"Try the standards," Click said as he sat at the desk next to her. He was greeted by the same screen requesting a password. "You know, 1234, password, iamgod, etcetera."

Laney frowned but tried the ones he had suggested anyway. "They're not working. There is no way I believe an employee at a secure government facility of dubious purpose would use such a weak password."

"Try big boobs."

"No."

"But uses zeroes instead of O's."

Laney geared up to punch him if not for the fact that it worked. "I hate you."

"I know. It worked on this one, too." After a few minutes of frantic mouse-clicking, he said, "I haven't found anything all that important. They have a folder labeled 'potential' with a few video files, but nothing too damning."

Laney found the same things. "See if you can find access to a network drive or shared folder or something on the cloud."

"Okay, but—"

Click stopped himself when the door by him opened. Senator Alistair Varney entered the room with another man.

Both Click and Laney sat straight in their chairs and looked intently at the monitors. Click started tapping the keyboard as if he were typing two hundred words a minute. *Idiot*, she thought, worried the camouflage of "dutiful worker" wasn't enough to conceal him. The true test came when Varney approached him.

Laney's heart stopped when Click looked up and asked, "Hey, boss. What can I do ya for?"

"Do you mind if I use your workspace?" Varney asked.

"No worries, boss. Angie over here needs my help anyway." Click shot Varney with a wink and a finger gun, then rolled his chair next to Laney.

Laney leaned forward as Click rolled up next to her. Barely louder than breathing, she whispered, "Finger guns? Have you lost your fucking mind?"

"I don't do well under pressure, okay?"

"Then keep your head down, plug in the drive, and copy over anything that looks even vaguely important."

As Click did what she commanded, she slowly turned her head and leaned back, making sure to capture Varney with her glasses. "Interesting."

"What?" Click asked, his face close enough to the monitor to fog it with his breath. "What's interesting? Interesting, good? Or interesting, bad?"

"The guy with him is one of the people who've been tagging along with the ninja granny. And who just fought Varney and his minions in that field in Georgia. They clearly don't like each other, but why would—"

Laney's question was answered before she finished it. The large monitors at the front of the room popped on. Four different scenes, horrific and amazing, played across the screens. She made sure to turn her head to each one while listening to their conversation. She then heard a name that was the missing piece to a puzzle she didn't know she was trying to solve. "Click? We gotta go."

"I copied a lot, but I don't know if I got anything—"

"We gotta go now." Laney grabbed his arm and dragged him away from the desk just as he pulled the thumb drive from the computer. She slid her glasses into her pocket as they went back to the door they had entered from. "And take your glasses off."

Once in the hallway, Laney needed the wall's assistance to steady herself. The butterflies in her stomach slammed into each other with such fervor, she looked around for a bench or chair just in case she collapsed. "Holy shit."

"Well, I agree with that. Those videos were crazy. Were you able to get them with your glasses? I don't think I got them. I was too close to the screen trying to hide from Varney."

"I did, but there's now so much more. We have to figure out a way to infiltrate Carol's organization."

"Whoa! Why?"

"She and Conner are heads of one of the places Varney was telling that professor-looking guy about."

"Are you sure?"

"Absolutely. Did you hear them refer to people named Matthew Matthews and Edward Edwards regarding the other facility?"

"Yeah? And?"

"Remember the tour that Carol and Conner took us on?"

"It really wasn't that much of a tour."

It wasn't. They had pulled into a parking lot of a three-story building as boring and plain as if they constructed it from the crayon drawings of a dull four-year-old. But while they were there, both Carol and Conner interacted with other building denizens. "Remember how everyone addressed them?"

"Ms. Carole and . . . and . . . oh, fuck . . . Mr. O'Conner." Color faded from his cheeks as the realization seeped in. "Their names are Carol Carole and Conner O'Conner. Oh hell. So, when Carol said Varney was the competition . . ."

"She meant that she and Conner were *making* people with special abilities, and Varney is swooping in and *stealing* them."

"Wow. I can't blame her for being pissed about it."

Laney punched Click in the arm. "Jesus Christ, what is wrong with you?"

"Oooow! I'm going to report you to HR, Angie, if you can't control your displaced aggression. I know the personnel department is at the end of the hallway. Or are they one hallway over? Are they even on this floor?"

Another punch to the arm. This time Click winced and rubbed the point of impact. "Same fucking spot!"

"Quit being a shit heel and focus."

"Focus on what, exactly?"

"Focus on what we're going to do with this information."

Click squinted. Laney hated that look, one that warned he would challenge everything she was going to suggest. It usually started with, "What do *you* think we should do with the information?"

"Use it to dig deeper."

"Dig deeper how?"

Laney didn't have the patience for this. Staring directly into his eyes, she grabbed his shoulders and squeezed. "We found ourselves in the middle of the most insane war ever. It's an arms race between a mysterious organization secretly using people against their will to manifest special abilities and the United States government stealing those people to use in the name of king and country. We have some pretty damning information on one side of the war, so all we need is information on the other side of the war."

Click chewed his bottom lip and nodded. "I hear you. I do, but this is a dangerous game, Laney. This is real life-and-death shit."

"Don't talk to me about life and death, Click. We witnessed an entire town get leveled by some form of military force, and then they swept it away like it never existed. Innocent people are having their lives seriously fucked with against their will by Carol and Conner and others like them. We can bring this to light. It has become our duty to find out what we can about Carol and Conner and get evidence."

Click paced in small circles, scrubbing his fingers through his hair. After a few laps along his imaginary track, he stopped. "Okay. I'm in. We have to do this. But first . . ."

"Yes?"

Click held up his temporary badge and said, "Can we stop at the cafeteria? I'm kinda hungry."

CHAPTER
34

Near Michaux State Forest, Pennsylvania

Michael couldn't see it, but he could smell it. Burnt grass. Where he had been standing when he killed Stone.

The rain had gone but didn't take the humidity with it, and a stickiness in the air clung to Michael's skin. Standing a few yards away from the house, he stared at that spot in the backyard. He didn't remember much—black gaps in between snippets of memory. An incomplete photo album of the events, not an ethereal cinematic retelling within his mind. Claire had filled in the missing moments. The way electricity jumped from the surrounding transformers to him. Into him. How lightning flowed around a column of air from his fist to Stone's chest. The hole that remained after Michael used his push to punch.

He didn't feel the electricity—not the way he should have. It should have burned or stung or *something* if it was strong enough to singe the grass around his feet. He didn't feel any of that, though. He felt the energy. He felt the power. The fury within him made manifest, a tangible part of who he was, a hidden appendage. A weapon that brought death. Again.

Michael taught himself that all life was valuable, meaningful. It was an effort to reverse-brainwash himself from eighteen years of Buck's teachings that hunting was a sport, "capital" was an acceptable form of punishment, and dying on the battlefield was an honorable way to go. Michael had now killed so many people he had lost count.

No! Not people. Monsters.

Michael clung to that lone piece of flotsam to keep from drowning in the raging ocean of moral ambiguity. The men in Mills Hook. They were clones of Ethan Steiger or some other inhuman abomination stemming from the same malevolent technology found within his own brain. Then Stone. Anyone willing to hold a child hostage and break her arms didn't deserve to be considered human. Michael hadn't killed men; he killed monsters. But he still killed, and that took a chunk out of his soul. Just when he thought he couldn't take any more hits, his father came outside and stood next to him. "Sarah's asleep in our bed."

Michael's throat constricted at the thought of what happened to his daughter, so he simply nodded. And waited. Buck couldn't handle silence, always needed to fill the emptiness with his opinions, so Michael just waited until his father started, "So . . . Claire filled me and your mother in on a few things."

Jut-jawed, Michael nodded again.

"And what your plan is."

Michael almost laughed. He stopped looking for his father's approval sometime in his teens, when he realized the only way he'd get it was if he were a different person. Now, decades later, he'd finally get it in ways he didn't want it, by being forced into violence and pushed into bravery. "And?"

"I don't think it's a good idea for you and Claire to go wherever it is you're going."

Michael somehow felt disappointed in not getting something he didn't want. There had to be a psychological term for that. "Jesus Christ, you can't be serious."

"I am. I don't think it's a good idea to put your daughter in jeopardy like that."

"You don't think it's a good idea."

"I don't."

"And your opinion is the only one that matters."

"I'm only thinking of my granddaughter, especially after what I witnessed tonight."

"Only thinking of your granddaughter."

"I'd kill for my granddaughter—"

"Would you, Dad? Would you really?"

"I was in the United States Army, Michael!"

"How could I ever forget? You made me feel like shit for literally two decades because I had no interest in serving my country, for putting my life on the line for corrupt politicians to use in defense of billionaires' best interests in some perversion of patriotism."

"I never meant to make you feel like—"

"No? Really? Never meant to make me feel like shit, to emasculate me with your snide comments about my job? Your little digs about me wishing the country were a welfare state, being a communist and socialist, being a pacifist hippie? Well, guess what, Dad? You may have served, but you never saw action. You hit that sweet spot where you were too young for 'Nam and too old for Desert Storm. You never had to fight for your *life*. You never had to kill for your family. *I have!* The latest man I killed was right on your fucking lawn! And there were more before that. There was a whole town made up of one guy. Hundreds of men all wearing the exact same face. I don't even know how many of them I killed to get out of there, to save Claire. Five? A dozen? I don't know. But what I do know is that you're a hypocrite. Noun. A person whose actions and private beliefs belie their public statements. You've always wanted me to be more manly, more macho, more like the person you proclaim yourself to be. But now, when I'm stepping up to be a macho manly man and fight instead of hiding behind my words and books, you suddenly think it's a bad idea."

Buck looked wounded, Michael's every word an arrow to his heart. "Son, I didn't . . . I didn't know about all of . . . *this*."

Michael snorted and wiped away his tears. "Why the hell would you?"

"Because you never told me, Michael."

"Because you never listen to me! I learned while very young not to share my feelings with you unless I wanted them belittled. I never asked for help, because there was only ever one way to do things. Your way."

"Hey! It's not like your grandfather was good at expressing or encouraging feelings. I did the best I could with what I got."

"I know. And you're a better manly man for it."

"Jesus Christ, Michael, what do you want from me? You want me to listen better? Well, I don't know how to do that. I didn't grow up with that, so tell me how to do that."

"Listening is easy, Dad. All you have to do is let the other person talk and keep your opinions to yourself."

Michael didn't wait for any form of rejoinder, not caring what it might be. He turned and went back inside and stormed through the living room. He assumed a few people might have overheard through no fault of their own, but he didn't care what they thought. His mother's tear-streaked cheeks made him feel bad, but he hadn't said anything she didn't already know.

"Michael," Claire whispered as she walked with him through the living room and kitchen. "That was really harsh."

"Not as harsh as it could have been."

"This whole situation is hard for him. Yes, it's hard for everyone, but we've had time to deal and adjust. In one night, your parents had to deal with their house being broken into, almost dying, almost losing their granddaughter, and learning that their son and his wife have abilities that aren't natural."

Michael stopped in front of the bedroom door; behind it, Sarah slept. As if the knob were an eggshell, he opened the door and regarded the tiny body in his parents' king-sized bed. In case Claire had forgotten she was there, Michael pointed to Sarah and said, "Well, *we* almost lost *her*. We had to watch a madman break her arms. We gave someone permission to rewrite her brain. Her *brain*, Claire."

"That doesn't give you the right to take it out on your father." Claire put her hand on his arm, and that was all she needed to do. It was permission to come out of his cage, to knock down the walls he had built over the past week. To acknowledge his feelings, give voice to his fears. To remember that he wasn't alone.

Tears flowed over his cheeks, waves of frustration crashing through the levies. He grabbed Claire and squeezed. She held him as he cried. "We almost lost her, Claire. Our baby. Our life. I don't care if the world burns. We can't lose her."

"I know, Michael," Claire whispered through tears. Michael wept, his emotions rushing from him to her. She absorbed his weakness and replaced it with strength. After he couldn't cry anymore, Claire continued, "Believe it or not, your parents feel the same way about you."

Michael's head and his heart argued about that statement, one believing it to be true, the other not. He had no idea which one argued the factuality of Claire's words, and he was too drained to care. He just trusted his wife with all his aching heart. "Okay. You're right."

Claire placed her hands on Michael's cheeks as if to keep his head from falling off his shoulders. "You've been through a lot. There's a lot ahead of us. Let's take it one step at a time. We'll go to this mysterious location and rescue Horatio. We have a couple hours. So, you take a nap. I'll handle your parents and everyone else, figure out who's coming along, and if anyone wants any sleep."

"Okay."

Claire smiled and wiped away the last of his tears. It was his turn to take her cheeks into his hands. He leaned in and pressed his forehead against hers. Closing his eyes, he inhaled. He savored how she felt, how she smelled. "Thank you for being so damn awesome. I don't know what I did to deserve you."

"Well, you filled out an extensive questionnaire to create a perfect woman and then paid for expedited shipping using a valid credit card."

Michael laughed, something he hadn't done in too long. He kissed her, then said, "You are perfect, by the way."

"You make me feel that way every day. Now, grab some shut-eye." She winked and made her way back down the hallway toward the living room.

Michael wanted to grab a ream of paper and a dozen pens to scribe a list of ways she was amazing. One of those points being her prudence. She was right; he could use some rest.

He curled up beside his daughter, his eyes on her angelic face. She stirred, shifting right back to the position she started in. Without opening her eyes, she whispered, "Daddy?"

"Right here, sweetie," he whispered back as he gently moved a lock of hair from her cheek to behind her ear.

"You wanna know one of the billion reasons why you're the best daddy ever?"

"I absolutely do, sweetie."

"Because you take my nightmares away."

Michael cried himself to sleep.

CHAPTER
35

Norfolk, Virginia

Emma threw up. Claire sympathized—her stomach also roiled from being at her in-law's house one second then three hundred miles away the next, the travel as easy as stepping through a door. Neither Michael nor Sister Angela suffered any ill effects. Of course, Emma might soon come face to face with the man who betrayed her. Betrayed everyone she knew by kidnapping a teenage boy. The good news was Kevin's "doorway" put them behind a set of bushes lining the farthest point of the parking lot. The witnesses to Emma's reversal of breakfast were limited to five.

"I'm so sorry," Emma muttered as she wiped her mouth with the back of her hand.

"No worries," Claire said. "I also found the trip unnatural and disorienting."

Marvin smirked and handed a handkerchief to Emma. "I'm a little surprised to see your group's resident ninja can't handle a little disorientation."

Emma snatched the handkerchief from his hand with a snap. She wiped her hand and mouth with it, then tossed it into a nearby trash can. "I'm a little surprised that a man with such power would be so cowardly as to have others do what he could. Well, if I didn't know you, that is."

"Wow, you have become quite acerbic now that your super friends have replaced you as the group's religious zealot," Marvin replied while looking at Sister Angela.

Nervously running her hands over her long black hair, Sister Angela looked away. Claire understood her unease. Marvin possessed great power and could be intimidating. Now that they were by the parking lot of an unnamed, unmarked building, she was visibly discontent. It didn't help that Jonathan was along as well and glared at her.

No one was happy he was there, but his talents were needed if they were going to be successful in their efforts. That didn't stop Michael from voicing his opinion. "I still can't fathom the necessity of bringing him along."

Jonathan moved his fiery gaze from Sister Angela to Michael as Marvin answered, "I'm sure you're a smart enough guy to know we need his abilities to give Kevin a better idea of where to open his quantum doorway within the building and where you should go once you're inside."

"Oh, I understand that. I just don't understand why he has to be here. Why can't he just look through all of the employee's eyes from your secret location? We all know his range is miles and miles and miles."

Jonathan scowled. "I don't know any of these people, so I have to be as close as possible. My range is miles only with people I know on a more intimate level."

Michael clenched his fists and stepped toward Jonathan. Had this been a year ago, Claire would have worried for Michael. He hadn't been one for fighting or falling prey to primal thoughts. But now? Michael put a hole through the chest of a man who was the closest thing to indestructible she had ever seen. If Michael lost his temper again, there'd be nothing left of Jonathan.

Claire stepped in front of her husband. As casually as walking through a park, she lovingly grabbed his arm and guided him in the other direction. "Let's go over here to let him do what he needs to do. Don't stoop to his level."

Her words had the desired effect. Jonathan's gaze fell to the ground, mournful.

"Let's just get this over with," Emma said, arms crossed over her chest.

A car door shut; an employee was ready to start their day. This was all Jonathan needed. Claire didn't know the specifics of what he could do, just that he could see through other people's eyes. No control, no influence over what they do, just a form of clairvoyance. He needed line of sight unless, as he previously stated, he knew more about the person he "hitched a ride with," as he had once put it. This random employee was his ride until they got inside the building and saw other people, and then Jonathan could jump inside their minds and see what they saw. Everyone waited in silence for fifteen minutes, plenty of time for Jonathan to get a good idea of what they could expect when they made their way inside the building. "Okay, it's a fairly standard, boring office building. It seems like the second floor is the least used, so your best bet is the stairwell at the back-left corner. The basement seems to be where you want to go."

"You keep saying, 'you,' as if you're not joining us," Michael said.

"I'm not welcome, remember?" Jonathan replied.

"I'm surprised you're so astute." Before Jonathan could reply, Michael approached Marvin. "That means you're up."

Marvin laughed. "Sorry, Michael, I'm management."

"Then you need to manage. Right now, I'm terminally exhausted, and I can't imagine my wife, even as amazing as she is, being any less so after witnessing our daughter suffer a severe atrocity. We have zero desire to go in there, but we're willing to do so for the sake of Horatio. Not for this." Michael reached into his pocket and pulled out the thumb drive.

"We had a deal. You plug that in somewhere and you and your super friends will be taken off my department's databases."

"First of all, without your lackey coming with us, what assurance do we have that you'll come get us once we plug that thumb drive in? We have no idea what it does or if you need it back. Second of all, it's not our priority, so there's a good chance we could fail this little task of yours. If you want something done right, do it yourself, right? Third, and most importantly, there's no real reason to come after any of us. You already have all of our abilities, so wasting resources to capture us hardly seems worth it." Claire almost gasped when Michael stepped closer to Marvin and concluded, "And believe me, Carver, your resources would be wasted."

"Look at the big balls on the killer."

"What? Afraid I can do it better than you?"

Marvin took a step back and winced as if he thought Michael was about to spit on him. "Jesus, Roseman, that's dark."

Michael tossed the thumb drive to Marvin and said, "Suck it up and come along. We don't care about your mission, and we don't trust you."

Marvin scowled while tapping away at his phone. A doorway opened to inside the same lab Michael had gone into last night. "Come on, then."

Claire took Emma by the hand and followed everyone else in. The doorway closed and the nausea was nowhere near as bad as the first time. Emma seemed better prepared for this trip, turning only one shade of green without vomiting.

Marvin went to a closet and retrieved five white lab coats. "These will help us blend in."

"Interesting how you didn't think to furnish us with even the most minimal of disguises until you decided to join us." Michael made no attempt to be coy with his sarcasm while putting on the lab coat.

"Sometimes all you need is a new perspective," Marvin said as his body started to change. His face shifted as he grew a few inches taller and wider at the shoulder. In less than a minute, he was a different person. His suit visibly strained against his new muscles, so he removed the jacket and replaced it with a lab coat.

Sister Angela turned pale, visibly shaken by what Marvin did. The ability for a person to change their body with a mere thought and then open a door in reality was unholy in every religion.

Marvin sent another text, and a doorway opened before them; on the other side was an empty hallway. For the third time in less than ten minutes, Claire and the others covered a great distance with one step. Before the doorway closed, Michael and Jonathan flipped each other off.

Their timing was perfect—just as the doorway winked out of existence, a group of three employees rounded the corner. Following Marvin's lead, they slipped into the stairwell and started down. "Have you devised a plan yet?" Michael asked.

"Since I had no intention of coming along until a minute ago, when exactly would I have devised a plan?"

"Just figured megalomaniacal geniuses always had a plan. You certainly seem to know where you're going."

"Jonathan said the labs were in the basement."

"And then?"

"Just act like you belong here."

The stairwell had no access to the basement, so they exited to the first floor. Claire suddenly believed his statement was far easier said than done. The hallway they found themselves in made a ninety-degree turn and opened up to a small cafeteria on the left. It was still early enough for employees to swing through and grab a coffee or breakfast snack. If not for Marvin, the surprise on the faces of the other four interlopers might have highlighted they didn't belong here.

To the casual observer, Marvin worked here. As tall and muscular as he made himself, his imposing form could belong anywhere he wished to be. He strode along as the few dozen people flowed around him. The number of people was a small surprise; a larger surprise was the number of guards. They all wore black shirts and pants, but what made them really stand out were the sidearms strapped to their thighs. A few stood sentry by the cafeteria opening while others walked around in pairs. Those mingling with the other employees chatted and smiled along with them, but there was no doubt that they would draw their weapons on anyone if needed.

Michael lost his sense of direction and bumped into Emma, which caused Emma to bump into a man biting into a muffin. Sister Angela cringed so much that it looked like she might drop to the ground and burrow her way through, especially after tapping shoulders with two other people. But once the jostled person took a look at Marvin, they simply turned away and went about their business as if nothing had happened.

The hallway opened up to a set of four elevators and an expansive lobby. Marvin slowed his pace, and the others followed suit. It was obvious the elevators were the only way to the basement, but it was also logical that the average employee or guest couldn't go there with the simple push of a button. They needed to figure something out quickly because their only other options were to take a left after the elevators through a set of glass doors leading to a cubical farm or go through the lobby and leave the building altogether. A pair of guards discussing their morning walked by, and Claire had an idea.

She whispered to Marvin, "Go to the elevators and hit the button."

She was a little surprised that he did as she instructed without question or hesitation. Maybe it was just Michael who made him so antagonistic? Her husband certainly had that effect on people.

All five stood in front of one of the elevators as a tight group and encouraged anyone needing an elevator to go ahead of them if there were others in the elevator when the doors opened. When one arrived with no one else on board, they quickly filed in and stood close to the door, giving the illusion that the car was full. Claire hit the "door close" button. Marvin cleared his throat.

"Don't worry. I got this," she whispered.

Watching the guards as they had passed, she focused on one of their badges dangling from a belt loop. She touched it with her mind, felt the plastic card, the simple alligator clip. When the doors only had a few inches to go before closing, she unclipped the badge and pulled. It zipped through the air, through the decreasing gap between the doors, and into her hand. She swiped it through the reader and hit the "B" button. It turned green and they descended. "I assumed that the guards had access to everywhere in the building."

"Genius. Noun. You," Michael said.

The elevator stopped and the doors opened. Claire grabbed Michael's hand.

Marvin had chosen apt disguises. The laboratories were separated by walls of glass, each housing machines, computers, and equipment, all being cared for by people in white lab coats. There were guards positioned around the massive, white-walled room, but none interacted with the employees like on the first floor.

"Remember, stay calm and act like you belong here," Marvin whispered as they stepped off the elevator.

"How about you use Derrick's ability to make us invisible to everyone down here?" Michael asked. "Like you did for us in Mills Hook?"

They walked down the main hallway that split the room in half, with other hallways branching away. None of the employees gave them more than a glance, too engrossed in the data displayed on the numerous monitors or making adjustments to the machines they were working on. Marvin huffed and answered, "Because it's uncomfortable to use other abilities than the one I was gifted with, especially Derrick's. It's . . . unsettling."

"Or it's because you can only use one ability at a time, and you don't like to be without your original since that makes you feel weak."

Marvin's only response was a tight-lipped glare.

Michael continued, "However, unless you actually have a place for us to wait without the people here noticing that we're just standing around not doing anything, then I suggest you put on your big boy pants and use Derrick's unsettling ability."

"Fuck you, Roseman," Marvin grumbled as he looked around the massive room. Claire assumed he was looking for the right time to work his magic. Red flags would fly should any employees notice five people blinking out of existence. She didn't know what to expect from this ability, but it was rather anticlimactic. "Okay, no one can see us now. We need to stay close together because it's easier to affect one small area than five individuals. But I don't know how to make them not hear us, so keep your voices down."

"Where's Horatio?" Sister Angela whispered.

"I don't know," Marvin answered as he led everyone down the hallway. He paused at an intersection of hallways, then went left, thirty feet to a door. The room was smaller than most of the others, but it had three workstations, each with a computer, and no one inside. "But if I were a betting man, I'd say you should keep an eye on the woman with the purple hair. Her name is Carol Carole, and I'm assuming the one in charge of this building."

Though Carol was on the other side of the room, Claire could see her through the glass walls.

"And how do you know all of this?" Michael asked. He seemed incapable of talking to Marvin without being sarcastic.

"I'm sure you can put two and two together, Michael. Even you can't be *that* bad at math. Mrs. Roseman? May I have an assist?" Marvin gestured to the card reader next to the door.

Claire swiped the card, and Marvin opened the door slowly so as not to draw attention. Everyone slipped into the room. Marvin went to a computer with its screen facing away from the activities in the main room and hit the space bar. The screen saver stopped, and the login prompt appeared. Marvin didn't need that and simply slid the thumb drive into a USB port.

"I thought you needed access to the computer itself to tell it to copy files?" Claire asked.

"Not when you have someone like Kevin on your team," Marvin answered.

"He should be paying for his crimes," Michael hissed. "Not aiding you in espionage."

"Paying for his crimes? You mean like capital punishment? What he deserves? Now that you're a killer, you certainly have a heck of a lot of bloodlust."

Michael clenched his fists. Claire put a hand on his shoulder and addressed Marvin. "I think now would be a perfect time to explore this nefarious basement laboratory and look for Horatio."

"Sorry, Claire," Marvin said, "Horatio is no longer my concern."

"We had a deal, Marvin," Michael growled through clenched teeth.

"A deal that you altered."

Claire looked at Emma to see if she'd be willing to add support, but the older woman remained quiet, arms crossed while looking absently through the glass walls. To Claire's surprise, Sister Angela said, "I thought you wanted to spy on this organization?"

"Obviously, I do. That's why I'm infiltrating their network and copying it."

"How long will that take?"

"About five minutes."

"Then why not look around this facility? It's an opportunity for you to learn how their operation works. We have five minutes to look at their machines and see how their scientists use them."

Marvin scowled as he looked toward the middle of the expansive laboratory. Sister Angela winked at Claire. She was smart enough to change people's minds without needing to use her abilities, and Claire needed to recognize that. She smiled and winked back. Marvin then went back to the computer. He huffed and whispered as he exited the room, "Blocking us from everyone's mind is quite tiring and uncomfortable."

"My overly sensitive, soft hippie heart is bleeding profusely for your anguish," Michael whispered back.

At the first intersection of hallways, Marvin started to go right, but Sister Angela went left. Marvin stopped and whispered, "Where are you going? There is a project in a work area over here that I want to get a closer look at."

"You said the woman with the purple hair is in charge and might have information about Horatio."

"So?"

"How can a man as smart as you not want to hear what the person in charge of this facility is talking about?"

Once again, Marvin's face displayed his frustrations as he acquiesced to Sister Angela's suggestion. He led the way to Carol Carole.

She stood at the corner of the laboratory, a small area with different floor tiles, a couch, and two potted plants. Another elevator and a unisex restroom were there. Another hallway led away from the laboratory, dimly lit with red brick walls.

Carol talked with a tall, statuesque woman, wearing slacks, a blouse, and subtle make-up. A man was with them. He looked out of place not only because his T-shirt and jeans accentuated his unkempt hair and beard but also because he looked exceedingly nervous while the two women held a calm conversation.

Marvin crept closer to Carol and her associates, their words beginning to coalesce, but stopped when Carol suddenly whipped around. She looked right at them and squinted.

Claire's heart raced as she tried to control her breathing. No one moved. Carol reached into her jacket pocket and pulled out what looked like a gun grip with a red button on top. Thumb hovering over the button, she stepped closer.

"What's that?" Michael whispered so softly that Claire barely heard him.

Just as quietly, Marvin whispered back, "If she hits the button, everyone within ten feet of her will lose their abilities for a few hours. Maybe even lose consciousness."

Carol reached out with her other hand and stepped closer but stopped when something behind her distracted her, something from down the hallway. She looked back at Claire and the others, smiled, and turned away while returning the device to her jacket pocket.

Claire breathed a sigh of relief, but her heart sped up again when she saw what demanded Carol's attention. Ed with Horatio.

"There he is!" Carol spread out her arms as if getting ready to hug him. "Just the young man I wanted to see."

Horatio squirmed from Ed's grip and backed away from Carol. "Get away from me!"

Ed grabbed Horatio's arm hard enough to make the teen wince in pain.

That was too much for Emma, who could no longer remain quiet and stand by passively. She yelled, "Get your hands off him!"

Her words caught the attention of more people than just Carol.

CHAPTER
36

Norfolk, Virginia

Confidence. Laney had been in high-pressure situations before and pretended to be calm when she was anxious. Those situations were different, though, trying to come up with ways to converse with a person on their level, act like they shared motivations, get a bit of information or talk her way into a place she shouldn't have been. This time was different. This time, she would lie directly to a woman who controlled a secret facility that created ways to give special, powerful abilities to regular people. Giving power meant she had power. Maybe nothing fantastical like strength or flight or speed or laser beam eyes, but control. Carol controlled everyone in this building and many people outside of it. And Laney was going to lie to her. She felt fucked.

No, she scolded herself as she and Click strode down a bustling hallway. The building was similar to the one they had just come from. At first glance, it looked like a typical office building: three stories, sprawling brick and glass with boring, blocky corners. The front entrance opened to a security desk standing sentinel before an atrium drowned in natural light cascading from the glass ceiling. Tall leafy plants invited people to sit on one of the benches scattered between the guard desk and the elevators. *You can do this. Stay in control.*

Laney and Click were gifted badges that allowed them to swipe their way through the turnstile just like the other employees. Eyes forward, Laney strode with purpose. Click, on the other hand, gawked like a tourist, peeking into any area with a window, then hustling to catch back up to Laney when he fell too far behind. They walked past the elevators and made a right when they reached the back wall; to the left was the cafeteria. This hallway provided more rooms and more doors to distract Click. They turned down another hallway, a smaller one that ended with an elevator and a set of stairs.

Click slowed his pace again and looked around. Up at the ceiling. Down a different hallway to an out-of-the-way exit door. He stopped altogether and then backtracked. Before turning down the hall they had just come from, he said, "Go on ahead. I'll catch up with you."

"Seriously?"

"I thought I saw something interesting. It's probably nothing, but I just want to check it out real quick. Like five minutes. Promise."

"She said to meet her on the second floor, by the atrium."

"Hey, if you didn't want to snoop, we could have taken one of the elevators by the atrium." Click gestured down the hall before he disappeared around the corner. This bothered Laney. It was bad enough she felt like they were behind enemy lines, but now Click was dancing blindfolded through a minefield. *Screw it*, she thought as she continued toward the elevator. Once she was on it, she ran her hands over her blouse, an unconscious fidget she disguised as shooing away wrinkles.

The second floor wasn't as busy as the first floor. More business casual but still plenty of lab coats and guards. Laney strolled to the banister surrounding the open area that exposed the first floor all the way to the glass ceiling. Sunlight hit the spot where she stood, warming it. It felt nice. She started to relax until she heard Carol from behind her say, "Where's the cute fur ball?"

"Bathroom. Explosive diarrhea. He ate some bad oysters for breakfast." The words flew from Laney's mouth so quickly that she almost laughed as if someone else had said them.

Carol smiled, a wry twist of the right side of her mouth. Laney had been hit on enough to know what that smile meant, where Carol wanted the conversation to go. "Oysters, huh? Interesting breakfast choice."

"He said he wanted to be ready for 'lunch.' I told him not to bother because nothing's available from the menu you offered him."

"I like you. Caustic levels of sarcasm. Hot." Carol crossed her arms over her chest, her gaze shifting to one of judgment. "But sooooo uptight. You were a model with aspirations of being an actress. Maybe pushed into the world by a dance mom? Your whole existence was based on your looks, but they couldn't get you as far as you thought or as far as Mommy dearest wanted. You rebelled against that world, wanted to 'make a difference,' and be judged by more than just your looks, so that meant you needed to be serious, sooooo serious, placing one hundred percent of your priorities into your career and none on your happiness."

Laney hated being such an open book that strangers knew her whole story by just perusing a few pages. "I'm sure you found all that out with a few internet searches. Plus, you're the boss in this building. You must have prioritized your career somewhere within the past few years."

Carol laughed, then looked surprised that it was a real one, not a prop used in persuasion or negotiation. "Oh, sweetie, I'm a sex-addled sociopath with a penchant for partying and no concept of what the definition of 'scruples' is. I prioritize my libido and ego. In this line of work, my bosses viewed me as a bizarre weapon, and they kept using me as such until I was in a position to take aim at them and fuck them over for their spot at the table."

"You shouldn't do that. A woman should never downplay her intelligence. There's no way you're in charge of an organization so super-secret that the government doesn't know its name and not be intelligent."

Carol's shark smile returned, a hunter baring her teeth, as she sauntered closer to Laney with a seductive roll in her hips. She reached for Laney's waist but pulled away, opting to clasp her hands together behind her back as if to resist temptation. She leaned in close enough that her lips brushed against Laney's ear as she whispered, "Of course I'm the head of an organization so secret that the government doesn't know its name because I'm an intelligent woman. You should know very well that the one thing men love to kill the most is an intelligent woman, so it's prudent that I hide. I just choose to hide in plain sight."

It had been too long since the warmth of another person's breath flowed over Laney's cheek and neck. It felt good. Too good. But she tamped down her confusing feelings and turned her head just enough to brush her lips over Carol's ear. "Speaking of your organization's name . . . I didn't see a sign out front. No signage inside, either. No logos anywhere. What's this place called again?"

Carol stepped away and laughed again. "Oh, you are such an evil little bitch, aren't you? Teasing me like that for information."

"I never said I was teasing." *What the hell?* Laney screamed at her brain.

"Then it's a quid-pro-quo situation? You shouldn't do that. A woman should never use her body as currency."

"And you don't do that?"

"Nope. I use my body for fun. I'd use your body for pleasures God hasn't even invented yet."

Carol's words were like a bolt of lightning to the base of Laney's spine, the electricity radiating downward. Almost as surprising to Laney was her response. "Now who's being a tease?"

Laney was surprised her clothes hadn't burned off from the heat radiating from Carol, the blush of her cheeks, the fire in her eyes, the lick of her lips. Then the cold, wet blanket of Click got thrown over them. "Hey, guys. What's up?"

Carol's gaze lingered on Laney before her expression shifted from playful to professional, at least as professional as a starving barracuda could be. "We were just discussing our plans after you two give me the thumb drive."

Click's eyes went wide, his lips pursed as if he had bitten into a lemon. Before she had to worry about his potential for incontinence, Laney cleared her throat and said, "About that . . ."

This was it, the moment of truth for the lie. Carol knew what Laney meant, her emotions a play acting out upon the stage of her face. Confusion. Anger. Disappointment. Frustration. "So, what we were talking about earlier was just a bullshit smokescreen."

"No. What we were talking about earlier was exactly what we were talking about. That has nothing to do with the failed mission."

Carol slid her hands into her pants pocket and worked her jaw muscles. "I'm listening."

"When we first arrived, the guard at the security check-in commented that we had matching glasses. He liked them and asked where we got them. We took them off after making our way through so we didn't draw too much attention. However, thanks to Click being Click, he got us access to a media analysis room. We plugged the thumb drive into a terminal, but shortly after that, Senator Varney showed up and asked to use the terminal we were sitting at."

"Um-hmm," Carol uttered.

"He had someone with him, one of the men Varney had engaged in the field in Georgia. His name's Michael. Click and I had no choice but to abandon the terminal."

The indignation melted away, replaced by concern. "Michael? Marvin . . . Senator Varney showed *Michael Roseman* the inner workings of his sanctum? What the hell is he up to?"

Laney and Click had been following Michael and the others from Williamsport. But who was Marvin? "I can't attest to Michael's last name or who Marvin is, but Senator Varney showed a man named Michael some individuals with special abilities from around the world. There was a guy who lifted more than half a ton. Someone who seemingly could control spiders. But Michael became very upset when the senator showed him a regular-looking man named Ethan Steiger."

Carol's eyes widened as she ran her hands through her hair. "We didn't get all the Ethans? Fuuuuuuuuck me upside down!"

Not sure if it would help or hurt, Laney stepped closer and put her hand on Carol's shoulder. The concern in her voice was genuine. "What's wrong? Who are Michael and Ethan?"

Carol looked at Laney's hand and then directly into her eyes. She then whispered, "You better not be fucking with me."

Laney wasn't sure if Carol was referring to the story about losing the thumb drive or the flirtations, but she was nervous either way. She squeezed Carol's shoulder before letting go. "I'm not."

"Okay. So—" A buzz from her pocket cut her off. Her phone. Whatever text she received made her smile, which eased the tension within Laney. But only a little. A shark was still a shark, no matter how happy it was. "More about that later. Christmas just came early."

They took the nearest elevator to the basement. The doors opened to a white wonderland of glass and machinery. Armed guards patrolled the hallways while employees in lab coats scurried around inside glass-walled rooms like insects. Laney wished Click had his camera and entertained the thought of trying to sneak her phone out of her pocket and secretly record this underground laboratory. She decided against it, feeling her life might already be in jeopardy.

Carol strode to the other end of the room to a small waiting area furnished with a couch and a couple of potted plants. A hallway lined with brick walls led away from the waiting area to an exit. Carol gazed down the hallway with a broad smile and said, "I'm not going to tell you what we do here, but I can give you the dirt on Senator Varney."

"I'm listening," Laney said as she, too, looked down the hallway. There was movement at the very end.

"Are you familiar with a Pennsylvania businessman named Marvin Carver?"

"I am."

"Well, he has special abilities."

Laney assumed that he did. She heard he had been involved with a building in Hershey that disappeared under unusual circumstances. He suddenly disappeared right at the same time the entire town of Mills Hook got destroyed and bulldozed off the map. "That would certainly explain his meteoric rise to success, wealth, and power."

"It does, because his ability is a very powerful one. He can manipulate biology, a human's anatomy, with skin-to-skin contact. Imagine making a rival businessman have a heart attack by simply touching him. Well, he can also control his own anatomy, meaning he can change his appearance to be anyone he wants to be. Say, a senator named Alistair Varney."

"Whoa," Click mumbled as his eyes widened. "You can't be serious."

"I absolutely am, Fuzzy. He—" Carol stopped and whipped around as if someone had snuck up behind her and tapped her shoulder.

Laney held her breath. Something wasn't right, but she didn't know what. Carol pulled out a handheld device with a red button and wielded it like a weapon. Were there . . . voices? Whispering? Carol reached out with her other hand. Laney almost jumped out of her skin when a man's voice came from the hallway, "Carol, I'm back. I have the asset."

The man looked familiar. Edward? The man Emma was dating. Why was he here now with Horatio, the kid from the field in Georgia?

Whatever Carol reached for no longer interested her. She returned the device to her pocket and approached the two newcomers with open arms. "There he is! Just the young man I wanted to see."

Horatio yanked his arm from Edward's grip and stepped back. "Get away from me!"

Edward grabbed Horatio's arm hard enough to make the teen wince in pain.

"Get your hands off him!" came from thin air, right where Carol had reached mere seconds ago.

Then a woman appeared out of nowhere. An older woman. Laney recognized her. Emma! Where did she come from, and why was she here?

"The fuck?" Carol snapped as Emma sprinted past her and leaped into a flying kick, her foot slamming against Edward's chest. Laney had seen Emma in action, but it had been through a camera lens. But to see her up close? Mesmerizing.

Edward was built like a professional athlete—tall and solid with muscle—and didn't go down after Emma kicked him. He was a foot taller, so Emma needed uppercuts and high kicks to connect with his chin. She landed a dozen before he could even react. Wobbling, he dropped to a knee and blocked his face with his left forearm while swatting with his right. He missed while Emma continued to land punch after punch.

"Fuck!" Carol yelled as she reached into her pocket and pulled out the device with the button. Before she could press it, the device shot out of her hand, flew through the air, and then disappeared. "Fuck!"

"Holy shit," Click whispered.

Laney would have commented as well, but she was afraid her words would somehow disrupt Emma, like popping a beautifully shimmering bubble by reaching for it. Alas, the spell was broken by voices from . . . nowhere?

In the general area where Emma had suddenly appeared, there was shouting.

"Emma! Stop!"

"Horatio! Get Horatio!"

"We need to go!"

"Shut up, all of you!"

Being outweighed by over a hundred pounds didn't stop Emma from driving Edward to the ground and into the fetal position, head tucked in his hands. Splashes of blood speckled the floor around him. She stopped and ran to Horatio. Emma then blinked out of existence.

So did Horatio.

"No!" Carol shrieked and ran to where Horatio had been standing. She reached and grabbed at the air as if trying to hug a ghost. "No! Who the fuck can turn invisible?" Carol barked at the guards to find the intruders. She pointed at one guard and then at the computer nearest to him. As she ran over to it, she yelled, "Infrared! Heat signatures! Find these assholes! Hurry!"

After a few seething seconds, Carol looked up and pointed to an area in the lab, screaming, "There! Six of them! There!"

The glass labyrinth confused Laney; every glass-encased room looked like the other. Everyone else must have known where she was pointing; the guards ran toward the location while the scientists ran from it. Laney guessed where the invisible interlopers were by the trail of collapsing guards.

All down one of the hallways, guards were falling like ragdolls. Laney didn't know how it was happening or if they were still alive—which she hoped they were —but any guard within the path of the unseen threat collapsed.

"Stop them!" Carol screamed. "They're going to the northeast corner! Box them in!"

Laney had always been a practical person. She never liked the stereotype of beauty queens and models being simple, easily duped. She looked at the world through cautious eyes, looking for the answer to any question. Magic tricks were nothing more than a set of calculated steps—every miracle had a logical explanation. But if what she saw next wasn't magic, then it was a miracle.

A hole. A portal. A doorway of some sort from this reality to another one. A circular window opened, like the one Senator Varney walked out of in the Georgia field, showing the interior of another room. A white room, similar to this lab.

"No! They're getting away!" Carol shrieked. "For fuck's sake, someone get them!"

The doorway closed.

Carol roared. No words, just pure emotion rattling the glass wall closest to her. She grabbed the computer and threw it to the ground. She reached into her pocket and pulled out her phone.

Laney grabbed Click's arm and hurried down the hallway that Edward and Horatio had come from. If there was a way to get into the building at the end of the hallway, there must be a way to get out. Laney and Click ran faster, chased by Carol's words, "Conner! Start phase one for your shop. Yes, I'm fucking serious! How many? All of them!"

CHAPTER
37

Marvin felt the heat but didn't back away from the box. Linda, Jonathan, and the dozen other scientists moved farther away as the inferno inside the box raged hotter. He heard the air whooshing into the box through the holes along the top. When the flames stopped, six scientists wearing head-to-toe flame-retardant protective gear rushed to the box and inserted tubes into the holes, the quickest way to deliver coolant and breathable air for the box's lone occupant.

The box had been created specifically for Sandeep, a contained way to experiment and run tests. Twelve-inch-thick glass walls formed a fifteen-by-fifteen cube, holes at the top to allow oxygen flow, and one door, currently too hot for anyone to touch.

"And?" Marvin asked, watching the billows of white overtake the gray smoke through the fire-stained glass.

Linda walked to the nearest workstation and tapped away at a laptop. "That was well over twenty-two hundred degrees Fahrenheit."

"Hook up the second generator."

"Mr. Varney, I respectfully disagree with such a request."

Hands clasped behind his back, Marvin turned around and peaked an eyebrow. "Oh?"

Linda gestured with her hands to the workstations and equipment around the lab. "We have a ton of data to pour through. We have to look at and understand what that data is telling us. We need to know what's happening and figure out what adjustments to make. I'm not saying we shouldn't do it. I'm saying we need to do it safely. This isn't like testing bathtub water by messing with the faucet and sticking your toe in to judge how hot it is."

Marvin took slow, languid steps toward Linda. Wearing the face of Senator Varney, he knew its best feature was the smile. Disarming. Charming. He could tell an army to march into an undefended village while smiling and they'd do it. "I hear what you're saying. I do. But this process is agonizingly slow. Each time we do it, we have to start from square one and go half a step further than the time before. For what? A hundred degrees here, a hundred degrees there?"

"Yes, it's a slow process, but that makes it a safe process."

Four scientists stood in silence, awaiting an order before they could move.

Marvin waved a hand dismissively, shooing away a toddler's concerns about monsters under the bed. "We have all the safety measures covered and you know that. This is about unlocking potential. My ol' Aunt Gertrude always told me you can't run a marathon by walking. I agree with her."

It had been a week since he had witnessed Michael pulling electricity from nearby transformers and using that energy to amplify his abilities. He had increased his strength by using electricity, enough to punch a hole through a man with impenetrable skin with air. By God, Marvin wanted that level of power boost. There was no telling what he could accomplish with that level of power! But how to harness it?

He wasn't about to experiment on himself. Kevin was far too valuable to experiment on, especially if the experimentation proved fatal. Amplifying Jonathan's abilities would be of little use. Sandeep was the perfect lab rat. If it worked, Marvin added more power to a weapon. If it failed, the loss wouldn't be catastrophic. So far, the results seemed promising.

Linda frowned, getting ready to add more to her argument, but Jonathan stepped up and said, "Hey. I got a crazy fucking idea. How about we ask Sandeep what he'd like to do?"

Still looking unhappy about it, Linda kept quiet and gave a curt nod of acceptance.

"Perfect," Marvin said. As he walked toward the box, he said to the idle scientists, "In the meantime, get the first generator charged back up and get the second one ready to use."

The coolant had plenty of time to work, and the scientists opened the door to the box. The billows of white roiled and evaporated. In his head-to-toe black specialized uniform, Sandeep stood in the center of the room.

Marvin clapped a hand on his shoulder and said, "That was great! We were just talking about jumping right into another test—this time with the second generator. What do you say?"

the

"Yes!" Sandeep replied. "Yes. Let's do this."

Eyes dancing with worry, Linda asked, "Are you sure? This test was more vigorous than the last test. How are you feeling?"

"Great!" Sandeep took his head covering off. He didn't look great. He looked maniacal. Sweat rolled over his face from his matted black hair as the right corner of his mouth twitched. He spoke faster than usual. "Yeah, I'm feeling great. The tests are going great. I feel like I need to jump right into the next one, so let's get everything reset and amp it up."

The reason he felt like he needed more was because he physically needed more. Addiction had that effect on people, which was why Marvin had used it as motivation when he was still Marvin Carver, businessman. With a simple touch, he had made his employees addicted to work. With another touch, he could reward them or ramp up their levels of addiction. His touch worked on everybody, except that bitch his ex-wife was dating. Bree. Not only was she immune to his abilities, but she also cured people of their addictions. Marvin pushed her out of his mind as he patted Sandeep's cheek. "You're doing your country a great service. Let's keep up the good work."

Sandeep's eyes widened; his pupils dilated. Sweat droplets splashed on everyone around him as he nodded his head. He pulled his head covering over his face and said, "Yes. More. Let's do it again!"

Marvin escorted Linda and Jonathan away from the box. The scientists buzzed around them like a swarm of flies, each doing their part for the greater colony. Once the door to the box shut, Jonathan moved away from Marvin. Sandeep paced back and forth, the bottom of his mask moving as if he were talking to himself. The technicians hurried to reset the experiment, checking their equipment and hooking the generators to the box. The generators were charged but not connected to anything other than the box. Marvin wanted to control what Sandeep drew power from and loathed to think what would happen should he draw from the whole building. At least not while inside the building. Outside on a mission? That could be interesting. First, he needed to know the limits.

"Damn it, Varney," Jonathan snarled. "You need to stop this."

"I agree with him," Linda added.

Still smiling, Marvin pressed his palms together and gestured toward the box. "How could you two possibly say that? You asked for Sandeep's input, and you both heard his response. Not only does he want to move forward, but he's excited to do so."

"I know Sandeep," Jonathan growled like an angry dog protecting its master. "And *that* isn't him."

"Just because an individual is overly enthusiastic about doing something doesn't mean they should do it. Especially something so dangerous," Linda added.

"You two are not going to change my mind or Sandeep's, so how about you do your job, and that way, you can control the situation and its safety. Or I can simply find someone who can do what needs to be done and you'll have no control over anything."

Linda set her jaw and glowered at Marvin, but that was all for show as she turned on her heel and marched back to her laptop. Marvin leaned close to Jonathan and whispered, "I know you're thinking about exposing me. Just remember, no one would believe you. Even if you got Sandeep to believe you, I could make you disappear but not before making your life Hell. So, sit back and enjoy the Kool-Aid. It's cherry-flavored."

Jonathan crossed his arms and walked away, glaring at Marvin while skulking in the nearest set of shadows.

Like a conductor with an orchestra, Linda guided the technicians and scientists through their routines. The reset went smoothly, and Sandeep bounced around the center of the box like a professional pugilist awaiting his next bout. A green light in the center of the room signaled it was time.

Everyone in their positions, Linda spoke into a microphone, "Okay, Sandeep, whenever you're ready."

Not wasting a second, Sandeep ignited. Orange and yellow waves of flame flowed over the black suit. "I'm ready," Sandeep shouted, barely audible through the thick walls of the box.

"Fire generator one," Linda commanded.

"Firing generator one," called out a technician.

The generator was twice the size of a car and hummed when it came to life. An insulated cable led from the machine to one of the holes in the box. A bright blue arc of electricity jumped from the end of the cable to Sandeep. He yelled and the fire grew.

"Add the second generator," Marvin said.

"Senator Varney—"

"I said start it!"

"Fire generator two," Linda said, her voice a wilted flower.

"Firing generator two," called out the technician.

Identical to the first generator in size and setup, the second generator unleashed a thin lightning bolt. This was the result Marvin had been searching for.

Sandeep screamed louder as the flames pressed against the walls of the box. The fire grew hotter, from orange to yellow to white. Blue streaks of electricity wrapped around the inferno like a ribbon on a present from the devil.

"Stop both generators!" Linda ordered.

"Generator one is off!"

"Generator two is off!"

Electricity still flowed into the box, into Sandeep.

The fire within the box raged hotter, leaving inky streaks on the walls of the box as it burned the glass. Oxygen whooshed in through the holes while black smoke rushed out. The furnace blazed so loudly everyone needed to shout to be heard.

"What the fuck is happening?" Jonathan asked.

"The generators are no longer *giving* him power," Linda shouted back, "He's now *taking* it!"

That was music to Marvin's ears. He decided he would experiment on himself, figure out how to draw power from other sources to amplify his abilities. That was, of course, if Sandeep survived this.

Small tremors shook the lab—nothing strong enough to move items on the workstations but felt by everyone in the room. Nervous glances were exchanged. The walls of the box were pure black, and one of the technicians yelled, "The box is melting! He's melting the box!"

Contingencies. Marvin needed contingencies. He slid closer to Linda, the only one in the room he needed. Should the box give way and release the conflagration, he could save himself and her. He'd be exposing who he truly was, but she was his top scientist. He readied himself for pain, a lot of pain, and to regenerate burned skin for Linda. Then the generators stopped.

The inferno lost its voice first, and then the flames died out. Thick black smoke poured out of the holes. Linda took control, barking out orders to the scientists and technicians. Marvin couldn't tell if Sandeep was alive or not—no response came from within the box when Linda called out his name. The holes at the top had warped from the heat, but there was enough room to fit in the tubes that delivered coolant and breathable air. It took a minute to cool the box enough to approach it without needing a special suit. Marvin hadn't been this excited to open something since Christmas day when he was ten. Finally, they opened the door.

The smoke flowed from the box and then to the air filtration system. Everyone approached, but no one crossed the threshold, too nervous about the health status of the lone inhabitant. The smoke lightened from black to gray. When it became white, a silhouette of a man appeared. Standing.

Each observer heaved a sigh of relief, even Marvin. He said to Linda, "See? All your worrying for nothing."

Had her frown been a punch, his nose would have been bleeding. "Are you serious? He continued to pull power from the generators after we shut them down and almost melted the containment unit meant to protect us. If that would have failed, or if his energy draw hadn't been limited to the generators . . . ? A catastrophe was avoided. We got *lucky*."

"But we learned a lot in the process. And I'm very impressed that his suit went through all that perfectly intact."

"It will withstand anything less than a nuclear explosion. Now, if you'll excuse me, I need to see how he's doing."

Marvin was about to join her until a timid-looking man approached as if Marvin were a viper primed to strike. He wore a T-shirt, jeans, and wireless headphones looped around his neck. He must be one of the analysts. "Sir? Have . . . has anyone made you aware of this yet?"

Marvin hadn't seen the tablet the analyst clutched to his chest until he showed it to him. A video played. Jittery, a recording from someone's phone. Marvin asked, "When was this recorded?"

"It's a live stream, sir. Happening right now."

Different emotions crashed around within Marvin. He needed to handle this now, and the timing couldn't be worse. However, this was also the perfect way to field test what Sandeep could do with what he'd learned. If things got out of hand, he could render Sandeep unconscious with a simple touch.

Marvin clapped his hands to get everyone's attention. "Okay, we have a situation we need to take care of. Sandeep is all ready to go. Jonathan, suit up. I'll get Kevin. We need to move in less than five minutes."

Linda issued her protests as she stormed toward Marvin. Not in the mood, he held up his hand and snapped, "This is not up for discussion or debate. This is an all-hands emergency we need to handle in . . ." he turned to the analyst for confirmation. The analyst's confusion lasted a few seconds until he realized what was expected of him. Eyes widening, he looked at the screen and said, "York, Pennsylvania."

CHAPTER
38

Horatio rolled the large green trash can to the end of the driveway. He smiled the whole time. How could he not? The past week had been the best of his life.

After being rescued from the woman with purple hair and a crazy smile, the group discussed what to do with him. The Rosemans decided he should stay with them. Staying with a nun made no sense, and poor Emma wasn't in the right headspace for company after being betrayed by her boyfriend. At first, he might have preferred to stay with Thelma and Bree. It made more sense that he stayed with the heteronormative nuclear family—a positive in the eyes of his parents.

The first couple of calls were contentious, Mother being the bitch he knew her to be, making threats and demands. Horatio got so sick of it that he had hung up on her once. Father was more understanding and actually listened to Horatio when he gave the details of being kidnapped not once but twice. Father even told Mother to "shut the hell up and do what's right for our son!" His change in attitude worked. That and Claire's smooth-talking.

Twice a day, Horatio talked to his parents via video conferencing. Whenever possible, he made sure either Michael or Claire said a few words to his parents to show them what a nice, morally healthy couple looked like. The best was when Sarah made an appearance, showing his parents that the people he was staying with were family people. Although he worried about Sarah.

She didn't remember seeing him at her grandparents' house. She didn't remember anything from that night. At first, he thought that maybe the trauma was so great she immediately repressed the memories of it. It was a blessing that she couldn't remember, but Horatio found it odd she wasn't at least affected by it. He was confused when she had come up to him and gave him an exaggerated, firm handshake. "Hi! I'm Sarah. Nice to meet you." He was downright concerned when she cheered, "Yes! We have a house guest! We have a house guest!"

Michael and Claire debated briefly what to tell him but decided that "full transparency" was the best course of action. If Horatio was honest with himself, he didn't remember much from that night either. Confusion. Fear. Panic. Disappointment. His abilities had failed him, failed Sarah. It was one thing to heal an overly willing participant, but it was something completely different when the other person was screaming and thrashing in an ungodly amount of pain. He had failed, but Senator Varney—a man everyone called Marvin—succeeded. But it was Sister Angela who saved Sarah.

During the car ride from Georgia to Pennsylvania, Horatio chatted with the nun the most. She was the most willing to answer his questions. He liked her, liked how she worshiped their mutual God. She did it the way it was supposed to be done, with charity and love in her heart, not with a hand out demanding money in exchange for His word. They discussed her abilities, but that conversation was brief, and he couldn't conceptualize the concept of "changing who a person is."

Michael and Claire explained to him what Sister Angela did to Sarah—*for* Sarah. She had erased Sarah's memory of that night. It freaked Horatio out a little that someone could do that, but he reconciled that if someone had to have that kind of power, he was happy it was Sister Angela. He was upset that she wouldn't be able to make it to today's meeting.

After taking out the trash, Horatio cleaned up for lunch and set the table. Claire insisted he didn't have to do that, but he wanted to. It was the least he could do. He even helped clean the living room in preparation for the meeting.

Michael's parents came over to pick up Sarah to spend the night at their place. Father and son didn't speak, the tension like a separate person standing between them. Sarah didn't notice it; she was just an exuberant girl excited to see her grandparents. Before they left, Buck said to Michael, "Son, we need to talk."

"Later," Michael replied.

Buck looked sad but accepted his son's words with a nod and left with his wife and granddaughter. Horatio didn't know the specifics of their relationship, but he could empathize with its complexities. He reflected on his own relationship with his parents, wondering if it would always be contentious or if it would grow over the years. Or end.

Thelma and Bree were the first to arrive. Horatio got a chance to talk to Bree, and she made his day. The blue hair and facial piercings alone would make his parents demand he keep his distance. Not being straight was only another reason for them to say she was going to Hell. But Horatio enjoyed talking to her, an ambassador to an alien world. She was an artist—a bonus in Horatio's mind; undoubtedly a negative in his parents'—and had a passion for music. The Rosemans gave him an older phone to use, like the one he used to have before his parents confiscated it. He used it to research artists to admire, music to discover. Their conversation ended when Emma showed up, causing everyone to gather in the living room. That was okay—Horatio was satisfied with his time talking to Bree.

Slump-shouldered, Emma aimed for an armchair in the living room and flopped onto it as if she couldn't have walked another step, which confused Horatio since she was the fittest person in the house. Horatio had three grandparents, all Emma's contemporary in age but definitely not stature. He had laid hands on them, curing their ailments, but they were still overweight and slow-moving.

Horatio sat at the butcher block island in the kitchen, but since there were no walls separating it from the living room, he felt he was close enough to everyone to be a part of the meeting. The only thing on the island was his phone, set to vibrate so he could hear the conversations better, although that seemed redundant once Colton showed up. No conversation was quiet after that.

Horatio didn't like him. He was aggressive for no reason and made sure everyone knew his opinion—the *only* opinion that mattered. Apparently, Michael had been a lot like him, not only having the same ability but sharing the same opinions on what to do with their special abilities. Maybe a week ago, but not now.

"I can't believe you kidnapped a high school kid," Colton fussed, sitting on the edge of the armchair.

"Oh, for fuck's sake," Bree fumed. "This is like the hundredth fucking time we said it's not kidnapping. His parents know where he is, and they're thankful that we *rescued* him from some top-secret facility that makes people like us."

"The only reason he was in that facility in the first place is because you took it upon yourself to interfere with a government operation—a *federal* government operation."

"The 'federal government' operation was to kidnap a high school kid, smart guy."

"They were doing that for his own protection and for the protection of the entire country."

"If you think the government should lock up people with abilities, go ahead and turn yourself in."

Colton huffed and rolled his eyes. "God, *you* complain about needing to repeat yourself to me. I told you a *billion* times that I don't use my abilities. Some people don't want them and won't use them. I don't want them. Michael doesn't want them. Right, Michael?"

Michael hadn't been engaged in the conversation, sitting on the couch and staring out the window.

"Michael?"

Michael ran a hand through his hair, then turned his attention to the conversation. His voice weary, he replied, "I don't know."

"Whoa." Colton's eyes widened, shocked by the words he had just heard. "What the hell?"

"Look, Colton, a lot has happened since our last meeting."

"No shit, that's obvious. First there's the kidnapping, and then what?"

Michael ignored Colton's barb and rubbed his hand over his face a few times. He spoke faster than usual, as if getting the words out quickly would save him from reliving any of the events. "When we came back from Georgia, we went to my parents to get Sarah. Stone was there, rambling like a madman. He hurt Sarah. Badly. We needed help and we contacted Senator Varney—who is Marvin Carver, by the way. He healed Sarah. Then I . . . Then I . . ." Michael took a shaky breath, "I . . . killed . . . Stone. Marvin then—"

"Whoa!" Colton interrupted. "Whoa, whoa, whoa! Don't try to gloss over what you just said. You killed Stone?"

"He didn't gloss over anything, asshole," Bree snapped.

"Trust me, I didn't want to," Michael added.

"It doesn't matter if you wanted to or not; murder is murder," Colton said.

Claire, Bree, and Thelma all snapped at Colton, each emphasizing that it was self-defense. Bree sniped, "Marvin took Stone's dead body, so Michael had the full backing of the governmental authority that you love so fucking much."

"Let's not forget, Colton," Claire added, "you weren't here. You chose not to accompany us to Georgia. You didn't have to hear our daughter's screams when a monster broke her arms."

Colton held out his hands to shield himself from everyone's emotions. "Jesus. Okay, you're right. I wasn't here. How is Sarah? You said Thelma's ex-husband—who is miraculously still alive, apparently—healed her? God, poor girl's probably an emotional wreck."

"She was," Michael answered. "Until Sister Angela used her ability and took away the memory of it ever happening."

Colton's face reddened as his jaw muscles rippled. The seconds of silence seemed like hours. Uncomfortable, Horatio shifted in his seat, getting ready for the impending explosion. When Colton finally spoke, he seemed pained that he was speaking instead of yelling. "You. Can't. Be. Serious. You let someone literally enter your daughter's mind and strip away a memory."

Michael frowned, his voice getting louder. "A life-altering one. A scarring one. A memory no human should have."

"What happened to you, Michael? We were in agreement with so much regarding these abilities. Don't use them. They bring nothing but trouble."

"Well, after hearing my daughter's screams and killing the man who caused them, I guess you could say I had a change of heart. I thought about having those memories removed from my head."

"Wow. I thought you had some level of conviction. I thought you were a person who stuck with what you believed in."

Michael pointed his finger at Colton and leaned forward. "Don't give me that nonsense. I did what was necessary to protect my daughter. This is my family we're talking about!"

"And that suddenly makes it right? That suddenly changes your entire way of thinking? Jesus, Michael, it's *always* somebody's family! Every point of conjecture about right and wrong is regarding someone's family! Welfare, immigration, taxes, the justice system, and every other political hot button you can think of always involve someone's family. You were against this, against having abilities, until it benefitted *you*."

"Oh, believe me, I did what I did for a necessity rather than benefit!"

Horatio thought Colton and Michael would use their abilities on each other and wondered what would happen if they did. He deduced it would never happen since Colton refused to use his abilities and wondered if he'd be able to survive if Michael pushed him through the wall behind him. Of course, someone other than Michael might use their abilities on him or put him through the wall. Bree, Thelma, and Claire joined in the argument all at once, Claire the most rational, Bree the most animated. Voices merged and Horatio could only pick out words or phrases. Then his phone buzzed.

He didn't think much of it until it buzzed a second time. Wanting to prove himself useful in this "community" he found himself in, he downloaded a police scanner app on his phone. If there were an incident involving someone from this community, he'd be one of the first to know. He opened the app and read the reports coming into the police. One word was repeated—monster.

This seemed serious, like an adult should know what was going on and decide about the level of importance. He loathed the idea of interrupting anyone. Emma. She wasn't participating. She seemed despondent, content to sit in the armchair and stare off into space. Horatio didn't want to disturb her either, but she was his only option.

He slid off the stool and slunk over to her. He whispered, "Emma?" A little louder. "Emma?"

Emma twitched as if he had roused her from a sleeping dream. She looked over her shoulder at Horatio and offered a soft smile. "Horatio? You startled me."

"I'm sorry, but something's happening nearby."

She still smiled, but her eyes showed that she'd rather go back to staring into space. "I'm sure it's nothing the police can't handle, sweetie."

He showed her the phone and pointed to the word that had caught his attention. "They mentioned something about a creature. A . . . a monster."

Emma jumped from her chair and made no apologies for interrupting the argument. "We need to put aside our differences and get ready to leave immediately. Something is happening that seems like something only people like us can handle."

Face still red, Colton threw his hands in the air. "Jesus, this is exactly the opposite of what we should be doing."

"Then don't come with us, asshole," Bree snapped.

"Where are we going, Emma?" Claire asked.

"York."

CHAPTER
39

Timonium, Maryland

The arrow hovered over the "send" icon just as Laney's finger hovered over the left mouse button, frozen and waiting for the command. "I feel like we need more."

"Oh, Laney, come on," Click snorted. "We have eyewitness accounts behind the scenes of Senator Varney's top-secret organization involving the pursuit and capture of people with other abilities, details on another organization even more super top-secret who are behind the creation of these people with abilities, a thumb drive full of documents from the one place, and pics and video from the other."

Laney spun in the office chair and leaned forward, elbows on her knees, to regard Click. He was across the room—it was his studio apartment, so the whole area was just one big room—on his couch with his coffee table pulled close, using it as an ersatz workbench. Next to him was a four-propeller drone, and he was hooking up an ultra-high-def camera so small that no one would notice if he put two in his pocket, which was exactly how he stole them from Carol's organization. There was another drone on his coffee table, the camera attached and working. Laney almost killed him for that stunt. He assured her that when he saw the storage room, the area was completely devoid of cameras and security. The door was open, and he couldn't pass up the opportunity. That only added to her paranoia, giving Carol another reason to hunt her down. "The problem with the eyewitnesses is that they're us. Not exactly what one would call credible sources."

Click waved at the drone. The laptop on the other side of him showed exactly what his hand was doing. Three black wires traversed his lap, connecting the drone to the computer. "Seriously? No one challenged the credibility of

Hunter S. Thompson when he spent time with the Hell's Angels. We're gonzo reporters!"

"We spent a few hours sneaking around suspicious office buildings. Hardly what I'd call gonzo journalism."

"Let's not forget that we talked to plenty of people when we embedded ourselves in Varney's cafeteria."

Laney rolled her eyes. "You talked to four people about sports while shoving a bear claw in your face and guzzling coffee."

"There was a lot of subtext."

"Subtext or not, we have no sources *on record* other than the two of us."

Click unhooked the cables from the drone and set it on the coffee table next to the other drone. Between the two was a police scanner intermittently crackling to life with random voices. Somehow, through the piles of wires and cords and tools and computer pieces Laney couldn't identify if her life depended on it, Click grabbed the drone's black casing. He also found the correct screws and reattached it to the drone. "Doesn't matter. We're adding narrative to our evidence."

"The documents on the thumb drive? They're certainly damning, but they could also be easily dismissed."

"What are you talking about? They included the names and addresses of people the United States government has targeted for having abilities. We have fucking hit lists."

"But they could be faked. We could go on the internet, toss a few hundred bucks to a few people, and have these exact forms in our inbox within a few hours."

"Oh, puuuuh-leez! The only people who would doubt their authenticity are those who think we faked the moon landing. Couple the video and pics we got at Crazy Carol's place, and we're gonna be in line for a Pulitzer."

Laney looked over her shoulder at the open picture files on the computer screen. At Carol. The intensity in her eyes, her upper lip frozen in mid-snarl right before her rage. She sighed and turned her attention back to Click. "I appreciate your optimism, but the only images we captured came from your phone."

Click leaned back and stretched his arms along the top of the couch's back. "Yeah. That makes me a fantastic cameraman for using what resources were available to me at the time."

"But it's obvious we used a phone camera. And what are they really showing? A weird lab, a few armed guards falling over, a weird doorway?"

Click tilted his head back and yelled at the ceiling, "Bullllllll*shit*, Laney! Add that to what we filmed in Georgia. These are solid stories. Send them to Dean."

"That could be the problem, Click. These are two separate stories. One about what Senator Varney is doing and one about what some secret organization is doing. We know they're connected, but we can't convey that through what we have, so it looks like two separate stories."

Click sat up straight and grimaced. "So? The stories will feed off each other. Hell, we don't need to state anywhere that they're related. People will make that connection automatically."

"I doubt it. The odds of people believing in both of them are slim to none. If a person dismisses one, they'll dismiss both no matter how much they want to believe the other."

Click rubbed his hands over his face, then scrubbed them through his hair. Over the years, she learned that was his Laney-is-working-on-my-last-nerve move. If she stonewalled him anymore, he'd probably get up and leave his apartment to cool off. "Jesus, Laney. This is what you've been obsessed with for months. It's almost like you're afraid to take that last step and send the—" Click stopped rubbing his face, but it had been enough to fluff his beard and send his hair reaching for all edges of the universe. "Are you? Are you afraid of this?"

Laney hadn't asked herself that question, yet she knew she'd been trying to deny the answer. She always wanted the big story, the one that brought attention to a wrongdoing, something that people talked about. But she always assumed it would be a slam dunk, a story with irrefutable evidence. And insulation.

Confirming the rumors that people with special abilities existed by exposing what the federal government was doing behind closed doors while also bringing to light that a secret agency was behind it all would certainly get people talking. But what would the conversation be? Did she have enough to make people believe? There would always be skeptics no matter how much evidence she presented. She didn't care about trying to win an argument with someone determined to be contrarian. She wanted the general public to pick up her pieces and solve the puzzle themselves. But at what cost?

Dean had a decent legal team to protect his employees, but what Laney was messing with far surpassed the protection Dean could offer. This was the U.S. government and a secret organization. Rules didn't apply to either of them.

Laney wanted to tell Click that fear came with the job, but her throat hitched, and the words never came out. What she wanted to say was a lie by omission. She exhaled slowly through pursed lips, blowing away any reservations. This was Click, after all. He deserved the truth. "Yes. I . . . I really think I'm afraid."

Click leaned forward and cocked his head. "That people won't believe you? Sure, there will be vocal skeptics, but—"

"No, Click. Think about who we're going after."

"Senator Varney? I'm sure he's well aware that, sooner or later, someone would give the rest of the world a peek behind the curtain. Hell, he'll probably be happy we're corroborating what he's saying, that there are people out there with special abilities."

"Or extremely pissed when we expose that he has people with special abilities working for him or extremely pissed we know where there are other people with abilities, and we didn't bring it to the government's attention. Plus, I'm not worried about him as much as I am about Carol and whatever the hell operation she's running."

"What she has going on is so secret she could probably empty the entire building and set up shop somewhere else within an hour. It would be a minor inconvenience."

"But we're not trying to inconvenience them. We're trying to expose them."

"That's what our readers and viewers are for. This will be one of the few times conspiracy theorists will be correct about something. Their fervor plus the education of John Q. Public will cause the government to investigate. The pressure on Carol's organization will be coming from sources other than us. Sure, we started it, but she'll be too busy battling the barbarians at her gates to worry about us."

Laney turned to face the computer screen. She double-clicked on one of the thumbnails to maximize the picture. Carol's face took up the whole screen, her eyes the focal point. Intense. Focused. Determined. Insane. Those were not the eyes of a woman who would stop worrying about someone who wronged her. "I don't know, Click. I just don't know. I know you're sick of hearing me say this, but I just want a little bit more."

Click had no response. The silence between them acted as a volume increase for the police scanner when it crackled, and a voice said, ". . . residents say it's some kind of big creature. A monster."

Click laughed. "Well, if you were looking for a sign as to what we should do next, I don't think you'll find a bigger one than this."

Laney and Click jumped up and hurried to grab everything they needed. He grabbed his camera equipment, she grabbed both drones, and they ran from his apartment to the van as they prepared to go to York.

CHAPTER
40

York, Pennsylvania

Claire looked at Michael as he guided their SUV off the highway toward downtown York. The look of determination on his face concerned her. The only other time she saw his face this rigid was when he decided to make sure Stone never threatened anyone again. *What was he doing now?* She wasn't used to seeing her husband like this. Or act like this. He was in charge and that *never* happened.

The moment they heard about something unusual happening in York, something the police might not be able to handle, Michael issued commands. At first, he wanted to leave Horatio behind, but the young man reminded Michael that he could heal anyone who might get injured and assured him he would do better than the last time he was in a tense situation. He'd be prepared. Michael acquiesced and made Horatio promise that he would do everything he was instructed to do. Everyone assumed Colton would opt out, but he stated he was coming along as a silent dissenter. Michael ended the debate about transportation before it began, saying, "I'm driving."

Then he really surprised Claire—he had forethought. Other than his math skills being subpar compared to a child Sarah's age, Michael had a level of intelligence Claire found in very few people. He could keep up during any conversation about any topic, and she loved that. But he was guided by an artistic soul, one who lived in the moment and rarely planned ahead. He'd rather react than act. Claire almost fell over when he suggested they stop at a sporting goods store halfway to York. A quick stop far enough away from their home so no one would recognize them, they picked up ski masks and goggles. Barely after noon in a downtown area meant people would be out and about, which meant cameras and phones. Claire and Thelma each bought a pair of yoga pants for comfort. Emma opted for yoga pants and included a microfiber sports top. Claire marveled at how fit this woman was at almost twice her age. Michael, Horatio, and Bree were comfortable in jeans and their shirts. Colton refused to buy anything, even something to cover his face, stating he wouldn't do anything illegal so he had no reason to hide.

The rest of the way to York, the silent dissenter was far from quiet, offering, "We shouldn't be doing this," every five miles, which was quickly followed by, "We don't fucking care," by Bree. The comments finally stopped when they exited the highway, the anticipation too much for anyone to speak.

The butterflies fluttering around in Claire's stomach crashed into each other, harder and faster the closer they got to downtown. "Straight through this light. Right at the next one." She gave directions, holding her phone on her lap, cupped in her hands as if Carol's and Edward's organization were trying to spy over her shoulder. "We're getting close, so let's park."

Michael eased the car along the streets, using his turn signals, never getting close to the speed limit, making no sudden movements. A left, a right, another left, and they found a public parking lot six blocks from the incident. Without a word, everyone exited the vehicle. Just regular people on a regular day. Nothing suspicious to the casual observer. Should someone apply more scrutiny, the bulges in their pockets from ski masks and goggles would raise suspicions. None of the women had purses or handbags. Michael, Claire, Horatio, and Thelma all wore ball caps. Emma said her gray hair made her invisible, while Bree said people never noticed a single facial feature of hers—they only saw her blue hair, piercings, and tattoos. Of course, Colton had nothing to hide, which made him stand out even more as the small crowd of seven walked tightly together along the sidewalks.

The downtown area desperately tried to shake off an unpleasant image. The sidewalks were old and uneven but clean, home to pleasant-looking trees and sculptures ranging from realistic statues to metal shapes welded together in abstract ways. Two- and three-story buildings lined both sides of the street, and first-floor storefronts supported apartments above them. Banks, convenience stores, clothing shops for men and women, a small hardware store, specialty restaurants, bakeries—no storefront was vacant, and very few "for rent" signs could be seen.

Claire worried they'd stand out as they walked as one, heads down, hands in pockets. People paid them no mind, though, too wrapped up in conversations with each other or whatever was on the phone in their hands. After two blocks, people began noticing the blue and red lights. One more block and people started walking in the same direction as Claire and her crowd. The next block was why. Two police cars were parked sideways behind barricades and yellow tape. Four officers manned the area, making sure none of the dozen onlookers tried to get past.

"What's going on?" someone asked.

"Just something we need to take care of," an officer replied.

A block down was a vehicle labeled "York County Quick Response Team" and more police cars. The half-dozen armed officers looked more like soldiers in their all-black tactical gear. They lingered around a tiny convenience store and pointed at the third floor. The white curtains were closed, but they rustled intermittently. Too far away to hear the specifics, Claire assumed the tactical team was going in the building soon.

"See?" Colton said, keeping his voice low. "The police have everything under control. We should just turn around and get out of here."

"If it's a situation where someone like us is involved, the police absolutely do not have it under control," Michael countered.

"You're such a traitor, Michael. You used to extol the virtues of law and order. A criminal is a criminal whether they're 'someone like us' or not."

"I opened my eyes. You should, too."

"We have no fucking clue if the person in the apartment is a criminal or not," Bree hissed. "In fact, we don't know if they're someone like us. So how about you quit being a whiny bitch, and let's see what happens before you start judging everyone."

The men in tactical gear gathered close to the building as if ready to storm in. The onlookers pulled out their phones to record the action. This was what concerned Michael. Claire looked around and found a spot a little farther back, an area behind the spying cameras of the onlookers but still close enough to see what would happen. She whispered to the group, "Let's stand over there."

As nonchalantly as possible, they moved, except for Colton. "I'm staying right here. I don't care if I end up on someone's social media page."

"Was I ever that bad?" Michael asked once they claimed their spot on the sidewalk near the corner of a building.

"Yes," four voices answered in unison.

"Introspection. Noun. Examination or observation of one's own mental and emotional state of being."

"You'll have plenty of time for that later, sweetie," Claire said while patting his arm. Her moment of levity was short-lived as the men in tactical gear rushed the doorway. She squeezed Michael's hand. He didn't pull his eyes away from the building, but he cocked his head to let her know she got his attention. She whispered, "I have 'the big, bad red button' in my pocket."

Michael nodded. "Hopefully we won't need to use it, but in case we do, we have to be smart about it. Undoubtedly, whoever uses it will be rendered unconscious and will need to make sure everyone else is far enough away. It'd be an unmitigated nightmare if all of us were knocked out in such an exposed environment."

Claire agreed, hoping they wouldn't need to use it. She hoped a lot of things. She hoped this was a false alarm, that the situation would end without violence. She hoped people with special abilities were not involved. She hoped they could walk away from this without the need to put on masks. She stopped hoping when she heard the shouts and gunfire.

Male voices from the third-floor apartment, barking orders. A woman wailing, pleading. An animal . . . roar? Then the pop, pop, pop of the guns. Everyone around the barricades winced and gasped, yet more phones came out to record the event. The officers ordered the bystanders away and came around the barricades when no one listened to them. More gunshots and the officers' demands became louder. The people backed away from the barricades this time, wide-eyed with concern.

An explosion of glass and wood elicited screams as one of the men in tactical gear flew out of the apartment with such force, he hit the building across the street with a meaty smack and fell like a ragdoll to the ground. Another figure appeared in the hole in the wall and jumped. Dust and debris puffed from the ground when it landed. It was big, two or three times larger than an average human. The body was shaped like a man's—chest, arms, hips—but its legs and head were anything but that of a man's. Cloven hooves capped off bovine legs while the head of a bull was between its shoulders.

"A minotaur," Michael whispered. "An honest to God, fucking minotaur."

The officers by the barricades drew their guns while the bystanders ran.

"Masks on," Claire called out.

Each person running by them was in a panic, their monomaniacal survival instinct making them too myopic to notice a group of six people putting on ski masks.

"Now what?" Horatio asked.

"I don't know," Claire answered, watching the scene, trying to determine how best to help. Something about the hole in the wall caught her attention. It was blurry. No, something within the hole itself was blurry. Before she could make it out, there was a streak from the hole to the ground, close to the minotaur. Two men in tactical gear appeared in the hole, guns trained on the beast below. Claire braced herself for the guns' noises, the burst of blood from the man-shaped bull. They never came. The minotaur grabbed a nearby motorcycle and threw it at the men in the apartment.

Claire's breath hitched. Stone had been stronger than a normal person, stronger than he should have been for his size. But this . . . this was incomprehensible even though she had witnessed it with her own eyes. This was truly the beast from mythology, if not for the blood running down its left arm to prove it was really happening. It . . . *No* . . . he! *This is a person*, Claire reminded herself. He clutched his arm. Blood from at least two bullet holes flowed over his thick fingers.

The blur was now on the ground and moved. Not so much moved but flashed from one point to a spot right in front of the minotaur. The blur looked . . . human? Yes, Claire squinted, focused. It was another person, vibrating so fast she could barely make out that it was another man. She couldn't see any specific features; he was moving too fast. He held out his hands to the minotaur, trying to calm him down. The beast took deep breaths, and his shoulders and chest moved with every inhale and exhale. The minotaur seemed to calm down, as did the vibrating man, slowing just enough to show he had black hair and a dark complexion. The situation was almost at the beginning of de-escalation until one of the uniformed officers shot at the minotaur.

The officer missed his target, the bullet striking the ground by the minotaur's left hoof. The officer now had the misfortune of drawing the minotaur's attention. In what seemed like a desperate act to regain the minotaur's calm, the blurry man jumped in front of the beast and held out his hands, an unspoken plea to stop. He must have been agitated as well because he started vibrating faster, almost disappearing from view. Roaring, the minotaur picked up a nearby car and lifted it over his head. *A car!* Four officers trained their weapons on the bull-man.

None of the men in tactical gear who went upstairs came back down, nor was there any sign of the woman who had been crying. The minotaur had bullet wounds. Lord only knew if the blurry man had been injured or not. Claire assumed that more than one person in the apartment was dead. That was too many. Too much bloodshed. She couldn't allow any more.

The minotaur threw the car. Michael must have had the same idea. Just as Claire used her ability to lift the four officers out of the way of the car flying at them before they could shoot, Michael used his ability to stop the car midflight, then dropped to his hands and knees.

Claire yanked the guns from the officers and dropped them into the closest trash can while she levitated the men up to the nearby rooftops. She crouched next to Michael and asked, "Are you okay?"

"I am," he answered as he got back to his feet. "Just surprised by the feeling of when I hit the car. I didn't realize I would feel anything."

"Umm, guys?" Bree said, pointing to the minotaur and the blurry man. "You're going to feel a lot of pain if you don't pay attention."

The blurry man moved toward them in his own way. He disappeared then reappeared ten feet ahead. He disappeared again and reappeared closer but twenty feet to the right. Spastic streaks, he zigzagged his way closer. It looked as if he were winking out of and popping back into existence, but Claire deduced he was just moving faster than her brain could register. If his ability manifested recently, he'd have no idea how to control it, how to stop vibrating, how to run at such speeds. He probably had to think about stopping as soon as he decided to start. Suddenly, he stood in front of Claire.

It was a ghost of a face, superimposed on himself a hundred different ways at a hundred different times, but Claire was close enough to make out his features. His eyes were exaggerated, too big, panicked, scared. His mouth was a perversion of what one should be, and his voice was distorted and shaky as he said one word: "Help."

Then he was gone, this time not by his own power. Emma flew through the air, her foot connecting with the vibrating man's chest.

"Emma! No!" Claire cried out. She reached out with her mind to pull her away, but the ground started to rumble, and she heard Michael yell, "Claire!"

The minotaur charged at her and Michael. Out of reflex, she used her ability to move Michael back just as he used his ability to push her out of the way. The minotaur didn't hit either of them, but Claire landed shoulder-first on the sidewalk and screamed in pain. Her vision blurred as a wave of nausea rolled through her belly. The whole left side of her body felt like a bag of glass, shattered and cutting deeply into the rest of her.

"I'm here!" Horatio yelled as he ran over and crouched beside her. The entire world rippled from the tears, but she could see his wide eyes. The fear was trying to convince him to run and hide. He was barely winning that fight. "I'm here!"

"Yes, you are," Claire forced through gritted teeth. The pain twisted its way through her body, her bones. She wanted to encourage Horatio, but she wouldn't be able to talk if she opened her mouth, just vocalize her agony.

"Don't panic. Don't panic," Horatio whispered the words like a mantra. Claire wasn't sure if he was talking to her or himself. "Don't panic. Don't panic."

After a few deep breaths, he placed his hands on her arm. *Don't panic*, she silently encouraged. *Don't panic. Don't panic.* Then she felt it . . . a coolness within the flames burning through her body. She felt Horatio's hands, the clamminess of his skin, the tightness of his grip. The relief radiated outward like the ripples of a stone thrown into a pond. She took a big gulp of air when the pain disappeared from behind her chest. Whatever had been broken was now repaired.

Horatio's tight grip started to hurt, and Claire almost chuckled at that. Eyes closed, he still whispered, "Don't panic. Don't panic."

"Horatio?" Claire said as she put her hand on his shoulder and shook to get his attention. His eyes snapped open, red and watery from crying. "You did it. You healed me. You did great."

"Yeah?" He tentatively let go of Claire's arm and sniffled.

"Yes." She looked across the street. Michael rolled back and forth on the other sidewalk, holding his arm and kicking. "Now Michael needs your help. He probably won't be as calm as I was. Are you going to be able to concentrate while he expresses himself?"

Horatio got to his feet and nodded. "Yes. I can help him. I *will* help him."

Claire got to her feet as Horatio ran to aid Michael.

The roars of the minotaur echoed between the rows of buildings. Thelma, Bree, and Colton distracted it. The three of them ran around it, keeping away from each other and staying away from the bull-man. Bree and Thelma yelled at Colton to use his abilities. He still refused. Claire didn't like that their lives were in jeopardy, but she believed there was only one way to get the minotaur to stop—the blurry man.

Emma fought with the blurry man, but it wasn't going well. As fast as she was, she couldn't land another blow. Flipping and spinning, she threw punch after punch and kicked whenever she had the opportunity. Nothing. The blurry man might be the one thing on the planet faster than Emma. Her blocks were just as useless as her attacks, unable to stop him from hitting her. Then again, it was difficult to block something she couldn't see.

Emma swung at the air as the blurry man zipped across the street. He zipped back faster than Claire could see and slammed into Emma, sending her flying backward. With a twist and a tuck, she did a graceful forward roll on the sidewalk and landed on her feet. Claire got in front of her and held out her hands before Emma could try anything else. "Stop. I think he's confused and scared. And I think he can stop the minotaur."

Fists up, primed for action, Emma's entire body moved as she breathed. Wild eyes came into focus as Emma relaxed and nodded.

Claire approached the blurry man as she would a feral cat, with slow, deliberate steps and hands out in front of her. "Hi. My name is Claire. Can . . . can you hear me?"

The blurry man nodded.

"Good. Okay. We're special like you and . . . your friend?"

Like a hundred different voices answering from one mouth, he replied, "Brother."

"Your brother. Okay. You're scared and he's scared. You're both confused. Trust me, we all understand. We all went through the same confusion, the same fear. We don't have all the answers. We have some answers, and we want to help you and your brother. We will try to get you out of the city. It'll be hard, but we can't help unless you and your brother calm down."

The man's vibrating slowed, not a great amount, but enough for Claire to see his facial features. He nodded again and then disappeared. In less than a heartbeat, he reappeared in front of the minotaur.

Michael stood up, healed from his wounds thanks to Horatio's help. He then extended his hands. Claire ran to him and yelled, "Michael! No!"

He heard her. Hands still in front of him as if her words were an arcane spell meant to petrify him, he didn't move until she joined him with Emma right behind her. "I shouldn't push the giant mythological beast ready to eat our associates?"

"No. He and the blurry man are brothers. They're both scared and confused. I told him that if he can calm his brother down, we'll try to get them out of the city."

The bull-man was panting, snorting as he shook his head, but he stopped trying to attack Bree, Thelma, and Colton. His breathing slowed as his shoulders slumped. His brother was getting through to him.

Michael relaxed, too, dropping his hands and turning to face Claire. Even with a mask covering his face, Claire could see his consternation. "That's a hell of a promise. Do you *really* think we're capable of doing that? I'm sure more police are on their way, if not the National Guard."

"I can get them up to the roofs and move them from rooftop to rooftop. If we go north, there might be enough trees to get to the dairy. Beyond that is a forest. They'll have to run, but I think they can make it to the trees."

"That's a big 'if.' The forest is pretty far away with a few farms between here and there. And what about us? How are we going to escape if we—"

Michael was cut short when the blurry man suddenly erupted into flames.

CHAPTER
41

York, Pennsylvania

Michael jumped back as soon as the vibrating man caught fire. His first instinct was to run, but he consciously told himself that was no longer a viable response. This man needed help. Maybe Horatio could help? No, he wasn't Marvin. He didn't have that kind of power or strength. If they extinguished the flames, maybe Horatio could help—if he were calm enough. Extinguishing the fire was the priority. Could he "push" the fire away? That seemed unlikely without pushing the man as well. Maybe if Claire used her abilities to keep the man in place, Michael could push the flames away? That idea was also unlikely, but it was the only one he had. Too bad he never had a chance to share it.

An inhuman warbling shriek echoed off the buildings as the vibrating man disappeared from in front of Michael to across the street. He disappeared again and reappeared on the street, half a block away.

The minotaur roared and ran toward his brother. The fire died down, then flared up again. This time, they could see the source. One of Kevin's doorways had opened in an alley. Michael assumed that the man standing front and center was Sandeep. Like in Georgia, Sandeep wore an all-black outfit that clung to his body, including his face. What gave him away was the line of fire streaming from his extended hand.

"Sandeep?" Claire called out. No response. He just walked forward, closer to his target, while he continued releasing a torrent of fire. Behind him were Kevin and Jonathan, also in the same black uniforms. Marvin, in the form of Senator Varney, stepped out of the doorway in a suit and tie, hands tucked in his pockets as if out for a leisurely stroll.

"Marvin! Stop this!" Michael called out.

Marvin nodded at Kevin, then sauntered over to Michael and Claire. Kevin pulled a phone from a pouch on his sleeve. After a few taps, the doorway disappeared.

"What are you doing, you maniac?" Michael shouted at Marvin when he joined them on the sidewalk. "You're killing him!"

Marvin shrugged. "Seems like a clear-cut defending people from a hostile threat."

"We were communicating with him," Claire jumped in with a tone of aggravation Michael seldom heard. "He can't control what he's doing, and he was trying to calm his brother."

"If you and your super friends were truly helping, we wouldn't have needed to intervene."

"You monster!" Thelma screamed from across the street. Bree had her arm around Thelma's shoulders. Michael couldn't tell if she kept Thelma from collapsing or holding her back from rushing headfirst into danger.

The vibrating man dropped to his knees; the horrid reverberating screaming stopped. He no longer vibrated; he was now a burning caricature of a human form. Sandeep kept blasting the man's remains from twenty feet away.

The minotaur bellowed while Sandeep reduced his brother to ash. He roared and charged, parked cars shaking as he thundered down the middle of the street. Halfway to his target, Sandeep finally shifted his attention and blasted the minotaur with a plume of fire. It didn't slow the bull-man.

On fire, the minotaur slammed the crown of his head into Sandeep's chest, sending him flopping along the street. Jonathan ran to Sandeep while Marvin intervened before the beast could charge again. Using Michael's ability to push, he launched the flaming man-beast over a row of cars and against the building behind them. Bricks and the windows of the neighboring hardware store and bank cracked from the impact, glass shattering. It wasn't enough to stop the creature.

The minotaur stood and shook his head, snorting. The flames died, flickering along his arms, but he seemed unfazed. Fists clenched, he looked right at Marvin and rhythmically scraped his hoof on the sidewalk three, four, five times. Then he charged. He immediately fell on his face, his right leg failing him. No, not failing—held in place by wires snaking out from under a nearby car.

The minotaur growled and yanked his leg hard enough to snap the wires. Before he could stand, more wires shot out from another parked car and wrapped around his arm, too many to break as he struggled to free his arm. An ax came down on the wires. Emma. She raised the ax over her head and swung again, cutting most of the wires, enough for the minotaur to break free. Behind her, Thelma and Bree exited the hardware store wielding their own axes.

The minotaur hurried to his feet and ran to the center of the street. The situation worsened for him. As if he had jumped into a chromatic snake pit, wires of all colors and thicknesses spiraled around his legs and slithered up his body.

Claire tried to help, using her abilities to pull him out of the squirming mass. She was able to get him a few feet off the ground, but the webbing tightened around him. Sparks flew as Thelma, Bree, and Emma used their axes to hack away at the wires. More wires and cables replaced the ones they cut away.

"Kevin! Stop this! You're hurting him!" Michael called out. "Marvin! Tell him to stop. You don't need to do this."

"On the contrary, Michael, this hostile creature killed at least one police officer, destroyed property, and attacked a federal agent. I have no other choice. Kevin, you know what you need to do."

The wires drew taut. The women cried out as they swung their axes. They cut dozens, but hundreds flowed from the buildings and vehicles along the street. Claire continued lifting the minotaur, trying to unsnag him from the net. The wires pulled tightly.

Like a blooming flower of gore, a burst of blood sprayed the area, and entrails splattered on the street as various limbs went in different directions. The wires tossed aside the severed body parts, useless hunks of meat now. The bovine head landed at Michael's feet, its tongue lolling out of its mouth.

"In fact, Kevin," Marvin continued, "I told the rest of them not to use their abilities anymore. Take care of them."

The ground rumbled. Windows cracked and broke. Screams came from the buildings. People ran from the stores and fell from their apartment windows. Kevin turned appliances into robots. Televisions merged with ovens to make machinations of jagged teeth. Washers combined with dryers to become clawing tanks. Machines became nightmares and threw people from the second and third stories. Propelled by cables and wires, registers and ATMs chased away the people who had been hiding within the stores.

Most of the wires that had slain the minotaur spread to the nearby vehicles. Three cars on the left side of the street creaked and groaned from their metal parts bending and merging. Like in the Georgia field, they formed a monstrosity with three arms, each ending with an engine block. On the other side of the street, two SUVs, two cars, and a pickup fused together, the parts shifting and reforming to create a second robot, this one bipedal.

"Marvin! He's hurting innocent people," Claire yelled. "People you should be protecting."

Senator Varney smiled—not the way a politician would, the way a madman would. "Just unfortunate collateral damage that happens when fighting a war."

"Asshole!" Michael shouted as he pushed Marvin, slamming him against a building across the street.

Michael turned his attention to the robots forming out of vehicles. "What the literal fuck am I looking at?" Michael whispered.

"We need to stop this," Claire said. "I'll lift; you push."

"Got it!"

Claire started with a car Kevin's touch hadn't perverted. She extended her hands, and the car floated off the ground as if it had turned to paper. Five feet. Seven feet. Ten feet.

As Claire worked her ability, Michael called upon his and stored it at the base of his skull, the tingle of electricity flowing up and down his neck. He was ready when she yelled, "Now!"

Extending his arms, the feeling of electricity rushed along his arms and shot from his fingers. The full force slammed into the car and sent it flying. Michael lamented not having enough control over his ability to aim what he pushed, but he was satisfied that he sent the car toward Marvin and Kevin.

They moved in opposite directions, and the vehicle crashed between them. Marvin jogged briefly to get out of its way while Kevin, on his four-legged mobile chair, skittered like an insect out of the street, over the sidewalk, and onto the side of a building. As he scurried along the building's side, Michael moaned, "You have got to be kidding me."

Emma distracted the large robots made from vehicles, too fast for either of them to hit, while Bree and Thelma did what they could to help the civilians flee the war zone and hack away at the wires connecting the smaller robots to the buildings.

"Do you think we're strong enough to topple the giant killer robots?" Michael asked.

"I don't know," Claire answered. "Lifting a car was difficult enough, let alone trying to move things made out of multiple cars."

"What if you did what you did at your parents' house?" Horatio asked. "You know . . . what you did to . . . stop . . . Stone?"

A pang of guilt danced through Michael's chest, upset at himself for losing track of Horatio until now. "I'd love to, but I don't know what I really did or how I did it."

"Oh," Horatio replied. "Wait! Colton! Isn't he able to do what you do? If the three of you use your abilities together, then maybe you can stop the robots."

That wasn't a bad idea, but it could only work if Colton were a willing participant. Or if they could find him. Even though the situation was contained to a couple blocks, there was too much happening to focus on finding one person, and that was if he hadn't run away himself. "I don't know where he got to."

"He's over there." Horatio pointed to the small alcove they had been standing in when this mess started. "He ran over there when the senator showed up."

"Colton!" Michael called out and waved his arms. "Colton!" Horatio and Claire joined in, trying to get his attention.

Crouched down and leaning against the alcove wall, Colton looked over and frowned. Michael gestured for him to join them and yelled, "Come here!"

"No!" Colton yelled back.

"Oh, for the love of all that could be holy . . ." Michael muttered and then turned to Claire. "Use your ability to bring him here."

"No," Claire replied, looking in the other direction. "Even if I did, he wouldn't help us. And we don't need him."

Michael watched the scene before them. The two larger robots smashed divots into the street as they unsuccessfully tried to stop Emma. The smaller robots chased civilians, using cables and wires to capture them, subdue them. They shoved the people that were still alive into the remaining vehicles lining the streets as if they were cattle crates. Michael had seen firsthand the horrors of what Kevin did to other people, the unholy monstrosities he turned them into. Kevin was using this situation as an excuse to gather more test subjects, and now that Marvin was posing as Senator Varney, he had the full support and backing of the United States government. If Colton had been willing to help, it wouldn't be enough to stop this madness. They'd need an entire army of people with telekinetic abilities, so Michael was a little surprised when Claire said they could stop this themselves. "How are we going to stop this?"

"By taking Kevin out."

"How? We threw a car at him and missed."

"Exactly. It was too big. We'll do what we did with the car, just with smaller projectiles. I'll lift; you push."

Kevin was in the middle of the street but behind the mayhem, a conductor for an orchestra of madness. He was the target now. Whatever his plans were, whatever motivated this monster, he needed to be stopped.

Claire started with a tangle of kitchen appliances joined together by wires and cables as they chased after a man with an injured leg. He cried out with every painful step, unable to stay ahead of the machine. Claire stopped it. She lifted it in the air and pulled it away from the man. As soon as she moved it between Michael and Kevin, he pushed.

Kevin dodged the missile. Claire yanked a dishwasher away from a crying mother with her arms wrapped around her child. Michael pushed but missed again.

The larger robots stopped targeting Emma. They both turned and faced Michael.

Claire lifted and moved two smaller robots this time—a refrigerator and an oven. Feeling the adrenaline rush of a prey animal being hunted by a predator, Michael pushed both at once, harder than before. Kevin avoided the refrigerator, but the oven slammed into the ground right by him and hit one of his chair's legs.

The massive robots paused to receive new orders. The bipedal robot stomped toward Kevin, moving closer for protection. The other robot slammed its three engine-tipped arms onto the ground, expressing its master's frustrations.

"Claire! The road!" Michael yelled as the three-armed robot started toward Michael, again slamming its appendages against the street. Each strike produced a divot of broken asphalt.

A dozen chunks of broken road floated between Michael and Kevin. Getting angrier, pushing faster, Michael launched two at a time, then three, four. Many of the chucks exploded into pebbles against the legs of Kevin's robot shield, but a few made their way past, forcing Kevin to make evasive maneuvers.

The three-armed machine got closer; Michael could smell the oil and gas of the chugging engines. All the remaining vehicles on the street revved to life while the people inside screamed and cried, pounding on the windows. He couldn't stop, couldn't let himself get distracted. "More!"

Claire complied. Pieces of road floated in front of him in a continuous stream. Michael didn't know if it helped him focus, but he extended his right hand, then left, then right. Left. Right. Sending chunk after chunk like bullets, Michael assumed the law of averages would kick in, and one would hit his intended target. He was right. A fist-sized piece of asphalt struck Kevin in the shoulder and bounced against his head. The obese man's arms dropped to his side as his head slumped forward. The robots, large and small, mimicked his action.

"One down, three to go," Michael said, panting and exhausted. The mask made it difficult to breathe, but he loathed removing it in public, no matter how distracted the other people were as they exited their vehicular prisons and fled. Assessing the situation, it was a little better than he had hoped. Sandeep's arm was around Jonathan's shoulders, wobbling with their every step. Michael didn't like seeing other people suffer, but he was happy that such a powerful weapon in Marvin's arsenal seemed out of commission.

"Varney!" Jonathan yelled as he helped Sandeep walk. "Varney! We gotta go. He's hurt. Bad."

"I'll fix him up in a minute," Marvin said. "There are still way too many vermin on the street."

Claire extended her arms, and Marvin started to levitate, but as soon as his feet left the ground, he extended his hands in her direction, using Michael's ability to push.

An invisible punch to his chest sent Michael flying backward. He hit the wall behind him hard enough to see stars. Claire and Horatio were hit as well. It was a struggle to get to his hands and knees, but Michael called out, "Claire!"

"I'm okay," she moaned.

"I can fix this," Horatio said as he crawled between Claire and Michael. He reached out and placed his hands on theirs.

The same warmth Michael had experienced earlier when Horatio fixed his shoulder spread through his body. The pain in his head and back diminished. He wondered how much pain Horatio was in, but there was still the pressing matter of Marvin to deal with.

Emma jumped onto the hood of a parked car, then jumped off again, doing a flip this time to get a little more momentum when she threw the ax at Marvin. With a flick of his wrist, the ax stopped within inches of his face. Another flick, and he sent the ax flying back at Emma. She easily dodged it but fell victim to his telekinesis, a gift he stole from Claire. He tossed her aside, and she landed hard on the sidewalk close to Michael. Horatio scampered over to her and placed his hands on hers, the only exposed parts of her body.

Marvin marched closer to Bree. "You're that blue-haired bitch who stole my wife, aren't you?"

Bree swung her ax at him wildly and screamed, "You're the asshole who tortured her every minute she was with you, aren't you?"

"I'm going to make you suffer in unimaginable ways." Marvin advanced closer, evading the ax with ease. He snatched the weapon by the handle and tossed it aside, then grabbed Bree by the wrist.

Nothing happened.

Michael breathed a sigh of relief and remembered that this had happened a while ago, that Marvin's touch didn't affect Bree. Marvin must have remembered as well. Tightening his grip, he yelled at her, "Why doesn't my ability work on you?"

"Because, asshole . . ." Bree grabbed his wrist and twisted her arm so she could hold onto him with both hands. "You're addicted to your abilities. I can cure addictions."

"Wha—? No!" Marvin tried to pull away, but Bree's grip was too tight. His face stretched as if he were going to scream, but no noise came out. The twisting didn't stop—muscles rippled and skin pulled. The face of Senator Alistair Varney metamorphosed into that of Marvin Carver.

With a roar, Marvin yanked his arm free, holding it as if Bree had scalded it. "You bitch! Just because my primary ability doesn't affect you doesn't mean—"

Marvin's words were cut short by the ax driving into his skull.

Thelma stood behind him, panting, while she pulled the ax from his head. And swung again. She hit the same spot, driving the ax edge halfway down his face.

Marvin dropped to his knees, twitching. Thelma pulled the ax back out and walked around to face Marvin. The two halves of his skull were in a "V" shape, his left eye bulging out of his socket. Blood and chunks of brain slid over his split nose and mouth, dripping from his chin. His body twitched in sporadic spasms as phlegmy gurgles came from his twitching mouth.

Thelma pulled off her mask and leaned forward. "I don't know if you can hear me or see me, but just in case you can, I wanted to make sure you knew it was me. Michael told me you created an illusion in Mills Hook. No illusions this time, Marvin. No tricks or use of your abilities. It's over!"

Bree flipped him off with both hands. "Yeah! Fuck you!"

Marvin's nose became whole. His left eye moved back into its socket, and both eyes moved closer together as the seam in his head started to close.

"No!" Thelma screamed. "Not again!"

Bree reached for Marvin's hand, but he slapped away her efforts. He shifted and planted one foot on the ground to stand up. Thelma swung her ax, this time like a baseball bat. The blade went halfway through his neck.

Grabbing his hand, Bree yanked hard enough to pull Marvin to the ground. "His head! Cut off his fucking head!"

Screaming, Thelma swung the ax. Again. And again. Harder, faster, each swing created an arc of blood, splashing herself and Bree like an executioner's paintbrush. Chips of sidewalk flipped through the air, and Thelma finally stopped. Bree kicked Marvin's severed head away from his body.

Michael couldn't believe it. Marvin was finally dead. He and Claire collected Emma and Horatio, and they walked over to Thelma and Bree. Michael couldn't tell if Thelma was crying or laughing, and Bree hugged her. He assumed she was crying, but he couldn't see any tears from all the blood on her face. Then he clenched his fists, and the base of his skull tingled as Sandeep limped closer, still supported by Jonathan.

"Was . . . was that Marvin Carver?" Sandeep asked. "Was Senator Varney Marvin Carver?"

"Yes," Michael answered. "The big bad god you worshiped was nothing more than a greedy little man."

"Fuck you, man!" Jonathan snapped. "We didn't have a choice. And he put Sandeep through a lot of pain."

"You did have a choice! You had the same choices we did, and you chose poorly," Michael countered.

"Ummm . . . everyone?" Horatio said, his voice timid. He pointed to where Bree had kicked Marvin's head. "I think we still have a problem."

Bree had kicked Marvin's head toward an area where three people had been killed by Kevin's robots. Marvin wasn't done yet.

Thelma screamed as raw meat tendrils sprouted from the base of Marvin's severed head, giving it the means to move. It scuttled along the sidewalk to one of the dead bodies. A few of the tentacles wrapped around the corpse's wrist. In an instant, the body twitched and jerked as if hit by a defibrillator. While it continued to spasm, its left arm broke in half, the snap of bone accompanied by a spray of blood. The arm shriveled like a squeezed tube of toothpaste as two lines of muscle squirmed free and reached for the second of the three dead bodies, causing it to spasm just like the first body. Its right leg cracked in half, releasing two more worms of muscle to wriggle to the third body.

In one spectacular twist, all three bodies pulled together. Flesh tore in some spots, then regrew in others. Muscles ripped free and reformed as bones snapped and shifted. Arms and legs poked out from random parts of the roiling mass as organs floated across the surface, flotsam and jetsam on a pulpy ocean. As the blob crept its way to another dead body farther away on the sidewalk, a small pool of bubbles formed in the center of the mass. Marvin's face pushed its way to the surface and smiled. "I feel as though I need to thank you, Thelma. Like they say, necessity is the mother of innovation. I never knew I could do this; never knew I could be *more* than I was until you forced me to think outside the proverbial box."

Thelma screamed again, almost collapsing if not for Bree holding her. Michael's stomach lurched and he swallowed hard to keep its contents down. Emma and Claire gasped while Horatio whimpered and moved behind Michael.

The mass of human parts moved close enough to the body to reach it with four sinewy tentacles. Like the others, the body joined the mass, arms and legs now vestigial, dangling from the thing's skin.

Michael tried to ready himself for a push, but the thing squirming across the street was so disturbing that he had a hard time concentrating. His mind simply couldn't fathom what he was looking at. Fire. The fire snapped him out of his stupor.

Standing without Jonathan's help and shooting fire from his fingertips, Sandeep doused the mass in flames. The mask helped mute the smells of burning skin, but Michael needed to cover his mouth with his hands. As did everyone else. Black smoke emanated from the thing as its flesh bubbled and charred.

Marvin laughed. As soon as the fire stopped, the skin healed. The blob made it to the next dead body and absorbed it. "Sorry, Sandeep. You can't kill me. *No one* can!"

"No!" Sandeep screamed. "No! You kidnapped me! Used me! Lied to me! *Tortured me!*"

He released a torrent of fire, the blaze consuming the entirety of the blob. But it didn't stop Marvin from laughing and moving toward the next dead body. Sandeep screamed again and the fire raged brighter. It still wasn't enough.

Michael couldn't blink, couldn't breathe, as he watched wave after wave of fire crash against a mound of flesh formed by an amalgam of five human beings. Then he heard a crackle, a buzz, coming from above him. The power lines that draped from building to building. Sparks burst from the lines as blue arcs of electricity jittered along them. Jagged bolts of lightning jumped from one of the buildings and struck Sandeep. The amount of flame flowing from Sandeep to Marvin doubled in size. A second and third streak of electricity leaped from another building and touched Sandeep. Like with the first bolt, the amount of fire Sandeep produced grew in size and intensity. And became hotter.

"Is . . . is that what happened to me?" Michael asked.

"Yes," Claire replied. She grabbed Michael's and Horatio's arms and backed away. "But you had a limited source. We should go. We should *all* go!"

An arc of electricity from one of the power lines attached to the nearest building reached down and connected with Sandeep and didn't stop. The conflagration grew to the point of consuming him and engulfing Marvin. Everyone gasped and screamed and backed away as one.

Michael could no longer see Sandeep or Marvin, but he still heard laughter. He didn't know if it was real or his imagination. "Claire, the button. I think we need to use the button now."

"It's too late. We can't get close enough."

She was right. The heat was unbearable and getting worse. "What do we do?"

Claire turned to Jonathan and asked, "Has he ever done this before? Can he control it?"

"This is the result of Varney's—Marvin's—experiments. He'd hit Sandeep with industrial-sized generators and make him burn. He only stopped when the generators stopped."

More electricity arced from the power lines and touched Sandeep. The fire consumed two buildings, expanding so fast that Michael held out his hands and pushed to keep the flames from touching anyone around him. He kept pushing as he and everyone else backed away.

"It's not likely that he's going to run out of electricity," Claire said.

"I didn't think he was impervious to fire," Michael said, generating a steady push to keep the flames away.

"He's not," Jonathan said. "But his suit is. The person who made it said it could withstand anything less than a nuclear explosion."

"Fuck!" Bree snapped. "Guys, there's a power plant ten miles north of York. And a *nuclear* power plant thirty miles south of here."

"We have to get out of here!" Michael yelled. "Kevin! He needs to make one of those portals to get us out of here."

Michael thanked God that Kevin was only a block away. Sweat drenched everyone's clothes as they ran to Kevin, still limp in his chair, crooked from the damage to one of its legs. Everyone yelled his name as Jonathan shook him. He removed Kevin's mask and tapped his face. Michael kept an eye on Sandeep as the situation worsened.

Thick fingers of electricity reached down the wires and grabbed Sandeep. The column of fire grew higher, wider, by half a block. It consumed more buildings and vehicles, liquefying the asphalt of the streets. The power lines disappeared like gossamer spider webs. The electricity feeding into Sandeep didn't stop—the sources simply changed.

"Claire!" Michael yelled and pushed as the wall of fire roared toward them. Standing next to him, she used her abilities to push as well.

The people who had remained in the buildings tried to flee. A few ran from each doorway. Some didn't make it, bursting into flame like a struck match. Others caught fire but kept running. Colton was one of them.

Finally deciding to leave the alcove, he ran toward Michael and Claire but was too far away. After a few steps, fire covered his entire body, his clothes shriveling and burning into his skin. A few more steps and he collapsed. Claire used her ability to grab him from the ground and bring him closer. Horatio reached for him but pulled his hands away. Colton was too hot to touch.

More lightning from power lines struck Sandeep. The fire grew larger, hotter, as it roared its way toward them. Michael and Claire created a wedge in the flames while everyone behind them tried to wake Kevin. That didn't stop the heat. Michael's hands throbbed as they turned red. The fire was all around him, all he could see. Getting hotter. Of all the ways he thought he'd die, even with putting his life in constant danger after receiving this ability, being cooked alive hadn't cracked his top-one-hundred list. How would his parents explain this to Sarah? How would his parents even find out? There was a good chance he and Claire would be reduced to ash. Claire. He was going to lose his wife. His daughter was going to lose her mother. No. No! *No*!

This time Michael felt it. The electricity. Not the tingle at the base of his skull. No. The electricity from the nearby power lines. The jolt invigorated him, made him feel more alive than ever before. He felt his heart, his lungs, the blood rushing through his body. He felt every cell in his body. And they wanted to live.

Leaning forward as if pushing against a wall, Michael yelled, driving the invisible wedge deeper in the fire. The burning lessened but only minimally and only for a few seconds. The fire increased in intensity again. It gained ground, grew hotter. Then a hand from Heaven reached out and touched him.

Claire. She moved closer to him and reached out with her right hand to grab his left. The power fueling him and Sandeep now ripped through her as well. Together they pushed the flames back. But they couldn't stop them.

The heat increased. The air hissed. The skin on Michael's arm bubbled. A few blisters popped, the liquid evaporating into steam. His fingertips cracked, shriveled, blackened. They cooked and burned down to the bone.

"I can fix this!" came from between him and Claire.

Horatio.

"I can fix this!" he screamed again, the throaty sobs of a boy telling himself to do what he didn't want to do, to face the monsters from nightmares, under the bed, in the closet. "I can fix this!"

Horatio placed both of his hands on Michael's and Claire's. He cried out when the power surged through him. But he didn't let go. Black turning to pink, the skin on Michael's hand grew back.

"It's open!" Bree yelled. "The portal is open."

"Not them!" Kevin yelled.

Voices raised in argument. Yelling. Swearing. A commotion.

Fighting through the pain of the surrounding fire wanting to burn him away, Michael turned his head. Kevin and Jonathan were almost through the portal, but they fought with Emma, Thelma, and Bree. Assholes.

"Hold on," Michael said through gritted teeth. "Claire, get ready."

Michael counted to three, getting himself ready for what came next. He lowered his hands, his focus, and pushed against the ground. The force sent him flying backward into Kevin and Jonathan. Claire and Horatio were able to hold on as they crashed through the portal. As he had hoped, Claire had the wherewithal to use her abilities to pull Emma, Thelma, Bree, and Colton along with them before the portal closed.

The room was white and filled with computer-lined counters and workstations. Michael lay wheezing atop one of the counters and assumed that Kevin had opened the portal to a laboratory in the building where Marvin, as Varney, had taken Michael before. He didn't know where it was. He didn't know what happened to Sandeep or to the city of York. He was alive. More importantly, Claire was alive. All he wanted to do was go home and pass out. Head hanging off the edge of the counter, he could see the door out of the room. All he had to do was summon enough energy to get off the counter, collect Claire, and walk out that door. If life were only that easy.

Kevin shrieked. Sitting on the floor, his chair against the far wall, he kicked his feet in a tantrum. "He's dead! He's dead! You killed him!"

The overhead lights flickered, and Michael knew he had to move soon, no matter how much his body didn't want to. Kevin screamed again as wires and cables burst from the ceiling and walls. Dozens of them snaked through the air, forming webs or reaching for everyone in the room. Emma was the only one fast enough to avoid their attacks, but she could do nothing more than jump or spin out the way.

Michael leaped from the countertop, avoiding a tangle of cables reaching for him. He suddenly found himself in a position to do something. Kevin was mere feet from him. The confines were too tight for a push. The best he could hope for was a hearty shove into a wall. Instead, something inside Michael took over, something primal, something driven by the anger caused by this man capturing Claire in a web of wires.

"Let go of my wife!"

Michael jumped on Kevin's back and wrapped his left arm around the obese man's throat. He weaved his right arm under Kevin's and clasped the back of his neck. He wrapped his legs around Kevin's body and squeezed every muscle he had.

"Jonathan!" Kevin cried. "Help!"

Jonathan rushed over and punched the back of Michael's head. Michael pushed. It was unfocused in all directions. The force knocked Jonathan backward. Kevin squealed again. "Pull him off me! Pull him off me!"

Jonathan jumped on Michael and slithered one arm around Michael's neck.

"Claire! The button!" Michael yelled, extending his left arm. He couldn't inhale; Jonathan's arm tightened around his neck. Panic from not getting oxygen pulled his mind in different directions, grasping at ways to get Jonathan off him. Not sure if it was a good idea or bad, he let go of Kevin's neck with his right arm to throw his elbow into Jonathan's nose. It was a sacrifice, but it worked. Jonathan released Michael's throat to grab his arm. A pull, a twist. Michael assumed there was a nasty pop or snap, but he couldn't hear anything from the explosion of pain in his shoulder. Razor blades radiated through his whole body in waves, squeezing his guts to the point of impending vomit. His vision blurred from tears and the threat of blacking out. But Claire got him the button, using her abilities to slide it into his hand.

Too close. She was too close. Through his tears, he saw her, a blurry image of her and the others struggling against the wires and cables grabbing them. He tried to inhale again but only made a sad wheezing noise. One last idea snuck its way through the inferno blazing within his mind.

Squeezing his fingers around the grip in his hand, Michael extended his thumb. And jammed it into Kevin's eye. The fat man screamed and squirmed, twisting his way out from Michael's legs. That didn't matter; what did was the wires falling limp. Almost blind himself, Michael aimed for Claire and pushed. A steady application of force instead of a hard burst. It was enough to get Claire through the door along with two others. Horatio and Emma maybe? That was all he needed.

He pushed the button, and his world went black.

CHAPTER
42

Baltimore, Maryland

Dean was so agitated Laney honestly wondered if he would see his next birthday. At the minimum, he'd have a gut-dissolving ulcer by then. He sighed, arms crossed and fingers tapping against his sleeves, as he watched the monitor on his office wall. Click and Laney stood next to him and watched along. Click was nervous as well, but for different reasons.

Dean wanted someone at the White House press conference, what they were watching, but there was so much happening in the office that he didn't have the personnel to spare. Laney reminded Dean that none of the millions of new subscribers they got would cancel their subscriptions because he didn't have a representative there. Plus, Laney had a feeling the president would take very few questions after the announcement.

"Five days ago," the president started, "a great tragedy befell the city of York, Pennsylvania. You have undoubtedly seen the video."

Click nudged Laney with his elbow and gave her a thumbs-up accompanied by a wry smile. She rolled her eyes and went back to watching the president talk. He went on and on about hearing the concerns of the American people, empathizing with their fears and confusion. He apologized for taking only a minimal interest in the existence of people with special abilities up until now. He insisted that he and the rest of the administration had been duped by Senator Varney, who was really a small-time businessman named Marvin Carver with grand designs for unfathomable power.

"This will not happen again on my watch," the president promised. "Which is why we shall continue with the task force and give it all the resources it needs to find and deal with these individuals who possess more power than any human being should wield. It is my duty to keep America and her interests safe, and I am proud to announce the new head of the task force will be Edward Edwards, a man who can make this happen."

The president began extolling the virtues of Mr. Edwards by listing numerous credentials. Laney wasn't convinced any of them were real, but the public would undoubtedly accept that they were. She was concerned about the man standing next to Mr. Edwards—Conner O'Conner. Click gasped when he saw him. Luckily, Dean was so fraught with regret that he didn't notice.

Questions from the reporters in attendance followed, and as Laney had suspected, they received zero meaningful answers. Dean tapped the remote to turn off the monitor and crossed his arms again. Awkward silence followed until Click whispered, "Well, *that's* a thing now."

"We should have had someone there," Dean bemoaned.

"No, we shouldn't," Laney countered. "You don't get millions of new subscribers by reporting stories that, literally, everyone else is reporting."

Dean sighed and leaned against his desk. He immediately stood at attention as two burly men entered his office. They spoke only to each other in a language Laney assumed was Russian. With only grunts, they promptly removed the desk.

"That's our cue," Laney said, punching Click in the shoulder. "Let's leave Dean to this and figure out what our next world-breaking story will be."

"Even though it was amazing, I don't know if my heart can take another one!" Dean cried out from his office as Laney and Click left, squeezing past the massive new desk waiting to be moved to its permanent home.

The rest of the office was in chaos. Dean had a staff of a dozen, yet it felt like the New York Stock Exchange floor as Laney and Click traversed the insanity of movers taking away the old and delivering the new while building maintenance was busy knocking down a wall to the neighboring office suite. Dean was a stickler for deadlines but a terrible planner.

Laney and Click slipped through the ragged hole between suites, stepping away from a world of noise into one of quiet. This side of the hole would have a similar fate as the other side tomorrow, but for now, Laney was happy to sit on an old, wobbly, leftover office chair in her new office, four times the size of the shoebox she had shared with Click on the other side of the hole. He got a new office, too, sharing in the fruits of their labor. They, after all, were the reason Dean had millions of new subscribers.

Thanks to Click stealing the ultra-high-def cameras from Carol's organization, they got Dean to upload a video of what went down in York mere minutes after it happened. Then the world changed forever.

Stock markets had halted trading. Servers from all over the world had crashed intermittently. Every foreign government sought an audience with the president for answers. The president sought answers. There were exhaustive questions from the FBI and what remained of the task force. Laney was sure there would be more once Edward Edwards got everything back under control. Neither the FBI nor the task force had tried any strong-arm tactics. After all, the Laney Pederson video was a worldwide phenomenon, and now the spotlight was too bright for the shadows to touch her. At first, Click had been upset that her name was the only one associated with the video, but then Dean showed him how much of a bonus he would receive, and he smiled nonstop for a full twenty-four hours.

Laney finally achieved her dream, her goal. She brought truth to the masses, to the world. She started discussions, debates. She opened people's eyes. She so desperately wanted to bask in the moment, but as soon as they entered her new office, Click blurted, "We're fucked. We're so fucked."

"Calm down. We'll have plenty of time to panic later, so there's no need to panic now."

Click ran his hands through his hair with such vigor Laney wondered how he had any left. "Did you see who's the head of the task force now? Did you?"

"I did."

"That was Conner, Carol's associate, standing next to that guy who brought in that kid when we were at Carol's secret evil lair."

"It was."

"Well, what the fuck?"

"What the fuck what?"

"What the fuck are we going to do? The President of the United States just put a man who literally kidnaps kids and is associated with a psychotic woman involved in creating people with special abilities in charge of an organization to hunt down people with special abilities. And where the hell was Carol?"

"Answering your questions in the exact order you asked them: not freak out, you are correct, and I don't know."

Hands through the hair some more. "How can you be so calm? There could be some very bad, very dangerous people after us."

"Yes, but fame offers a certain level of protection. First, if they want us dead and we die, then they're going to be investigated in a very public manner. That is something they don't want right now. Second, this is exactly what our next story will be about. We will investigate them. We'll start with the task force.

If they don't allow us access, we can easily whip the public into a frenzy about transparency."

Click stopped messing with his hair. Eyes wide, he now wrung his hands. "Okay. Okay. Okay. So, the hunted become the hunters. Good. Good, good, good. Good start. What about the super-secret special-ability-making factories? What about Carol?"

Laney shrugged. "Some good ol' investigative reporting. We were at Carol's facility, so we'll start there. Even if it's completely empty, it's a start. Plus, right after the York incident, there was a small fire in a building in Arlington. Barely made the news, and there was no mention of who owned the building or what company might be leasing it. Seems suspicious. The past few days have been insane, so I haven't had time to research, but I think it's the task force building we infiltrated."

Click nodded in agreement. He then leaned forward and rested his elbows on his knees. Whispering, he asked, "What about the people in the video? Thanks to the data we stole from the task force, we know who they are. So, what do we do with this information?"

Laney shrugged again. "They seem like regular people trying to do the best with what they got. We saw them try to stop the task force from kidnapping the kid in Georgia. We can assume it was them who rescued him from Carol's. In York, it seemed like they were trying to help until the task force came along. It would do absolutely no good to expose them. The same goes for the other names. We don't have the time to hunt down each one of them. I know you referred to it as a hit-list, but you and I can help them more by taking down the ones who are hunting them and the ones who made them. We have bigger fish to fry."

Click smiled. "I like it. I like it all. Let's wrap it up and ship it! Of course, now that you mentioned fish . . . wanna get lunch? I'm buying."

Laney laughed. "Of course."

As they left her office, Laney's phone vibrated. A text message. "Click? Things just got more interesting."

"Yeah? How?"

Laney showed him the text.

What you posted online, what you discovered, is only the beginning.

CHAPTER
43

Claire didn't want to see the video again. She had seen it a dozen times. But she stood next to Michael in silence and watched it again for the benefit of his parents. She assumed they had seen it before as well. There were over ten billion views, so it was quite feasible that a couple of them came from her in-laws. Michael insisted they all watch it together as a way to share the experience before they discussed the future.

Buck and Stella had been there for two hours and simply listened to Michael recap what had happened over the past year-plus. They didn't interrupt, didn't add their two cents. Stella went through a few tissues, and even Buck's eyes welled up, but they let their son get everything off his chest. After the stories, Michael set a laptop on the coffee table for them. He and Claire stood behind the couch while he played the video of Mills Hook first, then the one from York, by the same woman, Laney Pederson, a journalist for an online news company.

Buck clicked the play button. An aerial view, a view from a drone as it zipped through the city over the tops of the buildings. The scene started with a gathering of people by an intersection barricaded by the police. Claire had lived this scene.

Buck leaned forward and squinted. Michael said, "There's no evidence of us being there. We viewed this at least ten times specifically for that purpose."

His father nodded and leaned back.

The drone captured much of what happened next. The minotaur. The vibrating man. Senator Varney and his death squad showing up. Kevin's robots. The resolution was superb, capturing every detail of the screaming faces as people ran for their lives, some not making it. Claire had never been so happy to have listened to Michael about wearing masks. The only thing that made her happier was that he had yet to bring up the fact that he was right. Then came the part that started a long-lasting impact.

Not only did this video show the world that the rumors and conspiracy theories of paranoid people were true about individuals with special abilities and the necessity of Senator Varney's special project, but it also showed that those people weren't being paranoid enough. It showed that Senator Varney had special abilities as he turned into missing millionaire Marvin Carver. The bombshells didn't stop there—one of the masked people was none other than his wife, Thelma Carver. The picture quality was so crisp Claire could almost feel the splashes of blood as Thelma beheaded her husband with an ax. Just when a first-time viewer might think it was over, Marvin utilized dead bodies to become a monster. Then the true horror happened.

The drone captured Sandeep stepping up and using his abilities to set the moving blob of human body parts ablaze. Once Sandeep tapped into the city's power grid to enhance his abilities, the fire grew too great too fast and presumably took out the drone. The finishing clip of the video was from a different drone, one farther away, but it captured the mushroom cloud with just as much crystal clarity.

"Was . . . was . . . that a nuclear bomb?" Buck asked.

"No," Michael answered. "There are plenty of scientists all too willing to explain that a non-nuclear explosion can cause a mushroom cloud."

Claire and Michael had missed the last explosion in real-time, having been transported hundreds of miles away in a fraction of a second. The portal closed, yet the nightmare continued. Kevin used his abilities to make wires and cables come alive and grab everyone. Michael, God bless him, fought Kevin and Jonathan. He fought through the pain of Jonathan dislocating his shoulder. With one final effort, he pushed Claire and Horatio far enough away to be unaffected when he hit the button. Everyone else was caught in the radius of what the button did; Emma and Bree passed out, but Thelma was unaffected. Luckily, Horatio's healing ability worked on reviving them with abilities unaltered. Horatio needed a couple of minutes to heal Michael's shoulder.

Security came running, so they had to fight their way out of the building and steal an SUV. Again, Claire thanked God that they were all wearing masks. Within minutes, they heard on the radio what ultimately happened to York after they escaped. Halfway home, they realized they had forgotten about Colton but rationalized that there was no way he could have survived what Kevin did to the lab.

They picked up Sarah from Buck and Stella and told them they needed some time to sort things out before they could go into detail about what had happened. They needed to see whose radar they were on and who had crosshairs on them. They needed to confer with the others. Now that Thelma's face was all over the internet, she used her financial resources to disappear with Bree. Emma wanted nothing more to do with any of this. She needed to heal from Ed's emotional and mental damage to her. Sister Angela said she wished to help in any way she could. Horatio had gone back home to his parents, and now they seemed to be doing a good job of keeping him out of the spotlight. So, Michael and Claire had a long discussion. They decided their future and what they would do moving forward, made more poignant after the announcement of Edward Edwards being named head of the task force to deal with people with special abilities.

After that announcement, Stella could take no more waiting. Earlier today, she had called, asking questions through waves of tears. Michael and Claire invited them over to their house to go over everything.

"Okay, so it wasn't a nuclear explosion," Buck said. "What caused it? That fire man?"

"Yes," Claire said. "Apparently, we can draw power from sources of electricity to enhance our abilities. The man's name was Sandeep, and he was very nice. Marvin had experimented on him to exploit this nuance to the point of Sandeep not being able to control it."

"Marvin. He was that businessman who could control biology, right? And he became Senator Alistair Varney? Oh, this is so confusing," Stella said.

"Yes. He also could take on the abilities of anyone special like us that he touched. That was why he wanted to be head of the task force. He could collect more power by capturing people like us."

"Now that Edwards is in charge of the task force. He'll be coming after you two, won't he?" Buck started speaking louder and faster. Stella started tearing up again. "He knows who you are. He knows who we are! That man was in my house."

"He has no reason to come after us," Claire said. Michael had always told her that Buck liked her more, that she could tell him anything and he'd listen to her. "The average American citizen is scared and wants him to hunt down the people like us who are dangerous, like Sandeep and Marvin. There's nothing dangerous about a suburban couple. Nor a nun. Nor a woman in her mid-sixties. Nor a fourteen-year-old boy."

"What happens after he captures all the dangerous ones?"

"We're not entirely sure," Michael said. "But we'll be ready. Dad, you always joked that sometimes a man just needs to shut up and listen to his wife. Well, with this particular topic, you're right. Claire had always said that whether we like it or not, whether we admit it or not, people with special abilities, people like us, are a community. Claire and I have decided to be leaders of that community."

Both Buck and Stella shifted in their seats, uncomfortable with what they just heard. Michael held out his hands, signaling for them to wait until he finished. "We're not telling the world who we are. We're going to keep that a secret. But there are plenty of people who have abilities like us, many of whom just discovered them last week. They're going to be scared and confused. The government hunting them down won't make things any better. We're going to do everything we can to find them and help them. Surreptitious. Adjective. Stealthy, clandestine, done or made in secret."

Buck stood and Stella followed his lead. Clearing his throat, an obvious gesture to stave off impending tears, Buck nodded, then said, "Son, I'm proud of you. I have always been proud of you and supportive of everything you've ever done, even though it has become clear you didn't think so. The only thing that has changed between then and now is that I'm going to make an effort to let you know that more often. Your mother and I will do absolutely anything possible to help you and Claire and your new community."

"Actually, Dad, the good ol' boy network you're a part of could certainly come in handy."

Mother, father, and son all chuckled as they came together for a hug. Claire would never forget this moment. But one thing still nagged at her. The Mills Hook video was shaky, and when it first came out, it was widely disbelieved, thought to be fake. The York video, though, was a much higher quality, shot with better equipment. What bothered Claire was that the same journalist was witness to both events. How did she know when and where to be? Did she know who they were? What else did she know? Tomorrow she'd bring this up to Michael because the first thing they needed to do was find Laney Pederson.

EPILOGUE
1

Augusta, Georgia

Horatio smiled at the paper in his hand. He felt silly, but he couldn't stop himself. It was a permission slip for a class trip. Only a year ago, he thought they were annoying, tedious at best. Not anymore. This was his ticket to normalcy, and he'd never complain about it again.

His complaints had diminished significantly over the past few weeks. He liked being back at school, a feeling he never thought he'd have. Of course, before a year ago, he never thought he'd have the ability to heal people with a single touch and then have that ability exploited while painting a target on his back. But after his ordeal in York, Pennsylvania, a month ago, and the new government task force ramping up its efforts to find people like him, his parents realized it wouldn't be a good idea to draw attention through their church, no matter the sudden loss of income. Even his mother. It took making her watch the Laney Pederson video, but she eventually understood the magnitude of the forces involved. They'd moved to this area and signed him up for school immediately.

It was a typical high school, where rumors travel fast. Someone figured out it was him in "those healing videos," even though he now went by August, his middle name. Every time someone asked, he'd laugh it off and say, "Yeah, the kid sure does look like me, but if I could do that, do you think I'd be here?" The inquisitive person would always accept his answer, but Horatio heard the whispered conversations and saw the sideways glances while walking the halls. That didn't matter. He was no longer bilking money out of people who couldn't afford it, and, in his heart, he could now worship the Lord in far more acceptable ways. That made him happy.

In the short time here, he'd made friends. Not a lot, but he met someone new here and there. He even had enough to make plans with a few of them for the upcoming field trip. So much more exciting than rehearsing lines for a sham church service.

Horatio continued staring at the permission slip as he walked, as if it were a Golden Ticket. He was so enamored with it that he almost ran into someone coming the other way. His peripheral vision caught movement ahead, and he stopped and looked up. "Oh! Sorry."

One more step and there would have been a collision. The other person—a student, a girl—had been too preoccupied with her phone. Startled as well, she looked up, eyes wide at how close she came to running into someone. "Oh my God! I'm so sorry!"

She looked familiar. Why did she look so . . . ? "Molly!"

At first, she took a step back and squinted, clearly searching her memory for him. She found it and her eyes went wide. "Horatio?"

Hair much shorter than before and sporting glasses he didn't need, he looked over both shoulders and then held his index finger to his lips, the international sign for, "Shhh."

Molly put her free hand over her mouth and giggled. "Sorry. Is it a secret?"

Warmth bloomed within his cheeks. "Yeah, I go by August now. I don't do the church thing anymore."

Molly frowned, disappointed. "No? Why not? You were helping people. You helped me."

"I will always help people whenever I can. I'm just not going to charge for it anymore." He punctuated his statement with a wink.

Molly smiled and Horatio melted. He blushed again, for different reasons this time. "That's awesome. Do you go to school here now?"

"I do. But I don't know many people."

She gave his shoulder and playful squeeze. "You know me!"

"I do, and that's amazing."

Impossibly, her smile brightened, and her eyes sparkled. Horatio was happy she seemed to like his compliment. "Yes. It is. I have to run, but let's meet up tomorrow, and we'll sync up on social media."

"I like this plan."

"Okay, see you tomorrow. Bye."

"Bye."

Horatio's parents sold their ostentatious house and cars and opted for a more conservative residence a mile from the school. He enjoyed the walks to and from, even when the weather wasn't exceptional. But today was perfect, and he had to make a conscious effort not to start skipping across the parking lot once he left the school building.

After the parking lot, he went through a small copse of trees, then another parking lot belonging to a church. It was empty except for one van. Horatio knew better—every adult in his life had taught him to be wary of situations like this. But his mind was racing a million miles away, so he didn't hear the van roll up next to him. He didn't even realize the van was there until the back doors opened and someone jumped out.

It was only one person, not much larger than Horatio, but he was so unprepared that he was easily overpowered and tossed into the back of the van. It was a cargo van, empty in the back, nothing to use as a weapon, nowhere to hide. He scurried across the floor and threw himself into the far corner, fists clenched.

"Calm down, kid," his abductor said.

A woman.

With purple hair.

Horatio instantly recognized her as the woman who kidnapped him before, then remembered that Edward Edwards made her the number one most-wanted woman in America. She was trying to kidnap him again. He had no skills or training in self-defense, but blindly punching and kicking was better than doing nothing. He clenched his fists. "I'm not going easily."

Carol crawled closer but stopped within arm's reach. On her knees, she held out her hands in surrender. "I'm not kidnapping you, kid."

"No? Sure seems like it to me!"

Carol lowered her hands and started to unbutton her blouse. "Trust me, if I were kidnapping you, you wouldn't be conscious right now, and I would have drawn a dick and balls on your face. I need you, Horatio."

After the last button, Carol opened her blouse to expose her breasts. Electricity flowed downward from Horatio's chest while fire burned from his neck to his forehead. Out of courtesy, he averted his eyes and looked at the van's ceiling. "Wha . . . wha . . . what?"

"I have breast cancer. I need you to heal me. That was why I was so obsessed with kidnapping you. Well, that and I'm very mentally unstable, so I get obsessed easily. But I've reached the point where I now need to say something that I'm pretty sure I've never said in my life . . ."

A few seconds of silence was all Horatio could take before looking back at her. A lone tear escaped her watery eyes as she said, "Please."

"Okay," Horatio said as he gazed upward again. "Okay. I'll help. But . . . I don't . . . I don't need to touch . . . you there."

"What kind of fourteen-year-old boy says no to a grope? If I put my tits away now, it'll just make things awkward."

Horatio doubted that was possible as he made the situation more awkward by trying to lay hands upon her while studying the ceiling. He glanced down and then closed his eyes. Soft. Warm. With her breasts in his hands, he tried desperately to focus on the tingling at the base of his skull rather than the tingling below his belt. If he couldn't focus, he'd fail Carol the same way he failed Sarah. He suddenly remembered who he was touching and hypothesized that if he failed her, she'd do something inhuman to him, like cut his throat. That thought got him to focus.

As had happened hundreds of times before, energy flowed from the base of his skull along his arms. Carol gasped. It was done.

He opened his eyes, and Carol smiled, the wicked shark smile that would haunt his nightmares. "Got a cigarette?"

Cheeks on fire, Horatio flung his hands behind his back and looked up. "Sorry. I didn't . . . I didn't mean to . . . Sorry . . . Ummm . . . You . . . You're cured."

Carol's chuckle almost seemed sympathetic. "Nothing to be sorry about, kid. You cured me and that's pretty fucking amazing. You're a good person. Not many of those around. You can stop staring at the ceiling, by the way."

Slowly, Horatio lowered his chin, fearful of what to expect. Either she was pranking him and still had her blouse open, or she was going to kill him. No exposed breasts, no gun pointing at him. Just a woman with a look of relief and gratitude in her eyes. She said, "You're a weird one. Probably every teenager in America would kill their grandmother to have a gig like you had. Once your dipshit parents figured out how to take your act national, you would have been swimming in money. I mean, literally filling up an Olympic-sized, in-ground pool with hundred-dollar bills and swimming in it. Yet, you resisted. Hell, you did the one thing all parents fear—you took candy from strangers and ran away. Why?"

Horatio thought about telling her all his thoughts about exploiting those who have been exploited all of their lives or the feelings of being helpless and trapped while possessing so much power. But he knew that wasn't what she wanted to hear. He gave her the soundbite she wanted. "It was the right thing to do."

Carol laughed and shook her head. "Fucking teenagers."

Horatio was worried about what would happen next, how the motivations of a crazy person would affect his future. "How about you? It seemed like you went through a lot of trouble to kidnap me when all you had to do was come to one of my sermons and donate the money you clearly have."

"With the resources I had? You don't spend a million dollars on a kitchen to make grilled fucking cheese. I did what I did because I had the means to do what I did. Plus, you know, I was gonna sell you to the highest bidder."

Thoughts of punching and kicking resurfaced. He must have tensed up or done something to telegraph his thoughts because Carol rolled her eyes and waved her hand dismissively. "Settle down, kid—I'm not going to sell you to anyone. I don't have the aforementioned means anymore. Fucking Eddie. Burned me good, that son of a bitch. And Conner. That ginger fuck-face! Did you see the press conference? Did you how that smug little leprechaun shit stood right behind Eddie like they were best buds the whole time? Christ, Eddie hates Conner more than I do, and Conner did everything he could to put his dick in me. That fucking piece of—"

Carol refocused her eyes on Horatio as her gaze drifted during her rant. Clearing her throat, she sat straight and ran her hands over her hair. "Anyway, the moral of the story is that I'm not kidnapping you."

"I am certainly happy to hear that. So . . . what are you going to do?"

"Well, first, I'm going to let you out of the van and make some over-the-top threat about ripping your fingers off and force-feeding them to your pet hamster while making your parents watch if you ever tell anyone that you saw me, and then I'm going to hunt down Laney Pederson."

Horatio made the connection. If not for the Laney Pederson video showing the world that people with special abilities existed, then Edward Edwards wouldn't have come out of the shadows to expose Carol. "So, you're going to kill her?"

Opening the van door, Carol chuckled, and her face contorted as if that was the dumbest thing she had ever heard. "Kill her? Fuck no. I'm going to find her and marry her."

EPILOGUE
2

Mountains outside of Ashville, North Carolina,

Devlin Varney smiled as he turned off the main road. The smaller road meandered through the forest and came to a gravel driveway cut through a thicker part of the forest. Today was the day to tell everyone the plan.

His real name was Robert. No . . . his birth name was Robert. But Robert had turned into a rabbit. A human-shaped rabbit with hands and the ability to speak and walk upright. A few redneck hunters caught him, cut off one of his feet, and strung him up in a barn. But Marvin Carver saved him, cured him. Not only did Marvin turn him back into a human being, but he made him better. Robert was a weak teenager. Devlin was a strong man in his twenties. Handsome. Muscular. Rich.

He wasn't insanely wealthy, but he had access to Alistair Varney's wealth. Marvin killed the real Alistair and his son. The world knew about the first murder, but not the second one. He shed a few tears for the media, and he got all the sympathy pussy he could handle. Those girls were just a fun little distraction, though. What mattered was that Devlin was the sole heir to Alistair's estate. The formalities were yet to come, but there wasn't anything Devlin couldn't have access to, including this A-frame house in the middle of the forested mountain, where he had everyone holed up.

He parked next to the eighteen-wheeler. With half a dozen grocery bags, he went to the front door and rang the bell. Linda greeted him. "Hi, Devlin, let me take those for you."

Devlin thought it was a waste to have such a brilliant mind take and put away groceries, but there was nothing else for her to do until he and the others set his plan into motion. An amalgam of flesh and machine parts, Linda took the bags and walked toward the kitchen in jerky movements. Wires snaked in and out of her skin while one black cable protruded from the base of her spine. She moved like a marionette, her strings pulled by a drunken puppet master. Her body parts were still flesh covering muscle wrapped around bone, but her joints weren't real—black metal protruded from her limbs to create ball-and-socket connections. And her right eye was no longer there, replaced by a telescoping camera lens.

Devlin approached the dinner table and sat next to Jonathan as he drank a beer. Jonathan eyed Linda and whispered to Devlin, "She creeps me the fuck out."

"I know. Sorry about that. But it needed to be done. Just be happy we got him to wear clothes," Devlin whispered back while nodding toward the recliner across the room occupied by Kevin. In a T-shirt and shorts, Kevin lounged in it so deeply there was no way he could leave it without assistance. Wires sprouted from his wrist, connecting him to the nearby electrical outlet, allowing him access to everything in the house, including the seventy-inch television dangling from the ceiling in front of him. Even though Devlin thought that what Kevin did was the coolest cyberpunk sci-fi imaginable, he didn't think it was right that Linda walked around the house she was now tethered to while naked, so she ambled around in a T-shirt that came down to her knees. And he agreed with Jonathan that Kevin needed to wear clothes.

"Yeah," Jonathan grunted. "Still don't think she deserved this, though."

It was her fault, Devlin rationalized. She should have come with them voluntarily.

Devlin was in his father's headquarters when Kevin and Jonathan came through the portal from York, bringing those assholes with them. They did something to Kevin and Jonathan, knocking them unconscious. Devlin knew who Michael and Claire and the others were. Most of them were with Marvin when he helped Devlin escape from his father. They were also in Mills Hook, and Marvin helped them escape. They repaid his kindness by killing him and making Sandeep blow up York.

After the assholes recovered, they left, simply fleeing the lab and headquarters. Assholes didn't even stick around to take responsibility or help out. They caused enough chaos during their escape that Devlin was able to enter the lab and lock the door. He spent two hours waking Kevin and Jonathan back up. When he finally did, he realized someone else was in the lab with them, someone the assholes left behind. A man named Colton, whose entire body was burned to a crisp, but he was still alive.

While Devlin worked on waking Kevin and Jonathan, he devised a plan. His adopted father was dead, and the government wouldn't waste any time taking over the facility, confiscating all of his father's hard work. He shared his plan with Kevin and Jonathan. They couldn't think of anything better, so they went along with it.

First, Kevin connected to the nearest computer and downloaded all the task force's information to the hard drive. Declan disconnected the computer and let Kevin wreak havoc. He had destroyed every machine he had built, every project he had been working on, including the quantum entanglement teleportation device. He could always build another later; Devlin did not want the government to have this technology.

Devlin wanted to save Colton. He knew what he could do, and it wasn't right that the assholes did this to him and left him to die. There was an eighteen-wheeler at the dock, empty after its delivery. Devlin told Kevin to load up enough equipment—only essential machines and computers—to keep him busy for a month or so. He also instructed Kevin to create a mobile gurney for Colton. There was plenty of medical equipment in other labs, but Devlin didn't know what was needed or how to use it. Then he found Linda.

Linda didn't want to listen to Devlin, too busy trying to flee the building while Kevin destroyed everything inside. When she finally heard what Devlin was proposing, she called him as insane as his father. Devlin had no other choice than to have Kevin make her come along, loading her in the back of the truck like the rest of the equipment.

Getting the truck to the A-frame house was difficult, but once there, Kevin used what he took to modify it to their needs. Once he integrated Linda into the rest of the house, she helped save Colton.

Still sitting at the table with Jonathan, Devlin set up his laptop and asked Colton, "How are you feeling today?"

Skin knotted and twisted like the waves of a turbulent pink ocean, he sat up on his gurney. Thanks to Linda informing Jonathan of what was needed and Kevin knowing how best to use it, Colton's recovery was faster than normal. "Best I felt since we got here. I'll feel better when Kevin figures out how to manipulate the nanobots in our heads so we can do what your father did."

"Need a lab for that. And subjects for experimentation. And time," Kevin mumbled.

"Don't worry," Devlin said, his tone cheerful. "We can get started on that once the entirety of Varney's inheritance is officially transferred to me. In the meantime, I have some good news regarding our war with the new task force. We're going to do a two-pronged assault. Thanks to my father, we have names and locations of a few powerful people with special abilities." Devlin tapped away at the keyboard. Still images and videos took over the screens, including the television, of people doing amazing and horrific things.

"We've seen these," Jonathan said. "Who are we gonna start with?"

Devlin tapped away and a black and white video played of a man walking along a small-town sidewalk. Hands inside the pockets of his windbreaker, baseball cap pulled low to obscure his face. Across the street, a car tried to navigate into a tight parking space but failed and hit the front of another car. It must have been louder than it looked, because the man in the ball cap turned to look at the commotion, giving the camera a perfect shot of his face. The video stopped playing, and the man's face froze on the screen. "A man you and I have had personal experience with."

"Ethan?"

"Yep. Apparently, he survived the destruction of Mills Hook."

"Who's Ethan?" Colton asked.

"Every thirty days, he creates a duplicate of himself. Those duplicates also create duplicates every thirty days. I don't know if one mind controls them all, or if it's a hive mind, or if they exist autonomously, but when Jonathan and I last saw them, they sure as fuck seemed to work well together. A whole town— one or two *thousand* of them."

"Whoa. That's insane."

"Yes. One thing every war needs is numbers. We get him, we get numbers for days. Literally. I waited to tell you all this part of the plan because I needed time to continue what my dad was doing—looking for him. And I found him."

Jonathan finished his beer, crossed his arms, and leaned back in his chair. He smirked, which was the most emotion Devlin had ever seen him exude. "We should assume the task force will be going after him as well," Jonathan said.

"Probably. But we fucked up their headquarters pretty good, so we have a head start. And that brings me to our second prong. Our attack against the task force."

"You want us to attack the task force?"

Devlin pulled out his phone and winked. "No. I want someone else to attack the task force."

He thumbed the letters on the screen to type out his text and then hit "send."

What you posted online, what you discovered, is only the beginning.

ABOUT THE AUTHORS

Brian Koscienski & Chris Pisano skulk the realms of south-central Pennsylvania. Brian developed a love of writing from countless hours of reading comic books and losing himself in the worlds and adventures found within their colorful pages. In tenth grade, Chris was discouraged by his English teacher from reading H.P. Lovecraft, and being a naturally disobedient youth, he has been a fan ever since. They have logged many hours writing novels, stories, articles, comic books, reviews, and the occasional ridiculous haiku. To find out where they may be skulking next, visit them at www.novelguys.com. If you happen to see them at one of the various conventions they participate in, feel free to stop by their table and say, "Hi." They're harmless!